patterns of
the heart

and other stories

WEATHERHEAD BOOKS ON ASIA

WEATHERHEAD BOOKS ON ASIA
Weatherhead East Asian Institute, Columbia University

For a list of titles in the series, see page 277

patterns of the heart
and other stories

CH'OE MYŎNGIK

TRANSLATED AND INTRODUCED BY
JANET POOLE

COLUMBIA UNIVERSITY PRESS   NEW YORK

Columbia University Press wishes to express its appreciation for assistance given by the Pushkin Fund in the publication of this book.

This publication has been supported by the Richard W. Weatherhead Publication Fund of the Weatherhead East Asian Institute, Columbia University.

COLUMBIA UNIVERSITY PRESS
Publishers Since 1893
New York   Chichester, West Sussex
cup.columbia.edu

Library of Congress Cataloging-in-Publication Data
Names: Ch'oe, Myŏng-ik, 1903– author. | Poole, Janet, translator.
Title: Patterns of the heart and other stories / Ch'oe Myŏng-ik chŏ ;
    translated and introduced by Janet Poole.
Other titles: Pi onŭn kil. English
Description: New York : Columbia University Press, 2024. | Series:
    Weatherhead books on Asia | Includes bibliographical references.
Identifiers: LCCN 2023041832 (print) | LCCN 2023041833 (ebook) |
    ISBN 9780231202701 (hardback) | ISBN 9780231202718 (trade paperback)
    | ISBN 9780231554671 (ebook)
Subjects: LCGFT: Short stories.
Classification: LCC PL991.18.M9 P5613 2024 (print) |
    LCC PL991.18.M9 (ebook) | DDC 895.73/5—dc23/eng/20220711
LC record available at https://lccn.loc.gov/2023041832
LC ebook record available at https://lccn.loc.gov/2023041833

Printed and bound by CPI Group (UK) Ltd, Croydon, CR0 4YY

Cover design: Chang Jae Lee
Cover image: © Hee Seung Chung, Untitled #02, 2018, from the series
    Remembrance Has Rear and Front

Contents

Introduction: A Dislocated Art and Life

> The factory where Pyŏngil worked lay just outside the city wall,
> as did his room on the opposite side of the city.
> Although the two sides of the city might be said to oppose each
> other, the angles of the wall did not form a perfect square, and his
> thirty-minute walk to work barely scraped past one corner of the
> inner city midroute.
> Once he left his boardinghouse, he had to walk for about ten
> minutes down a narrow, steep path, which did not appear on the
> city government's borough map.
> —Ch'oe Myŏngik, "Walking in the Rain"

The opening lines of the debut work of fiction by Ch'oe
Myŏngik (1903–?) seem to foretell the career that was to
follow. The story begins with a description of Pyŏngil's daily
commute to work. An aerial view carefully locates his route in
relation to the city walls—denotative of authority, commerce,
and the history of the walled town—before the narrative view-
point switches to the ground and the sights encountered by the
walker each day. It is as if a camera has zoomed in and then

become the eyes of this solitary man. The texture of Ch'oe's writing in this story, as elsewhere, is indelibly shaped by the technologies of cinema and photography, which were still relatively novel on the Korean Peninsula at that time. The resulting effect of precision takes its aim at the relations of power and wealth that govern a city in the midst of dramatic material and social transformation brought on by the dynamics of early capitalism. At one point Pyŏngil just manages to gaze through one of the four city gates toward the lights that illuminate the inner city, but his route continues along the periphery, marked by the slum and a newly developing factory district. The material accumulations of this center of capitalist modernization—the "new city of commerce and industry"—are represented with all their disruptive and dislocating effects exposed. Ch'oe leads his reader off the city government map and into the alleys with no whiff of nostalgia or romanticism but instead with cool-eyed observation from the margins of power. Throughout his later work the focus was to lie on those sidelined and displaced from the authority of the center, whether on the edge of the city or empire: young women in rural communities, young men sent to the battlefield as martyrs for the liberated nation, sons falling out with their fathers, the war evacuee. In all these instances Ch'oe was a meticulous and creative detailer of the life of the marginalized and the disaffected.

In 1930s Korea, Ch'oe Myŏngik garnered a reputation as an exquisite architect of the short story form. His stories reveal a craftsman's attention to detail combined with a consistent experimentation that distinguished his writing from that of his contemporaries. In later essays on his writing philosophy, Ch'oe stressed his belief in the virtues of precision in writing, stating that there was no such thing as beauty immanent to language, that "the beauty of words, if it exists, is the name for words placed exactly in their right place . . . expressing objects precisely."[1] Yet this philosophy of exactitude and order existed alongside an attention to rupture and the interrupting moves of an avant-garde ethos. As far as we know, Ch'oe was not a formal member of the Pyongyang-based avant-garde literary coterie known as Tanch'ŭng, to which his brother belonged, but his stories nevertheless align with that coterie's self-translated appellation, *La dislocation*. Ch'oe shared the group's pioneering interest in psychology and sought to detail a consciousness he believed to be ruptured. For him, this entailed the portrayal of those dislocated by the modern transformations on the peninsula—by the rise of a petit-bourgeois ideology propounding economic and self-development as a prized goal, by the violence of colonial occupation and its suppression of opposing movements, and by the sacrifices demanded and exacted during the tumult of wars in the mid-twentieth century. He was equally attuned to revolutions of style and of economic structure. Most recognizable for their dense yet finely delineated detail, his stories reveal the extent to which the modern visual arts of cinema and photography revolutionized literary writing in early twentieth-century Korea, as they did around the world. Simultaneously, he tracked the fortunes of the political revolutionaries who opposed the colonial government and later sought to build a brave new world in the northern half of the peninsula. Words had to be placed exactly, but to the purpose of detailing the dislocation of everything else.

Despite being one of the most adventurous of Korea's modernists, Ch'oe is not well known in South Korea today, and his work has not been translated into English previously. His lifelong residency in the city of Pyongyang is surely the cause for his erasure according to the logic of the Cold War, which endures on the Korean Peninsula and still shapes the world of Korean-to English-language literary translation. In the 1930s, Ch'oe's decision not to move to Seoul granted him some distance from the busyness of the booming publishing scene in the colonial capital, allowing him to establish his reputation as a somewhat aloof, pristine writer who was uncontaminated by the commercialism of Korea's largest city. Perhaps that distance also granted him some protection during the Asia-Pacific War from mobilization activities driven by the colonial Government General, which was headquartered in Seoul. His stories reveal a geography unfamiliar from previous translated Korean literature from this era, one that is centered on the north of the peninsula and Manchuria. Although Ch'oe was geographically marginalized from the Seoul literary scene, he was deeply affected by the visual aesthetics of a globalizing modernism, and this impact hardly diminished as the prototypical second city of Pyongyang transformed into a new state capital in the late 1940s. His own transformation from peripheral Korean writer into an author at the very center of North Korean life and literature in the early years of the Democratic People's Republic does not always appear to have been easy for him. His short fiction offers unique insight into the political and artistic life in the new socialist capital emerging from decolonization, forcing readers to rethink the "origins" of North Korean fiction and its relationship to global modernist styles.

Ch'oe's career maps onto an often chaotic and violent, yet equally creative and dynamic, period in Korean history. At the beginning of the twentieth century, Korea was a kingdom increasingly subject to encroachment from external powers—China, Imperial Russia, and especially Japan. The unequal trade treaties that had been imposed on countries throughout the Asia-Pacific region had also channeled Korea's diplomatic and commercial relations with the United States and European imperial states. Increased traffic between nations had led to greater awareness of the powers and threat posed by imperialism, as well as a proliferation of often competing and contradictory social reform efforts from the court, from elites and from the peasantry. If Europe, and increasingly Japan, emerged as militarily superior in their displays of power, an appropriate response was sought through knowledge of the institutions, technologies, and education of the victors. Koreans traveled overseas to the United States, Europe, and Japan to study, and what was known as the "new learning" or "Western learning" began to reshape Korean educational institutions. Expertise in European epistemology was deemed necessary for survival in the new age, alongside developing the technologies of the railroad, gunpowder, and trade. Inequities in power were accompanied by an intellectual maelstrom: encounters of ideas, styles, and forms that inspired artists and thinkers alike to forge their own creative pathways. The brutalities of a thirty-five-year colonial occupation by Japan shaped a popular communist movement in response. By the 1960s, when Ch'oe published his essays on writing, the peninsula had been sundered into two by opposing occupations under the United States and Soviet Union in the wake of the collapse of the Japanese Empire, and it had then seen the two resulting states go to war in the famously unended civil war, known in English as the Korean War. The North Korea of the 1960s was an industrializing postcolonial socialist state, widely understood at that time to be more viable than the poverty-stricken, dictator-led state located to the immediate south.

Anyone who lived through the early twentieth century in this part of the world experienced the force of social transformation at an enormous speed. Ch'oe Myŏngik was born the middle of six children on the outskirts of Pyongyang shortly after the turn of the century and most likely in 1903, although his exact year of birth can only be inferred from his later essays. His childhood was spent in relative wealth due to his father's trading business, taking wild ginseng from the regions around Pyongyang down to Chinese merchants in the port of Inch'ŏn, next to Seoul. But Ch'oe's father passed away when Ch'oe was fifteen, just one year after he had moved to a dormitory to attend Pyongyang High School, and Ch'oe later described himself as having been shaped more by his mother, who lived another ten years in less comfortable family circumstances. Little is known about Ch'oe's private life, perhaps due in part to his reticence to follow contemporary trends toward semiautobiographical fiction. Yet he did publish a dozen-odd short essays during his lifetime that hint at a life split between business and art. His memories of childhood include scenes of his father inviting a storyteller to the family home, on which occasions all the elderly men from the area would gather to enjoy the entertainment. Perhaps passing on this love of storytelling was one way in which his father did indeed influence him, he later reminisced.[2] When Ch'oe himself was older and had begun to publish his own work, he lamented being unable to devote as much time as he wanted to his own writing because of the financial necessity of running a family business, apparently a small glass factory. Other essays attest to his interest and participation in events of national importance; as a young man he was in Seoul for the famous reading of the Declaration of Independence, which began what became known as the March First Movement opposing the colonial occupation.[3] The initial demonstrations led to protests across the nation, and in the Japanese metropole too, leading to violent suppression and thousands of arrests. Some reports suggest that Ch'oe's own mother and brother were caught up in the resulting imprisonments.

In the late 1920s Ch'oe began to write in leftist publications. There are just four brief short stories, known as *contes*, from this period, along with a short essay on the writer Yi Kwangsu (1892–1950). It was not until 1936 that Ch'oe was to attract wider attention and the admiration of critics and other writers with his debut short story, "Walking in the Rain" (Pi onŭn kil). Over the next five years he was to publish a total of seven short stories at an approximate rate of one per year and a roughly equal number of anecdotal essays. Few writers at the time attained his degree of renown with such low productivity. His first collection of short fiction did not appear until 1947, when two book-length collections were published—one, in the north, comprising new stories and the other, in the south, anthologizing his earlier colonial-era fiction. Ch'oe does appear to have picked up his writing pace in the newly formed Democratic People's Republic, publishing collections of new short fiction in 1947 (*Maengyŏng*, The Barley Hump) and 1952 (*Kigwansa*, The Engineer). In 1956 he published the historical novel *Sŏsan daesa* (Great Master of the Western Mountain), which was followed by four more short stories in the early 1960s. In 1964 the collection *Kŭl e taehan saenggak* (Thoughts on Writing) gathered essays that he had written over the previous decade on his writing practice. As is the case with so many writers who live in the Democratic People's Republic, it is difficult to obtain exact information on Ch'oe's publications, let alone to locate all copies. Similarly, we have no idea when Ch'oe passed away.

Despite his attestation of distance from the literary scene centered on Seoul, Ch'oe accrued a particular following among the intellectual classes during the late colonial period. In 1949 the southern-based critic Cho Yŏnhyŏn (1920–81), reviewing the republication of Ch'oe's earlier fiction in a single volume in the south, claimed that Ch'oe's relentless focus on "despair, unease and impotence" had resonated widely under the colonial occupation.[4] He heralded the characters of Ch'oe's fiction for their cohesion in displaying what he termed the "tragedy of self-consciousness"—the angst and sense of dislocation they experienced in their lives. Reading through Ch'oe's fiction, with its frequent references to Baudelaire, Dostoevsky, and Nietzsche, among others, it is clear that Ch'oe was steeped in the decadent art of the European fin-de-siècle, which resonated so powerfully in Japan and Korea alike during the interwar period. Aficionados of Japanese literature from the time will also detect in his work traces of the motifs and concerns of the great modernists

Natsume Sōseki and Shiga Naoya. Ch'oe forged a style that was resolutely his own, but he was undoubtedly well read and self-conscious in his aesthetic and political concerns and interests.

Cho's review feels a touch nostalgic for a time when intellectuals could share even despair in common, and who could blame him? By the time he was writing in 1949, two competing states had been established on the peninsula, and populations on both sides were engaged in vociferous debate and increasingly violent skirmishes. In the south, multiple political parties and independent candidates had competed in the first Constitutional Assembly election held in 1948, suggesting the severe extent of fragmentation in southern society; any sense of commonality and agreement had long since vanished. The year following Cho's review, the civil war was to officially explode. By 1949 Ch'oe had published a collection of new stories in Pyongyang in which the atmosphere of despair, unease and impotence had noticeably dissipated, except perhaps in the title story, "The Barley Hump," translated here, which attempts to narrate the transition from colonial into postcolonial time. After liberation from Japan and throughout the Soviet occupation Ch'oe had remained in his hometown of Pyongyang, which became the new capital of the Democratic People's Republic in 1948. There is evidence that he was treated as a VIP and invited to official welcoming dinners with Soviet dignitaries in the early days of the Soviet occupation, and he continued to publish extensively into the mid-1960s, long after many of the better-known modernist writers and artists who had moved up from the south had fallen out of favor, been sent into internal exile, or, worse yet, been executed during Kim Il Sung's consolidation of power in the mid-1950s. Yet Ch'oe appears to have maintained some distance from the center of power in Pyongyang, just as he had from the colonial capital earlier in his career. As the writer who during the 1930s had produced perhaps the most detailed aesthetic depictions of the streets of Pyongyang, he would have been hard to dismiss in the new state capital, and his previous rather aloof stance may possibly have saved him too.

The zeitgeist in the new capital of an emergent revolutionary regime did not favor the decadent atmosphere that Ch'oe had earlier explored in his work, but neither did Ch'oe allow the goals of the revolutionary regime—many of which he most likely shared—to overwhelm his own writing concerns. The stylist in him continued to flourish, and his experiments in writing inflected by the language of cinema persisted. If anything had changed by the time his second collection of new stories appeared in 1952, it was the appearance of a palpable sense of melancholy and pathos informed by a devastating personal experience of the civil war. Ch'oe's later essays reveal that his beloved elder sister lived in Seoul, and because of the embargo on communication across the border they were unable to share even letters with each other; his was one of millions of families separated when the partition of the peninsula hardened. His dearest wish, he wrote, was to spend the rest of his life near his sister and her family, but this wish was not to be realized.[5] A public letter from 1952, addressed to his son and only surviving child, reveals that the young man had not been heard from since August 1950, when he joined the People's Army. Ch'oe and his wife had themselves evacuated Pyongyang for several months during the temporary occupation of the city by the southern forces in the fall of 1950. His wife apparently died shortly afterward. The civil war and ongoing division, which persists to this day, tore Ch'oe's family apart. As for the final days or years of his life, we can only imagine how he may have passed them.

I n the early twentieth century Pyongyang was known as the most modern of Korea's cities. An early center for Protestant missionaries and home to new educational institutions, Pyongyang was at the forefront of the "new learning." By the 1930s it was also considered a hive of burgeoning industry. In a magazine roundtable discussion from 1939, a visiting journalist describes the wonderous sound of knocking and chipping to be heard when walking down a street as residents busied themselves with manufacturing and the home industries that set the city apart.[6] Other participants in the discussion located Pyongyang at the center of Asia on the strength of newly opened shipping lanes between Pyongyang and Shanghai and Pyongyang's key location on the railroad leading from Japan, via the Shimonoseki ferry, up from Pusan, Seoul, and farther into Manchuria. The railroad enhanced Pyongyang's position as a prime site for imperial tourism, and Japanese guidebooks from the time extolled the beauty of the female entertainers known as *kisaeng*. Such exoticism was not always dismissed by Pyongyang natives such as Ch'oe, who admired the serenity and architectural sophistication of the pagodas located along the Taedong River.[7] But the railroad also solidified Pyongyang's strategic importance once the Second Sino-Japanese War broke out in 1937, since it was the railway that transported soldiers and materiel out into the far reaches of Manchuria. The cacophony of influences, old and new, inspired the well-known avant-garde coterie named Tanch'ŭng, *La dislocation*. Ch'oe's brother, Ch'oe Chŏngik (dates unknown), was a member, contributing both fiction and an expository essay on D. H. Lawrence and the question of "sex and self-consciousness" to issues of their eponymous journal, which appeared briefly in 1937–38. Advanced industry and arts characterized the then third-largest city on the Korean peninsula.

The Pyongyang depicted in Ch'oe's debut short story, "Walking in the Rain," displays the ruptures of a developing city, literally "breaking through the old city walls" but with only half-developed, lopsided streets located on the other side: haunted by the spirit of the ancient city gate, animated by disagreement between young and old over customs and traditions, and challenged fundamentally by the driving ideology of self-improvement, promising a future that is far from guaranteed. The story's juxtaposition of a photographer who propounds the joys of building up his own business and saving money for the future with the artistic yet disaffected clerk Pyŏngil, who is struggling to obtain a reference from his employer, suggests something of the situation of Ch'oe himself, who often lamented the fact that he could not devote himself entirely to his art. But perhaps this was precisely what positioned him to write his elegy to Pyongyang and the disquiet embedded in the bourgeois aspirations of its inhabitants.

Ch'oe's best-known stories were written between his debut in 1936 and the onset of the Pacific War in 1941, which led to a harsh crackdown on publishing outlets in Korea. Stories from this time display a deep interest in exploring the schisms that characterized an increasingly divided colonial society. The gap between those who believed in the power of self-improvement through financial accumulation and those who sought meaning in life elsewhere appears to have been a particular preoccupation. "A Man of No Character" depicts the conflict in a fraught relationship between a drifting young intellectual and his dying father. Here the rupture is depicted as generational with the moneymaking entrepreneur having earned the disdain of his son, a highly educated teacher who nevertheless cannot find a target for his own desires. Although Ch'oe continually casts doubt upon the values of the entrepreneurs driving the development of the northern city, here the son discovers a new respect for his father's will to live, if not his passion for money.

The gruesome descriptions of the father's ailing body reappear in "Patterns of the Heart," where another listless drifter confronts a former revolutionary leader dying of heroin addiction in the Manchurian city of Harbin. Possibly the most memorable depiction of the fallen revolutionary in the wake of Japan's crackdown on Korea's communist movement during the 1930s,

"Patterns of the Heart" seems to signal that the revolutionary spirit, while violently suppressed, did not die but lived on in the shadows in the form of resistance to the state-led mobilization that characterized the years of the Asia-Pacific War throughout the Japanese Empire. Where other leftists famously "converted," rejecting socialism under the extreme pressure of torture or the enticement of financial incentives, Ch'oe's dying protagonist offers up recalcitrant refusal. So whereas the decadent atmosphere of decay in the story might seem at first reading to foretell the end of socialist opposition, a sign of resignation and defeat, it is more appropriately juxtaposed to the contemporary fascist ideal of "bright, clean, and healthy" living propounded by the imperial wartime state.

Ch'oe's work is notable equally for its attention to the gendered nature of the dislocations of modernity. In "Spring on the New Road" the schism between old and new cultures is moralized and spatialized onto country and city, but the ultimate victim of urban deceit and betrayal is a young peasant girl. "Ordinary People," meanwhile, presents the shocking scene of a sex worker being trafficked across the border into Manchuria. An unfamiliar and expansive geography of Korea within the Japanese Empire emerges, where Pyongyang links as naturally to Harbin as to Seoul, but the "north" is presented as a lawless region where violence rules without constraint. Ch'oe directs his focus toward the complicity of the passengers in a rail compartment, who witness the woman's transportation only to sneer at her. The morality of the common folk themselves is brought under scrutiny. This depiction of the heartlessness of the crowd surely resonated in an age of war and jingoism, but what makes the story even more extraordinary is Ch'oe's spirited and alluring female protagonist, whom Ch'oe resists any urge to present as a silent victim.

With the end of the war and collapse of the Japanese Empire, Ch'oe remained in Pyongyang, now administered by the Soviet

Union. As befits an event of immediate historical significance, liberation from colonial rule inspired much reflection on the recent past and hopes for a better future. Told from the point of view of a writer named Sangjin, "The Barley Hump" describes the final months of the war, when Sangjin evacuates to a rural village, through to his return to the village after the war to witness a community being reborn under collective, peasant rule. The semiautobiographical feel of this story, and similar stories by other writers, encouraged readers to read them, rightly or wrongly, as confessionals that attempted to explain—even exculpate—writers' actions during the period of the greatest wartime suppression before then describing a changed attitude to writing in the postcolony. Another such story by Yi T'aejun (1904–?) has been translated as "Before and After Liberation" and features more direct confrontation with wartime mobilization on the part of the colonial authorities and negotiations with a multitude of postwar factions by a writer deemed a cultural leader in the capital.[8] But Yi was a more controversial figure than Ch'oe in 1946 because of his previous and ongoing centrality to Seoul's literary scene and his then recent defection to the northern zone. Ch'oe was a Pyongyang native, and "The Barley Hump" focuses as much on the transformation of the peasants as it does on Sangjin's reappraisal of his role as a writer in society. The story offers a different but no less fictional version of the emergence of the new regimes that will intrigue readers interested in the history of the era and those who wish to understand the longer trajectory of writers such as Ch'oe who lived through the transition from a colonial to a socialist society.

The final three stories translated here originate from Ch'oe's 1952 collection of wartime stories and show something of the range and creativity of his continued experiments as a writer. It is common for readers and scholars alike to group stories from North Korea by theme or plot and then to dismiss them as propaganda, as if their content overwhelmed their stylistic

creativity and their messages were unitary and coherent. War—
and perhaps especially civil war—always demands taking sides,
but it also brings the challenge of new technologies and experiences to which the writer must respond. "Young Kwŏn Tongsu"
opens with moving scenes of the destruction visited upon the
city of Pyongyang, which was burned to cinders by aerial
bombing. It then offers a story of cunning resistance to wartime
occupation. The intensely cinematic "The Engineer" revisits
Ch'oe's earlier concern with the entanglements of visual images
and writing, this time within the drama of civil war. It is hard
not to sense a trajectory from the opening pages of "Patterns of
the Heart," where the speed of a train conjures up the fantasy of
a painting formed by accumulated scenes rapidly passing by the
window, to the closing lines of "The Engineer," where the dying
protagonist gazes upon the catastrophic and visually dramatic
tableau his actions have created. Yet the lonely depiction of the
dying hero casts doubt upon the martyrdom demanded by the
new nation-state. The revisions to the ending of the story upon
its republication one year after its first appearance—translated
here—show an apparent need to align the hero's fate more decisively with the new nation-state.

Finally, the sense of terror and devastation experienced by
those targeted by wartime bombing missions—iconized in U.S.
films from the time—is movingly depicted in "Voices of the
Ancestral Land," which is perhaps based upon Ch'oe's own
experience of having to flee his city as the frontline advanced. It
is hard to imagine a more poignant figure of the human body
under fire from twentieth-century weaponry than that described
in this story, where U.S. fighter jets open fire on a column of
evacuees fleeing the city of Pyongyang.

Toward the end of "The Barley Hump," Sangjin encounters
the peasant Ingap at a ceremony marking the first time the

anticolonial March First Movement has been celebrated since the collapse of the Japanese empire. Ingap holds a large streamer that reads, "Land to the peasants!" The story glosses Sangjin's thoughts: "He had perhaps always been vaguely conscious of this demand, but he had been unable to formulate words for it other than through suggestion or paradox. Today it had taken shape in a clear slogan; its time had come to be pronounced clearly and concretely." The scene highlights the centrality of land reform to the political agenda in the north, where its accomplishment was acclaimed as a great achievement in the wake of colonial rule and one that was not matched in the south. Yet the scene also attempts to describe a condition of consciousness and expression: with peasants now freed from the constraints of colonial censorship and educated outside of colonial institutions, clear demands could be not only understood but also expressed without resort to indirection. Given the centrality of irony and gesture to so many of Ch'oe's colonial-era stories, the statement might be said to apply to Ch'oe's writing as well. To a certain degree, his later stories seem to shy away from the opacity of suggestion to move into more direct forms of address, and yet we see in a story such as "The Engineer" how demands are not necessarily more concrete, only differently situated.

To readers in Korean today, Ch'oe's language offers a special challenge; its opaqueness occasionally defies comprehension. Partly this reflects the evolution of written Korean in the interim, and partly it reflects Ch'oe's erudition and his dedication to placing words in their rightful place. Ch'oe was well attuned to the subtleties of language, whether the properties of northern dialects, the multilingual nature of colonial life, or the classed variants of speech. Intonation, pronunciation, and the subtle hierarchies of the multilingual situation clearly fascinated him. It is difficult for an English translation to show a Korean character speaking Japanese with a Korean accent, or mixing Korean and Japanese in daily conversation, as happens repeatedly in "Ordinary People," or a younger educated man struggling to understand the colorful language of an aging peasant. This translation attempts to at least suggest that the writer is playing with the lack of transparency inherent in the everyday use of language. Likewise I have retained Ch'oe's penchant for inserting parenthetical question marks after words he would like us to approach with caution, particularly in "Patterns of the Heart."

A further challenge for the translator of Ch'oe's writing comes from the lack of definitive reprinted editions. The palimpsestic nature of colonial and Cold War censorship has meant not only that particular aspects of the base text may be contested but also that the texts themselves can be hard to find. The texts used for these translations were found in libraries in Seoul, London, and Washington, DC, as well as in personal collections. Many of the stories have been published several times—in 1930s colonial magazines, in single volumes from both north and south in the 1940s, and sometimes in contemporary South Korean reprints. Versions vary slightly, and so the edition used as a base text here has been noted in a bibliographical note at the end of the volume.

Ch'oe is one of several significant Korean authors who participated in a thriving modernist literary scene in the 1930s only to disappear from the historical record in South Korea. All writers who either defected to the north or, like Ch'oe, simply stayed in place there found their works banned until 1988 in the south. While other writers who defected from south to north, such as Yi T'aejun, have been rehabilitated to some extent, perhaps Ch'oe's elegiac records of life in what was to become the northern capital made restoration to a South Korean history that much harder. The world of English-language translation has tended to follow the literary canon of South Korea. Even today access to North Korean publications from outside the country remains inconsistent, and only a portion of Ch'oe's oeuvre is easily available. For a writer so attuned to the subtleties and complex conditions of historical location, it is ironic how arbitrarily Ch'oe himself has been located in later history. With this first translation of Ch'oe's works into English, I hope to offer a new perspective on the modernist experiments that flourished in Korea in the mid-twentieth century and to share some of the fruits of Ch'oe Myŏngik's creative genius.

NOTES

1. Ch'oe Myŏngik, *Kŭl e taehan saenggak* [Thoughts on Writing] (Pyongyang: Chosŏn munhak yesul ch'ongdongmaeng ch'ulp'ansa, 1964), 98.

2. Ch'oe Myŏngik, "Sumŭn ingwayul" [Hidden Rules of Cause and Effect], *Chogwang* 6, no. 7 (July 1940): 228–30.

3. "3.1 ŭi hoesang" [Remembering March First], *Kŭl e taehan saenggak*, 81–92.

4. Cho Yŏnhyŏn, "Chaŭisik ŭi pigŭk: Ch'oe Myŏngik ron" [The Tragedy of Self-Consciousness: On Ch'oe Myŏngik], *Paengmin* (January 1949): 132–37.

5. "Na ŭi nyŏmwŏn" [My Heartfelt Wish], *Kŭl e taehan saenggak*, 62–71.

6. Kim Yŏnok et al., "Nae chibang ŭi t'ŭksaek ŭl malhanŭn chwadamhoe: P'yŏngyang p'yŏn" [Roundtable Discussion on Regional Characteristics: Pyongyang], *Chogwang* 5, no. 4 (April 1939): 260–82.

7. Ch'oe wrote about the many different meanings of the Taedong River for Pyongyang natives such as himself in a short essay, "Yŏrŭm ŭi Taedong kang" [The Taedong River in Summer], *Ch'unch'u* 2, no. 7 (August 1941): 196–98.

8. Yi T'aejun, *Dust and Other Stories*, trans. Janet Poole (New York: Columbia University Press, 2018).

patterns of
the heart

and other stories

Walking in the Rain

The factory where Pyŏngil worked lay just outside the city wall, as did his room on the opposite side of the city.

Although the two sides of the city might be said to oppose each other, the angles of the wall did not form a perfect square, and his thirty-minute walk to work barely scraped past one corner of the inner city midroute.

Once he left his boardinghouse, he had to walk for about ten minutes down a narrow, steep path, which did not appear on the city government's borough map.

That path ran between tiny houses packed so tightly together they seemed to rub each other's backs and past alleys so narrow that even on a summer's day the rapidly rising dawn sun barely illuminated a hand's width beneath the eaves on the western side.

Perhaps it was always quiet, but Pyŏngil, who only walked this way in the dark mornings and evenings, saw hardly anyone except for the dogs loitering around the toilet holes at the foot of the back walls of the houses on the eastern side and the half-blind women who would throw dirty water into the alley from the kitchens on the western side.

Pyŏngil's legs were already weakened by beriberi and wished for nothing more than a wide and flat road, even if it meant walking a little further. In truth, it was hard work to make his way down this path.

In the spring the ice would melt, and the path would turn into slush. In the summer the seasonal rains rushed down the narrow alleyway, transforming it into a dirty stream. With the first snow of winter the children would polish the path and slide down the ice.

Pyŏngil would walk along as if he were crossing a log bridge, his arms flaying every which way as he tried to balance his body weight upon his fragile legs.

Once the snow had melted and the summer rains were over, the rocky path remained. Pyŏngil constantly scuffed the toes of his precious shoes in the dark.

Whether looking up, distracted by the sound of an airplane, or head bent and deep in some thought, he would inevitably step in some malnourished child's feces, even in broad daylight.

In the spring, small stalks of grass would shoot up one by one at the foot of the gloomy walls.

The moss spread like fungus on the tiles of the old houses packed into the alley and sometimes glistened green with the damp of the morning dew, but it was the young stalks of grass creeping along one by one and decorating, albeit poorly, this rocky path, which renewed the feeling that even this slum belonged to an earth welcoming in spring.

At night, a house on the western side might have a lamp hung over the door opening onto the path. A sign would read, "Land-Houses-Workers-Introductions."

These signs moved around. A lamp anticipated on one corner would have disappeared, while a new lamp would unexpectedly appear on a previously dark corner.

Recently another new lamp had appeared. Each evening the sound of a young girl singing to the accompaniment of a drum drifted out from the house.

Once the lamp was in place, rickshaw men holding lanterns could often be seen waiting outside the door.

And then this summer, a silk gauze mosquito net, large enough to fill the entire inner room, had made an appearance one early evening.

The other houses were still burning dried mugwort to repel the mosquitoes.

This house had also burned mugwort last year. Each time Pyŏngil walked home through the alley thick with mugwort smoke in the evening and caught a glimpse of that green mosquito net with its red trim, his mind invariably conjured up the thought of a watermelon with its stalk sliced off.

After passing through the alley, he emerged onto a wide dirt road, recently leveled according to the new city borough plan.

This road had knocked down one corner of the city wall, but it had yet to acquire the feel of a city street.

A single row of new houses, all whitewashed walls and galvanized iron roofs, stood as if to screen the older, tiny houses, which were spread out forlornly beneath the crumbling city wall, like opened tombs.

There were no houses on the other side of this lopsided barrack-style street, where various merchants still used the empty land outside the city wall to sell fuel and timber and earthenware pots in open-air stores, and where factories manufactured cement pipes.

The developing city had begun to break through the old city wall and penetrate the grassy land beyond.

The ancient gate to the city stood not far away, and the once yellow earth of this not yet fully established road had been blackened and bruised each day by soot and footprints. Through that gate the city streets themselves were visible, pierced at right angles by the newly built road.

Pyŏngil walked past the outer side of the gate and entered the factory district of the city, which was known as a new city of commerce and industry. This was where the factory in which he worked was located.

Pyŏngil had walked this road for more than two years now. This was the shortest route from his home to the factory each morning and back home again in the evening.

Though he had been employed for two years, Pyŏngil had still not managed to find a guarantor.

Each evening he would add up the cash-on-hand column in the account ledger while his boss counted the money in the safe. The day's work was not finished until the figure Pyŏngil recorded in the ledger matched exactly the amount of cash his boss had counted.

Once his boss had locked the safe, Pyŏngil would pick up his hat and step outside the office door behind his boss, who would then make sure to lock the door.

After a day spent working as a combined office boy, errand boy, and scribe—sweeping and wiping the floor, bringing tea to visitors, tidying up after lunch, writing some dozens of letters, and keeping track of the accounts—Pyŏngil would return to his boardinghouse room, his head and legs weighing him down like heavy flasks of water.

He would bid his boss farewell and step outside the factory gate, but instead of feeling the relief of liberation from a day's toil, he would invariably be overcome by an unspeakable sense of desolation as he stood beneath the tiny stars sparkling in the sky.

He would inhale deeply on the cigarette that he had resisted smoking in front of his boss and ponder once more the problem of a guarantor, which he had been seeking unsuccessfully for the past two years.

As far as responsibility was concerned, it was simpler not to be able to touch the cash or the documents inside the safe, but faced with the ongoing, relentless surveillance by his boss, Pyŏngil had felt an equally unremitting sense of displeasure since his first day at the office.

Upon first encountering this surveillance, he had felt apologetic and grateful for the goodwill of his boss, who had employed someone so unworthy as himself with no guarantor.

Then, for a while, he had harbored resentment and antipathy toward this boss, who still could not trust Pyŏngil's simple sincerity.

Recently, he had come to realize that it was due to an ill nature—that his boss distrusted not only Pyŏngil but everyone else too, even his own wife—and so Pyŏngil had tasted the satisfaction of being able to truly despise someone.

He tried his best to ignore the despicable and unrelenting scrutiny and not be upset.

However, from the early days when he had felt grateful and apologetic through his subsequent feelings of resentment and antipathy and up until the present, when he merely despised his boss and tried to ignore him, Pyŏngil had never been able to suppress the displeasure that inevitably arose in response to unrelenting surveillance.

Even now, Pyŏngil's empty stomach would churn with nervous exhaustion at the mere thought of his boss's large fingers noisily jangling the keys to the safe while checking the ledger one final time.

Pyŏngil looked up at the old city gate, towering over him like an enormous shadow. He saw the black contours of the eaves, which seemed poised to take flight into the dark sky, and then he gazed once more through the gate at the brilliant city lights, and he tried to conjure up those amazing population figures—one hundred thousand, two hundred thousand!

"They are all preoccupied with their own problems." With this thought, he looked up at the sky once again and watched the bats flit around in the darkness. They were flying out from the black gate tower and disappearing back inside again. It was as if the spirit of the ancient history of the old city gate were still alive and roaming through the night.

By the time Pyŏngil walked this way it was usually dark, and few people were to be seen. Yet even those he passed by every day remained mere strangers on the roadside.

Nothing ever seemed to change, not even the face of the old woman sat inside a shop window on the lopsided street, nor the crab apples piled up at her side.

A gentle rain began to fall. The gate tower was still visible through the rainy mist, but its contours merged with the darkness, as if the whole thing might melt away into the black clouds that seemed to harbor an eternal rain.

And yet a single lamp, hung high up on the observation deck, still cast its light onto one corner of the eaves.

Those tiles yet to be covered by moss glistened, and clumps of tall grass, which had sprouted up through gaps in the roof, waved in the slanting streaks of rain.

Pyŏngil had reached the lopsided street, where he took shelter under the eaves of a house. A lamp hung in the small entranceway. A square had been cut out of a whitewashed wall to one side and glass inserted to create a show window.

"So, there's a photographer here!" Pyŏngil smiled at himself for not having noticed before. A cheap sixteen-watt bulb lit up the show window. Blue wallpaper with a gold foil pattern decorated the interior, which was filled by small photographs, the size of a business card, pinned up in a circle surrounding a larger wedding photograph. They were mostly portraits of young girls who probably worked at the rubber factories or rice mills. Their nostrils looked as if they had been painted on with ink.

"Must be because the photos are pinned at the top, so their faces are all bent back . . ." Pyŏngil shared this small joke with himself.

Flat noses pushed down by low foreheads and squashed between dull eyes and protruding cheekbones. Gazing at them, Pyŏngil pictured to himself the rough hands resting on laps.

He lit a cigarette and turned around to look into the dark empty lot on the opposite side of the street, all the while listening to the sound of the rainwater rolling off the eaves and splashing at his feet. From time to time, a gust of wind sprayed the rainwater onto Pyŏngil's trouser legs.

In the shop window next door, polished green crab apples shone in the light, as if they had been brushed with oil. In their midst the old lady half-dozed and half-puffed on a long pipe while watching the smoke rise up into the air. A thin line of blue smoke wafted up toward the top of the window.

The wisp of smoke would scatter and vanish into the shiny cheeks of the crab apples with each swish of a reed fan that emerged from the dark shadows.

Each swish made Pyŏngil shiver, as if the harsh whine of a mosquito had pierced him like a steel needle.

Other than the sound of falling rain, the evening was quiet.

He turned back to face the photographs in the show window, yawning repeatedly. Suddenly the back insert onto which the photographs were pinned was pulled back, and an enormous face appeared.

When the eyes met Pyŏngil's face they gazed at him through the glass for a while, and then a pair of red hands proceeded to sweep inside the show window and even dust the light bulb. A spider's web, as fine as a thread of silk wool, stretched from the light bulb to the ceiling.

The man put down his brush and set to chasing flies out of the window with a fan; his large rosy face glistened under the direct light. A deep furrow in his brow looked as if it had been carved out by knife, his messy eyebrows might well have been pasted fragments of a shoe brush, and a large shadow resembled spilled ink cast from the nose to the furrow of his upper lip; in fact, this face belonged less to a living being than to a silhouette cut out of white card and painted with ink brushstrokes.

Pyŏngil wondered whether this face, and those he had seen in the photographs earlier, were not all tricks played by the poor light. He recalled how streaks of rain had seemed to dampen only one end of the eaves on the old gate tower, which disappeared into the stillness of the dark.

He stood listening to the sound of water rushing off the eaves outside the door of his consciousness, and then he turned to face the bloodshot eyes on the caricature created by the light in the show window, the eyes that now glanced at him through the glass.

A sudden gust of wind splattered rain onto the glass between them, and the water streamed down, drawing long lines.

"Sweat running down a caricature!"

Pyŏngil tried to conjure up such an illusion. He had felt a slight antipathy toward the bloodshot eyes, which had been stealthily watching him.

The face seemed surprised by the rain and retreated from the show window. And then the door opened.

Holding the door open, the man first looked up at the sky and next addressed Pyŏngil, who was also looking up at the sky, "It's really pouring down. Why don't you come inside out of the rain? Yes, do come on in."

A plump stomach peeked out from beneath his summer jacket. The protruding stomach rankled Pyŏngil's sensitive nerves, much like the swollen sky that continued to drop rain so relentlessly, but then he thought that it was probably the nature of such a plump stomach to show kindness to a stranger, and so he stepped inside the entranceway as bidden.

The man offered Pyŏngil a seat and began to unpin the photographs from the insert, which he had earlier removed from the window, all the while whistling away.

The sound of the rain falling on the galvanized iron roof made the narrow, messy room seem all the more forlorn.

The shoe brush eyebrows frowned, deepening the lone furrow on the brow still further, and the whistle seeping through those puckered lips grated on Pyŏngil's ears.

Pyŏngil flicked through the pages of an album placed on a table while he listened to the whistling merge with the sound of the rain.

Then the photographer stopped whistling and turned to face Pyŏngil, saying, "There's going to be a lot of rain this year."

"Really . . . ?"

"Just you wait and see. There'll be floods for sure this year."

"Really . . . ?"

Pyŏngil could think of nothing else to say.

"They say that the gatekeeper snake at the West Gate has been out and about."

Pyŏngil said nothing, and the man stopped his work as if he were about to explain the details of a great event. He began with the words, "Yesterday evening, when a gentle rain was falling . . ."

Someone was walking under the West Gate, holding an umbrella, when suddenly some tiles from the gate scraped the side of his umbrella and landed at his feet with a crash. He looked up to see an enormous snake, sprawled across more than ten of the wide furrows in the roof and brandishing a head the size of a rice scoop. Crowds of people gathered around. An agile young man from the crowd climbed up onto the gate and attempted to catch the snake. All the old people were causing a fuss, saying that if the gatekeeper snake were hurt something terrible would happen. While the old people kept saying to leave the snake alone, the young people gathered around, laughing raucously and shouting out directions to the young man who had gone up onto the gate—it's here, no, it's over there—while the snake slid around and evaded the cracking whip. Finally the snake had slipped between some of the tiles and disappeared. The youngsters grumbled about the escape, but the old people, although relieved, began to worry that the floods would be severe this summer.

The story ended with the words, "The old people's warnings usually come true."

"Really?" Pyŏngil felt awkward that he had now uttered the same response three times in a row. On the other hand, it would be most bothersome if he were to say, "Do you really think so?" and the talk turned into a futile complaint about the ignorance of young people.

Just then a small food box was delivered to the entrance. The man had been busy pinning up new photographs, which he must have developed that day, but now he put his work aside, placed the bottle of rice wine and food dishes from the food box on the table, and pulled up a chair.

"Well, let's eat together. I'm afraid I had already ordered this . . ."

And he poured a drink, which he offered to Pyŏngil.

Pyŏngil leaned back from the cup, which almost touched his nose, and declined, saying, "I'm sorry, but I don't drink."

"Oh, don't say that, just have one cup. I've already offered it to you, so why not just have one . . ." It was quite unpleasant the way he pestered Pyŏngil to drink without even having introduced himself. Pyŏngil refused several times. Yet there was no reason to think the drink was offered out of anything other than goodwill and, moreover, Pyŏngil could imagine all those super-stitious customs of such drinkers—about wine cups having to be passed around, or never refusing a drink once offered—and so he could not hold out indefinitely.

There was no option but to empty the cup and place it back in front of the man. As long as Pyŏngil poured a drink and passed the cup on he would be playing his part in this drinking party, and he placed the empty cup back down.

"Well now, try some of this. I'm afraid I had already ordered, though."

The man poured himself a drink while he said this and pushed the chilled chicken soup toward Pyŏngil. "Yes, do try some." He urged Pyŏngil again, then fetched another set of cutlery from out the back before trying the soup himself. "Oh, that's refresh-ing. Nothing beats a drink after a hard day's work."

Pyŏngil swallowed the word "really," which was about to leave his lips one more time, and instead tried to offer his sym-pathy. "It must feel good when you're tired."

"Oh it feels good, all right. As you know, the photography business is all about technology and so it's not the kind of work that brings on aches and pains, but you do have to be in the dark room every day using your eyes and brain. Then, to have a drink like this . . ."

He poured another cup, emptied it, and passed the cup to Pyŏngil, who was already asking, "Do you have very much work?"

"Just enough to keep me from getting bored. And if there's no work and I make no money, then I don't drink but just go to bed early. Ha ha . . ."

From the way he laughed so contentedly and downed cup after cup, he must have made a lot of money that day.

Pyŏngil emptied the cup once more. By now the photographer was a little inebriated and poured Pyŏngil yet another drink.

"So, what's your business, sir? Oh, but we haven't introduced ourselves yet, have we? I always see you walking past. Although this is the first time we have sat down together. Well, my name is Yi Ch'ilsŏng. I'm very pleased to make your acquaintance."

After their long introductions were over, the photographer proceeded to address Pyŏngil as Mr. Kin[1] and poured him a drink in an even more familiar fashion.

"Mr. Kin, you should start your own business. I was a salaryman too until several years ago."

And he began to recount his life story.

Pyŏngil thought it distasteful that the photographer was suddenly acting his senior now that he knew Pyŏngil's position.

Rather than listening to the photographer's story with respect, he regretted sitting down and even began to feel something approaching disdain and annoyance.

According to the life story, the man must be twenty-five or twenty-six years old.

His achievements during the decade that had passed from the age of thirteen until opening this studio three years before amounted to his photographic skills (?) and this independent business, which Pyŏngil could now see with his own eyes.

At the end of the story the man pushed open the paper sliding door behind him, saying to Pyŏngil, "This is the studio." He then stood up and offered a tour.

One side of the ceiling was built of glass, installed at an obtuse angle. Through this glass ceiling the sky outside looked dark. The rain pounded on the glass with a heavy sound that did not linger.

A background had been hung on the facing wall. The electric light from the room outside cast a dark shadow from a sofa

1 The photographer now addresses Pyŏngil as Kin-san, *Kin* being the Japanese pronunciation of his surname Kim, followed by *san*, "mister" in Japanese.

onto a tree, which was painted in grey on the background behind. In front of the sofa, there was a small table on which a pot of narcissi and a large book written in a Western language had been placed, just like in a still life painting.

The photographer turned on the light and stepped into the studio, where he proceeded to stroke his camera, which was covered with a black cloth.

"I don't have that much equipment. This is the most expensive thing and would cost me three hundred and fifty or sixty won if I had to buy it today. I bought it on monthly installments, although I've paid it all off now . . ." He explained with great satisfaction how grateful he was to his boss of more than ten years—from his days as an errand boy and then an assistant—for acting as a guarantor so that he could buy this camera in monthly installments, and how the camera was now all his, ever since he had paid the final installment last spring.

Then he turned the light out in order to step back into the front room, and Pyŏngil found himself looking at an ink painting as he stared at the narcissi in the now dark studio. The photographer patted him on the shoulder. "It's quite simple really. That's all that I've got to call a background, but I sit the customers in front of that landscape, place the narcissi in front of them, and then take their pictures while they quietly hold the book open."

He laughed loudly and, sitting back down again, added, "I must get around to making a better background." He certainly did not seem to be making fun of his customers but rather laughing at everything with an unbearable sense of satisfaction.

Even the scarlike furrow in his brow appeared to smooth away when he began to cool his face with a fan.

The photographer's mood seemed only to improve. While chattering on and on, he kept twisting his right ear with his right hand, most likely a habit of his when drunk.

Pyŏngil yawned and stared at that right ear, which was now as red as a tangerine slice.

Taking hold of the ear once more, the photographer continued to talk. "Mr. Kin, you're strong enough that you probably don't feel the heat. Maybe it's the drink, but I've been putting on weight since last year . . . oh boy, is it hot . . . as the old people say, if you get fat and make some money, then when the night comes . . ."

Stroking the stomach that spilled out from beneath his jacket and all the while laughing loudly, he began to talk about matters of the bedroom, of which Pyŏngil was still innocent. When he saw that Pyŏngil was blushing madly, he urged, almost admonished him to start a business, get married quickly, and discover the joys of life.

Pyŏngil wanted to ask more about those joys and what he would have to do to find them, but the thought of listening to more of the sweaty photographer's words made him utter a simple "really" yet again, and glance at his watch while stretching.

It was past ten on a summer's night. . . . At some point the rain appeared to have eased somewhat.

The photographer urged him to wait for the rain to stop completely, but Pyŏngil borrowed an umbrella, promising to return the following day.

He had not walked many steps when he turned around and saw that the light in the show window had already been turned off. All the shutters on the storefronts were closed on the dark lopsided street. Streaks of rain glistened, like threads of silver in the light that seeped out faintly from between the gaps in the doors, and fell noisily on his paper umbrella.

The night air hit his cheeks and the raindrops struck his palms, bringing a sudden recovery of clarity to his senses, which had turned all too hazy.

A couple of frogs croaked in the empty grass plot. Pyŏngil stood still and strained his ears. He did not have to wait long before he heard another croak.

He could picture those frogs—eyes blinking from the raindrops beating down, white stomachs wobbling under the water with each croak.

That bastard of a frog's stomach! Suddenly these words slipped out, and Pyŏngil felt a disdain for the photographer that he had not noticed before.

A foul taste of saliva filled his mouth, as if he had actually licked the white stomach of a cold and slippery frog, so that he had to spit with each step he took. The stench of alcohol steaming past his nose with every breath sickened him, and his steps faltered when he tried to turn his face away.

Am I drunk? This thought brought him to his senses somewhat, but the splish-splash of each step through the muddy water sounded like someone was following behind, and he kept turning around anxiously.

That bastard of a frog's stomach! He turned into the narrow alley, spitting once more at the thought.

Once in the alley, the sound of the rainwater falling off the eaves on both sides made him feel dizzier than had the noise of the rain itself.

On the eastern side the back walls were crammed together more tightly than tombs. From the west the sounds of crying children and gossiping women merged with the smell of the hot air, which pushed out through doors that opened into dark rooms.

Here and there, in rooms lit by small oil lamps, wizened old limbs, like dried snakes, poked out from beneath dirty quilts, there was a hacking of phlegm, and snores reverberated.

To Pyŏngil, walking up the alley with his umbrella scraping on both sides, everything seemed even more dismal than it was in the mornings and early evenings.

Were these the joys of life? That frog's stomach of a bastard! He mumbled to himself and spat as he walked along.

A bell rang out from behind. A rickshaw lit by a yellow lantern was approaching.

Pyŏngil did not want to be seen tottering in front of it and stood to one side. Once it drew closer he could see that the lantern was flickering under some kind of small rain hat. The rickshaw passed by, scraping the umbrella that he had half folded down, and a voice inside lamented, "Oh, why do these alleys have to be so narrow?"

"Madam should buy a big house on the road below and move there," gasped the rickshaw man in reply.

"Oh, that'll be the day . . ." The kisaeng's voice broke off, but Pyŏngil could picture her sat beneath the dark awning, straining her ears to hear the rickshaw man's reply.

"Why, with the amount madam must earn . . ." Catching his breath, the rickshaw man stopped midsentence to blow his nose.

"I wonder how much a big house would cost . . ." Suddenly, her voice took on a desolate tone as she talked to herself.

"It wouldn't take more than three or four years for someone who earns as much as madam." He finished his sentence in a comforting voice, but there was silence inside the awning before she spoke up in an even more desolate tone.

"But it's expensive to feed and clothe a large family." Silence fell once more, broken only by a heavy splash each time the rickshaw man stepped in one of the muddy puddles that glistened faintly in the lantern light.

The rickshaw stopped before a small gate, where a tiny round lantern shone like a white grape floating in the rain that poured off the edge of the dark eaves.

The kisaeng stepped down from the rickshaw and swiftly rushed through the gate to avoid the falling water. She briefly peeped back out to say goodbye to the rickshaw man with a childlike smile before disappearing inside.

In the light of the lantern held by the old rickshaw man, Pyŏngil caught a glimpse of her tiny hands, half covered by sleeves, and a red jacket tie hanging down over her colorful skirt, which she had gathered up around her waist. Her outfit matched her pale young face, making her look younger still.

And yet the words she had just exchanged with the rickshaw man and her desolate voice, which had concluded their brief conversation with a confession of her difficult life, were hardly those of a child.

That voice still lingered in Pyŏngil's ears long after she had disappeared inside, and the face flecked with the soft down of a freshly hatched chick still hovered before his eyes; together they reminded him of a blade of grass on which he had cut his finger as a child.

When that green grass, so soft but so sharp, passed before his eyes, his nerves seemed to finally cast off the effects of the alcohol.

He even found himself smiling with bemusement when the rickshaw passed by him again and the light of the lantern revealed the dirt on his trousers.

When he reached his room he lay down, resting his head on a couple of books to hand.

Gazing up at the ceiling, he watched again those scenes of life he had witnessed and heard on that road, where it was raining tonight, the unchanging course of his life that he had walked every day for the past two years.

This was nothing new. And, of course, it was nothing unusual. It was so ordinary and unremarkable that it was rather he who was strange for storing such things in his head and thinking about them. Yet, although that dreary reality spread out before him was prosaic, he also thought he could sense some more powerful rhythm. The rhythm seemed to transform into the force of a grave criticism bearing down on Pyŏngil's chest.

I have neither the elasticity of a frog's stomach nor the spirit and sharpness of a blade of grass, do I?

His head full of such reflections, he closed his eyes, urging on the sleep that would come only with difficulty, it seemed.

The dreary rains dragged on. It was the kind of persistent rain that provokes the yearning for a violent storm ambitious enough to wash clean the face of the sun, the blue sky, and the earth.

That sun had not shown its face for several days. Even when the rain did clear up for a while, the feverish sun behaved like an ill-tempered invalid.

Children rushed out in joy at the sight of a long-absent rainbow stretching across the sky ahead of them, but they were soon chased back under the eaves in the treeless streets.

Even the stars in the night sky rarely switched on their lights. An endless stream of black clouds rushed by like herds of wild beasts. And then the rain fell again. A myriad mosquito larvae wriggled in the rainwater pools, like amputated nerves.

Recently Pyŏngil had completely lost all strength to read.

One night he had fallen asleep very late after reading *The Idiot* and had dreamed of Dostoevsky spitting up bloody phlegm after a long empty cough. He was leaning over a chair, eyes closed and semiconscious, blood and spit spattered all over his beard. Pyŏngil saw the dark circles around the eyes, the sunken cheeks and beads of sweat gathering on the broad forehead threaded with black veins, and he could still hear the exhausted breathing when he opened his eyes. The only sound in the room was the dry chime of the unoiled wooden clock, striking four o'clock.

Having woken like this, Pyŏngil took one more look at the biographical note on the author at the front of his copy of *The Idiot*. It was just as he had remembered; the only chronic disease recorded in the note was the epilepsy from which the literary giant had suffered.

The bloody phlegm dotting Dostoevsky's oriental-looking beard must have been a phantasm produced by the memory of Pyŏngil's own father's death when he was young.

Recently, even when he was tidying up the account ledger at the office, he would see Nietzsche pacing up and down like an enraged bull in a backyard, clasping a mossy green rock to his chest and striking his own head. Pyŏngil would feel himself on the verge of a groan, and a shiver would run down his spine.

Each time this happened he would glance over at his boss, who would be smoking a cigarette while turning the pages of the newspaper, and he would be envious of those who seemed happy living with no other ties to print but the newspaper. Recently, in fact, his books, which he had once so coveted and purchased with the few coins left over from his salary after paying his rent, felt more like a burden.

His nerves must have been exhausted by the stimuli of literature, by the rampant proliferation of piles of words compressed into type.

Every day when he arrived home from the office exhausted he would grumble to himself about when the tedious rains would draw to a close.

He had always stopped to look up at the gate tower on his way home, thinking that this was now "his time" to do as he liked, but these days he would more often than not simply pass by, sheltering under his umbrella. On the occasions he remembered to look up, not even the bats were flying out of the tower, which was bathed in endless streaks of rain. The story about the snake knocking down tiles brought a sense of gloom upon him, as if he had seen the dead body of a family member.

He lost the courage to sit down in front of the black type crammed into books in his airless room, where all that awaited him was the whining of mosquitoes, the smell of bedbugs, and fleas intermittently leaping around, and he began to visit the photographer, as if lured by some kind of temptation.

The photographer welcomed Pyŏngil's visits. Drinking and desultory chat would ensue.

Pyŏngil was new to the delights of alcohol, and he felt a certain satisfaction that he could drink his share and give and take in the exchange of idle gossip.

While listening to the photographer's rambling chatter, Pyŏngil would suddenly remember the book waiting for him at home, left open from the night before, and he would glance up at the clock, but the sound of the rain would help calm a sense of unease, arising from nowhere in particular. Each time this happened he would reach for the cup, forgotten while the photographer was caught up in the excitement of his own words, and down gulp after gulp.

When he set off for his room just before midnight, Pyŏngil felt almost relieved to be caught in the rain. "What am I doing?" He wondered, as he stood beneath the stars, which peeked out from between black clouds. It was easy to blame his actions on the rain, to think, "This life is only temporary. It's all because of the rain."

When he sat down at his desk, he would realize yet again that all of "his time to do as he liked" had evaporated.

He needed to sleep in order to rise early the next morning, but he could almost hear the snores of the photographer, who would already be fast asleep, and then he would be unable to sleep himself.

Lately there had been times when the photographer had declined to drink. He had decided to abstain for a while, because he was making so many mistakes during the development process on account of his shaky hands. With no customers due to the rain, he too seemed to be feeling melancholy. But if Pyŏngil bought some rice wine and encouraged him, after three or four cups he would soon cheer up.

On one of those days when he had grown lively, he passed the cup to Pyŏngil and asked, "What do you do in the evenings, Mr. Kin?"

Up until now, most of the subjects the photographer had raised consisted of tales and boasts about his own past and lifestyle. There were times when Pyŏngil felt embarrassed by the excessively private nature of the stories, but he listened patiently and smiled.

However, in the past few days the photographer had evidently been trying to steer the subject of conversation toward Pyŏngil's life, maybe because it was Pyŏngil who had been buying the drinks.

Two days earlier he had asked how much Pyŏngil earned.

The previous night, after inquiring about his rent, the photographer had done some calculations: since Mr. Kin was not taken to wasting money here and there, he must be saving seven or eight won a month, even if he spent as much as six, consequently, over the past couple of years he must have put aside at least two hundred won all told. When Pyŏngil had laughingly replied, "Well, that would be good if it were true, but I haven't saved a penny," the photographer had hastened to add, "I'm not someone who would try to borrow money, so there's no need to lie." Then he had grown really curious, "Well, if you really haven't saved anything, how did you spend all that money?"

Pyŏngil guessed that this curiosity had prompted today's questioning and reluctantly answered, "I read books when I'm bored." He turned the scowl on his face to one side on the pretense of exhaling the smoke of his cigarette. The photographer looked at Pyŏngil and, with no hesitation, continued.

"Books? Are you studying the law? All that money . . . on books? Maybe you're not telling the complete truth here, but do you really mean that you use all that money yourself without putting any aside?" His bloodshot eyes widened in a stare.

Pyŏngil was well aware that after a few drinks it was the photographer's wont to expound, or even insist, upon his own beliefs in an excited tone with sentences that began with the words, "It is in the nature of human beings that . . ." Pyŏngil had listened half-heartedly before, but he found it extremely unpleasant now that he had become the object of the prying and advice.

A little drunk himself, Pyŏngil thought of saying, "What business is it of yours?" But he did not have the courage; it would feel like using someone else's words that did not fit this occasion.

He could say, "What would become of my life were I to refrain from buying even books in order to save money? Do I have time to go to the library these days? You may well ask why I read books, but I don't have any particular objective." Or perhaps, "I also used to try to find answers to such questions as how to live without any regrets, or what is the nature of man, but now that this weak body of mine is no longer able to work its way through school and a rancorous resentment has built up inside me, brought on by my boss's insults over the past two years . . . in other words, in this world where everyone is absorbed in their own business, reading is simply my way of devoting some time to my life." But, if he were to do so, he knew that his voice would quiver and the photographer would yawn, and so he just smiled bemusedly and instead he responded, "So maybe I should start saving the money that I spend on books? I could seek happiness in watching my savings account grow bit by bit each month, instead of in books . . ."

"Of course, now that's happiness! As they say, save a little, earn a lot."

Pyŏngil interrupted, "Ha ha, turn time upside down and enjoy the thousand won I'll have in ten years' time now, ha ha . . ." And he swallowed the contents of his cup, which had been sitting a while, and poured a drink for the photographer, as if to cut him off.

The photographer accepted the cup with a grave look that suggested he had been hurt by these barbs and was trying to maintain his composure in the face of Pyŏngil's hollow laughter, but then he steeled himself, rolled his eyes, and forged ahead bravely.

"Ten years is no time. Ten years is ten years, whether you save money or live recklessly, so shouldn't we save our money like other people do . . ."

At this Pyŏngil's eyes shone for a moment, and he asked, almost defiantly, "Like who? How come?"

Up until this point, he had been listening with indifference, but now he suddenly wanted to hear just what exactly this happiness was of which the photographer dreamed.

"What do you mean, like who? Mr. Kin, just listen to me. I'll put it another way. What I mean is that the greatest pleasure in the world is to sit in your own home, however small it may be— as long as it is yours and not rented—and then, you maybe run a business and feed yourself and save up anything left over little by little."

The photographer wet his throat with another drink and passed the cup to Pyŏngil.

"Now just think about it. If I can keep going like this for three years, I think I can get my own house, and by then it will be time for my oldest son to start school. It doesn't matter if the house is in an out-of-the-way place, so long as it is near a school and I can set up shop on a big street, then just you wait and see. I won't be envious of anyone, not even that Ch'oe Ch'anghak."[2] He laughed with delight. His eyes momentarily met those of Pyŏngil, who was holding the cup and staring back at him, and the photographer stopped laughing a little awkwardly before smiling again, as if nothing had happened.

"How about it? Am I right, Mr. Kin, or wrong? Ha ha ha."

And he pushed Pyŏngil's shoulders so hard that he almost spilled his drink.

Pyŏngil emptied the last few drops of wine onto his tongue and seemed to taste its full bitterness as he swallowed. Then he placed the cup back down on the table with a slight knock, lowered his head, and uttered the word, "Well."

"What do you mean, well?" The photographer seemed to be scolding Pyŏngil for such an insipid reply. "Your problem, Mr. Kin, is that you do not take other people seriously. From what I can see, you have no intention of saving and setting up a home." The photographer looked across at Pyŏngil as he spoke, shaking his head as if to affirm his own words.

Pyŏngil could only agree.

Even before the photographer's lecture, Pyŏngil had been well aware that these hopes and goals were those of the happiness idealized by a certain social class (to which he himself was also fated to be subject).

No matter where he went he invariably heard and saw that the lifelong efforts of this class should be directed toward the attainment of this happiness. He himself could not believe that this was true happiness. And yet whenever he tried to think about his own hopes and goals, he came up with nothing, as if his brain had frozen. He could neither imagine other hopes or

2 Ch'oe Changhak (1891–1959) was a contemporary gold-mining billionaire and supporter of Japanese business interests on the Korean Peninsula.

goals nor understand why it was that he could not believe in this happiness to which everyone in his class aspired.

Pyŏngil felt himself in the lonely position of wavering without any direction, caught up in the waves of people struggling and fighting to achieve such hopes and goals. Yet he could just manage to whisper into his own ear that a lifetime's goals should not be decided upon so thoughtlessly.

How much support the photographer must derive from his own confident words in comparison with such whispers! Hopes and aspirations, whether expressed in words or in writing, tended to weaken with age and lose much of their passion and attraction, so when Pyŏngil saw that the photographer had, on the contrary, found ever more faith and happiness in his own words, he could conclude only that the photographer must truly be happy.

With this conclusion Pyŏngil could feel himself succumbing to that ideal of happiness. And yet, he could not subject himself with all his heart. Just like a slave in revolt, the drudgery and flogging that fate visited upon him seemed as if it would only be more severe.

He was not able to make plans for even one confident step into the future but had instead, under the whip of a cruel fate, become a slave to living itself; whenever he thought of his own life, however long it might be, he would break into a sweat all over, as if he were trapped in an endless nightmare, groaning. Such were the oppressive thoughts distracting him when suddenly the photographer turned to face him with the words, "Oh, Mr. Kin, there's a favor I'd like to ask you . . ." Pyŏngil watched a beaming smile spread across the photographer's large oily face, as if a page had been turned and a new picture revealed.

"Mr. Kin, do you happen to know any gentlemen in the newspaper business?" His expression was now urgent.

"No," replied Pyŏngil, to a more disappointed click of the photographer's tongue than expected.

"But it is in the nature of human beings that they should make connections as widely as possible." And the photographer continued, laughing, "Mr. Kin, you are very self-involved!"

The photographer laughed again and began a lengthy explanation—while repeating the phrase "gentlemen in the newspaper business" with every sentence—about how it would increase his income considerably, and what a great honor it would be for his studio, if he could only hang up a "Designated Studio" sign bestowed by some powerful newspaper's branch office. In fact, only a few days earlier, he had been outraged by an article in the local news section concerning the fuss caused by a three-foot-long snake that had appeared on the West Gate, and he had ranted to the effect that if it really were a journalist's responsibility to report such a small thing as a big event, then what kind of stupidity was it to write that the gatekeeper snake, which had lived there so long, had measured only three feet.

"I have been thinking about this for a while, but the reason why I'm bringing it up now is that, well, an opportunity might . . ."

He lowered his voice, as if to confer about something.

"The owner of XX studio has been suffering from consumption for quite a while and could leave us any day." (He explained that this was his former boss, whom he had previously mentioned.) "There's not another studio in the city as big as his and, what's more, it's perfectly equipped. With this opportunity, if I could just get a Designated Studio sign from a powerful newspaper and move into his studio, there's nothing else I could possibly ask for . . ."

He continued. "Mr. Kin, if you could just spare a little effort at this opportunity and help me get that sign . . ."

Pyŏngil smiled. "This opportunity? When exactly did the boss say he would die?"

The photographer glanced furtively at Pyŏngil over his cup. "Oh, Mr. Kin, this is why I say that you do not take other people seriously.. I said any day soon, and even if it doesn't come to a quick end, I can hang that sign up now right there, so please don't make things any more complicated than they are, just try to exert yourself . . ."

Pyŏngil did not like the way the photographer looked at him. He turned away to slowly exhale his cigarette smoke up toward the ceiling, and said, "Well, I'm not making things more complicated. When I played tennis at school and had to go second, I also used to wait impatiently for the game before mine to finish. Ha ha ha . . ." His laughter was quite exaggerated.

"Of course, that's how the world is!" The photographer laughed with delight. He shook Pyŏngil's wrist and urged him once more to ask a "gentleman in the newspaper business" for a Designated Studio sign, even if only through an introduction by a friend of a friend.

By the time Pyŏngil stepped out into the street amid the photographer's entreaties to come back the next day his head hurt, and he felt unspeakably depressed.

He turned around to find the show window already in darkness. When he had turned around that first night it felt as if the light had already been switched off by chance, but ever since it had invariably been dark by the time he reached the spot where the frogs had croaked. Pyŏngil usually set off for his boarding-house room around the same time, but the show window light would be extinguished after a set time, as if the photographer were counting how many steps Pyŏngil had taken.

Even though he knew very well that the light would have been turned off, he would still turn around to find it already dark.

Once when he was drunk and feeling jovial, he had stopped early in order to wait for the light to be turned off, and watching it happen, he had smiled and murmured, "But how could it be otherwise?"

Each time the light went out, Pyŏngil felt an unfathomable loneliness, as if the two of them each stood alone before a curtain, which had been drawn closed according to the order of their own lives as the business of the day came to a complete end.

The only thought remaining in Pyŏngil's aching head today was the refrain, "The photographer must have gone to bed already." He found himself mumbling the thought under his breath.

In no time at all he had entered the narrow alley, where someone was knocking at the door with the round light and a puddle at its foot, calling out "Ranhŭngi, Ranhŭngi."

The light illuminated the tall silhouette of two rubber boots stood side by side in the shadows of the eaves, not moving. A man knocked carefully on the door two or three times and then, equally carefully, called out again, "Ranhŭngi, Ranhŭngi." He seemed to be quietly waiting. Pyŏngil strained his ears with each call. He realized that for some reason his heart was pounding.

The man knocked on the door several times, called out "Ranhŭngi, Ranhŭngi," and then waited for a reply that never came. Finally, he gave up and turned around, shooting a glare at the onlooker, so sharp it seemed to slash Pyŏngil's face; dazed, all Pyŏngil noticed was the handlebar moustache beneath the man's nose. Pyŏngil lowered his head, as if in flight, and returned to his room, where he pulled back his quilt and lay down. He felt feverish, and his whole body trembled.

The fever raged for several days before he could return to that road, but he did not visit the photographer again. He realized that during those visits he had behaved like a hot, sweaty horse searching for some dust in which to roll. And it had not been somewhere he could roll in peace.

His nerves were raw, as if exposed on the surface of his skin; it had been painful to encounter the life of the photographer, whose nerves seemed to function more like the strong suckers of an octopus.

Yet, having decided not to visit the photographer again, he felt uneasy each time he passed the studio. He thought the photographer must be displeased that he had suddenly broken off contact after visiting every day. More than anything, Pyŏngil was sorry. It was as if he was slighting the goodwill of the photographer, who had seemed to like (?) him. Not knowing the reason why Pyŏngil stayed away, wouldn't the photographer misunderstand and presume that his request for a Designated Studio sign had been a burden? Unlike the hero of a novel, there was no way that he could talk of his true reasons for avoiding the photographer, who likewise was no novelistic character. But once he had been overwhelmed by so many thoughts, Pyŏngil finally started to feel annoyed by the photographer's carefree existence in the middle of this road, which gave Pyŏngil a rare opportunity for contemplation in his life. In the mornings, of course, the studio door was closed. Perhaps the photographer had drunk all alone last night and was still asleep? On the other hand, his was hardly the kind of business that needs to open its doors from dawn, thought Pyŏngil. Yet, whenever he caught a glimpse of a pale human shadow inside the open door of an evening, his hair would stand on end, as if he were stepping over the sprawling corpse of a snake.

For the past few days the studio door had been closed in both the morning and the evening for some reason.

When the door remained closed on several hot summer nights, Pyŏngil grew curious. He even thought of stopping by just once to see the photographer but decided that it was better not to repeat such a painful episode from the past, and he walked on feeling rather glad that the door was shut.

Almost a week passed by in this fashion. On the first dry morning in a while, Pyŏngil sat at his office desk reading the newspaper.

"TYPHOID FEVER RIFE IN PYONGYANG, MANY DEAD," read the large headline of the article he was reading, where he saw the name Yi Ch'ilsŏng on the list of those who had died at the city's quarantine hospital. Pyŏngil did not at first believe his eyes, but judging from the address and occupation this had to be Yi from the Ch'ilsŏng Studio.

Pyŏngil felt empty, as if someone had been talking to him and had suddenly left in the middle of the conversation. Now that story would always remain interrupted in his memory. The shrill tone of the phone reverberated, and he picked up the receiver, but even though his pencil ran across his notepad he found himself wondering if this was the nature of human beings after all, and having lost attention he could say to the caller only, "I'm very sorry, but could you repeat that, please?"

He had no way to mourn the death of the photographer. All he could do was look toward the far north, where black smoke rose up from the crematorium on Ch'anggwang Mountain.

Two days later, he saw a cart loaded with luggage in front of the studio.

A young woman was carrying what looked like a little girl on her back and holding the hand of a small boy about five or six years old while they walked behind the heavily laden cart. Pyŏngil guessed that this was the photographer's family.

He followed after them and watched until they disappeared inside the city gate.

Once they were out of sight he continued on to the factory, mumbling to himself, "People survive somehow until they die." He recalled the feeling of not being able to go on living when, as a child, his parents had died.

The lamp in the entranceway was already gone by the time he walked home in the evening. A crooked piece of paper bearing two large words, "To rent," had replaced the photographs inside the dark show window.

The awful news of the typhoid epidemic died down after a while. There was no flood, and the tedious rainy season began to look as if it might end soon. Even when Pyŏngil was caught in a late rainstorm he did not seek shelter under any eaves. He wanted strangers on the roadside to remain strangers on the roadside forever.

And he walked that road planning from then on to devote himself to his books.

A Man of No Character

When a telegram urging him to come home quickly followed just two days after the letter that informed him his father had taken to bed for the last time more than ten days earlier, Chŏngil went to the hospital to say goodbye to Munju. His intention had been to leave soon in any case, and Munju was well aware of that, but the sight of her lying alone in the hospital room prevented him from uttering the words, "I am leaving." Perhaps it was because she was wrapped in a white bedcover and lying on a white bed in a white room, but Munju's face, which was also resting on a white pillow, looked even more thin and pale, definitely sicker than upon her admission the previous morning. When he realized that simply the idea of being in hospital had depressed her spirits to that extent, he began to regret having pressed her to go to the hospital against her wishes. Eventually he showed her the telegram and said he must leave, explaining that back at home everybody would be expecting him to arrive on the next express train now that they had sent this urgent missive. Munju nodded and told him not to worry; she even made an effort to smile when Chŏngil took hold of her hand, which was resting on the bedcover. Then, while the dispirited Chŏngil caressed her hand, she asked whether he would be late for the train, and suddenly turned away on the pretense of needing to cough. Chŏngil hurriedly said goodbye and turned away himself, afraid of seeing Munju's tears, but once he had left the room and reached the entrance to the hospital, he asked the old servant, who had followed behind him, to keep Munju company; Munju needed to remain absolutely calm and not become lonely and sad at any cost. He then jumped in a waiting taxi and reached the station with three or four minutes to spare. Once there, he found a public telephone and called the Arisa tearoom in the hope of finding Munju's older cousin Unhak, to no avail. All he could do was to ask the boy who picked up the phone to contact Unhak and urge him to visit Munju as often as possible. Then Chŏngil rushed to board the train. Waves of exhaustion rolled up through his head as he dropped his body down into a corner of the relatively empty second-class car. He leaned against the window and closed his eyes. He was not likely to fall asleep, but still he placed a hand-kerchief over his face so that no one would see it crumpled by a grimace, and he attempted to calm his mind. While his body shook in time with the rumbling of the wheels, all kinds of dis-ordered thoughts raced around inside his head behind his closed eyes. He desperately regretted the mistake of taking Munju to the hospital against her wishes. But did he have any other choice?

When Chŏngil received the letter two days earlier, his first concern had been about leaving Munju on her own. He should have rushed straight home, but instead he adopted a rather liberal interpretation of the phrase "Come back as soon as you can" and decided that, before setting off he would either find Munju a temporary place to stay or admit her to a hospital. If he left her in the boardinghouse, it was clear that she would find the isolation unbearable and would begin to roam about outside, when what she needed was absolute calm. There was the additional problem that Munju had already despaired of her illness and was not the type to take her medicine at the appropriate time, unless pressed by someone else to do so. Moving her elsewhere all by herself did not make much sense, and so finally he had her admitted to the hospital. Munju was by nature afraid of solitude and did not want to be alone in a hospital room, separated from everyday life; she also said she did not want to feel indebted to expressionless doctors and nurses, whom she had never seen before and with whom she felt no connection. Chŏngil had cajoled and begged her to go to the hospital, saying that he wouldn't be able to stop worrying if he simply left her where she was. In the end she agreed and threw her chronically fevered body onto his chest, sobbing that if he left this time, wasn't it to rid himself of the burden of her forever? Once his father had died, she continued, he would have to look after his mother, and that meant his returning to his wife. She was willing to go to the hospital because he was paying the bill, which would remain the only reliable proof that they had not in fact broken up. Ever since Chŏngil had returned home a couple of months earlier, upon first receiving the news that his father had been diagnosed with stomach cancer, Munju had alternated between laughter and tears while constantly asking him when he would leave her. This had continued right up until the previous evening, but now that he really was leaving and he witnessed her mournful effort to smile before turning away to hide her tears, not even urging him to return to her as quickly as possible, he wondered whether she might not just die a lonely death while he was gone. If that were to happen, even he would feel he was really discarding her and running away. By forcing her into a lonely hospital room without any prospect whatsoever of recovery, was he not merely attempting to ease his own worries?

Everyone must have taken their seats, because the dizzying cacophony in the carriage quietened, and then the reverberation of the wheels gradually faded as well. The train had left the polluted city behind and was running among green hills and fields. Outside the window, green waves of barley rolled past, like flowing oil. Chŏngil lit a cigarette and felt himself lighten up, as if a fresh breeze had blown into his head at the nostalgic sight of this rural landscape. But after no more than two deep intakes of breath the dizziness returned; he threw his cigarette out the window and closed his eyes again. Thoughts kept rising to the surface in his mind, like opaque bubbles boiling up in stagnant water on a hot summer's day; such thoughts seemed to be the way his exhausted brain discharged its accumulated refuse. The dying father whom he would see in just a few hours, the groans and stench emanating from a body aging and long sick; his mother's teary eyes; the sound of the wife he hated, who would see this as an opportunity, as granting her permission to cry and pour out all of her worries; the filthy chamber pot . . . and then, there was the blood Munju hacked up, her hysterical laughter and crying . . . and he could hear the sounds produced by twisted human emotions, and picture the gloomy scene in the hospital, darkened by death's shadow. If the thought of his father dying threatened momentarily to force its way to the surface above the dizzying cacophony in his head, it soon disappeared, leaving behind no reverberation in his heart; just occasionally he would catch himself in the middle of this game of emotions, and he would smile and murmur with a sentimental flourish: *My father on his deathbed!* He wondered about his inability to feel sad about his dying father; was it perhaps due to his own age, now approaching thirty? His heart must be even more heavy and dark than he had supposed, congested and mute, like a vase that made no noise no matter how hard you beat it.

Outside the window, the small stations through which the express train passed without stopping looked arid, like red fragments of earthenware breaking up the spring greenery of the mountains and fields. How many times did he see porters, like small dolls cast from lead, emerge from beneath the eaves of red station roofs bearing the full light of late spring and casting thick shadows at sharp angles, and dazzling tracks, running alongside empty uncovered platforms on the opposing side? Some passengers were preparing to alight at the approaching K station.

Munju had accompanied him this far when he had returned home a couple of months earlier after receiving a letter informing him that his father had vomited blood and been diagnosed with stomach cancer. Back then, she had not yet lost confidence in her own health or fallen into despair. "Aren't you leaving me forever now that I've become a burden?" She had sobbed the night before he left, before announcing she would accompany him as far as K station, instead of resting at home as he had suggested. From there she planned to catch a train back in the opposite direction and in fact had done so in the end. Until this point, though, she had gazed out the window, mostly silent and with no fuss, and then she had smiled, as if struck by a sudden new thought, and jokingly proposed that now they had come this far she might follow him all the way to his hometown for a change of scenery, so that she could accompany him on his return. Chŏngil was taken aback by her words, almost as if he had been stabbed. He did not know what to say, because he did not want to reveal the extent of the jolt he experienced. There had been times before when Munju would jokingly propose something like this and Chŏngil had simply accepted it as playful, with the result that Munju would suddenly straighten her face and scold him for not taking her seriously, and then she would pester him to turn her joking suggestion into reality. This was a habit of hers. If he were to tell her such words were futile it might well arouse her strangely stubborn nature, but if he were to speak rashly, as had occasionally happened before, when they had laughed and said, "Okay let's do it then," he might end up really having to take her all the way to his hometown, because there was more than a trace of true feeling harbored within her playful words. He could hardly beg her understanding as long as she was still joking, and he did not want to look too serious too soon by arguing that he was in no position to take her home when he was visiting his sick father. While Chŏngil had hesitated, trying to think of a way to turn Munju safely around at K station, he could feel her eyes fixed on his face; his anxiety multiplied when he caught sight through blinking eyes of the scenery outside the window and the station, which was gradually drawing closer. Munju had observed him with an insistent smile that contrasted starkly with Chŏngil's frozen face—*Look, just pretend that I'm a nurse and take me to your house, and then*—she started saying that she, who could not even recall what her own parents looked like, wanted to nurse Chŏngil's father as if he were her own and that she was confident she would be able to look after him better than any nurse from the countryside, even though she had only completed the first year of medical school, and then she burst into fits of laughter. As her arguments grew longer and her laughter gradually stronger, Chŏngil was first relieved and only later able to play along. By the time he was certain Munju was laughing at her own expense . . . just at that moment the train once again drew into K station, the source of so much anxiety for Chŏngil back then.

Now he looked down at the platform through the window; it was the same platform upon which he had stood then too, after stepping down from the carriage with Munju to wait for her train, which would arrive from the opposite direction, and although they waited no longer than three minutes, he must have taken out his watch several times. Chŏngil had been taken aback by Munju's hysterical laughter, which he had understood only when it grew in intensity and she had said, "Stop looking at your watch and get back on the train. I'll wait here alone." He had put his watch away without even checking how many minutes were left; clearly he was anxious to move on. Then as now there had only been two minutes remaining, but Chŏngil had kept pulling out his watch, anxious to escape as soon as possible from Munju's side and from her unrelenting surveillance of his heart and his gaze. Tears had welled up in her eyes, which did not relinquish their fixation on his, until finally she turned away with the words, "I know you are in a hurry, but you might just spare some thought for me." And she stepped up into the train, which had just pulled in. They stared at each other through the train window in silence, faces devoid of all expression, like two cups of cold water, until finally the signal for departure had appeared. Chŏngil had quickly entreated her to rest and not worry herself, before jumping up onto his own train. When his train started to move and he looked back out of the window, Munju was already heading back along the tracks in the direction the two of them had just come. At the moment the window of her carriage disappeared behind the moving town wall, he had caught a glimpse of a white handkerchief, fluttering like the wing of a white butterfly against the black body of the carriage. Yet more outrageous behavior! He tutted to himself but then recalled the tearful smile that had hovered on her ashen lips. At last, the tail of her train vanished around the corner of the hill. With Chŏngil's eyes losing their focal point, the fields had seemed even more expansive than before. His head had emptied, as if the memory of Munju had left along with her. But that completely empty head had felt equally heavy, as if all his thoughts up until that point had fallen into a deep slumber and he was sensing the entire weight of a suddenly idle brain.

Chŏngil leaned his heavy head against the window and closed his eyes, feeling the wind graze his face. The wind felt fresh because of his hair beating against his neck, even icy when he imagined the racing train slicing this same air into pieces. He remembered how a brand-new straw hat had been blown off his head while he was looking out of a train window like this back when he was at university. At that time everything had seemed too precious to miss by closing his eyes as he did now. Even the loss of his hat had been a mere coda to the entertainment of gazing voraciously down upon a constantly evolving landscape.

Wasn't it only three or four years ago when he had passed an entire summer hatless? His pride still might not allow him to recall his student days with any hint of sentimentality, but when he thought about the last couple of years of his life, and especially his relationship with Munju, wasn't it simply honest to admit that his self-respect had rotted away as definitively as that straw hat had disappeared back then? His relationship with Munju! His life, which now revolved around Munju! There was no reason for any of his former pride to linger as long as he was still playing the baby at the age of thirty, leading a decadent life on money he received so indecently from his mother, notwithstanding his father's loud complaints, as if being an only son were some great thing.

The first year of his teaching life had seemed like an extension of his student days until he gradually began to lose interest in his studies and lacked direction once he had dusted off the chalk for the day and stepped outside the school gates. Sometimes, when he had nothing to do, he would sit until late in a tearoom just in order to rest his legs, which were exhausted from wandering through the streets. All around him, young people passed the time yawning and gazing at the cigarette smoke that wafted up from the tips of fingers propping up chins, their gloomy poses huddled beneath shadows, projected like rocks onto the wall by the faint electric light. Chŏngil, too, would gaze mindlessly at his own shadow, magnified to enormous dimensions by the angle of the light, and soon he realized that he was no longer satisfied by the stimulus of the coffee clutched in his puffy hands and wanted to drink alcohol instead. From time to time he would admonish himself, reminded of Zola's complaint of having slowly grown too fat to have any energy left for worrying about the future, and then Chŏngil would tell himself that, although an occasional drink was fine, the day after not drinking was even better; and yet, those teetotal days would soon turn gloomy again if they continued for too long. He would take to drinking again and wonder whether he had become an alcoholic, because it seemed to him that his ennui and depression were caused by his craving for alcohol instead of his consumption of alcohol's acting as a solution to help him forget his ennui. Each time he picked up a glass, he would promise only to drink a little, but would invariably finish up drunk. The following day he would barely make it through his classes before stumbling through the congested streets on shaky legs with a cloudy head, like some kind of ghost. Occasionally, he would enter a bookstore on these wanderings. This was the one habit that still remained from his student days. But now this habit was drenched in nostalgic sentiment. He was no longer searching for a vital book, given that any structured research and plan for reading had long since evaporated. He would absentmindedly cast his eyes over the books leaning aslant on the tall, wide bookshelves, and he would gaze at their covers: the classic Ming-style type and the new sensibility of cursive writing, which looked as if the ink had only just dried. A vague glance at a newly released collection of writing from someone he had once loved and respected would evoke a sensation of remembrance, like the body warmth of a woman who had once captivated him. Occasionally he would pull out a newly published book by an author whose name he recalled from something he had read in the past and peruse the table of contents, only to discover a missing link far too gaping to allow for any connection with the book. He would return the book tidily to its place and gaze up at the bookshelf in frustration, as if he faced a wall he could not break through no matter how many times he threw his own bloated body against it. And yet, when he took a step back and looked up at the bookshelf again, he could also feel a sense of joy and majesty, as if he were gazing upon the pyramids or the grandeur of the Great Wall, solid bodies forged from sweat and blood. He recalled a time, seemingly now long past, when he had harbored the ambition to place a stone of his own atop this tower of culture. That ambition had vanished like a shooting star, drawing a momentary line across the night sky with its dazzling light. Once the trace of gold across the night sky fades away, a black line takes its place, and when even that black line disappears, we cannot help but sigh. This was how Munju had appeared in his life! When Munju had pressed him to die with her he had agreed, as if he would always listen to her. At her first request he could feel the teeth of a poisonous snake bite down on his chest, but though he thought the sentiment far too extreme, hadn't he gone and buried his face in her emaciated chest and cried? Back in Tokyo, when Unhak had introduced his cousin and laughed while he explained that she had made the leap from medicine into the arts of dance, Chŏngil had thought that such irrepressibly shining eyes could not possibly belong to any doctor. Last autumn, when he had encountered her again after a three-year interval, this time as the madam of the Arisa tearoom, he had taken one look at her pale face, at her almost translucently white, slender fingers, her lips as round as clams even with no rouge applied, and the shining eyes that yet seemed always tired and unfocused, and he had thought that Alissa must have looked like this when she wandered through that ancient garden in the gathering dusk, calling out Jerome's name. But whereas Alissa's shining eyes possessed an otherworldly angelic beauty beneath her black mourning veil, Munju wore a green Western-style dress over a body so slender that the curves seemed to flow without a single crease, and the sparkle in her eyes seemed almost wicked, like a poisonous mushroom beneath the light of the moon. One day late in the autumn, he had asked Unhak whether it might be all right to befriend her, and Unhak had looked at him carefully before replying, "That's up to you, but do you really want to be a fish who can no longer swim in pure waters, seeking out the Dead Sea where fish float so well? If only that hysteria, stemming from her uncultivated decadence, were less seductive . . ." Despite

Unhak's warning, Chŏngil had begun to meet up with Munju, who would sometimes be happy when he agreed to die with her in response to her pestering but at other times would writhe around tearfully, asking why he wasn't strong enough to lift her up and urge her to live even as she begged him to die. Her sobs would inevitably culminate in rounds of hacking, and after that blood. Each time this happened, he would lay her down in his arms, dab her forehead and chest with a cold, damp handkerchief to try to cool her down and wipe the blood away before telling her to rest; these were the only words of comfort he could find. After going through this several times, he had realized that whenever Munju's health improved slightly and she felt more confident about life, she would say she liked him because he would die with her, but whenever her health declined or, even if that were not the case but she simply felt anxious about her health due to her terrifyingly overdeveloped sensitivity, then she would throw a fit and ask why he was unable to beg her to keep on living. He could find no way of knowing in advance when such moments might arise. He did wonder whether her behavior might be connected to her menstrual cycle, but since they were not married he had no way of knowing whether that were the case. In fact, he could find no pattern at all: when she vomited blood at the beginning of one month, he would pay attention at the beginning of the next month, then luckily nothing would happen and he would wait for the following month, to no avail. Sometimes she would cough up blood at the beginning of the month, but then a month or two later her coughing would become severe at the end of the month. Given the situation, the best course was probably to always make a decided effort to comfort her and argue they should live, no matter the time in the month, but she continued to be most delighted at his promise to die with her when her health was at its best and she felt confident about life. He could conclude only that it was the pain in her heart emerging through such words, which were clearly not spoken for words' sake, nor were they fully self-conscious. Her eyes would shine, her clam-like lips would tremble, and she would cling on to him with a strength so frightening he could hardly remain unaffected and would agree to die with her when she asked. If he managed to muster the composure to reflect at such moments and ask her why she felt this way, albeit in an effort to comfort her, her disappointment would stretch beyond measure.

Of course, at such times it was all but impossible to summon up such composure.

Even though he could not suppress a frown at the thought of their life, his feet would head toward Munju's place whenever he walked out of the school gates; he pictured himself defeated by the lure of some kind of decadent intoxication, like an addict drawn to an opium den.

Back when Chŏngil had arrived home later that day, his father was not groaning in his sickbed as expected but was seated in his study as usual and meeting with his debtors, broker, and scribes, although he did look a little thinner than before. The doctor, who had diagnosed him with stage 2 symptoms of a now inoperable stomach cancer, said that it helped that the cancerous growth was in the lesser curvature rather than the cardia or pylorus, meaning his father was still able to digest food and water, but above all it was due to the patient's immense determination that his spirit remained unbroken in the face of such advanced symptoms. The old man had taken great pride in the fact that he had reached the age of sixty without even knowing the taste of medicine, and now he seemed to have taken a dislike to this doctor—who took a more serious view of the indigestion, which the old man did not even consider an illness—and subsequently, he was of a mind neither to take the hospital medicine nor be seen by the doctor again, rounding out his complaints with the question: "What do these new-style doctors know about anything except lancing an abscess?" He would let the old herbalist feel his pulse and declare simply that the source of the illness lay in congestion or roundworms in the stomach, and then he would accept the cup of medicine with the constant gripe, "What, more medicine!" When Chŏngil urged his father to go to the hospital to recuperate, with the hope of perhaps slowing down the progression of the disease a little, even if a complete recovery was beyond hope, his mother had supported him by saying, "Chŏngil will take care of the household affairs." This had provoked an angry interruption from the father, who shouted back, "What does that kid know about the way things work?" The fuel for the old man's anger lay not only in the son's mistreatment of the daughter-in-law who had been loyal through all difficulties but also in the fact that this son, whom he had funded with great effort through to "university study," had yet to attain any government post that might bring glory to the family, nor had he become a high-earning lawyer or a doctor. Indeed, he had rejected his father's advice to give up his poorly paid teaching job in order to help back at home and learn the ins and outs of trading; instead, he continued to use up even more of his father's money to fund his shabby nomadic existence away from home. "I keep telling you this, but just look at your brother-in-law Yongp'al!" All the father's reprimands would begin with the same comparison between his useless son and his son-in-law Yongp'al, whom he could not praise more highly. This Yongp'al, whom the father trusted so much, had originally been the old man's clerk. As the clerk gained the old man's trust in his role as a kind of secretary and advisor, the old man, who had a reputation as an ignorant, mean, and greedy miser, now earned additional complaints that his cunning and hard-hearted behavior was unbefitting his plump appearance. When Chŏngil had heard the news in Tokyo that his little sister was to marry this Yongp'al, whose cunning and cold countenance he had despised from first sight, he struggled to picture them as a cozy pair of newlyweds and was too depressed and angry to congratulate them properly.

Even before this he could hardly bear to look his little sister in the face without grimacing, because her right eye was as opaque as a weathered stone. But it was especially difficult for him to think of her eyes as eyes of love, so disconnected were they from the world of light and so incapable of illuminating the workings of her heart. Far from feeling gratitude toward Yongp'al for marrying his sister, who had hidden herself away in a kitchen corner on account of that one eye and missed out on her flower-like youth, he had instead wondered whether Yongp'al's heart might be just as opaque as his sister's right eye. And yet, whenever he saw that same little sister these days—now a mother who carried her head high and smiled at everyone with pride, revealing the face she had been so ashamed of as a child—he could not help but feel a warm sense of gratitude toward Yongp'al in the small corner of his heart that still retained some scorn for his own neurotic and fastidious nature. This Yongp'al had now begun to interfere in Chŏngil's domestic affairs as well, in an attempt to keep them in check and having clearly developed the confidence to hold Chŏngil in disdain as someone who failed to understand the value of money and misused the funds that the mother-in-law was handing over under Yongp'al's watchful eye, even though Chŏngil already received a decent monthly salary in his nevertheless shabby position as a teacher (to borrow the father-in-law's words). On this particular day, Yongp'al had come to discuss something with Chŏngil's father but had skirted over the surface of the issue when he found Chŏngil in the room, as if trying to avoid sharing business secrets. When he stood up to leave he flashed a wildcat smile at Chŏngil while saying, "Though it has been a long time since you were here, elder brother, you must find it awfully boring." This made even the old man wonder whether his reprimand had been too harsh, and his eyes settled heavily on his son, who sat kneeling before him. *Why am I this angry right now?* It was not so much the thought that he hated his son, but some kind of unfortunate premonition lurking somewhere in his heart, which made him explode in anger and feel flustered and annoyed beyond words. But this realization only exacerbated that anger, and he struggled to calm down when he realized he was banging a full pipe on the floor and screaming at his son, "You good-for-nothing!" While Chŏngil listened to this scolding, he had to suppress the urge to smile and joke back in return, "You're so right, father, I'm a good-for-nothing. I think so too, you know."

On that visit, Chŏngil had left again after two or three days. When his mother had begged him to give up his job and stay at home to take care of his father, who did not have long left to live, Chŏngil countered that it would be irresponsible for him to suddenly resign, especially since the doctor had said that his father's illness was not absolutely urgent, providing there were no unnatural stimuli. Then Chŏngil added, "I'm sure my brother-in-law will take good care of household affairs." He returned to Seoul.

Chŏngil went straight to Munju's boardinghouse when the train pulled in that evening and found Unhak there. The two of them looked surprised to see him: Munju stared without saying anything, and Unhak asked why he had returned so quickly—after all, once he'd gone that far, why would he return so quickly? "Perhaps I was chased out." Chŏngil lit a cigarette and smiled for no particular reason. Unhak looked bemused before forcing an heroic yet half-hearted smile. Munju remained silent until she asked them both to leave, explaining that the thick smoke made her cough and she planned to sleep soon anyway.

A few days later, on a Sunday, Chŏngil had taken Munju out of the city when it started to rain, forcing them to take refuge in a farmhouse before returning only late in the evening in a car sent to pick them up. Inside the car, Munju leaned back into one corner and closed her eyes as if to sleep, silent, as though she had forgotten Chŏngil was at her side. Despite the spring, a cold wind rolled around inside the narrow car, which felt even more frigid because of the rain streaming down the windows and the sound of the storm outside in the dark, mist-shrouded country-side. Munju coughed from time to time, but her eyes remained closed. The sudden rainstorm could hardly have been predicted, but Chŏngil still felt apologetic and could only watch on silently. Her face seemed paler than ever, with her closed eyelids shielding the light from her eyes and her blue eyelashes casting a deep shadow. When Munju slept like this, Chŏngil struggled to imagine any human warmth in her body, which looked like a blade of grass propping up a fallen white petal of a face. Another coughing fit forced her eyes open, and she saw that Chŏngil was watching her; she gazed into his face, her eyes unfocused yet still shining, and barely managed to breathe out the words "Don't worry" before shutting her eyes again, leaving a faint smile to linger on her closed lips. Chŏngil had to look away; he stared out through the streaks of rain rolling down the window and realized that tears had inexplicably gathered in his own eyes while he watched that faint smile disappear from her lips. In the mist that hovered over the apparently sleeping city, only the streetlights had opened their eyes, and the shining tram tracks stretched out into the distance in the empty, rain-washed streets.

As soon as they arrived back at Munju's room, Chŏngil spread out her bedding and told her to sleep soon, worried that the harsh coughing fits might erupt again at any moment, but she protested that her cough had improved and that she felt fine. She did not want to be left alone on a rainy night and begged him to stay with her, so he sat down again with the words, "If you have a pair of scissors, I'll trim your nails for you." He was bothered by the silence between them as they sat across from each other with only the noise of the rain outside in the night. After com-plaining that she was hardly likely to own a pair of scissors, Munju rummaged around in a drawer for her tweezers, which she had apparently lost, and finally took out a razor blade. Chŏngil then held her, as he would a small child, and began to tidy up the nails on her slender fingers, which still trembled from her fever. He stilled his breath and quietly trimmed her rather short nails, but he grew frightened by the deep silence between the two of them; he could hear the sound of her beating heart and even sense it through his hands and his arms, which held her hands and her waist. He forced himself to listen to the rain outside, but when he looked up to search for the discarded nail trimmings, he caught sight of Munju's face in the mirror, leaning against him as if to burrow into his chest. The smile in her eyes suggested she had been watching him, and now he saw that he was blushing, and so he covered her eyes with his hands and asked her, "And what did you see in my face?" She buried her head deeper into his chest in order to escape his hands, which were attempting to screen her, and she stayed still for a while before answering, "Earlier in the car, I liked what I saw in your eyes very much." "Were those eyes that would die with you, if you were to ask?" He could not bear for the silence between them to accrue added weight and forced himself to laugh out loud while shaking her shoulders. She simply nodded without raising her head from his chest. The silence returned. A pair of flies that had been circling around the light now settled on the mirror, with the male on top. Chŏngil could feel himself sinking back down into the silence, which he had actively resisted by concentrating on the sound of heavy rain outside, but now he heard Munju's breath lighten, as if she had fallen asleep, and so he laid her down with the words "Go to sleep now." And then he got up and left.

Chŏngil had not sensed such a silence between the two of them before and, once out in the rain, he walked straight into a stand-up bar. He could not understand what had just happened; it was as if he had woken from an enchanted dream, in which his subconscious had been freed from some terrifying obsession, and now he had no idea at all what thoughts were circulating inside his head; he could see himself stood there, drinking and blinking repeatedly, as if his head were completely empty. He drank more and more, convinced that the more inebriated he became the more likely he was to choose some kind of extreme act, which would confirm whatever thoughts were in his mind. When he was finally done with drinking, he walked away and pictured himself again, this time striding down the street with his coat collar raised while he whispered to himself, "Am I really going this way?" The rain continued to fall. It was pouring off the sodden hat that he had pulled down over his head and was seeping inside his raised collar. Water splashed all over his shoes as he strode forward with only a vague sense of direction, oblivious to any distinction between narrow alleys and wide roads. He was drenched through to his underwear and shivering, despite warm air puffing out from his nose and mouth. His body felt heavy. Had that feeling he'd had when he left the bar subsided a little? The urgent desire for vengeance and impulse to rebel, his anger at something, perhaps even himself. He was beginning to sober up. Thinking it might be best to turn back to home, Chŏngil walked on and decided that if, "just if," an empty car were to drive by in the opposite direction then he would readily hop in and go home. Several cars passed by. None of them were empty. Here came another car. This one was empty. He stared straight ahead at the approaching empty car and realized that he had already reached his destination. In an instant the empty car sped by.

He walked through a gate and bought himself the fattest piece of flesh on offer. He could hear himself groan as he threw his body down in the room in a state of collapse. He let out several more groans. "Are you feeling all right?" He merely grunted in reply to the girl's question and closed his eyes. Eyes shut, he asked himself whether he was sparing Munju's weak body. Or was he avoiding her germ-infested breath? While mumbling such questions to himself, he could feel the intoxication spread throughout his body once again, chased into his internal organs by the cold rain, and he could feel his excitement growing. If it had not been for that germ-ridden breath misting around his cheeks, Munju's eyes would not have looked so silvery when he had been trimming her nails, her clam-like lips would not have seemed so sad, her heart so pure, and the flow of her emotions would not have seemed so melodic nor her intuition so sensitive . . . he murmured all this to himself while picturing Munju in his mind's eye, and it occurred to him that the heated ardor he had felt in her body, which should not by rights hold any human warmth, might well have been the fever caused by the deadly toxic tubercular germs; and all the time he was thinking these thoughts, he fondled the fat flesh lying by his side until the heroine of this obscene painting began to snore. Chŏngil felt rather relieved at the sound and called the madam to pay the additional fee required for a full night's stay before lying down neatly beside the fat body. He silently voiced out Munju's name, as if to see how it tasted on his palate, while he watched his arm, which was stretched across the nameless flesh, move up and down according to the waves produced by resilient lungs, and as he did so, it occurred to him that those endlessly voluptuous breasts formed a square where flesh and flesh could meet. In no time at all, he fell asleep too, relieved by the thought that Munju's eyes, which seemed to analyze his heart as if illuminating a prism, seemed to lack any sense of the flesh.

In the wake of Chŏngil's visit home, Munju's health entered a gradual but clear decline. While Chŏngil would visit daily in order to sit at her side, there were many days when she was absorbed in her own thoughts, as if she had lost all hope. When Chŏngil urged her to take her medicine she would refuse, either with a wan smile and a shake of her head or with hysterical sobs, interrupted by the admission that she had lost all confidence in life. Finally, on the evening when Chŏngil had received the letter telling him to come quickly because his father had taken to his sickbed, she had burst into tears and asked whether he was now relieving himself of her burden forever. Even if he were to return, she said she could not wait and would die in the interim. Afraid that another fit was about to begin, he consoled her by saying that they should try to live bravely together; he would be back soon, and it was his intention to go with her wherever she wanted, so she should not dwell on such ominous thoughts. Munju had stared at him vacantly while he tried to console her, but now she writhed around crying, "Do you really think that's any comfort to me in this state? Do you think I don't know that my cousin told me to break off with you because you asked him to? All of these lies . . ." She broke into a bloody cough in the middle of shouting these accusations, before rushing up to him and rubbing her bloodied handkerchief into his face with a shriek, "You liar!" With blood still splattered all over his face, Chŏngil coaxed her to lie back down, and then he wiped her face and forehead in an attempt to cool her fever. Once she was calm again, she asked him to turn out the light because it was dazzling her eyes. She lay Chŏngil's hand on her chest and caressed it with both hands—her face almost blue in the pale light of the waning late spring moon which bathed the window—and then those clam-like lips trembled, and she whispered, "Let's die." Chŏngil nodded silently while gazing into her eyes and pressed her tear-strewn face to his chest. There was nothing else to say. Her body trembled and she sobbed from time to time, like a young child trapped in a dream. Though she was still awake, her breath was still; she appeared to be thinking. *She must be thinking about death! She might get up in the middle of the night to search for the razor blade I used to trim her nails in the evening, and she will shake me awake, or even leave me to sleep on . . . whichever takes her fancy . . .* Surprisingly, Chŏngil's excitement subsided while he murmured like this to himself, and he realized he was falling into a deep sleep, like a sick person released by a fever. How much time had passed? The window was already bright when he was woken by Munju's embrace and the sound of her crying;

a clear dawn had seeped in alongside the chill and, by his head, the razor blade sparkled white, like a trickle of dewdrops across the floor.

The train left the last scheduled stop. Chŏngil lit a cigarette and quickly tossed the match down at his feet; then he watched it slowly burn down to the tip, bending at the waist until it emitted a last gasp of smoke and turned to ash, when it extended its waist once more before complete collapse. His thoughts returned to his father on the eve of death. The old man was almost seventy! He had lost weight and vitality from his long illness, but would his fate be quiet enough to simply close his eyes and evaporate into smoke, like the match that had burned all the way down before its spark was extinguished? He had moved in with his wife-to-be's family and worked as a farmhand until he was more than twenty, but once his mother- and father-in-law had died, he was left alone with his wife who, though an old woman now, back then was a slip of a young girl with a sniffly nose and barely ten years old. They had no choice but to leave the land the family had farmed as tenants, because they could not manage all the farm work, and they drifted toward the city where they still lived today, bringing along with them nothing but an A-frame and four or five brooding hens. At first the hen basket was loaded onto the A-frame, but they had barely reached the entrance to their village when his future wife swapped places with the basket, which he carried with his hands for the rest of the long journey toward the city. There they settled down in a hut in a slum outside the city wall. From this lowly beginning as an A-frame carrier he had spent his whole life amassing a fortune of some hundreds and thousands. In other words, he was someone who had busied himself all his life for the sake of money. He lacked the cultivation to reflect upon life and was far too energetic to even think about death, so how could he not be panic-stricken when the prospect of dying suddenly reared its head? Chŏngil imagined his father wailing from pain and despair. But then, he thought, perhaps it would be a peaceful death enjoyed by someone who had worked hard for the sake of goals and responsibilities he had chosen for himself, no matter the nature of the business. Even if that were not the case, as someone who had been ill for a long time, perhaps he would be quietly waiting for death, in time with his weakening body. Chŏngil had heard how difficult it was to watch someone die but had initially felt curious about observing death for the first time, yet now that he was faced with the duty of keeping watch over the death of his father, his heart was heavy and dark. His only hope was that his father would go quietly, whatever the cause.

Such dark thoughts still lingered in his mind when he walked into his father's sickroom, only to find his whole body suddenly quake at the nauseating sensation of fetid air pouring down over his face. This was the odor of death. It was the same odor that wafts on sultry air whenever a funeral bier passes by in the summer. His mother dabbed at tears on her bony face and said that his father had just fallen asleep. Upon seeing Chŏngil enter the room, his wife had stood up mechanically and hesitated for a moment before rushing out to empty a chamber pot yet to be used. Chŏngil could not suppress a grimace at the rear view of his wife, dragging herself along without any confidence, and he thought he would retch if he had to sit in that air for long. Although his father had just fallen asleep, he now opened his eyes. Those eyes no longer seemed like windows through which he might see something in the dark and empty room; neither did they reveal any thoughts or emotion. A frown appeared on the sick man's face, and when he opened his parched lips to search for water, his tongue all but fell out of his mouth. Just one drop of water from a thin rubber tube affixed to a glass kettle provoked a fit of violent retching, and he had barely recovered when his eyes seemed to focus for the first time. That was when he saw Chŏngil and asked, "Did they ask you to come?" "Yes." Hearing Chŏngil's simple answer, he asked again, "Did they send a telegram?" His eyes hovered somewhere between Chŏngil's face and hat. Despite noticing out of the corner of one eye that his mother was about to say something, Chŏngil thoughtlessly replied in the affirmative once more, at which the slits of the old man's eyes narrowed and he spoke clearly, "So I'm about to die . . . I don't want to die." Aghast, Chŏngil could only look at his mother.

One month earlier, the herbalist had inserted an acupuncture needle into the old man's stomach in order to release the accumulation of fluid, but the cancer had ulcerated and the cancerous cells spread rapidly throughout his entire body, with the result that his condition was now grave with final stage symptoms. His intestines had congealed and hardened, and even the muscles in his legs had contracted so that he could no longer lie down flat. Because lying on his side placed too much stress on his body, he was made to lie down flat on his back several times each day. But almost as soon as he was stretched out, his abdominal lining and congealed intestines would pull down on his stomach like a stone, and the pressure on his spinal cord was unbearable. Unable to withstand the pain, he would twist his body, at which his legs, bent by their contracted muscles, would lose balance and fall to one side. At that point his bony upper body would collapse in their wake. Each time he was moved during the day, red patches would be revealed where his skin made contact with his bed and black and blue bruises would form, as if an infection were spreading. Only his sallow forehead, nose, and the skin above his lips remained as pale as before, while dark bruises had appeared on both sides of his face from the pressure of the bed, rendering the contrast between pale and dark skin ever starker. Between the pallor of his forehead and the ridge of his nose his eyes still shone, huge and terrifying now that the whites protruded out from between sunken black temples. The dark surfaces of his body had gradually expanded, as if the black shadows of death were attacking those shining eyes from the left and the right. The old man would look at his bruised shoulders and arms and fretfully ask why there was no electricity even though it was the middle of the day. When he saw that his body still looked black under the bright electric light, he asked what kind of shadow this was and tried to wave it away with his hands, in distress. Whenever he regained consciousness, he always asked for water. Water was all that he could drink now that he was unable to digest food through his mouth; nutritional fluids were poured in through his anus and saline solution and glucose were injected into his veins. Soon even the water that was poured drop by drop into his mouth would no longer slide down his throat. Finally, they dipped some cotton in water and used it to wet his tongue, which lay black and stiff inside his mouth. But the retching fits this provoked were so harsh that it was as if his hardened intestines were being wrung out, and when his body finally settled down again he would barely manage to shout out that he did not want to die. Chŏngil could not suppress the frown on his face when he heard his father shouting that he did not want to die, which happened frequently, no matter whether he had just returned to his senses and opened his eyes or was groaning and talking in his sleep with eyes closed. Each time Chŏngil was overwhelmed by the stench of death washing over his face as he entered the room and then heard those words emanate from his father's pillow, it felt so horrific that he had to stifle the impulse to shout out, "Are humans really animals?" But then something happened that made him realize just how superficial these thoughts of his were. It was one morning several days after his return. One of Yongp'al's several daily visits to the old man's sick room had ended with his asking to talk to Chŏngil in the front room. "You're not looking so good," Yongp'al said, as he sat down across from Chŏngil and looked at him with eyes that seemed to say, "And you're looking like this after just a few days?" Then he took what looked like some newly created documents from a large envelope and asked whose name should be put on the title deeds. Yongp'al could tell from Chŏngil's expression that he did not understand what Yongp'al was referring to, and so prefaced what he had to say with the phrase, "I am sorry to have to say this when he is still sitting nearby," before explaining that since Chŏngil's father's illness was all too real and all of his assets would be bequeathed to Chŏngil soon anyway, he, Yongp'al, had thought it would be simpler and cost less in fees if he were to draw up the title deeds to some land that had to be registered soon in Chŏngil's name instead of his father's. He had gone ahead and done so and brought them here today, at which point he flicked through the papers to note several places where Chŏngil's name appeared. While listening to Yongp'al's long explanation, Chŏngil was taken aback above all to learn that his father had speculated on buying more land as recently as the previous month. "My father bought land a month ago?" Chŏngil murmured as if to himself, somewhat to Yongp'al's surprise. Yongp'al explained further, all the while stressing his own important role at every turn in the scheme: how the land had great prospects, how there was no land broker who did not desire this particular land, and how Chŏngil's father had fought off several competitors in order to buy the land, all while lying in his sickbed. Yongp'al seemed frustrated to see Chŏngil listening to the explanation as if in a stupor. He took a small abacus from his jacket pocket, cleared it with a sharp click, placed it carefully on the floor, and proceeded to calculate the stamp duty and acquisition tax that would be owed on the title deeds to the land, which was already a considerable amount. With inheritance tax added in imminently, well, wouldn't the unnecessary expense be too much? And, using the specialized vocabulary of his judicial scrivener's training, Yongp'al began to run some more numbers through the abacus. Chŏngil could feel an inexplicable anger rising in his heart while he listened to Yongp'al's explanation in reply to his own expression of surprise, an explanation that missed his own meaning entirely. Yongp'al's smile was cold, as if he were trying to diffuse Chŏngil's not surprisingly tense and excited expression, and he began to push the abacus beads around again, after saying, "You would not understand as much as I do, brother. But even if we count just the larger pieces of land that you will inherit . . ." Chŏngil was disgusted to hear Yongp'al seemingly try to hand over the assets which the old man still controlled, all within view of the terrifying sight of his father groaning in the inner room. At the same time, he was conscious of himself quietly watching the beads on Yongp'al's abacus rise and rise again with no sign of hesitation, and when Yongp'al pushed the abacus before him saying, "This is just a rough estimate," their eyes met and Chŏngil could feel his face redden with the sudden surprise. "Given that the inheritance tax on this amount will already be enormous, may I suggest you follow my recommendations to avoid having to hand over this land too?" Yongp'al now spoke decisively and placed the power of attorney in front of Chŏngil to be imprinted with his seal. Chŏngil's disgust deepened. His nerves were without a doubt suffering from lack of sleep, but it would have been impossible for him to find words to describe how much he detested that smile, which seemed pasted onto Yongp'al's face as long as they looked directly into each other's eyes. *You little man! Since when did I agree to conspire with you in such a plot?* He felt a flash of indignation and the impulse to slap Yongp'al on the cheek. In the same instant, he felt a slimy smile pass across his own face. Was this feverish anger brought on by his weakened nerves? It couldn't be righteous indignation, nor any kind of fastidiousness, such things were futile . . . in one tiny corner of his churning heart, for just one second, he thought, what's going to happen if I relinquish all common sense? And once this glimmer of a thought had appeared, like a hint that could be easily missed, Chŏngil hurriedly handed over his seal with the words, "Well, just put it wherever you like, since I don't know where it's needed."

He heard himself laugh nonsensically after blabbering these words and wondered if he were not now suffering from an even stronger fever, and suddenly his words and smile, his entire expression, vanished all at once. After Yongp'al had imprinted the seal, he handed it back politely and stood up, saying, "I will talk to your father about the balance." Chŏngil watched Yongp'al's rear view disappear through the door and felt a sudden urge to call him back. He shifted his haunches as if to stand up and even gestured with his hand, but no words came out of his mouth, which hung open listlessly. In his haste, he couldn't decide what to call Yongp'al. Judging from his rear view, Yongp'al was a little nervous as he walked through the door, like a friend who leaves you behind when you lose the courage to go along with a joke you've cooked up and says, "You won't do it? Well, I will." Once Yongp'al had disappeared through the door, Chŏngil regretted not calling him back, but at the same time he thought to himself, "If I truly regretted this, I could still go after him and stop him, couldn't I?" As soon as Yongp'al had started talking, Chŏngil felt the anticipation that something was about to happen, something which he had somehow already sensed with his body, and now he stilled his breath to listen, as if awaiting the results of some experiment. For a while he was so tense he could not hear anything at all, although the distance was far enough that he would not be able to hear any regular conversation anyway. Would his father now finally submit to death? Chŏngil's escalated tension was matched only by the emptiness of his despair, and he was just about to light a cigarette when a furious scream from his father threatened to blast his ears off. He could not make out what his father was actually saying, but a further bellow was followed by the old man bursting into sobs. Chŏngil sat still, aghast at the shocking sound which far exceeded his expectations, but when he heard footsteps rushing out of his father's room, he jumped up like a ricocheting spring and hid behind the side door. The hurried footsteps stopped dead for an instant while Yongp'al glanced around the empty front room, his restless eyes rolling uneasily, and then he left again with a scowl on his face. Chŏngil peered through the gaps in the side door and watched as Yongp'al exited through the main gate; then he let out a long sigh. His efforts to avoid the embarrassment of Yongp'al's scowling eyes catching a glimpse of him hiding behind the door, his feet firmly planted on the ground, seemed almost a confession that he had been the one to instigate Yongp'al's actions, and now he didn't think he would be able to come out of hiding without someone first calling for him. He heard this only after the fact, but according to his scornful younger sister, who sounded as if she resented her brother for bringing shame upon her husband, Yongp'al had said that Chŏngil looked just like a hanged man stretched out with his two feet stuck flat on the floor. Standing behind the side door like that, Chŏngil recalled how he used to play hide-and-seek with his friends when he was a child. Once, when all the other children appeared to have been caught, the seeker passed right by the place where Chŏngil was hiding, chattering away with all the children he had already caught, and although Chŏngil realized they must have forgotten about him and moved onto some other game, he still could not bring himself to come out of hiding but remained stuck there, tearful, just as he felt now. While he listened to his father's violent retching, he wondered whether he really was crying like that child again, but his thoughts were interrupted by the surprise of his mother calling for him, and he was at last able to make his first move out from behind the side door. She said that his father wanted to see him, and she turned away as if to avoid looking at him, while she added, "I know that it is not all your fault, but knowing your father's character, why did you have to act so rashly?" Chŏngil's mouth dropped open in surprise at the word "rashly." *Rashly! Was I too rash?* Murmuring this to himself while he walked into the inner courtyard, he saw the reddish-black bloodstains on the bedding his wife was hanging out on the clothesline. An unbearable pressure bore down on his mind, like that flimsy line holding up all the dirty wet rags hung up in a row, and then he saw the thin steam rising from the washbasin placed on the deck outside the room; the basin was half full of a reddish-black fluid. It was not the first time he noticed this, but this time he felt it had been left deliberately within his sight. Normally such thoughts would anger him, but this time he felt that, for once, he might even be able to listen acquiescently to his father's reprimands.

Outside the window, the late spring sunshine seemed to belong to a different world, which made the sickroom, full of the scent of death, feel all the darker as a result. Chŏngil still found the air in the room unpleasant and was simply unable to repress a grimace when he sat down by his father's pillow and looked into his face. The once shining red hairline and high forehead had dried out and yellowed, like a crumpled scrap of oilpaper, and the high and fleshy nose had shriveled up, leaving behind an enormously swollen nostril hole in its place. His temples and cheeks had hollowed out into blackish bruises, while enormous black earlobes stretched out beneath his white hair like bat wings. White spots dotted across the black hole of the ear protruded like a skeleton emerging from a rotting corpse. Chŏngil took one look before having to turn away for a moment. A patchy mark, something like the rot on the skin of a fruit, was clearly visible on the depression beneath his father's nose. The skin beneath the nose had already decomposed. His moustache was now sparser than ever, because the roots had risen to the surface and would fall off at the slightest touch. So here was the source of the stench of death in the room. The doctor arrived to inject glucose and a saline solution into withered veins, and then he applied a heart stimulant between the bony ribs. This made the sick man regain consciousness, and he begged for water with his stiff tongue. The doctor said that drinking water now would make the retching start again and gave instructions for them to insert a few drops of water onto the tongue and into the mouth using damp cotton wool. Going forward, he said, the patient was to drink no more water.

Having regained consciousness, the old man now gazed at Chŏngil's face for a while, as if struggling to focus his eyes, before the blue veins on his crumpled oilpaper of a forehead bounced up and the pupils of his eyes glared so fiercely they looked as if they might drop out, and he pushed his bedcover away with his knees while bellowing something between a shout and a cry, "You bastard, you treacherous bastard." Then he began to sob so hard that his exposed ribs lifted up, provoking the fear he might choke. His chest continued to heave from his sobs, now dry of all tears, and, inhaling deeply between each word, he barely managed to exclaim, "So you bastards are haggling over my money already, without a thought to cure your own father? I won't have it." Clearly exhausted, he closed his eyes, but the heaving lingered for a while. Eventually, all signs of life appeared extinguished, and he lay there as if dead. Only the tremble of the yellow nose hair outside his wide-open nostrils suggested a persistent breathing. A heavy silence had accumulated around those watching the sick man with bated breath, and then Chŏngil heard what sounded like the sigh of a tensed heart breaking. At the end of the sigh Chŏngil's mother spoke, "So this is how hard it is to die . . . at least we enjoyed life for a while!" She wiped the tears from her eyes with her skirt tie, stood up, and left the room. Chŏngil was left kneeling alone and watched a fly land briefly on the sick man's decomposing upper lip. He remembered what Munju had written in her letter, which Unhak had passed onto him.

As she grew weaker by the day, she hoped that her death would not be in vain but would remove the barriers blocking Chŏngil's path forward in life. She hoped that he would laugh at such presumptuous words. She hoped that he would discover the audacity to laugh at her and think: because of you, Munju, my life was going to be ruined, but our relationship amounted to no more than a passing flirtation in a dreary life. Even if that were not possible, if after her death, a second Munju were to appear before him, then wouldn't they be able to fall in love again? Since she was worrying like this and hoping that her death would set him free, she hoped also that she would die before he returned, and if this proved indeed to be the case, then she asked him not to visit her dead body. It was as if she had carefully folded away the razor blade, which she had taken out in order to kill him one night, and adopted the pose of the good wife who would use a blade like that to shave his face instead. He mulled over her words and wondered whether he would be able to put them into practice. He then looked at his father and frowned, amazed that the old man could still resist death, having reached this state, when Chŏngil himself, far from possessing some kind of cultivation that delivered him from the terror of dying, simply lacked the willpower to continue living. He realized that his father was able to fight death like this because not once in his life had he doubted he would survive or felt the need even to think about dying. There were times when Chŏngil found himself awestruck by this enormous willpower he witnessed in his father's suffering.

Around that time . . . after such severe nausea that the old man could no longer swallow even one drop of water or have his tongue moistened without severe retching, he said he wanted to be able to look at some water. Chŏngil raised his father's sickbed by doubling up the mattress and placed a large vessel of water nearby, easily within his father's sight. But once he grew tired of looking at that vessel, the sick man wanted to see water wherever he looked. Chŏngil placed large fish bowls around the room and filled them up with water. The old man's eyes moved from one fish bowl to another, as if licking up the cool sensation, but then he became dissatisfied once again and said he wanted to see fresh running water. So Chŏngil placed a large jar of water within his father's gaze and used a small bowl to gather some of the water and let it pour back down into the vessel like a small waterfall, and he repeated this again and again. When the old man watched the water fall with rapturous eyes, his black, shriveled tongue drooped out of his mouth. Chŏngil struggled to control his own tears at the sight of his father's eyes. He had never seen such eyes before. And on his father's face! It was completely unexpected to see his father look so enchanted, his eyes pierced with such longing. Perhaps his eyes had looked like that when he had counted out his money. Chŏngil turned away in order to hide his tears and recalled the image of his father's back while he was counting money, something Chŏngil had at some point come to consider a miserly act. Whether alone or surrounded by people, it was the old man's invariable habit to turn around to face the wall whenever he counted out money. Chŏngil could still picture the sight, which had filled him with shame when other people were around, and with disdain if he were alone with his father. This must have been how the old man's eyes had looked each time money had come into his hands, thought Chŏngil, and he turned back to look at him again. His father was still gazing at the falling water with those same eyes, licking his dried lips with his dried tongue, tasting his lips, and then grinding his teeth, before calling out, "They say I'm dying. . . . I think I'll live on some more."

Chŏngil kept pouring water all through the night, wherever his father's gaze was directed. Occasionally he lifted up his father to lay him down elsewhere so that his bedding could be changed; it had become soiled when the nutritious liquid poured into his anal passage flowed straight back out again unabsorbed. Although Chŏngil would flex his arms, his father's body had grown so light he hardly felt he was lifting anything. And his father felt even lighter when Chŏngil recalled how, when healthy, his father's body had been hefty, like the huge Maitreya at Unjin without its crown of stone. This body now seemed to have lost all trace of the instinctual desires of fleshly life. That this body still wanted to live on and was in fact still alive despite its complete loss of the functions of life, surely this could only be the effect of a willpower that exceeded the instinctual desires of fleshly life? And wasn't this willpower boundless, refusing to renounce affection for the world it had built and now extending the life of a flesh already in ruin? Such was Chŏngil's conclusion when he examined his own emotions and tears brought on by the sight and sound of his father's rapturous eyes and the shouts of not wanting to die. Like a machine propelled by this invisible energy called willpower, the old man's body grew ever lighter and smaller. More fluid seemed to flow back out of his anal passage than was initially placed in, and it took on a lumpy consistency, as if his intestines themselves were collapsing. One day, while Chŏngil was cleaning up just such a mess, a group of women, who had come to ask after his father before being quickly ushered back out onto the deck, had been silenced by the sick man's shouts of not wanting to die and stood staring at each other. When they saw Chŏngil place something dirty outside the door, one of the women, perhaps thinking it a good opportunity to break the awkward silence, turned to Chŏngil's mother and said, "Of course, you have such a filial son, don't you?" From then on, whenever his father's eyes focused on him, Chŏngil would turn away and flee quickly back out the door, fearing that some kind of expression of affection might fall out of his father's mouth, moistened by his son's own hands.

The old man died on the evening of the same day a telegram had arrived from Unhak announcing Munju's death. Although Chŏngil thought that according to the saying that the dead should bury the dead he should be the one to bury Munju, he took care of his father's coffin instead.

Spring on the New Road

S pring had arrived for the first time since the new brides had moved into the village. Kŭmnyŏ and Yugami could still picture the small hoes and baskets they once used for gathering spring greens, hanging on the posts in the cowshed back in their family homes.

And yet it seemed that caterwauling heralded the onset of spring in this village, too.

I t was only one year earlier that the two girls had encountered a cat yowling under the sorghum fence by the vegetable patch on their return to the village at dusk. They had been out picking greens, and their arms swayed from exhausted shoulders while their hands clutched hoes and baskets packed full of the day's harvest.

The cat contracted its stomach, arching its back so high that it almost squashed its neck, where the fur now stood erect and tall, and then the yowling began.

The crying ceased several times while the girls watched on. In the silence, the wind rustled their hair and pushed its way through the sorghum fence, whose stalks whistled like willow pipes. At each shrill sound the cat resumed its noise. Then another cat from across the way joined in. The two cats slowly approached each other, feeling their way with their cries, each flattening its ears in response to the other.

By now the moonlight had reached inside the whistling fence and glistened softly on the stems of the green onions, like the wet on fingers sucked in babies' mouths. The two cats merged. They came together and, still entangled, rolled down the grass hill, as if falling.

Yugami blushed. She could not see well in the dark, but she could feel Kŭmnyŏ's embarrassment.

"Let's go, ok . . ."

"Ah . . . tchoo . . ."

Kŭmnyŏ sneezed and ran away in a fit of giggles.

This spring Kŭmnyŏ and Yugami heard the caterwauling in the village once more. But only Yugami chased the cats away with a poker and sometimes even gave them a kick if she came across them mewing at home or on the path to the well.

Kŭmnyŏ and Yugami had grown up in the same village, and both moved to this village upon marrying the previous autumn at the age of fifteen.

Their mothers were each determined that her own daughter would be provided for better than the other. If Kŭmnyŏ had a summer jacket in pink rayon gauze in her dowry, then so would Yugami, and if Yugami had a double-stitched padded jacket in the delicate green of pine pollen, then Kŭmnyŏ was to have nothing less.

Yet when Yugami moved to the village a few days after Kŭmnyŏ, a large silver ring had emerged from the midst of her wedding gifts. Lacking any such ring, Kŭmnyŏ had burst into tears. Her mother immediately summoned the matchmaker and gave her a roasting. The old lady then hurried to Kŭmnyŏ's in-laws, where she kicked up a fuss. But the real trouble occurred at Yugami's in-laws.

Yugami's mother-in-law was so upset to learn that her son had secretly sent a silver ring to his bride while his parents were barely managing to survive that she refused to eat for three days.

Instead of a silver ring, Kŭmnyŏ's mother-in-law snuck an extra swath of cotton cloth into the bottom of her girl's wedding chest.

Once another brooding hen had been counted in, Kŭmnyŏ found herself wearing a silver ring, just like Yugami.

The women of the village referred to the two girls as "the twins," because the two of them would meet up at the well to draw water wearing exactly the same jackets and skirts and identical silver rings on their fingers. If either girl were to appear alone, the other women would playfully ask the whereabouts of her twin.

The two bridegrooms, on the other hand, could hardly have differed more.

Yugami's husband—the one who had secretly sent the silver ring—was a strapping young man of nearly thirty years of age. At the wedding ceremony he was fully drunk before the main dining table had even been cleared away and had used a cigarette to set fire to the paper showing the hour and date of his birth, which the schoolchildren had presented to him when they came to tidy up.

Kŭmnyŏ's husband was a couple of years younger than her and no more than a child. When the dining table was cleared away at their ceremony he had kicked up a fuss, crying and insisting he return home with his father, who had accompanied him to Kŭmnyŏ's house.

Consequently the villagers had labeled Yugami's husband a drunkard and Kŭmnyŏ's new groom a crybaby.

Once they were married to such different bridegrooms, Yugami started to avert her gaze, her head bent low as if bowing under the weight of her newly raised hairstyle, while Kŭmnyŏ carried on much as before, her red hair ribbons fluttering in the wind like a chick's newly sprouted cockscomb.

In the spring, Yugami's breasts began to swell and her waist to thicken. She would throw her water pitcher down onto the bank by the well and set to retching tearfully. If she was alone with Kŭmnyŏ, she would burst into fits of sobs before eventually lifting the pitcher back onto her head. For her part, Kŭmnyŏ would shudder involuntarily at the sight of Yugami in such a desperate state. She had only a vaguely awkward sense of the trials that led to Yugami's tears; that sense raised its head whenever she saw Yugami's husband rushing over to the well, holding both oxcart handles with one strong arm while he gulped down a whole bowl of water, and then quickly running off again, leaving a stench of sweat and alcohol behind in his wake.

The well where Yugami and Kŭmnyŏ drew their water sat beneath a willow tree on the bank of the new road, which just clipped one edge of the village. Delivery cars would often stop by the well before continuing their daily journey along the new road, which headed out into the wide plain after rounding this final corner of mountainside.

One day, Yugami and Kŭmnyŏ noticed an unfamiliar driver joking around with the women at the well.

"Those damn cars sure drink a lot of water. How many baskets is that now?"

A woman stood holding an empty jar, waiting her turn for the basket that the assistant driver was using to draw water for the car.

"Just look at that car's body. We have to fill up that whole huge belly. How many jars would it take to fill up your belly, lady? Ha, ha, ha."

The driver was sat, legs splayed, on the bank next to the well and laughed as he cracked his snide joke about the woman's swollen belly.

He passed by at almost the same time twice each day, accompanied by his assistant, and each time the women would be forced to push their basins of rice and greens out of the way in order to avoid the soap bubbles that flicked off the men when they washed their oily hands and faces.

"Ugh, that musk smell just makes me feel sick . . ."

The women complained and pretended to hold their noses, but still they fetched more water to pour over the men's hands and heads.

Soon Kŭmnyŏ, too, was kind enough to switch her small water jar for the large basket the women normally used for rinsing rice and poured her first basket of water for the men, saying, "Here, this is easier."

"He keeps his moustache trimmed so tidily, don't you think?"

Occasionally Kŭmnyŏ would try to talk about the driver with Yugami after he had driven away. His face was slender and dark, but his eyes sparkled, and every time he washed his hands he never failed to wipe both them and his face dry with a bright white artificial silk *habutae* handkerchief, which he had neatly folded into the top pocket of his Western-style jacket.

"That's one smart handkerchief, isn't it?" One of the women remarked.

"Really."

"And isn't it always the same style?"

"Let's take a look."

"Ooh, it's so soft!"

This last exclamation came from Kŭmnyŏ.

"And you say you're a widower. Some girl must be looking after you."

"And who says a widower can't have a smart handkerchief?"

The driver retorted and laughed when the women at the well started talking about his handkerchief yet again.

"How many of those 'chiefs do you have, then? Or maybe he just gets it out to look good when he comes here."

A woman with an unusually red nose teased him, to which the driver replied, "Hardly."

He carefully shook out his handkerchief before folding it up again. His young assistant chimed in, "Hardly . . . what d'you mean, hardly? You're right, lady, there's a girl at this well who Mr. Kim likes, so he stays up all night just ironing his 'kerchief!"

With these words he ran off, followed by the driver, who gave the assistant's freckly face a shove as he got into the car.

"Very funny, eh?"

The driver looked back down at the women, who fell about in fits of laughter, and his eyes came to rest on Kŭmnyŏ. Yugami was almost blinded by tears when she caught a glimpse of Kŭmnyŏ in the midst of the women, blushing with confusion as her eyes met those of the driver. Yugami struggled to lift her jar onto her head before turning around.

"Sister, wait."

She could hear Kŭmnyŏ calling from behind.

It sounded as if Kŭmnyŏ were still two or three steps away, but from the distinctive knocking sound of her water jar and gourd bowl, Yugami knew it was her. Even more conclusive was the fleshy smell that always emanated from her; even when there was no breeze to speak of, that smell would still pierce Yugami's nausea and pique her senses.

"Sister, wait."

"Mm."

Yugami responded, but for some reason she hated the smell of Kŭmnyŏ, no matter how much it differed from the smell of her husband.

"Sister, you haven't ridden in a car either, have you?"

Yugami didn't bother to answer. Kŭmnyŏ listened to the sound of Yugami and her water jar in front of her and kept on talking, as if to herself: "It must be amazing. If you go all the way down the new road, there's Pyongyang, and then there's the sakura everyone talks about? They're supposed to be in full bloom at the moment."

A few days earlier, Yugami had gone to fetch water and found the freckly assistant driver standing on the bank above the car, whistling. At her approach he blew an extra loud whistle and coughed. Soon two heads peeked out from below the bank, glancing in her direction. By the time Yugami reached the well, the driver had already dropped a spray of blossom down onto the stone and driven away in his car, after wiping his hands with that dazzling handkerchief of course. All she heard were the words, "You're out of luck today."

Yugami wasn't quite sure what the assistant driver meant by these words, which he had casually tossed out the window, but she felt angry, as if she had been scolded or insulted, and wanted to grab hold of Kŭmnyŏ and shout at her, "You stupid girl." So you're feeling all upset because you can't see the sakura? But then, the thought of Kŭmnyŏ's sniffling crybaby of a husband made her feel uncomfortable, almost as if she understood the source of Kŭmnyŏ's restlessness. She had felt equally uncomfortable, saddened even, when Kŭmnyŏ stopped using her name and began to call her "elder sister" instead. Yugami often felt nauseous and dizzy recently and would cry easily; each morning when she woke up she felt as though her belly were about to explode. She had presumed it was her aching body that made her cry, but now she wondered whether her tears stemmed from her sadness at being called elder sister. The words seemed to force some kind of distance between the two of them. The thought that instead of acting as stupid and immature as Kŭmnyŏ it was she who felt that Kŭmnyŏ was immature and wanted to shake some sense into her, that thought made her feel the saddest of all.

K ŭmnyŏ's household had borrowed an ox from Yugami's family in order to mill their grain, and today was Kŭmnyŏ's turn to return the favor by helping Yugami's family with their grain. As she walked behind the ox, tapping its haunches with a switch to keep it turning the yoke, she gazed into the distance toward the golden evergreens surrounding the village shrine on the hill, across to the azaleas on the mountain behind the village, and over the chimneys of the houses, poking through the apricot blossoms; and she felt like launching into a tune she had often sung as a child.

To marry
or not to marry,
Gourds and vines,
See how they cover the roof!

She wanted to laugh and to cry and to sing out at the top of her voice.

Yugami rushed around with an old broom, jumping in and out to avoid the ox's haunches so that she could sweep the yellow millet grains, which had been pushed out to the edge of the bed stone, back under the runner and pick out the stalks that had gathered around the spindle, all while using her sleeve to wipe the sweat dripping from her brow. From time to time she had to put down her brush to wipe her nose with her skirt. Kŭmnyŏ offered to take over. But Yugami declined, saying, "The grain isn't dry enough, if we're not careful it will stick."

Yugami was dragging her heavy body around and speaking as if she were the only one who understood about the grain, and how often it was necessary to clear the millstone to stop it from getting blocked, and how much grain exactly to load onto the winnower, which her husband was turning. The gourd for carrying the grain was heavy, but if she happened to spill any while struggling to pour it up onto the high winnower, her husband Ch'unsami would twist that thick neck of his and shoot her a furious glare.

"Dammit, have you broken your fingers or something?"

And all the blood would drain from the quaking Yugami's puffy lips.

The sky was crystal clear. In each of the village houses the cocks were cheerfully crowing their daytime chorus. The children and the calves and the chickens and the dogs were all dozing, as if drunk from the sun's rays, or jumping about, the tips of their toes dangling tiny shadows, which looked like pieces of black cloth stuck to the ground. A fresh breeze grazed Kŭmnyŏ's neck beneath her ears and swayed the white skirts of the women who were carrying lunch baskets and water jars along the path by the field in front of the village.

Under the midday sun, the roof of the mill covered every last bit of shade; inside that shade the ox's snorting breath flashed white for about the width of a hand, while a dazzling light reflected back from the plows, which leaned against the ridges dividing the distant paddies.

Kŭmnyŏ had been gazing out across the fields when suddenly, out of the corner of one eye, she caught sight of a goods vehicle emerging from the purple haze that bathed the mountain. The vehicle had grown just a little bit larger each time she managed to coax the plodding ox around one more circle and could look out toward the new road once again. She chivied the ox through the semicircle from where the road was invisible in order to keep an anxious watch on the vehicle, which was growing larger at every glance—just like a young girl who goes to bed early each night in order to count on her fingers the days remaining before a festival in an effort to speed time up.

With each glance Kŭmnyŏ became increasingly anxious that the growing vehicle might pass by the well before she could leave to fetch water. Finally, her hard switch broke when it landed on the ox's rump.

"Get a move on, you ox, dammit."

Ch'unsami had guessed that the young bride had broken her switch after becoming frustrated with the slow saunter of the ox, and now he too shouted and slapped the ox on its haunches with one of his enormous hands. The ox leaped forward in surprise and raced twice around the circle, leaving an even longer trail of cloudy breath in its wake. Yugami was left dizzy and gasping for breath after being chased around the circle twice while trying to push the grain back under the runner.

When she saw that Yugami's already puffy face was now bright red and her chest was heaving up and down, Kŭmnyŏ resolved not to watch the vehicle any more. But then Ch'unsami caught a glimpse. Taking his pipe out of his mouth, he murmured, "Dammit, get yourself stuck in a ditch. You dirty butcher."

He had more than one reason to despise this particular vehicle.

One day in the spring, Ch'unsami had been driving his oxcart outside the village when a delivery vehicle coming toward him had driven into melting ice on the road and become submerged up to its wheels. At first it snorted like an enraged bull, but finally it was unable to move at all. The driver had asked Ch'unsami for help. Ch'unsami had arranged stones and broken branches on the wet road in order to gain some traction before tying the vehicle to his ox and pulling it out. The driver had given him a Mako cigarette and gone on his way.

A few days later Ch'unsami had been drinking heavily in town and was returning home on the hard new road. Seated on his empty cart with the spring wind gently grazing beneath his ears, he had nodded off, his reins slackened. All of a sudden he was startled awake by a crash and discovered that same vehicle had driven into the back of his cart; the driver jumped down from his vehicle, glaring furiously, struck Ch'unsami on the cheek twice, perhaps even three times, and then drove off.

Something else had happened a few days earlier. Ch'unsami was once again driving his cart outside the village when he heard the sound of a car horn approaching from behind. He was still furious on account of previous events but had little choice other than to move off the road. The driver and his assistant were swaying their bodies to a song and looking pleased with themselves. Huge smiles were plastered across their faces. Ch'unsami felt his fists clench and wanted more than anything to smash the car window. But the car had already raced past him before he even had time to raise a hand. And that's when the wind carried these words toward him.

"I wonder if Kŭmnyŏ and Yugami will be there today."

These were the words of their song, if it could be called that. Ch'unsami's eyes opened wide in surprise at the very moment the assistant driver pushed his face out of the car window and poked his tongue out while singing the words "Kŭmnyŏ and Yugami" even more shrilly. The vanishing of the tongue heralded an explosion of laughter. That sound of laughter disappeared into the distance along with the car.

This third incident cast an enormous shadow over Ch'unsami's daily life. From that day onward, whenever he went into town to offload his goods, he had to resist using the money he had earned to seek comfort in a tasty drink. Although he was mostly silent by nature, after a drink or two his lips would loosen, and he knew all too well what would happen if he were to become completely inebriated. He was terrified that one drink would start him talking, and that more drinks would lead him to beat his wife. But abstaining from the alcohol that he craved so badly only made Ch'unsami feel more troubled. No matter how much he pondered the problem, he couldn't figure it out. How could the driver possibly know Yugami's name? Even he had not voiced that name out loud since registering their marriage, and she was his wife. And yet, that driver had somehow stolen the name of his wife, a name that he oughtn't to know . . . ? Or perhaps he hadn't stolen it, but his wife, who had yet to smile at Ch'unsami tenderly even once since their wedding, had told the driver her name as a sign of affection instead of offering up her jacket tie? Such thoughts drove Ch'unsami wild and made him want to beat the truth out of her at the first opportunity. Yet he forced himself to restrain his emotions. "That baby in her belly is clearly mine." With this thought, he realized that his wife was as valuable as his ox, which formed the bedrock of his living.

As Ch'unsami well knew and perhaps had experienced himself, it was quite common for the girls in this village to undo a jacket tie or an inner ribbon at some point as a sign of affection, or to drop their baskets full of spring greens down on the hill by the village. There were even girls who would try to break free and run away, like fattened mares. The husbands and parents-in-law of such girls would have no choice but to rein them in and wait for them to return to their senses. But once these troublesome girls became pregnant, the eyes that had formerly cast amorous glances sideways would begin to look straight ahead, and the handkerchiefs that had once been worn at a nonchalant angle would return to their rightful place. The girls would become mothers and then for the first time wives, and finally they would fulfill the role of daughter-in-law and forget their youth entirely. And so, the husbands and in-laws of such young brides and daughters-in-law would wait anxiously for them to be impregnated and relax only after the girls had given birth.

Such were the thoughts that Ch'unsami was struggling to forget right then, but when he looked at his wife's rising belly and heard her retch, he felt himself calm down and thought, "Huh, just you wait and see, you bastard." He kept a close eye on

Yugami, who was still running around attempting to push the grain back in, all while the vehicle was gradually increasing in size. Yugami had also realized the car was approaching and that Ch'unsami was glaring at her in an unusually harsh fashion; as a result she didn't dare look up from the mortar. Meanwhile, beads of sweat were gathering on Kŭmnyŏ's tense brow.

Yugami went in first for lunch and was already stepping back out, carrying a water jar, when Ch'unsami crossed her path; with one eye on the approaching car, he scolded his old mother, who was busy at her spinning wheel.

"Why didn't you fetch the water, mother?"

"I'll go."

Kŭmnyŏ took hold of the jar and rushed out through the bamboo gate.

She was annoyed that her rubber shoes were sticking on her sweaty heels and that her skirt was not tied neatly. Her face looked like a willow branch heavy with dew; two or three lines of sweat trickled down over the flecks of grain that were caught in the soft down of her cheeks. On top of her raised hair, which glistened in the sunlight, red ribbons fluttered as they crossed the path running alongside the vegetable garden. "They must have left already." Kŭmnyŏ speeded up.

The car appeared to be waiting by the bank at the well. The assistant driver was blowing on a handmade willow flute, and the driver was smoking a cigarette. The red sun had now settled down in the middle of the well; white clouds floated past.

The driver glanced around before asking, "Did you come alone?"

His assistant quietly disappeared in the other direction. The driver sat down in front of Kŭmnyŏ while she drew her water, and then took hold of her wrist as he spoke.

"We'll go to Pyongyang like I promised, eh? . . . Just name the day, and I'll come over at night and be waiting for you out on the hill behind your house."

In the silence that followed, he lifted Kŭmnyŏ's lowered head with both hands and kissed her on the lips. When he pulled away, after all but suffocating her by squashing her nose, a soft smile was revealed.

"Baby!"

Growing more confident, he wrapped his arms around her waist and pulled her toward him.

"If you just name the day, I'll sleep at the hut over the ridge and come to the hill out back during the night, okay? Yes, and then we'll go to Pyongyang together."

"But I'm just a country girl. What'll I do if you take me to the city and leave me there all by myself?"

"Do you think I would abandon Kŭmnyŏ?"

"Then what will you do?"

The driver hesitated before saying, "Shall I go to your room?"

"No! I want to see Pyongyang."

She said this, but she herself didn't know if she really wanted to go to Pyongyang. She simply crawled into the driver's arms at the dreamy thought of being swept away in a car. The driver looked down at her and said, "You sleep in a room with just your husband, don't you? Then tonight I'll go to your room. I will!"

"No, don't! What if we get found out!"

Kŭmnyŏ's eyes widened in surprise at the driver's suggestion.

"So what if we're found out? What's that good-for-nothing husband of yours going to do?"

"What'll he do? Do you want me to die of shame?"

"But who's going to kill you?"

"So I won't die?"

Kŭmnyŏ felt sure she would die, even if she had no idea who would kill her. If she were caught, she thought she might even die at the hands of that crybaby, though just as the driver said, he could barely fulfill the role of a husband; or her mother-in-law or father-in-law might slice off her nose or scald her with the iron; or her own mother and father might kill her out of shame. And if no one else killed her, she might just end up dying all by herself.

"What'll happen if I *don't* die?"

The driver took one look at Kŭmnyŏ's ashen face, about to burst into tears at any moment, and quipped, "If we really are found out, your father-in-law might come running after us with his sickle!"

He quivered and looked Kŭmnyŏ in the face again. Her eyes were even larger now and rounder, filled with a sense of terror.

"We like each other . . . so what if we die?"

The driver continued, without a smile now.

"Isn't that right?"

He tried to take hold of her once more. But she had grown scared of him. She tried to push his arms away and stand up. He pulled her even closer to him with more force.

"It's true, if I can just go to your room, so what if I die? If you don't come out onto the hill tonight, I'll go to your room, bang on the door and you'll die of shame."

Kŭmnyŏ's mind darkened upon hearing this.

"Don't! Please. I really will die."

The driver glared at Kŭmnyŏ, who had barely managed to extract herself from his embrace and was now pleading with him, and then he threatened her angrily.

"If you just come to the hill tonight, everything will be all right. If you don't do as I say . . ."

At that moment, a loud whistle from the driver's assistant resounded from across the way. The driver leaped up onto the bank by the well before he could complete his sentence. Kŭmnyŏ's husband was heading in their direction, leading a calf. The driver turned back to Kŭmnyŏ, as if his startled reaction had been unnecessary, and then turning away again, he murmured, "If you think I'm lying, just come out into the front garden this evening. I'll be off now, but I'll be sure to be back tonight on my bicycle."

He seemed to be talking to himself, yet he enunciated each word distinctly, one by one, before driving away in his car.

K ŭmnyŏ was so worried by the prospect of the driver's appearance that she went out to the vegetable patch immediately after dinner and pretended to be weeding so that she could keep watch on the new road.

Whenever they had met by the well, she had not once worried about being alone with him, but now he seemed absolutely terrifying. Not in her wildest dreams had she imagined he could be so frightening. She wondered if he was merely putting on an act to scare her, but the way that he had uttered that threat when he had seen her husband approach, that had been no joke for sure. At the same time, she was furious—furious because he had dismissed her husband as a child, and furious that he seemed to be insulting her as well. He did not seem like a man who would be bothered by her humiliation, by her nose being cut off, or even worse, if she were to die. She was terrified of what might happen when night fell. She gazed over toward Yugami's house, wondering whether she should go seek advice. The house was some distance away, but she could see Yugami's husband sweeping the yard with a broom. Some flames flared up; they must be burning rice sheaves in the middle of the yard. With each flare of flames Yugami's face lit up before she disappeared into the flickering darkness once more; she was throwing all the rubbish they had swept up onto the fire. Soon the flames would leap up again, illuminating the two of them. They stood facing each other and appeared to be talking. Perhaps if Yugami were alone. Even then, talking to Yugami felt a bit like talking with her mother-in-law, given that Yugami seemed to think she was immature. If they did talk, Yugami would probably just say,

"You brought this upon yourself!" She was not likely to come up with any solution. The glare of the flames blinded Kŭmnyŏ's eyes and made the fields appear even darker; the only sound she could hear was of frogs croaking.

The croaking sounded like water bubbling up in the front rice paddy, where a crescent moon in the shape of a trunk latch cast its reflection, like a broken piece of mirror.

"Surely, he won't really come," Kŭmnyŏ murmured to herself as the night grew darker and the frogs croaked on, yet she kept her eyes on the horizon, where the tail of the new road disappeared into a faint light, which looked like dawn gathering in the eastern sky. Although she had heard that the faint glow which hovered on the horizon even on the darkest of nights belonged to the city, she had never been there, and it seemed an infinite distance away.

Suddenly a small spark seemed to fly toward her out of the gradually brightening glow.

No cigarette ember could walk that quickly. A firefly would not glow with such a bright, red tone. That was, without any doubt, the light of a bicycle.

Realizing it must be the driver, Kŭmnyŏ ran back home as if she'd just seen a tiger, as the old folk might say.

No sooner had she stepped inside the gate than her mother-in-law called out from her room, before the room went dark.

"Get yourself off to bed quickly, and don't forget you've got the rice to cook for morning."

Kŭmnyŏ entered her room and sat down beside her husband, who was already fast asleep. If he were anything like Yugami's man, the thunderbolt would have already struck, because he would have guessed what was going on even though he hadn't heard the driver's words earlier. Kŭmnyŏ thought that might be preferable. Now, when the driver reached the back door, he would knock quietly at first, but then try to push his way in, if the door didn't open; after a while, he would call out Kŭmnyŏ's name, so that she had no option but to go and open the door for him. Once inside he would leap on her, and given their tiny room, how could her husband not wake up, no matter how deep his sleep or how successfully she suppressed the urge to shriek? And then, once awake, he would be sure to either shout, or burst into terror-stricken tears, and her father-in-law would come running across from his room with a sickle . . . as she extinguished the light and lay down to bury her face in her quilt, Kŭmnyŏ could picture everything so clearly in her mind's eye. Her mind went blank for a while, but she soon returned to her senses, and her thoughts raced on: perhaps she'd better just lie down and pretend to be dead, no matter how long the knocking continued; or, at the first rattle of the door, should she call out "thief, thief," kick the door to her room open and run into her mother-in-law's room? She tried to calm her breath and realized she would not be able to call out, "It's a thief," when she so clearly knew who it was had come knocking. Even if the driver were to run away, she would be subject to the shame and humiliation of village gossip and her in-laws bustling about complaining that no ordinary thief would come to a young woman's room; and if he were caught and said that Kŭmnyŏ had invited him to her room that night, then, despite this being a lie, she would feel unable to deny it or defend herself. No matter how much she tried to explain, Yugami was not likely to ever believe her—not the Yugami who had warned her to "pull herself together" whenever she had gone down to the well late during the day. Then there was Yugami's husband, and the women at the well; it didn't seem likely any of them would believe her either. She wasn't even sure she believed herself that she hadn't invited him. If he were to lie and say that she had indeed asked him, it would be hard for her to deny; after all, although she had told him she didn't want him to visit her tonight and was afraid that they would be found out, she had still waited up for him, as if he really would turn up tonight of all nights.

By this time the shadow of the acacia tree had disappeared from the window on the back door, a sign that the moon had already moved on. A faint light glimmered in the dark corner by the back wall. Kŭmnyŏ's eyes were glued to the back door, her ears pricked up for any sound; at any moment there could be a rustling of footsteps, followed by a black shadow staring right into the room.

Suddenly a dog barked. There seemed little doubt that the sound came from the hill out the back.

She could no longer remain still. She decided to go out before the driver reached her room.

Stepping outside the gate, she didn't even notice the dewy acacia leaves brushing her cheek or the branches catching her skirt. She simply walked forward. She had no idea if she were afraid, or sad, or even happy. She had often dreamed of walking this path when she yearned for the driver at night, but now that dream had been shattered and she felt utterly bereft, and yet still she walked on as if this were a regular event, paying no notice to the tears streaming down her cheeks.

She had not gone far before she walked straight into the driver, who was approaching from the other direction. She slumped to the ground. She didn't even hear him say, "I upset you earlier, didn't I?" He quickly pulled her into his arms and explained how he had wanted to be sure she would come out to meet him. When his lips fell upon hers, the stench of alcohol from his nose and mouth made her want to retch, and then the dizziness struck and everything went black.

The cock was crowing for the third time when Kŭmnyŏ returned home. By the time she had hidden her soiled clothes and socks, which were drenched in dew, she could hear her mother-in-law coughing in the room across the way and her father-in-law clearing out his pipe on the doorsill. She went into the kitchen, where she prepared the rice for cooking and sat down in front of the stove to light a fire. Steam drifted up, like smoke, from the back of her hands and from her hair. As she watched that steam float up from her hands and wrists, which had turned red from the cold dew, her eyes brimmed with tears.

Spring passed once again, and the late-blossoming acacia trees began to drop their flowers.

In the end, Kŭmnyŏ had taken to bed. For a while, the pains in her stomach had been so bad that she would bend over double and have to keep going to the toilet. She had no idea what was wrong; her only concern was that someone would notice she was ill. And so she forced herself to endure and tried to work harder. But then her painful stomach had begun to swell as well. When she tried to walk, she felt dizzy and unsteady, as if the feet that she could just glimpse beneath her ever-expanding belly were treading along a path through fog or across the cloud tops. Everything before her looked yellow and blurry, like the gloaming when it resists the onset of darkness, even though it was still morning or the middle of the day. She gritted her teeth and tried to hide this sickness which she did not understand, until finally she could bear it no longer and collapsed.

The calf sent as part of Kŭmnyŏ's trousseau died the night before her. Kŭmnyŏ's young husband had taken the calf out only that morning and left it tied to the acacia tree on the embankment; then it had suddenly died. Her mother-in-law wailed and lamented the loss of their main source of income. Her father-in-law blamed his son and beat him. The whole village was in uproar at the rumor that some unknown cattle disease had spread to the village. The following morning police from the market and leaders from the township agricultural association were dispatched. No one understood why the calf, which had been chewing cud well and bellowing magnificently until the morning it died, had suddenly collapsed. Every inch of the field where the calf had been grazing was examined. Finally the calf's stomach was cut open on the suspicion it may have damaged its intestines by swallowing a sharp piece of wooden poker or iron skewer. But all they discovered was a stomach full of undigested acacia leaves and bark, and no wound that could be isolated as the cause of death.

Kŭmnyŏ passed away in the evening, when the whole village was awash with rumor and anxiety over the incomprehensibly sudden death of the calf. She died listening to the sound of bitter-smelling leaves boiling on the stove, prescribed by the doctor as medicine for edema. The frogs in the front paddy field had croaked especially loudly after a storm had passed through early in the evening. The sound of raindrops and of the spring cats still pairing up beneath the acacia tree behind the house amplified the noise. Whether Kŭmnyŏ could hear all this or not, the tears never stopped falling from her dimming eyes. She squeezed Yugami's hand and indicated that she should come closer to her side. Then, summoning all her remaining strength, she begged Yugami not to allow her underwear and trousers to be changed when she was buried.

On the day that Kŭmnyŏ's funeral cortege set off on its journey, a newspaper arrived at the house of the district head containing an article in which it was claimed that a calf had died after eating bark from the toxic acacia tree.

Soon everyone in the village was concerned about their oxen and pigs and looked askance at the acacia trees, which had spread from the hills to the fields to yard corners, and even over walls into kitchen gardens, despite the villagers' having neither planted them nor gone especially near them.

The acacia tree originated in America, according to the newspaper article, and this provoked a furor.

"So those trees came from those ugly bastards. America . . . isn't that where those Yankees live? So somebody brought those trees all this way, and now they've gone and killed one of our calves! That's just not fair."

"Not fair? That's fate. First a perfectly healthy calf dies, then a daughter-in-law they'd welcomed only yesterday."

"That's what I mean. Even if the calf died from eating the American acacia, why did that pretty girl die as well?"

Such was the chatter among Kŭmnyŏ's funeral party as it wound its way along the new road. At the back of the line, Kŭmnyŏ's mother was wailing. Her mother-in-law was also in tears. Yugami followed behind them, hiding her sobbing face in her skirt. She appeared on the verge of collapse, and the older women held onto her in an attempt to console her.

"It's just awful. You two were like twins. But you have to keep going."

Suddenly a car's horn sounded from the rear. All the men carrying Kŭmnyŏ's bier tried to make way by moving to one side of the new road. But Ch'unsami was at their head and stood his ground.

"Who gives a damn about the car? Let's keep going. Bastards."

"Really?"

"Yes, come on."

Some of the young ones refused to move and stood their ground. This resulted in Kŭmnyŏ's bier tilting to one side, until one of her husband's uncles came up from the rear and entreated the young men: "Once we've built the burial mound we'll have some drinks, so please don't do this, let's just do it right."

"Who said we're doing this because we haven't had a drink?"

Ch'unsami grew even more annoyed, but he had no choice other than to make way. The car had to slow down in order to pass the cortege. All of a sudden Yugami burst into a wail. All eyes widened. As soon as the car had passed the cortege, it speeded off again. A cloud of yellow dust blew up in its wake, as if a whirlwind had passed through. Kŭmnyŏ's cortege made its way through the dust.

"All these strange new diseases, they come from the West, you know."

The man who had earlier asked why the pretty new bride had died finally managed to open his mouth again after being choked by dust.

"But those bastards' disease came by car, didn't it?"

Ch'unsami had the final word.

Patterns of the Heart

E ven the larger platforms where we might stretch our legs simply raced past the window of our express train, which was traveling at some fifty kilometers an hour. Mountains, fields, rivers, small towns, and telegraph poles; pedestrians, oxen, and horses on long, straight asphalt roads. I conjured up the rich painting that would result if a wall were to block off the space and time through which we were passing at such great speed and all these things were to hit that wall one by one, like oil strokes beating down on a canvas. From time to time carriages, swollen with people, lingered on opposing platforms, but those freshly swept platforms and glittering, orderly rail tracks passed momentarily, indifferently, outside the window like scattered ruins; even the engines resembled pieces of junk, despite the fresh vigor of pistons heaving up and down in the wake of the inertia left behind by the screeching brakes; and a rabble of squashed faces evoked accident victims, splattered onto the windows without so much as an inch to separate them. All these things, too, would turn into specks on that canvas blocking off the space and time through which I passed.

Such thoughts hardly constitute a significant or novel observation. I am not traveling far or leaving behind my hometown for a long period of time, and neither am I indulging in sad illusions. This is not a journey that could offer any prospect of advancement in life or the excitement of some kind of business fever, thus I am not brimming with enough hope to allow my arrogance and sense of superiority to summon up pity for everyone around me. Given my hopeless nature and situation, there are no words to describe these illusions; they are too idle to constitute true despondency, but they are not pleasant either. This could all simply be a result of the *thrill* brought on by *speed* itself.

While I sit in this carriage speeding along recklessly (?), I can experience the illusion of adventure and enjoy that thrill in safety, because I trust this train and the skill of the driver. To enjoy the thrill of an adventure that is guaranteed to be almost one hundred percent safe, that is a kind of sensual game. It is like listening to a famous violinist play notes so shrill and elongated that they take your breath away, but instead of being absorbed by the melody you are struck by a spine-tingling sense of fear: "Now! Any second now!" Surely a string must break, you think. This, too, is a sensual game and a form of musical appreciation not to be entirely disdained. To experience the reckless speed of the express train and imagine the scenery receding ever further into the distance, until finally it hits a wall and transforms into a painting in which the passengers are mere specks of oil, seemingly abandoned among ruins—this may not seem particularly fortunate as far as the thrill of first journeys go, but neither is it an illusion to be despised.

Racing along at speed, I simply have no way to anticipate what kind of wall I will hit and when, or in what kind of genre painting or human drama I will be left behind as a mere stroke of oil in the background.

When we approach the border, the transport police demand to see my ticket and business card. Imprinted only with my name, Kim Myŏngil, my card provokes a look of scorn on account of its uselessness. The policeman takes out his notebook and inquires about my occupation, address, and the reason for my trip to Harbin. He starts to probe further, bothered by my lack of occupation and apparently disbelieving my statement that I have no fixed abode, and so I tell him the truth: having graduated from art school, I can lay claim to no title other than that of painter; as for my abode, I have been staying at various inns ever since selling my house when my only daughter moved into her school dormitory in the spring, my wife having passed away the year before last. But now, I add, in an attempt to make my story sound better and as if it is some great aspiration of mine, I am heading for Harbin to visit my old friend Yi—a successful businessman—in the hope that I might learn something from him about how to hold down a fixed job and address. This is not entirely untrue either. To tell the truth, I can no longer bear the burden of my rootless existence.

After my wife, Hyesuk, died three years ago, I packed in my job as a middle school art teacher, and since then I've been unemployed, having merely painted a few pictures that have yet to sell. My lack of a fixed address stems from my having sold the house, which Hyesuk and I had built at the time of our marriage more than a decade ago, just as soon as I had moved our daughter Kyŏngok into a dormitory last spring.

I was not often at home and kept all too irregular hours, rising only after Kyŏngok had left for school in the morning and returning home after she had already gone to bed. She had been lonely since her mother's death as a result, even though she lived with me. And then my lifestyle hardly exerted a positive influence on a young girl who was growing up and entering a more sensitive stage of her life. My sister had offered to take care of her, but a classmate was living in the dormitory, a close friend of hers from elementary school days, and Kyŏngok had decided quite happily to move there too. With only our old housekeeper at home, there was no longer any need for me to keep a house.

After my wife died, my sister kept urging me to remarry, saying that I should at least keep a mistress and hold onto the house, but I felt it would be awkward to see a new wife or even a mistress in the old house, which Hyesuk had looked after for more than ten years. What if I were to carelessly call out "darling" and another woman were to appear in place of Hyesuk? It would be unspeakably depressing. And wouldn't young Kyŏngok feel even more desolate if she lived in a dormitory in the same town as the old house where she had grown up? Surely she would only miss her mother more if on her much-anticipated visits home she were to see another woman in her old home.

All these thoughts had prevented me from remarrying, so I really should have stayed at home by Kyŏngok's side. Even though I had resigned from my job with precisely such good intentions, I had only made Kyŏngok feel more alone by spending all my time traveling, or to be more accurate, winding my way through a dissipated life—drinking, playing around with women, and sleeping in late.

I had occasionally painted (paintings that no one would buy) and found solace in comforting my daughter by decorating her room with portraits of her mother. That was my life. This time I again departed as if to roam, but I also hoped that I might find some new stimulus in life by meeting Yi, who had himself wandered off to Manchuria ten years before and was now a successful businessman.

Once we make it safely through customs and across the border, I move to the dining car. It is jam-packed, and I barely manage to find a seat opposite a middle-aged woman who at first sight can only be described as stern. She peers over khaki-colored glasses at my constantly tilting beer glass. She is wearing what looks like a nun's outfit over a body as voluptuous as that of the soprano Miura Tamaki. I cannot help but feel estranged by the small New Testament she is perusing, and while I continue to drink and curse my bad luck, the scenery outside the window suggests we are approaching Wulongbei. The patterns woven by plowed furrows and ripening, autumnal rice paddies begin to alter their expression by human design until the fields gradually lose their nature as fields, betraying the increasing touch of hands, and just at the point where the fields suddenly leap into gardens, a hot-spring hotel built in the Western style rises up, and steam from the overflowing springs floats all around, like heat haze beneath the high blue fall sky.

We pull into a platform where there is no sign of weary legs exhausted by wandering, no tense and harried faces, and no bundles suggesting the harshness of life; instead several couples alight, the women in flower-patterned *haori* jackets walking beside gentlemen with gleaming faces. Even this train, which has been racing along recklessly, its belly ninety percent full of shadowy lives—bustle, vagrancy, war, illness, and death—even this black train reveals an elegant face, not unfamiliar with such leisure. I have in the past taken advantage of this other side of the train's nature and been left with a memory of Wulongbei.

I had boarded this same train last spring on a trip where I was to have a model pose for me for the first time in a long while. By my side was Yŏok. There were rumors that a certain young resistance fighter had been her lover back in the days when she was one of those young female students in Tokyo who adore literature.

I had met her when she came to work as a hostess at a tea shop I occasionally frequented and had brought her along on that trip for my own pleasure: yet another woman to enter and leave my dissolute life.

Her beauty originated more in her character than a perfect body, and yet I had never before had so much trouble trying to master a model's personality.

Usually when I face a model for the first time, my brush strokes either take on a life of their own, propelled by the force of some personality that I feel instinctively, or impulse strikes and I muster the courage to accentuate some characteristic of the model and freely create a personality for her. Thus, a living character appears through my own interpretation and intention as an artist, and yet I could not get a handle on Yŏok on that occasion. Perhaps our relationship was too prosaic to allow me to forge a clear and unified impression. By prosaic, I do not mean that we had tired of each other. Instead we had parted before my interest could dissipate. My impression of her at that time was too scattered to coalesce into a painting: sometimes I would be intoxicated by her, whereas other times I would find myself observing her ardor with dispassion.

In the bedroom Yŏok was a whore of mature technique whose whole body smoldered with passion, but in the daytime her dazzling eyes shone coldly with an air of some cultivation, and her prim lips upheld the silence of a virtuous wife. Whenever she handed me something and I touched her fingers in passing, they were ice-cold, so cold I would have to take a second look at her face. Perhaps those cold hands seemed too intellectual; they certainly made me pause when I tried to caress her during our solitary strolls in the deserted spring hills. Those brilliant eyes and silent lips, together with the nose sitting haughtily between them, would come together in an expression so chilling that the previous night would feel like a dream until finally, perplexed, I wanted to slap her.

"I might be falling in love with you, Yŏok."

I stroked the ice-cold fingers resting tidily in my palm as I spoke, but she looked bored, as if she might yawn at any moment, as if this were none of her business.

Once again I experienced the bittersweet feeling of seeing my dead wife in Yŏok's face. Not so much as a frown seemed to have passed across Yŏok's face in the twenty or more years of her life.

After her death too, Hyesuk's face was pure and generous, displaying not the slightest wrinkle or blemish. I had behaved badly more than a few times while she was alive, childishly relying on the hope that the pure intelligence on her face would remain as generous as a mother's breast. Yet, despite having married such a man, Hyesuk had never once contorted the beautiful silhouette of her face. I often thought that her gentle nature must have something to do with her ears.

To gaze upon her ears was like contemplating those of the gentle Buddha: pure and warm like brilliant jewels, Hyesuk's earlobes seemed to calm any wave that disturbed my heart, bringing peace when I was exhausted by my dissipation and illuminating her grace ever more brightly.

As I looked at Yŏok's smaller but equally resplendent ears, this Yŏok of the daytime seemed so sweet and graceful that I could hardly believe her passion in the bedroom. Given her slender body and tiny face, should I dress her in white mourning clothes and paint her as a lily, virtuous and simple? Or should I transform her into a bunch of roses, wearing a deep red skirt and green jacket? While I pondered the portrait, I repeated my earlier words.

"Is that not so? Mightn't I really fall in love with you?"

"I don't know. Do you mean in the day or at night?"

That was her reply. If I found her a completely different person in the daytime and the nighttime, clearly she felt the same way about me. It wasn't so much that our already vague feelings were losing more focus, but that we could only watch from a distance as each of our hearts began to rupture into two, each half belonging to the day and the night separately.

Faced with such a model, I would proceed stroke by stroke as I tried to bring focus to the montage of double-layered observations and impressions that hovered over the canvas in a dizzying fashion, but I always ended up throwing down my brush when the emerging portrait grew closer to the Hyesuk in my head than the Yŏok who stood before me.

The first time this happened Yŏok asked if I felt unwell; afterward, whenever I smeared white paint over the face on the canvas, she would ask whether there was something displeasing about her as a model. Once she saw a picture that had not yet been completely defaced and asked, "Who's that? Perhaps she's the woman of your dreams?" From that time on her eyes would not meet mine for even an instant when she posed, and a sardonic smile hovered around her lips. Although she faced me head on, it was clear that in her heart she was avoiding me, and I, in turn, would grow more and more flustered until finally I would paint over the canvas with such anger it would tear. Yŏok would then turn around with a swish of her skirt and disappear into her room. If I followed after her to apologize, she would be lying on the bed and staring at the inner mechanics of her wristwatch, having removed its back cover. The watch was not broken; it was simply her habit whenever bored and alone or angry from quarreling with me to look inside the watch or to hold it to her ear and listen to its ticking. This could even provoke a kind of capricious cruelty in me. Other times I thought her childish games cute and would look at the watch with her; sometimes we even spent a whole afternoon taking turns to listen to it tick, as she held it to our ears with those ice-cold fingers of hers. On one of those occasions, Yŏok, her own heart aflame, told me that she had once placed her ear on a man's breast and listened to his heartbeat until dawn; her head had throbbed for more than four days afterward.

From such words I concluded that tender feelings for a tiny life were not the force that pushed her to gaze upon the living machine, which was crawling along inside that sparkling, bejeweled watch; neither was she drawn toward the novelty of watching cogwheels tread through the abstract notion of time. Her habit seemed to derive from a kind of capricious cruelty, the desire to see into the inner workings of the head and heart of the man whose heartbeat she had listened to all night. To tell the truth, I was curious about this almost symbolic behavior and wondered over whose heart she was standing guard and whose heartbeat she could hear.

Following her into the bedroom, I imagined drawing her cartoon-style, with the curvaceous lines of her back, waist, and legs rising up out of the duvet on the enormous double bed, and she holding not a watch but a large doll wearing a felt hat. I all but whispered to her, "What do you think about when you look inside that watch?"

She responded with another question. "And who do you paint when I pose for you? . . . Is it your wife? It is, isn't it?"

"You're thinking of your old lover, aren't you?"

"And whose fault would that be?"

"Mine?"

"Well, is it mine? . . . I must apologize . . . for getting in the way and not helping you to dream about your unforgettable wife."

She hurled the watch across the floor before turning her back to me and bursting into sobs.

I did not try to comfort her, but I did feel sorry for her. I felt both sorrow and guilt at using someone for my own entertainment who was so strangely sensitive, though not particularly smart. Perhaps it was not her nature to be so different at night from during the day, but rather a necessity brought about by my own lack of sincerity and refusal to surrender myself to blind love. Was our lack of passion and sincerity not insulting to both our characters and our pride? Could it be that her cold demeanor in the daytime was not her body's reaction to her passion at night, but a rebellion against my refusal to accept that passion with sincerity? It was up to me to respect her hysterical behavior, drop the fantasy of imposing Hyesuk's face and ears onto hers during the day, and love Yŏok for who she was. From the beginning of our relationship there had never been any expectation of marriage, because she understood my situation and feelings well, but this meant that I should accept and love her passionate nature all the more.

This was how I decided to go to Andong the next day and purchase the art supplies necessary to paint Yŏok through new eyes. By the time I returned in the evening, she had already left alone on a train headed north. She had entrusted my wallet to the hotel owner, along with the following letter.

Even I am surprised by my decision to leave suddenly like this. When I think about it though, this has always been my fate and I am merely following the road I was meant to travel. Please do not try to look for me. I do not know where I am heading or what I am looking for. I have taken some money for travel, and the ring you gave me.

Yours,
Yŏok

She must have taken this train back then. At the time I felt only relief, as if a weight had been lifted from my shoulders, and I would probably never even have thought of looking for her. Naturally, I heard no more after we had separated in this fashion.

But just over one month later, a letter arrived from my friend Yi in Harbin, and it concluded with an unexpected announcement: he had heard I was not unfamiliar with a certain beautiful cabaret dancer named Yŏok and sent his congratulations on my luck with the ladies at my age. This was how I had guessed her whereabouts.

Yet I certainly have not undertaken this journey with the intention of meeting her. For years, Yi has been urging me to come to Harbin and I too have wanted to visit; I have neither the desire nor any interest in trying to meet up with Yŏok. On the other hand, if by any chance our paths happen to cross, I will not go out of my way to avoid her.

Although I say I am not interested, that also feels a little forced. It is not really true to say that I have no interest whatsoever. Harbin is not simply a place where Yi is waiting to welcome me. Perhaps this is the passion of love after all, because when I think of Yŏok fleeing there after the struggle with her own complicated emotions, then Harbin is no longer just a place that might satisfy my curiosity in the exotic, or where the pleasure of meeting an old friend awaits. Harbin seems to harbor some dismal fate instead. And fate has the habit of throwing consequences at us without clear causes. Even when there is a cause, it may be as abstract as the phrase in the middle-aged woman's New Testament, the one that reads, "Sin gave birth to death." If fate is the name we give to those real consequences, such as death, which arise from abstract causes, then all we can do is to tremble in its face.

In my by now slightly inebriated state, I experience another kind of thrill when I think of this train racing toward Harbin as some kind of monster in conspiracy with the terrifying fate that awaits me there. As I chew on a piece of fried fish and conjure up the scene of fish swimming into an enormous whale's mouth, I wonder what part of the fish is in my mouth; and then I look across at the middle-aged woman, who is swallowing the last bite of part of a cow which has been made into a steak, and I watch as she wipes the blood from her lips.

Harbin . . .

At the risk of repeating myself, I did not hold out any great hope that this trip would amount to anything other than my usual kind of roaming around, but neither did I ever think that it would turn out as grim as it did. The fantasy of an adventure or a terrifying, fateful plot, which I had indulged while sat on the train, turned out to be no mere fantasy but a relentlessly accurate premonition.

I met Yi there, of course, and I listened to stories from his decade in Harbin, about his current success, his business, and his plans for the future, and I was impressed by his determination and congratulated him upon that. But this record of my journey is neither wholesome nor bright, and not because I enjoy dwelling on dark events or covet stories of novelistic interest and effect.

Yi's "tales of success" became quite irrelevant to me, the hero of this story, when I became embroiled in an incident which was all too close to me. I have to tell that story first, and it is, of course, the story of Yŏok.

With Yi as my guide, I went out to see Harbin. "Since you're a born consumer, let's start with the entertainment district." With these words, Yi set off with me in tow on a tour of the famous cabarets, restaurants, dance halls, and the so-called erotic grotesquerie that we associate with Harbin. By the time night fell, we were more than a little drunk.

"Now what was her name? She's quite a beauty. Don't you have to meet up with her?"

"You mean Yŏok? Well . . ."

"What do you mean, *well?*"

And he dragged me along, saying that everyone's glad to meet old friends when they're far from home. But he didn't seem to know for sure where she was, judging from the way he mumbled to himself, "Now where was she?" Apparently he had been showing someone else around when he had been surprised to meet a Korean dancer in some cabaret and had struck up a conversation with her. It turned out she was from our hometown; naturally, they had talked some more, and finally he had guessed her relationship to me. But he didn't seem to know anything about the circumstances of our separation. When I asked how she was, he replied that he didn't really know because he had only seen her that once, but since she was dancing in a third- or fourth-rate cabaret, her income could not amount to much and she must be barely getting by, unless she had some man keeping her. He added that I should have her show me around the next day and get the inside story, for surely she would be pleased to see me.

"I think it was here," he said, and we walked into a noisy basement cabaret in some back alley. It was the third or fourth place we had tried.

Glittering chandeliers hung from a high ceiling, a floor polished up like a mirror, and in between, a brilliant panorama with dancers riding on waves of music . . . perhaps my expectations had been too high, but Yŏok's cabaret was a most shabby affair. What with the noise of the small five-piece jazz band and the smell from alcohol splashing underfoot, my head began to throb almost immediately. Three or four clusters of customers lurked here and there in the otherwise empty hall, and almost a dozen dancers huddled together in a far corner. Some wore Chinese dress, whereas the white girls were draped in kimonos. Yŏok approached our table, walking behind the Manchurian waiter we had instructed to fetch her, but the moment she saw me she stopped dead in her tracks, eyes opened wide.

"Look who I've brought to see you. Take a seat."

At these words, Yŏok seemed to recognize Yi and understand what was going on. She regained her composure and sat down in front of us with the greeting, "It's been a long time." She did not raise her bowed head for a while.

Yi ordered drinks. Not only was he unaware of the details of our relationship, but perhaps on account of the continental habits he had acquired during his ten years in Harbin, he seemed oblivious to my awkward expression and Yŏok's response. Smiling and drinking merrily, he arranged for me to pick her up the next day between noon and one o'clock so that she could take me to all the places she wanted to show me. He would expect a phone call by three or four o'clock and we could all dine together. Yŏok replied that she didn't have anywhere in particular to show me but would wait for me if I stated a time, and then she wrote down her address and drew a map of the route from my inn to her apartment.

A nd so I went to her apartment at the agreed time. (Some readers may feel repulsed by the words "and so," and even despise me for acting on such a paltry excuse. It's for those readers that I am writing this now.) I had no particular reason to avoid meeting her again. When Yŏok had agreed with no apparent hesitation to wait for me, I had thought that rather than simply being polite she might be hoping for a quiet opportunity to apologize for her behavior the previous spring. There was no need for an apology, of course, but why else would she sacrifice her pride by meeting me at home and disclosing her pitiful lifestyle, especially as we had nothing in particular to say to each other? To tell the truth, the previous night she had looked worn down by the struggles of the past six months; even her pale, skyblue dress looked dirty, not fresh. There was no sign of the ring that I had given her, though it would have matched the scarlet nails so common to women in her profession. I could only presume that she must be destitute.

Yŏok's apartment really was a shabby affair. In the middle of the room, four wooden chairs were scattered around a circular table bearing only a porcelain ashtray; a long sofa stretched out beneath two small slash windows facing onto the street, its stuffing poking out through worn velvet at the corners. "Stretched" really is the most apt word to describe the sofa, which had clearly once been a majestic and luxurious piece of furniture, with its deep purple upholstery and the sleek pattern of the grain and delicate carving on its sturdy wooden legs; it was far too big for such a small room. A wooden divide screened off the far corner of the room, where the flower-patterned wallpaper had completely faded and an equally worn dressing table with a trifold mirror stood askew. The dressing table, too, had clearly once been a splendid piece of furniture, despite the flaking varnish on its wooden frame, scratched carvings, and wrinkling in the thick glass at the center of the mirror, where the silver had torn and crumpled. Such furniture could not have been so worn down by Yŏok on her own. It had not been intended in the first place for someone whose slender body floated around so lightly.

I looked up at the dark ceiling, which seemed all the more distant in this cramped room with its majestic furniture and boarded off corner, and I was taken aback by the desolate nature of Yŏok's life in Harbin. If she had taken to collecting such furniture, there was nothing to be done for her.

A green mandarin dress clung to the curves of the body I remembered so well, a body that now sank down into the purple sofa, elbows rested on the open window sill, a cigarette propped between the fingers. The short-sleeved dress revealed wrists that were terribly thin, shriveled even, while painted fingernails shone like rubies on the tips of her fingers; it was like gazing at a row of beeswax candles. I sat in silence, unable to think of anything to say, and watched the cigarette smoke waft up from those fingertips. Yŏok also seemed to be deep in thought. Because I knew that was her wont, I did not consider her impolite; instead I turned to look down upon the scene outside the window. A dazzling afternoon sun bounced off the windows of the houses across the street. Western women dressed in primary colors of red and blue passed by under the harsh sunlight; the hollow clicking of their heels resounded noisily upon the scaly patterns of the granite pavement; even the dust they kicked up glittered like gold in the sunlight. The women dashed nimbly past like tropical fish or goldfish, swimming through the valleys created by the tall buildings. Here and there clumps of coolies sat in the middle of this street of mermaids, like rocks on the ocean floor, indifferent to the coming of spring and winter and helpless in the face of the passing seasons and waves of history. My absorption in the scene was broken by the sudden cry of a bird in a cage hung next to the window. A patch of the clear sky in the distance peeped through the roughly woven bamboo of the cage. A skylark had tiptoed up onto the top bar and was hopping anxiously up and down on its perch, its head and neck extended as it tweeted and cried repeatedly. It flapped its wings as if to fly but had to be satisfied with hopping up and down the perch again, chirping constantly. For some reason the noise of this bird unsettled me, and an awkward silence followed while I could think of nothing to say. Yŏok dabbed her nose with a handkerchief and polished her nails on her green dress. Those vulgarly painted nails—no doubt a professional requirement—gleamed more and more with every polish, but I was shocked when I suddenly caught sight of the bird's spur claw. It was abnormally long, over an inch. It resembled those fingernails belonging to a certain Master Wang or Master Chin, the ones that are always hidden by long flowing sleeves, and prompted me to ask, "Is that a Manchurian lark?"

"Mmm. It was bought here, so I suppose it must be. Its claw is really long, isn't it?"

"Abnormally and repulsively so."

"If you say it's abnormal, then I suppose it is, but apparently it wasn't born that way. It's just like my fingernails."

She held up her red nails for show and smiled. Then, she explained that the long claw was not for decorative purposes, like those of Master Wang or Master Chin, but had simply kept on growing because no one had trimmed it and it did not wear down naturally in the cage. Long claws were a sign of long ownership, and such birds were deemed precious.

"With a claw like that, you can say that it either grows because it can, or the bird's been turned into an invalid by human beings . . . Isn't that what we call the power of one's environment or circumstances?"

She shuddered, as if her own words sent a chill down her spine, and then looked up at the cage while dabbing at her nose.

It occurred to me that this lark's claw could not have grown so long while in Yŏok's care, and I looked around the room again, wondering who else lived here. She sneezed several times and wiped her nose and watery eyes.

"You seem to have caught a cold. Do you feel a chill?"

"No."

She looked me in the face again, an ineffable smile taking shape on her lips and in her eyes, which she quickly lowered as if embarrassed.

This was similar to the smile at Wulongbei, which had asked whether I was dreaming, but there was no reason for Yŏok to tease me again with that old smile. I checked again, but the smile remained.

Could she be confusing day and night right now? I could not help but wonder, because this was her nighttime smile. I had never observed this smile in the chill light of day, and I wondered whether the force of Harbin and her current circumstances, to borrow her words, had brought her to the point where her impulses were uncontrollable. Was that capricious smile trying to seduce me? As I watched her with doubt and wonder, she returned my gaze, her eyes still smiling but eyelids slowly drooping, and then she gradually tilted, until finally she rested her shoulders on the arm of the sofa and closed her eyes, all but lying down.

There was no longer any room for doubt. I could disdain the decadence of her behavior to be sure, but when I looked into her face, I caught sight of a single tear clinging to the tip of her lashes. While her thin shoulders shook with the sound of soft laughter—ha ha, ha ha—this tear had slipped out from behind eyelids so translucent that her pupils were almost visible. I dropped my head down into my hands and closed my eyes while a shiver crept down my spine, and just then it happened, the cage above my head shook with a loud shriek, like that of a rat. Startled, I looked up to see that the lark had fallen from its perch and was shuffling around the floor of the cage. Each time it lifted its body in an attempt to fly back up to the perch it would fall back down again, frantically scratching with its long claw and flapping its stumpy wings, while letting out a dismal ratlike screech. It repeated this several times, rattling the cage, until finally its legs gave way and it collapsed in its own droppings, eyes shut. Stupefied, I watched the wretched sight of the bird's heaving breast.

"Please bring me the cage. Hurry."

Yŏok shook my arm.

Then, holding the cage in one hand, she pressed her other hand against the wall to support herself and disappeared behind the wooden screen, which blocked off the far end of the room. Moments later, puffs of smoke began to waft up over the screen that surely concealed her bedroom, and the room filled with a smell like burning animal fat. Soon I heard the sound of flapping wings and the even brighter sound of birdsong.

Yŏok returned with the revived bird and hung the cage back on its hook before sitting down.

"I'm funny, aren't I?"

A broad smile appeared on her blushing face, and she laughed awkwardly.

"Isn't it funny? I've got no shame."

To tell the truth, I did not know what to say.

"What can I do but laugh?"

She pushed the cage to make it turn and spoke to the bird, "Look at the state of us, we couldn't even last that long."

I followed Yŏok out onto the street. We dropped in at some cabaret bars and restaurants, where we sipped strong coffee and Johnnie Walker. I had already begun to tremble due to my inability to handle strong stimulants, but my desire to drink evaporated completely when Yŏok, sat across from me, broke into a fit of coughing upon merely wetting her lips. She blew her nose several times before taking a white powder from her handbag, pushing some into a cigarette and smoking, laughing silently, gaze averted as if to say, "What's so funny?"

Along the way we passed the museum and went inside, but first Yŏok and then I began to sneeze, and we moved on quickly. Inside the dimly lit building the long periods of time preserved in the pottery, the Buddha images, and the mammoth skeleton—all on display in chronological order—merely cast a cold and empty breeze over us. I wanted to examine this history more thoroughly, but I worried I might not be able to muster the courage to return after rushing through the displays like this. As long as Yŏok was in the lead, it seemed that all my sightseeing in Harbin would take a similar course. I was wondering to myself what on earth was going on between the two of us, when she strode ahead, saying, "Let's go to the Songhua River next." I had no choice but to follow.

We headed toward the river wharf after passing through Kitaiskaya, an area renowned for the erotic and grotesque, which the name Harbin suggests, and where many Russians and Jews are still living alongside the exotic establishments of pleasure and consumption. We walked side by side, so close together that the feather on the hat perched aslant Yŏok's permed hair brushed my cheek, but the comments we exchanged were dull indeed.

"It must be three or five times as wide as the Taedong River, maybe even ten times."

"Hmm . . . it certainly looks enormous."

I looked down at her, not so much from my greater height as from my mind, and not with any kind of sympathy but instead observing her dispassionately, and as if I were engaged in a public discussion, I asked myself, "What will this girl's fate be?" Our tedious silence felt awkward, but we walked on. At the wharf all the coolies gathered around us, pointing to the light boats, which floated like ducks on the water, and gesturing toward the swimming pool on the other side of the river. They tried to entice us with gestures and incomprehensible phrases and with broad smiles, which could not be frequent visitors to their lives, as if to say, it really must be fun if even we are smiling. Yŏok waved them away without even asking me if I wanted to take a boat ride. When they followed us, she shouted at them "*buyao*"—don't want—even going so far as to stamp her feet.

"You must be tired?"

"Oh, I'm okay."

But she kept pulling out her handkerchief, and so I hailed a carriage, saying, "Yi must be waiting for us."

Four o'clock had long passed by the time we reached the lobby of her apartment building. On the way she had suggested I wait in her room, and we climbed the stairs together. After leading me down a dark corridor to a door, she was fumbling around in her handbag to find the key, when the door suddenly opened. I could not help but be startled. She also seemed surprised.

"Do please come in."

A hoarse voice resounded heavily. The autumn sun had already sunk behind the tall building across the way; in the middle of the room, which was by now as dark as a cave, a long and thin, ghostly face looked back at me.

"Please go in."

Yŏok's distinct voice brought me back to my senses and, finally, I stepped inside.

"Let me introduce you. This is . . ."

But the man interrupted her.

"There's no need for introductions, this must be Kim Myŏngil. Well, take a seat."

And with that, he sat down first.

Yŏok appeared to be at a loss for words and said no more. The man lit a cigarette and showed no sign of introducing himself. Perhaps it never occurred to him, or he kept silent on purpose, nevertheless it was not hard to guess that he was most likely her old lover Hyŏn.

At such times cigarettes can prove useful. Faced with his attitude, which was more insulting than arrogant, though he did not look as if he would pick a fight, I had no choice but to light a cigarette, exhale slowly in his direction, and play the supporting role in this wordless play. He rested his elbow on the table and barely inhaled on the cigarette burning in his hand. I could tell from his face that he was entirely engrossed in thought. I could not help but feel even more insulted when I realized that he was intentionally ignoring me by silently indulging his own thoughts, despite sitting in front of a guest he was meeting for the first time. Then it occurred to me that, if this really was Hyŏn, he might not mean to cause offense but, as one corner of this love triangle, might simply be preoccupied. If that were the case, he was far more self-possessed than I was in my solitary excitement.

The pale face hardened into a plaster bust, long and emaciated due to a high forehead; suddenly he stood up, stubbed out his cigarette, and began to pace around the narrow room. A midnight-blue cotton Chinese robe tumbled down to his ankles from his thin shoulders, elongating his gaunt body and gathering the ever-deepening darkness of the room around him. That darkness seemed to congeal into a tall shape and sway before my eyes.

I wonder why he doesn't turn on the light? I did not like the illusion created by the darkness, but all I could do was keep on smoking, while the tips of his long, thin, bony hands looked as if they might morph into daggers at any moment.

"You have probably heard about me from Yŏok. My name is Hyŏn Iryŏng."

He stopped suddenly in front of my feet to say these words before continuing to pace around the room.

"I'm an absolute failure, and now I'm an incurable opium addict as well. . . . But there was a time when I was a brilliant young freedom fighter and a theoretical leader."

He pressed the switch by the door to light up the room. But the light from the small unshaded bulb, which dangled from a cord in the center of the ceiling, could hardly be said to be bright. He flopped down on the sofa, took some white powder out from the sleeve of his robe, pushed it into a cigarette and began to inhale. It was the same smoke and burning smell that had drifted up from behind the wooden screen earlier. A joyful song, as pure as the chime of a silver bell, resounded from the birdcage, which Yŏok had placed on top of the dressing table before disappearing behind the screen.

"You have probably heard of Hyŏn Hyŏk, even if your interests lay elsewhere. I mean the famous Hyŏn Hyŏk, who once held theoretical sway over the left. The Hyŏn Hyŏk who was so famous that no member of the intellectual classes at the time had not heard of him. Wherever he went, Hyŏn Hyŏk was always surrounded by youths who idolized him."

At the repetition of the words Hyŏn Hyŏk, I recalled seeing the name in newspapers and magazines from time to time. It could be because I have never been famous, but I wondered whether Hyŏn Hyŏk was really such an attractive name that he wanted to savor it again and again. Perhaps he was drunk? I wondered whether morphine could excite someone the same way alcohol does and observed him carefully in the dim light, but his pale face seemed to have shrunk even more and his eyes narrowed to mere slits.

"Yŏok was one of those students who worshipped the famous Hyŏn Hyŏk. At that time, the ambitious Hyŏn Hyŏk was a champion in love too. Love is no different from politics. Politics is about fighting and conquering. And women are more apt to worship and submit the stronger a man's power to fight and conquer. It is not a question of the formalities of marriage or of being man and wife. Yŏok was separated from Hyŏn Hyŏk for five or six years while he was in prison and afterward, too, when he roamed here and there, but she never forgot him and has followed him here. Now that she is here, she works as a waitress and dancer to pay for his keep. Today Hyŏn Iryŏng even buys opium with the money that girl earns. You may well ask why I use opium. Well . . . it's become even more precious to me than food and I cannot go even half a day without it, so I am beyond the point of worrying about using her money, keeping face, doing my duty by her. But, you protest, why did you take up opium in the first place . . ."

By now I could hear Yŏok sobbing quietly behind the wooden screen. Hyŏn tossed his cigarette stub down, stood up, hands clasped behind his back, and resumed his speech while striding around the room.

"It is only natural that you should ask that, Mr. Kim. Now everyone has deserted me . . . all my old friends and comrades . . . and Yŏok too, when I met her again, used to ask the same question and plead with me to stop even now, alternating between tears and curses. Sometimes I would come to my senses and ask myself that same question, protesting and crying and even shouting at myself.

"Of course, I have no shortage of reasons to turn to opium. Illness, poverty, loneliness, hopelessness, despair—can these be called reasons, or are they mere excuses? Of these, I suppose the biggest reason or motivation would be despair.

"Illness, poverty, loneliness, lack of hope—most people suffer in this order, and then they despair, but I don't believe that is inevitable.

"Illness and poverty are not so easily controlled, but to despair or not depends on the person concerned. Many friends of mine in equally dire straits have forged their own destiny according to the saying, 'Never say die.' Some of my old comrades have found new paths, even if it meant a one-hundred-and-eighty degree turn. I certainly don't say this to flatter them.

"But I was the only one who despaired. Out of despair I made the fatal turn to opium, something you should never do, no matter how sick or poor you are. And that's how I reached this final stage of addiction, how I came to be beyond saving.

"What I mean is, there is no age or environment that has the power to bring a man to ruin. On the contrary, the ruined man has a fatal flaw, which will cause him to ruin himself, no matter the age or environment.

"I have neither cause nor courage to curse this environment, neither am I so presumptuous as to blame our age. All I can curse is my own weak and despairing character.

"Even such reflections have become unbearable now. To tell the truth, what use is reflection to me now? It almost makes me laugh.

"Perhaps it's my vanity which has made me ramble on so tediously at our first meeting, Mr. Kim . . . my wanting to boast of the last dregs of my old cultivation. Or maybe it was just a chance to enjoy talking about my former wisdom, or should we call it cultivation?"

Apparently too tired to talk or walk anymore, he dropped down onto the sofa and clutched his forehead with both hands. For a while he listened to the sound of Yŏok's sobbing, and then he lit up some more of the white powder.

"To tell the truth, now I live like this on morphine vapor and memories of old dreams. Exhausted by reflection, my so-called conscience and reason have long since been paralyzed, and I float on a lake of time, exaggerating a poor romance in the style of a popular novel and painting the old Hyŏn Hyŏk's reputation even more heroically. That was the person to whose embrace Yŏok returned when she abandoned you. She must have been enticed by the memory of her first love. . . . I believe she was attracted to the brilliant and famous Hyŏn Hyŏk of old, to the ambition and power that could conquer anything. If you ask her, she will tell you so. My memories of the past have only become more dazzling and the food for my dreams has become ever richer. This way I can experience happiness even in my current situation. As long as I still have Yŏok by my side, I will be happy until my dying day. And she will not leave me until that day. That is how it must be.

"But I wonder why you have suddenly appeared before us, having already let her slip through your grasp? No matter how much you try to tempt her with your money, you're not man enough for her to ever follow you. Not only that, I'll never . . ."

He suddenly leapt to his feet and walked right up to me.

"I will not let her go without a fight, ok? I won't. Do you understand?"

His high-pitched voice quivered with excitement as he placed both hands on the table and bent over, glaring at me with eyes full of hatred.

"Ok? I said, do you understand? I will not let her go without a fight."

He struck his own chest and hit the table while shouting these words at me.

It looked as if my earlier premonition would be realized before my very eyes, and I had no idea what to do about it. A long and complicated explanation would be required to clear up this misunderstanding and ease Hyŏn's pathological excitement, but there was no time to do anything other than stand up to confront his glaring eyes and clenched fists with my own. The stand-off lasted a mere instant.

And then Hyŏn's frail shoulders shook, and his breathing grew labored. Yŏok ran out from behind the screen and inserted herself between the two of us before taking hold of his fragile waist to sit him down, where she collapsed at his knee, sobbing.

I reached toward the table for my hat but froze when I caught a glimpse of the tears pouring down Hyŏn's cheeks. Was it that I couldn't just leave them there in that state, or did I feel a certain cold curiosity about the tears shed by these ghostly shadows? I pulled up a chair and sat down again.

If I stood up and left now, having just heard Hyŏn's long monologue but made no effort to clear up the misunderstanding, which had resulted from his confused psychological state, then the insult would have been too great, and so I searched for words with which to explain the situation concisely. Yet, in order to clear up his mistaken notion that I had come here in order to seduce Yŏok once more, I would have to declare, above all, that I no longer loved her. In fact, I would have to go further and say that I had no feelings for her whatsoever. Since his excitement derived not from simple misunderstanding but from a self-abasing jealousy, which arose in turn from comparing himself in his fallen state to me, nothing less would suffice. But although such an explanation would assuage his excitement and misunderstanding quite effectively, how could I say such things in front of Yŏok? There was her womanly pride to consider, and I was concerned that such honesty might also offend Hyŏn's sense of self-respect.

At a loss for words, I inhaled on another cigarette and listened to the occasional chirp from the bird. Eventually Yŏok stood up, straightened her dress, and spoke in a tearful voice.

"Just look at me now. How can you talk about seduction and jealousy, isn't it all just ridiculous? Mr. Kim, please leave now."

I had no more reason to hesitate. I picked up my hat and left.

I was once more surprised by Yŏok's intelligence, for with one sentence she managed to forestall the long and clumsy explanation that I would have to begin in order to clear up the misunderstanding. But instead of relief, I felt even more depressed when I thought about how much more unhappy her intelligence and intuition must make her feel.

When I met Yi that night, he told me that he had finished work early and, not wanting to wait until four o'clock, had phoned the office at the apartment building looking for Yŏok. A male voice had offered to pass on a message to her when she returned, and so Yi had mentioned my name and the fact that she was probably with me and had asked the man to give her the message that Yi was waiting.

It was not in the least strange, therefore, that Hyŏn had recognized me at first sight. If that was how it all began, then the door suddenly opening before us, the unexpected appearance of his grotesque figure and strange monologue and excitement, and the one-act play, which had ended in tears just as the action scene was about to begin, hadn't it all been a ridiculous melodrama dreamed up by a fallen political youth? If this were true, then perhaps I was the one who had been drugged by whatever they were smoking, and perhaps that was why I had experienced a kind of eerie, strange pressure, before finally finding myself moved (?) by some kind of attraction to their sad life.

This thought, together with my habitually acute nervous exhaustion, caused me to lose all my powers of judgment and repeatedly empty my glass even without the encouragement of Yi, who was sat across from me. And Yŏok's tears and intelligent words? I comforted my shaken heart with the explanation that it had probably all been a ridiculous comedy written and performed by Hyŏn alone. And so I found myself sneering at him, thinking how much I hated those so-called political types who are so caught up in their own intrigue that they cannot say even one honest word or perform a single honest act. Yet I could not help but hear a shallow echo behind my sneers, and I found myself laughing louder and louder in an attempt to drown out that echo. My laughter must have surprised Yi, because with wide-open eyes he commented, "Even though things didn't go well, you seem pretty happy to have met your old lover."

When I woke up late the next day, the bellboy ushered in Yŏok, explaining that she had been waiting in the lobby for a while.

Wearing a green skirt and pink jacket that dated from our time at Wulongbei, she stepped into a room already bathed in full midday sunshine; even the perfume wafting around her evoked a new memory. Only her eyes had shed their brightness.

"I apologize for having bothered the two of you yesterday."

My words sounded awkwardly formal.

"Please don't worry about it."

She began in an equally formal fashion and then continued.

She was not deliberately trying to hide her current lifestyle, but she was sorry that I had been confronted so unexpectedly with things unnecessary for me to know on such a short trip. As all had now been revealed there was nothing more to hide, she added, and told me everything that had happened. Then, explaining that she had a favor to ask, she begged me to listen some more, prefacing her request with these words: "Perhaps such shameless thoughts are common in addicts like me, but . . ."

If I were just to offer a hand for a while, she hoped to hold onto it, to lean on me, and rescue herself from her present life.

"It might simply be an addict's shameless nature that makes me ask this . . ." Tears gathered in her eyes while she repeated this phrase and said there would be no more hope for her if she were to miss this chance, now while she was still aware of her own lack of shame and still possessed the will to save herself.

Upon hearing these words and witnessing her tears, I discovered in her expression the focus of a passion and yearning for renewal more unified than that unfathomable split consciousness, which had always threatened to rupture my own state of mind. This made me think that there was still a chance for her. I had seen her tears on the previous day too, but then they had been tinged with a pathological ennui and had quivered with her nihilistic laughter.

Now I saw pure tears and emotion flowing from a unified consciousness, and I wondered in what way and for how long I would have to hold out the hand for which she was asking and what would happen to her relationship with Hyŏn. It seemed too selfish to ask about conditions right now; furthermore, I was concerned that were I to offend her pride, then her determination, which deserved respect, might burst like a bubble. All I could say was, "I admire your determination. You must do this. And I will do my best to help you."

Yŏok's eyes had already been brimming with tears, but with these words she buried her face in her knees and began to sob. After observing her heaving shoulders for a while, I ventured further, "Why don't we talk about what we are going to do?"

"Yes . . . Thank you."

She wiped her tears and, looking out the window, continued, "I have to get out of here. That's the most important thing. . . . If it's at all possible, please take me with you to Korea."

I listened in silence.

"I'm certainly not thinking of anything improper, like before. It would be like looking after a sick person . . . because actually this is an illness. If you could please just take me as far as Korea, as if you're looking after someone who's mentally ill. It's not just that I'm scared to go on my own, but the temptation of the drugs, and . . . I don't think I have the confidence to abandon everything."

The temptation of the drugs, and . . . She hesitated to complete the sentence, but what did she mean by everything? Hyŏn? Was it her lingering affection for him? I could not help but recall the sight of her, collapsed in tears at his knees the previous evening. However much I had looked down at the two of them with disgust, as if looking at a clump of ghostly shadows, I could still feel their sense of rapture with each other and their deep emotion in the midst of sad, tearful lives, adversity, failure, and despair. I even felt a little lonely, as if the gate to such deep human connection had been closed to me. Was this jealousy? A result of my lingering feelings for Yŏok? "It can't be," I thought, and I brushed the idea away at once.

"You saw for yourself yesterday what a megalomaniac Hyŏn is . . . sometimes he even looks like the devil to me. It was Hyŏn who forced me to start using morphine."

She told me their story. He had been a leading thinker, well-known both in Korea and among Japanese comrades and an agile participant in the radical underground movement; she had been his lover back then, but he had been imprisoned and they lost contact for five or six years, because he had roamed around following his release; during that time she had moved from place to place working as a waitress and running her own tearoom—she had been an orphan—before coming to Pyongyang where she had met me; shortly afterward, she had run into an old friend of Hyŏn's from Tokyo and heard that he was in Harbin; but at that time neither her health nor circumstances allowed her to muster the courage to seek him out after five or six years of silence. But then, "Wulongbei was not far to go really, and just the thought that we had crossed the border made it seem as if Harbin was closer. . . . As you know, circumstances led to my really coming here."

She blushed and laughed. I laughed along with her. After we had both finished laughing, as if it were all truly ridiculous, I said, "It probably doesn't mean much to say this now but what happened was entirely my fault. I was lacking sincerity. You were entirely justified to feel insulted by my attitude and to run away like that."

She wiped away the new tears that these words of mine provoked.

"It was only natural for you to feel that way. If, on the contrary, you had said you really loved me, then I would have felt overwhelmed and not known what to do." She hesitated before continuing, ". . . I can't stand it any longer."

She took some more powder out of her handbag and turned away with tearful eyes to smoke.

Having revealed her feelings this much already, she could no longer disguise the situation simply with an embarrassed smile and appeared unable to hold back her tears.

"Even though I feel this way now, at the time my pride was hurt in my own way, when I saw that you were not even trying to love me but were trying unsuccessfully to rid yourself of old fantasies, even if just for the sake of your painting. It's only natural that I too began to yearn for my old dreams, as an act of rebellion . . ."

And so she had run away, but the Hyŏn she met here was a hopeless addict with neither work nor regular income, although he was ostensibly employed in a lawyer's office. After many years of an irregular lifestyle and overstrained nerves he had become addicted to narcotics, which were the most effective and available medicine for someone in his penniless condition to ease his frequent stomach convulsions and the neuralgia that constantly afflicted his face.

She had begged and cajoled him into visiting a treatment center for addiction, but on the first attempt he had shaken her off at the gate and fled, and on the second attempt he had managed to persuade her to give in, and they had returned home together.

I asked, "Why on earth were you persuaded?"

She replied, "It may sound strange, but there were circumstances I could not refuse."

By circumstances she referred to the terrifying pain and spasms brought on by neuralgia and convulsions the minute the effects of the suppressants wore off; these symptoms on their own were enough to turn him into the cripple he now was. He would die an addict, but he did not have long left anyway. Given the situation, he would rather live without pain until his death. At least, they were trying to rationalize their current lifestyle in this positive fashion.

Historical predictions and ideals are always demonstrated right or wrong by history, and the truth is only proven by the past; it cannot exist in the present, let alone the future. People are not duty bound, therefore, to make of such ideals their goals, or to be governed by the ideology of truth, and neither is there any need to be so serious. It is wiser to look to the undeceiving past than it is to undertake an exploratory adventure into the empty future. With these words Hyŏn had encouraged her to take the drug with him, saying that his contemplation of old dreams through a smoky narcotic haze had transported him into a realm of ecstasy and happiness.

There was no reason for Yŏok to listen to such talk. She was already exhausted from working as a dancer and cabaret waitress day and night in order to support the two of them. She could barely manage to fall asleep before three or four in the morning, but whenever she was woken by one of her severe coughing fits, he would invariably be sitting up in clouds of smoke.

Then, one night, she felt a hot steamy breath float across her face and began to cough; her throat felt constricted, as if she were paralyzed by a nightmare, but her limbs were so relaxed she could not move. Finally, she managed to open her eyes . . . it was as if she had walked into a wall in thick fog—his face almost touched hers, and he was exhaling smoke up her nose. When she realized what he was doing, she tried to scream and run away. But she was too weak to free her wrists from his grasp; all she could do was shake in fear and cry from grief at his cold-heartedness. It was a hellish scene.

Hyŏn had adopted a most serious tone.

"I'm sorry. I'm a bastard who deserves to die. But do you think I can live without you now?"

If he did not do something she might leave him anytime, perhaps today or the following day, and he could not bear the uncertainty. And so, he tearfully begged her to succumb to addiction and stay with him until he died.

It was not clear whether he meant that he loved her so much he could not live without her, or that he could not survive without the money she provided; nevertheless, she could not help but feel pity for him in his pathetic state.

She blushed once more and smiled.

"Please don't laugh. Just say I can't live without you, and a woman will fall for even a snake coiled around her body."

From then on she had become an addict as he pleaded, and she satisfied herself with the pride, if you could call it that, of a woman who still has a complete hold on a man's heart and, what is more, the heart of the first man she had ever loved.

"If that's the case, what about your determination to leave for Korea now? What will you do about Mr. Hyŏn?"

I finally asked the question that had been bothering me for a while.

"Listen to what I have to say."

She had continued to support the utterly dependent Hyŏn, but whenever she recalled that her own life was being destroyed, she would shudder and cry uncontrollably. When he saw her in this state, he would say, "What's wrong? Do you still yearn for the other world? Am I such a burden? Of course I am, but think of your fate as that of a mother of a crippled child. I will die soon, and if you forbear just a little longer, then you will be free forever." He was probably trying to comfort her, but listening to these words she guessed what he really meant by not being able to live without her, and gradually her fear of her own destruction increased, and her tears grew more frequent. Recently, whenever she cried he would fly into a rage, saying that because he was not trying to deprive her young body of its liberty she should not cry before him like this. She did not know whether such words revealed his true feelings or resulted from the shock of his body weakening day by day, but she was indescribably saddened to discover so clearly what he thought of her.

She continued, "Please don't misunderstand me. I just wanted to be able to feel that he needed me, for whatever reason, maybe to try to recover some self-respect as a woman after you had rejected me."

Hyŏn did not need to steal from her, but he would take money when she was not looking and even obtain advances from the owners of the dance halls and cabarets where she worked. Of course, there was not much money for him to steal anyway, since they could barely survive on her pitiful earnings, and even when he could get hold of an advance, no one would give much to him as an addict. Still, on such occasions he would not go home but hole himself up secretly in some inn, where he could smoke opium of higher quality than this white powder until all the money was gone. Because of this, she had not expected him to be at home the previous day.

She had not the slightest intention of trying to save herself if it meant abandoning him. She had planned to look after him until the end and forgo the rest of her life, accepting her fate as the mother of a cripple, to borrow his words.

But after I left he had kept asking whether I had come to look for her. His tone and attitude did not seem to stem from simple jealousy, and she had replied, "Maybe he has."

Hyŏn had said he was certain this was the case and seemed satisfied that his conjecture had been proven true.

"You haven't forgotten this Kim Myŏngil either, have you? Well, to tell the truth, however much of an nihilistic egoist I may be, I have no intention of sacrificing you for this corpse of mine."

If I would swear before Hyŏn that I still loved her, he would quietly step aside, he had said, and he asked her to confess her feelings honestly. She had asked in return, "Then can you live without me? Am I no longer any use to you?" He replied that this was not the case; if he had his way nothing would make him happier than to have her by his side until he died, but if he saw with his own eyes that the two of them were in love and had a chance at a bright future together, then he would no longer be able to satisfy only the desires of the living corpse he had become; and so the two of them should speak honestly in front of him. She replied to the effect that honesty was not something he should demand only of her, but he should try practicing some himself—"Isn't it because you need money more than you need me that you plan to extort money from Kim Myŏngil, if he says he loves me?" Her demand seemed to take Hyŏn by surprise, for he had denied everything, saying that although he had doubtless sunk low, he still had the pride of Hyŏn Hyŏk and would never go so far as to sell his own lover. He had burst into tears at her cruel suggestion.

"It really does seem like you are twisting his intentions, doesn't it?" I asked.

"Perhaps I am," she said, and changed the subject.

"Please, will you go with me now and tell him that you still love me, just as he said? I'm ashamed to admit this, but with one word from you, maybe I can free myself from him and start a new life . . . please take this and give it to him if he asks."

She took three hundred-won notes from her handbag and placed them in my hand. "This is what I got when I sold the ring you gave me." She added that she had not treasured the diamond ring I gave her as an ornament but had kept it hidden from Hyŏn in case bad luck should strike.

So the money that was supposed to pay for Hyŏn's funeral was now going to buy her freedom, I thought to myself, but when I started to say, "Surely . . . he won't . . . ," she interrupted me and stood up.

"I'm sorry . . . if you could come now . . ."

What on earth is about to happen? I mumbled to myself, realizing there was no time to hesitate when I saw her determination.

Her body swayed slightly in the carriage, but her mind seemed as calm as a lake and her eyes did not blink even once, fixated as they were on one spot with resolute determination, perhaps looking into that serene lake, untroubled by a single cloud of thought.

Sat beside her, I felt guilty, but I could not help finishing in my mind the sentence she had interrupted, "Surely, he won't ask for money?" I had uttered those words out of politeness, expressing doubt in an effort to save her pride; what I really wondered was, what would she do if he surprised us by not mentioning money at all? Of course, the presumption was that he would demand money, and if that presumption turned out to be correct, then the proper order of events would be for Yŏok to lightly dismiss her feelings for Hyŏn, who had just exchanged her for money, and for her to follow me back to Korea. But what would she do in the unlikely event that he abandoned her for her own happiness? Undoubtedly she would go back to him. If she followed her current determination and went with me to Korea,

PATTERNS OF THE HEART

123

whether he demanded money or not, then the curtain would fall for good on this drama, but if she stayed with him, then wouldn't I be left alone on the stage, abandoned by the heroine in the middle of the scene, and what gesture was I to make then?

This felt like some kind of tortuous comedy in which I would have to stand before that grotesque character Hyŏn and answer yes when he asked me whether I loved her, despite this being no wedding. There was no knowing how events would transpire. I fought to suppress a bitter laugh, which broke out when I thought of Yŏok sitting so chastely at my side like a new bride and realized the performance had already begun here on the streets of Harbin, as if we were on a *hanamichi* passage leading up to the main stage. A gypsy girl caught my expression and came running after me, smiling and holding out her hands. I reached into my pocket and threw her a coin, along with a smile. A short while later I felt as tense as Yŏok, who now seemed sad and nervous about her fate, and I was just beginning to contemplate the possibility that these events might have no small effect on my life too, when the carriage arrived at the entrance to their building. My heart pounded with every breath as I stood before the door, which Yŏok opened and entered ahead of me.

"Do come in."

It was the voice from the previous evening; Hyŏn had come to the door and now offered me his hand. I was hardly delighted at the sight of his long fingers with their protruding knuckles, as white as those ghostly hands that appear in paintings, but it was even more unpleasant that I had no choice but to grasp that hand, which turned out to be unexpectedly warm and sweaty, as if it were playing some kind of trick on me.

"Yesterday must have been quite a surprise."

This was true, but I could not think of a suitable reply to his greeting, and so I remained silent.

"Well, take a seat."

He offered me a chair and sat himself down first.

The early autumn north Manchurian sky was covered in fine, silvery cloud, and the sunless room felt frigid, as if we were submerged in water. Seen close up and in daylight, the skin on Hyŏn's high forehead and cheeks was dull and wrinkled, like an old sheepskin. I averted my eyes from the dandruff, which looked as if it might take flight from his sparse hair at any moment, and asked him, in passing, "So, how is life in Manchuria?"

"It's not good manners to ask someone like me such a question, ha ha . . . Have you been to the Songhua River?"

"Yes, I was there for a while yesterday."

"When I was at university, I once studied the economic history of agriculture in Manchuria. But now . . . take a look at this."

He stood in front of an old map of Manchuria, which was affixed to the wall.

"When you look at a map like this, the water from the Sea of Okhotsk flows into the Heilung River instead of flowing up toward the northeast, and then one branch becomes the Songhua River and flows down into Manchuria, where it keeps splitting, until finally it turns into streams so small that they cannot even be drawn on the map. Fascinating, isn't it?"

He laughed senselessly. It would have been polite to laugh along with him, but I refrained. I regretted asking the stupid question that had provoked this nonsense and smoked a cigarette wearily, worrying in advance that the conversation might take an even stranger turn, given that he was the kind of person with whom you never could tell where talk might lead or what conclusions might be drawn.

Yŏok sat listlessly on the sofa, blowing vapor over the birdcage.

All this time, Hyŏn had been pacing back and forth between Yŏok and myself, stamping his Chinese shoes on the worn linoleum floor, and now he began to talk again.

"Since you two have arrived together, you must have heard about my proposal from Yŏok, so there is no need for me to listen to what you have to say. Yesterday I became excited and even shed tears in front of you, Mr. Kim, and, as you know, Yŏok sobbed out loud. While I was crying, I thought about why I felt so sad. Ruin, despair, my crippled condition . . . as I said yesterday, there is no reason for such things to bring me new sorrow. So it must have been because you, Mr. Kim, had appeared before us."

Startled, I looked up at him, my eyes wide open.

"Just listen to what I have to say."

He was still pacing back and forth.

"At first, Yŏok left you to return to me, but now she is unhappy with this life and full of regrets. I am no longer your enemy, Mr. Kim, because it would be too simple for you to steal her from me. And even if she were to cast off your temptations— perhaps this is the wrong choice of word—and she were to swear to stay by my side, she would not feel the same as before. Her melancholic sense of resignation would grow ever sadder and her sympathy for me would demand a more conscious effort. There would be the pain of having to bear her steadfast sacrifice and my bad conscience that I had not treasured this sweet woman but had turned her into a cripple instead, even though a gentleman such as yourself had followed her this far, unable to forget her . . . even worse, deep down in her heart, she would resent me anew.

"If all these worries do not derive from you, Mr. Kim—you who have appeared before us—then whose fault are they?

"Even though you say you did not come looking for her on purpose but appeared before us by mere chance, you have shaken her heart and deliberately aroused, then beaten and twisted, the pride and self-reflection that I had tried so hard to forget, until you shattered for good our life together, our life which had been peaceful in its own way, though it may look less than human to you.

"Is that not so, Mr. Kim, or is this merely the hallucinatory thinking of an addict?"

He pulled up a chair and sat down in front of me, staring into my face as if waiting for an answer. I had no idea what to say. He was claiming that I had shattered their lives, even if I had only appeared before them by chance, so there was no need for me to deny that I had come to "seduce" Yŏok, as he put it. Even if I had felt the need for denial, I was in no position to make such a statement given my promise to Yŏok. Yet Hyŏn had just demanded an answer as to whether or not I had shattered their lives. I had no choice but to respond.

"I suppose you could think that was the case. But that would be nothing more than a supposition."

"Nothing more?"

He glared at me for a moment.

"I suppose you might think so, Mr. Kim. Whether your appearance was planned or not, you do not believe that you have consciously humiliated me. You can say it's nothing, because you feel no sense of responsibility. However, my humiliation is clearly a fact, as is Yŏok's shaken heart and the shattering of our lives. Is that not so?"

I could only wonder to myself whether this was all my responsibility, even if what he said were true.

"These are facts. Even if you say you did not consciously humiliate me, what are we to do about the humiliation and suffering that we have faced as a result of your appearance? If you are not responsible for the humiliation I have received because of you, then what am I to do?

"I suppose I cannot blame you entirely. My humiliation is that of someone incomparably weaker than you. But is it really possible for me to become strong enough to erase the humiliation and torment that I have suffered at your hands? Aren't you now sitting before me asking me to let Yŏok go? If that is not torment and humiliation, then what is it? There is no way for me to muster the strength to avenge this. It will never be possible . . .

"Since I am unable to humiliate you in return, to wash away blood with blood so to speak, I have no choice but to wash away the humiliation you have brought upon me by humiliating myself even more thoroughly. I will withdraw and leave Yŏok to you.

"Rather than suffer the humiliation of keeping her at my side now that her heart is wavering because of you, it is easier for me to step back in self-abjection. I am not doing this for the sake of her happiness in going with you, nor to wish you well in your love, Mr. Kim. I told Yŏok this in the morning. I have no such humane thoughts left in me. Merely the abject nature of a cripple, who is no match for you. . . . There is no need for me to stay any longer. I will go now."

With this Hyŏn stood up.

I had not expected his long explication to conclude in this fashion. I glanced across at him to see whether he would act out his own conclusion, and watched as Yŏok, who had been silently crying on the sofa for a while now, stood up and blocked his path.

"There is nothing more to say. That you brought Mr. Kim here today says it all. Anything else would just mean deceiving yourself and me . . ."

With these words Hyŏn walked past Yŏok to stand before me.

"Mr. Kim, in order to humiliate myself I have to be thorough . . . you will need this now."

He reached into his sleeve and pulled out a key, which he placed on the table.

"Yŏok and I each have a key to this room. It is of no use to me now, but you will be needing it. Please pay for it. Whether a thousand or ten thousand won, you will need this and will have to pay for it."

He looked me in the face. He looked surprisingly calm. Perhaps this was to be expected given the conclusion of his long speech. I glanced at Yŏok. Her face was buried in her hands. She could not bear to watch the money being exchanged. I realized there was no need to hesitate any longer. And so I threw the three notes she had given me earlier down on top of the key.

"Thank you."

With no comment as to whether it was too much or too little, Hyŏn grabbed the money greedily, as if it was more than he had expected.

"I'm satisfied with humiliating myself like this. Now I will go."

And he disappeared out the door, as if in flight.

Once his footsteps were no longer audible, Yŏok collapsed on a chair and began to sob. Having no words to comfort her, I sat in a daze, watching her heaving shoulders.

After a while, she wiped her tears and sat up.

"I'm sorry. That all went as expected. He will be happy to have so much opium, that's what money means for him. He's an intellectual, so he has to come up with a fancy speech to defend his lack of shame, which is a symptom he shares with all addicts. Perhaps he seemed excited by his own words and even sad, but now he'll just be happy to be rich and will have forgotten everything. . . . I must think about what I am going to do."

She wiped away fresh tears.

I told her to lie down and get some rest, since she was exhausted by all the tears and excitement, and then I returned to my inn. By the time I had taken a bath and eaten dinner, night had already fallen. I also felt tired and not up to visiting Yi, so I went to bed early and a little inebriated from my drink at dinner. But I could not fall asleep properly after all that excitement. All the problems that I wanted to forget about for the time being kept floating around my murky head in fragmented confusion: What would become of Yŏok? What would she do? Was she really going to follow me back to Korea? Should I take her with me? What would happen after we arrived? Finding a hospital

PATTERNS OF THE HEART

for her would be the first priority. And when she was better? Then what would happen to her? Would we be together? It was not impossible. You never know what will happen between people. . . . Such jumbled thoughts kept repeating themselves.

How much time had passed? Just as sleep was finally creeping up on me, I thought I heard a knock on the door and sat up with a start. Somebody really was knocking on my door. The bellboy led in a white messenger boy, who handed me a thick, square-shaped, Western-style envelope before leaving. It was a letter from Yŏok.

I am sorry to ask you this, but I would be grateful if you would come to see me early tomorrow morning. If the door is locked and I am not there, please wait in my room. The key is enclosed.

The key was in the envelope alongside this simple message. What was this all about? If she had something to say she could easily find me, so why go to the trouble of sending a messenger and asking me to go there?

Could she be sick? But if she couldn't come herself because she was sick, then what was the meaning of this "if I'm not there" so early in the morning? These thoughts crossed my mind, but the answers would only become clear the next day. I went back to sleep.

Yi phoned as soon as I rose the next morning. He said he had called the night before, but he had not dropped by when told I was asleep; could he come over now? I had to visit Yŏok first, so I suggested I call on him after I had seen to some business. He burst out laughing, asking me what kind of business I could have in Harbin, and could it possibly be calling on Yŏok? I said he was right and laughed too.

The day was pleasantly bright. By the time I arrived at Yŏok's apartment it was already nine o'clock. I coughed and knocked on the door, only to receive no answer. So I did need the key, I thought to myself, with an absurd illusion of gratitude for her meticulousness; even the sound of the key in the lock seemed cheerful as I stepped into the room. A cold air immediately enveloped me, pressing down heavily on my chest. She must have not opened the window after waking up, I thought, because a sickeningly stale narcotic smell hung in the air, and a chill breeze, lacking any human warmth, swirled around my chest with an oppressive, unpleasant feeling. Yet I had to wait for her, and so I sat down on the sofa and lit a cigarette. It was when I opened the window and looked out that I remembered the skylark, which should be in fine voice on such a clear day. I looked around the room to find no sign of the birdcage. That was when I noticed. From behind the wooden screen, in what I presumed was the bedroom, I could hear the sound of flapping wings and a dull screech. It was that same dismal shriek that I had heard on the first day. Left to itself, the bird would spread its legs and lie down in its own feces. If Yŏok did not come and breathe some morphine vapor onto it, it would die. There was more flapping noise as the bird apparently tried to lift its body up, followed by a mouselike squeak. Where could she have gone? With these anxious thoughts, I decided I had to take a look, even though I knew there was nothing I could do.

I pushed the screen door open. Yŏok lay inside. She was asleep, sprawled out on a double bed squashed into the narrow bedroom, just like in a picture. The birdcage was on the bed.

In front of me a hand grasped the bedcover, as if to tear it with red fingernails. On the floor beneath the hand lay a letter addressed to Mr. Myŏngil Kim. The letter was crumpled, as if it had originally been clutched in her hand.

Slowly returning to the sofa, I opened the letter.

Even though I have no sense of shame, I did think of going to the Songhua River or to the railway tracks to spare you this trouble, but I was worried I would fail with so many people and guards around. And so you will witness this ugly scene. I thought of waiting until you had left or quietly leaving to find somewhere to die, but I had neither the strength nor the courage to carry this death somewhere and wait for the right time. I was too lonely and scared. I know this is inconsiderate of me, but when I thought of some stranger taking care of my body, I just felt lonely and scared.

I have given much thought to the trouble this will bring you but have decided to trust you and leave this way. I had even dreamed of a new life.

I meant it when I said I would return home with you.

When you said, "Surely Hyŏn won't . . . ," I too shared your doubts. My determination was not so firm as to remove any concern that I might go with him, if he were to surprise us, and yet I yearned for a new life. He did as I expected. I know that it was his (incurable) sickness and not his heart's desire, so I am not dying from a broken heart, having been rejected. It's just that I feel so alone. Even if I said I would return to him now, he would already have forgotten our love and would sell that key to anybody, if the opportunity arose.

And if I could cure this sickness of mine (addiction), with a fresh and clear mind I think the world would feel so strange and empty that I would only feel more alone. The dream of a new life seems like momentary excitement. Now what is there to hide? Perhaps I sound fickle, but though I regret that I cannot win your heart, all I can do now is try to forget you.

If I were to follow you and recover, what kind of hope would await me? Please stay safe and well.

Yŏok
Six o'clock in the evening on the X day

After reading Yŏok's suicide note, I went back into the bedroom.

I looked down at her face, which displayed not a single blemish or wrinkle, and I even felt a kind of comfort, as if I were gazing upon my dead wife Hyesuk's face again.

Their dazzling faces reflected the beautiful patterns of their hearts.

Yŏok died with no one to offer her heart! I had been unable to accept that heart! I could hardly suppress the sadness that such thoughts provoked.

Placing her cold hand back under the bedcover, I considered how it had been Yŏok's fate not to follow me into a new life but to die like this instead.

Ordinary People

O nce all the rowdiness and confusion from the bustling platform had been packed into its carriages, the train departed. The chaos in the overexcited third-class carriage began to settle, too, while memories of the station faded into the distance.

Those with seats sat down, and those with no choice but to stand found their own spot.

I was sitting at the far end of the carriage, just inside the door, and now found myself with the leisure to light a cigarette and take a look around.

"Where could all these people be going to create this much commotion? What is their purpose?"

Whenever I found myself standing in the midst of a crowded platform or on a quay, it was my habit to murmur such phrases to myself. Of course, this could lead to some sentimental thoughts, such as, "Some are sure to be leaving on a dark journey, carrying with them sorrow and worries unimaginable to others."

This time, more than anything, I was feeling annoyed at being stuck in the middle of these mountains and oceans of people. But it was not a sense of annoyance that prompted me to now look around. Neither was I driven by curiosity or the hope of discovering the sorrowful expressions of those leaving on a desperate journey—although if I did find any such thing, it would no doubt have satisfied my unoccupied eyes.

It seemed I was not the only one who was feeling more relaxed. As the tension eased, people returned to their original selves, and in doing so they each began to recover their own habits.

Those newly recovered habits caused a country lad among us—he had wrapped a knitted scarf around his head in place of a hat—to commit no small mistake. His saliva, spat out in his usual manner from where he stood in the aisle, had by chance managed to land on the toe of a shoe belonging to a middle-aged gentleman seated across from me. But what turned this already considerable mistake into a major blunder and made everyone look on with startled eyes was the reaction of the shoe.

In an instant, that shoe almost stamped through the floor of the aisle. But the toe was quite rough, and nothing was easily dislodged. Becoming even more irate, the shoe began to kick violently into the air. Even I received some splash damage. The young lad was at a complete loss for what to do, merely stepping back to avoid the spit leaping toward him. At this point, the old man who appeared to be his travel companion tore a handful of old newspaper from a bunch in his cloth bundle and handed it to the lad. Clutching the newspaper, the lad then carefully reached out a hand toward the toe of the shoe, as if he were about to stroke a wild beast that might kick or rush forward and maul him at the slightest opportunity. The shoe did not attempt to bite nor to kick, but it flinched as if to avoid the hand. And then, slowly, the soft white paper began to wipe the shoe. That paper seemed plentiful and spared no effort.

Those watching on seemed more taken aback than when the shoe had been kicking up a fuss, and now they were all occupied observing the steady growth of a heap of paper in the aisle. With wipe after wipe, and yet more superfluous wiping, it seemed the lad was trying to erase the unpleasant memory more than the actual spit. That continual wiping also seemed to be a conscious effort to apologize. Or, rather, it seemed to attest less to the dirtiness of the shoe than to the dirtiness of the person who had committed the blunder.

All the observers now pouted and turned away. The young lad blushed wildly, his humiliation deeper than any sense of regret, and he stared up at the ceiling, just occasionally exhaling with a sigh. Across the aisle from the middle-aged gentleman, a baggy-trousered man kept stealing sideways glances that revealed the whites of his eyes and the nostrils of a prominent nose, flared as if he were more than a little disgusted. But whenever his eyes crossed those of the gentleman they would quickly change direction, and that mighty nose would point up toward the ceiling. Baggy Trousers was not the only one trying to avoid eye contact with the gentleman, whose glaring eyes shifted around enough to make anyone feel uneasy, no matter how mighty their nose. Those eyes were either deliberately trying to assume a dignified air, or they were in the habit of attempting to project a commanding presence, or, alternatively, they might simply be shifting around in spite of themselves, a sign of slight paranoia. Whatever the cause, they were not easy eyes to confront; when the old man with a pipe, the one who had earlier offered up a bunch of newspaper, was caught stealing a sidelong glance while trying to light up, his attempt was thwarted, and he quickly blew out the match before his pipe had properly ignited.

With no obvious topic of conversation, our carriage had been silent since our departure, but now the atmosphere grew increasingly uncomfortable. Of course, this was not the kind of place where anyone was responsible for taking the initiative to break the silence.

Just then a young man in a leather jacket, seated next to Baggy Trousers, turned to another young man wearing a cap who sat opposite him and asked, "Have you got any *chirigami*?" "Yes, I do," Cap replied, but just as he pulled some out, Leather Jacket said, "Oh, I've got *chirigami* too!" And he pulled out a bunch of tissue with which he proceeded to blow his nose. Cap laughed, blew his own nose, and then threw the tissue onto the pile of paper already accumulated in the aisle.

Baggy Trousers smiled, but there was no other reaction. In front of me the gentleman's eyes continued to shift around, and he yawned loudly two or three times. This may seem a little rude, but from where I was sitting opposite him, that yawn felt like the yawn of a toad in one of those strange, old tales where the toad's breath spreads a foul smell or a mist, which then casts a spell over people.

Now that I have made such a rude comment, I might add that the gentleman really did have something toadish about him. I had nothing to do but to observe him in even greater detail. As I mentioned before, his shifting eyes first caught the attention, followed by the unpleasantly flat lips, which remained firmly sealed, the double chin that kept gulping as if to swallow hard phlegm, and his nose, whose existence was so vague it could be omitted altogether if you were to draw a caricature. Surely even toads have noses, which must be somewhere on their faces, though I have yet to see a nose on a toad's face. According to the same rule by which a toad still has a proper face, this nose was the only feature of the gentleman's face that was so weak as to be inconsequential; it merely sat there, humbly upturned, failing to assert its own presence. Perhaps it was a truly noselike nose, provided for the sole purpose of breathing.

As for those so-called high-ridged noses, such as the one belonging to Baggy Trousers, they tend to either give the impression of utter conceit or are useless things that turn red at the slightest hint of cold.

The earlier incident of the mistake was not the sole prompt for me to steal enough glances at him to attempt this rather meaningless record of his facial features. Of course, it was true that his extreme fastidiousness (?) had both attracted our attention and aroused our animosity, but even without that, he would still have been the most eye-catching among us. If this were a class picture drawn by an elementary pupil, then he would be class leader, magnified larger than the other children. Not only was he the biggest and the best dressed of all of us—and by us I mean we four enemies in the same boat, sitting facing forward and backward on either side of the aisle—but his breathing made the loudest noise each time it propelled that fat stomach up and down.

Now this eye-catching gentleman yawned for the umpteenth time, reached behind the young woman sitting next to him by the window, and pulled out a flat bottle of sorghum wine, which was wrapped in paper the color of pine cake. He poured some wine into a teacup lid, as if measuring out bitter medicine, and swallowed it with a grimace that traced a myriad creases across his greasy face. After hurriedly pouring another lid of wine with trembling hands, he gulped that down too, and then his whole body shook with a convulsion so severe it felt like water might spray off the coarse otter-skin trim on his camel coat. Reaching down once more behind the woman, he pulled out a slice of dried meat, as if from under her buttocks, tore off a strip, and began to chew. The strong smell of alcohol wafting through the air inevitably attracted all eyes onto him again. Drops of sweat rose like crab eggs on his brazenly uplifted, receding forehead, where a few pathetic hairs fluttered like the eyelashes of some microorganism, while he noisily chewed away. Soon we were struggling for air in the hot carriage on account of the heat and smell emanating from him, and then, while we watched on, the chewing began to slow, the rolling of the glaring eyeballs stilled, the corners of his lips drooped as if to dribble, and suddenly he was asleep. This may seem a bit of an exaggeration, but it was like the Maitreya Buddha falling off the lotus dais. He startled himself awake—his bloodshot eyes opened wide, like a toad dreaming he had been placed on the stone for pounding rice cakes—and immediately he checked on the woman at his side before stretching with apparent relief. Next he quickly stood up as if he had forgotten something, removed his coat, took some tissue, and, rubbing it between both hands, disappeared into the toilet.

All eyes shifted onto the young woman, who until then had been huddled in the far corner of the abruptly vacated seat, hiding in his shadow. That is not to say that we noticed her for the first time. Neither have I been saving her up like a star player only to have her appear in a suitable scene. From the beginning of our journey she, like the rustic woman seated opposite her to my side, had said or done nothing worthy of record but had been silently dragging on a cigarette.

She stared out the window, seemingly unaware that she was now the object of our attention; a gray coat was draped somewhat decadently across her shoulders, and she twisted her permed hair behind her ears with her near hand, as if by habit. Although she appeared to be staring out the window, it was already dark outside, and the double-layered window merely reflected the shadow of her deep purple jacket, which shone back at us like a stoked-up furnace. This description might seem a little extravagant, but her shadowy face radiated a glow, like a white porcelain vessel placed on top a furnace; in the center a cigarette burned red while she exhaled smoke through pursed lips, as if to extinguish the flame.

Just then the door next to me opened, and the conductor entered, asking everyone to show their tickets. When her turn came, the woman did not even look around until the inspector prodded her on the shoulder and called out, "*Jyōshaken,* tickets please." After a brief glance, the woman quickly turned away again, speaking in Japanese, "The person I'm with has it."

"And where is that person?"

"In the toilet." She did not turn around to answer, but merely pointed with her thumb toward the wall at the back.

The conductor asked why she was not looking after her own ticket. "That's not allowed," chimed the young inspector curtly, in awkwardly pronounced Korean.

The woman glared into their disappearing backs and then turned away again with a frown. She looked on the verge of tears. Her expression was tense, hysterical perhaps, causing me to wonder why such a small thing had upset her so much. Later on, I realized she probably wanted to cry and complain, "What can I do when he bought the tickets and he's holding onto them?"

With the tickets checked and the "inspection"—the very word provokes unease—safely completed, everyone looked relieved at having survived this slightly tense excitement. Inevitably, we now paid even more attention to the woman, since she was the only one to have caused a problem, and she still did not seem to have recovered.

She can't be his daughter. A concubine, maybe? Just as I was thinking this, Baggy Trousers spoke up: "They say the money's good selling women in Manchuria and up north."

We had all been sitting quietly, but now that an interesting topic had finally emerged, all eyes fell upon the man. Leather Jacket, who was sat by his side, was the first to respond.

"Oh, the money's good all right, but you need capital. 'Cause even a cheap woman costs a thousand won, they say."

"And even in today's money, a thousand hwan is still ten thousand nyang, ain't it?'"

Of course, it was the old man with a pipe who seemed surprised. Then the lad of the mistake joined in.

"What's a thousand hwan nowadays? A decent cart ox don't come for less than that."

This time he carefully spat at his own feet.

"But back in the old days, didn't an ox always cost more than a woman?"

"You mean, when they used to sell their daughters off as future brides in the village? . . ."

Our eyes all followed his chin to settle with renewed interest on the woman. Even I could take a guess at her identity.

All this time she had been smoking and staring out the window, but her shoulders flinched, as if our words and glances lashed an invisible whip on her back. She pulled her coat up around her shoulders. The rustic woman, who had moments earlier been feeling the hem of the woman's jacket and examining her skirt, pulled back her hand in surprise and dusted off the front of her own skirt.

"Everyone gets by in different ways."

"Of course, how else could it be?"

"What do you mean?"

"Well, it's got to be different because we all get by according to the way we are."

"So some people are made to be whore merchants?"

"You don't know by looking?"

"Looking how?"

"Well, he's got that woman by his side, ain't he?"

"Ha, ha."

"Ha, ha, ha."

Leather Jacket and Cap bantered back and forth, laughing loudly.

And then: "It might sound funny, but you really can tell just by looking at people."

Baggy Trousers pointed at the empty seat with his chin, as if to explain that this talk of whoring, which he had been first to bring up, had not been started on the basis of nothing.

"Just take a look, he may well sit there with his head held high, trying to look like he's decent, but there's something indecent about the way the sweat glistens on his face."

"Now that you all say so, that does seem to be the case. There's something wrong with his face but still, I thought he must be a county official somewhere, dressed up as grand as that."

The old man tapped his pipe against his rubber shoes to empty it, while Baggy Trousers laughed.

"Dressing grand don't mean anything these days. All you need is money, and you can dress up fancier than any county official."

"Just ask him, what would he say . . . I . . . I mean, to people like us . . ."

The lad of the mistake didn't finish his sentence. He looked up at the ceiling and his face turned even redder than before for some reason. Everyone burst into laughter.

"Were you scared back then?"

Cap stopped laughing for a moment to ask the question before exploding into fits of laughter again. Baggy Trousers responded with some scorn.

"Well, it's the decent people who are really scary. What's there to be scared about people"—pointing at the empty seat again with his chin—"just pretending to be decent? Just think about it. Didn't you notice that earlier? You saw him hiccup after taking out that wine—he couldn't last without it. People like that just look unpleasant; once you get to know them they're all right, really."

The gentleman in question had dozed off after drinking the sorghum wine, but he had not hiccupped. And yet, the criticism sounded even more true than the truth.

"He hiccupped?"

Leather Jacket pressed the point. Everyone laughed again.

Just then the gentleman returned from the toilet. Once back in his seat he looked around as if to check whether there had been some change while he was away, and then he put his coat back on again. Everyone wiped the smiles off their faces and stopped talking.

The inspector must have been keeping watch, because he now came running up to inspect the tickets and repeat his previous scolding in Japanese.

"You caused us some trouble."

The embarrassed gentleman blushed wildly and kept repeating in Japanese, "Oh I'm sorry, I'm really sorry," and his smile revealed something closer to subservience than sheepishness. His eyes gently creased as he returned the tickets to his inside pocket, and then he began to speak, addressing no one in particular but as if entreating everyone to listen.

"Damn it, I'm so constipated, I'm always *** ***. Surely it should come out more easily than this."

He laughed raucously. (Writer's note: Even though I abandoned my fastidiousness when I began this work, my grace of character forces me to omit his sound effects.) His voice was gentle. And his smile friendly. Such words spoken alongside that smile had no small effect.

"Now, that is a problem. When it's really bad, it's like a tiny woman pushing out her first baby."

Baggy Trousers took the lead in expressing his sympathy. Soon all those eyes, which had been so ill disposed toward the gentleman previously, lit up with smiles instead.

"Well, since it's likely the drink if not any kind of sickness, can't you give it a rest for a few days?"

Cap offered this advice with impetuous friendship.

"That's all well and good, but how can you tell the gentleman to stop drinking when he has visitors and official business to take care of?"

The old man with a pipe spoke respectfully, and Leather Jacket agreed, "That's right, that's right."

Having obtained such empathy and cordiality all at once, the man belched several times before continuing, "Of course that's true, too, but it was the drink that helped me through the cold winters during the ten years I spent wandering around Manchuria and up north, and now I can't quit the habit, even though I'm out of there."

He picked up the bottle of wine at his side, gave it a little shake, and proceeded to stroke it.

"Is your business in Manchuria or the north?"

"Well, there's nowhere I haven't been. I was up at the frontline for four or five years, then it got too difficult, so I came to Taeryŏn, then to Singyŏng, where I got my kids doing the work. I got out of there last year."

"Business must be a worry?"

The question came from Baggy Trousers.

"Well, not really . . . they've been pretty good up 'til now . . ."

He went to put the bottle he'd been stroking back behind the woman, when the old man with a pipe, who had been watching on with interest, came and sat down, saying, "Well, how's about we share a drink then?"

"Oh, I'm sorry, I didn't even think to offer, I've been so rude. Let's have one together now."

And so, with smiles and pleasantry and exclamations of—oh, this is a surprise—well I might just have one—ha ha ha—an unexpected drinking party broke out in the carriage.

I was the only one who refused the cup as it was passed around—I cannot tolerate alcohol at all—and I was quite grateful when they did not press the matter. Despite the fact that they were good people, rather than sympathize with me for not being able to drink, their friendship simply didn't extend to me on account of my having remained silent the whole time. They seemed to distance themselves from me. This was not a simple distance, but something closer to the antagonism and suspicion they had previously felt toward the gentleman.

Of course, the topic of conversation dominating this unexpected drinking party was the gentleman's personal history and business.

". . . to tell the truth, there's probably no better way to make money than this. Still, the girls can be very difficult. When you have twenty or thirty to take care of, you get to see everything. . . . They get sick and take to bed at the slightest thing, but they're human after all, so you can't refuse them medicine; then, expense after expense mounts up and business doesn't go well; if you're lucky they get better, but if they die then that's more than a thousand won gone to the devil, as you have to shell out on extras, like the burial, on top of everything else. And so it went.

"It's not that they want to die. And those are the better ones . . . others fall into bad habits. They keep saying they're going to die, and then either they go kill themselves with someone or they run away . . ."

He accepted the teacup lid midsentence, asking, "Is this my fifth now?" as if he really didn't want to drink but would force himself to do so out of friendship. Having made the decision, he gulped it down with a heroic expression. His body trembled, and his bloodshot eyes opened wider still.

"I just can't believe it, my sons have been all over Manchuria looking for this bitch. . . . When I think of the money I've spent and the amount of trouble she's caused me, I could kill her . . ."

All of a sudden he raised his fist in anger. Everyone was aghast to see the fist about to fall on her head. But the moment passed. Everyone roared with laughter. The fist had quietly pulled away, and its owner began to laugh as well. I'd had to close my eyes, but now I managed to steal a glance at the woman.

She was inhaling so deeply on her cigarette that it seemed as if even her shadow might ignite. There was not the slightest sign of relief or gratitude for the fist's forgiveness. It was as if nothing had happened. It had only been for one moment, just one moment.

Raucous laughter reverberated around the carriage. But I knew they were not laughing out of malice. It was the laughter of good people, relieved that the violence had stopped and full of wonder at the gentleman's almost magical magnanimity, which had allowed him to joke instead of continuing with the abuse. Then why was it that their laughter seemed to inflict even more abuse upon the woman's spirit than the fist had?

Just then the train pulled into a small station. The lad of the mistake and the old man with the pipe both exited. They rushed away, still laughing, and the train continued its journey. No one had been waiting at the dark station to replace them.

"At any rate, that must be hard work. I have enough trouble trying to look after my family, but you must have a hell of a time with all those cunning women."

Baggy Trousers started up the conversation again in his twangy voice.

But the gentleman merely opened his sleepy eyes for a moment and then closed them again without speaking. The still unemptied wine bottle now passed around the three men opposite.

"While we're at it, why don't we get her to pour us a drink?"

"Shut up. Didn't you hear what he said?"

"What?"

"Do you think she wants to pour your drinks when she's just been dragged away from her lover down south?"

"If she's had such a *tsurai shitsuren* she can't pour me a drink, then why didn't she go kill herself?"[1]

"You think dying's that easy?"

ORDINARY PEOPLE

1 At this point many Japanese phrases intermingle in the conversation. *Tsurai shitsuren* means "difficult breakup."

146

"*Nani wake nai yo.* . . . Really, if he was good enough to run away for, I mean, if he was her *koibito* that she had to *issho ni naru*, even if it meant running away, then why did she leave him? Why didn't she ask him to kill her when she was caught, eh? You should have bit your tongue right there and then, isn't that right, *kimi*?"[2]

She turned away, her face pale with disgust. Those eyes, which had been watching the men, now seemed to say, "Who are you to say such a thing?" But the men were so drunk that they didn't stop, even when their eyes met hers.

"That's right, you know, if she was a good girl she wouldn't run away so easily."

Baggy Trousers' invisible words lashed her face like a whip.

"Well, let's drink up. What's the point of worrying about things that are none of our business?"

Leather Jacket seemed the least drunk and passed the lid as if to intervene. The young lad took their drinking cup and burst out laughing when he struggled to sit up straight.

"But *kanojo*, she's a *tenka no* whore, *ja nai ka*? Why's she none of our business?"[3]

The train came to a stop once more, and a row of lights appeared outside the window. The two young lads seemed to come to their senses and rushed off, laughing.

"This is our stop."

"We had a good time."

"*Sayonara.*"

Some new passengers took their seats, and the train departed again.

The bustle had disturbed the snoring gentleman, who now jolted awake in confusion.

2 *Nani wake nai yo*: "What are you talking about?" *Koibito*: lover. *Issho ni naru*: to be together. *Kimi*: you.

3 *Kanojo*: she. *Tenka no*: a natural. *Ja nai ka*: Isn't that so?

There being no one left for Baggy Trousers to talk to, he yawned wearily before getting off at the next station. When the rustic woman next to me also left the train, I moved into her seat to sit facing the young woman.

The gentleman then took down his bag and hat from the rack, as if in preparation for the next station. He retied his shoelaces and wiped his eyes and mouth with a handkerchief, all the while mumbling as if to himself.

"Now you know you made a mistake, don't you?"

". . ."

"Always taking advantage of my absence . . . well, we'll see about that."

". . ."

She kept on smoking. The new occupants of the carriage had no idea what had happened earlier and so were unable to jump in and amuse themselves at the woman's expense. Nobody talked about her, or even looked at her, until the train arrived at S station.

I expected the gentleman and woman would get off, but instead he opened the window and leaned out so far I thought he might even fall. He looked around as if searching for someone on the busy platform before shouting out. After several calls, a young man appeared at the window.

"What are you doing here? Your brother said he would come."

"He's had to go to XX."

"Why?"

The young man was flustered by the question and scratched his head with his hand, which was holding a woolen hat.

"Okju's run away again."

"What?"

"I said Okju's . . ."

"Damn you."

The hand, which had been leaning on the window frame, suddenly struck the young man's cheek. The young man stepped back in surprise.

"We'll soon get her back . . ."

"I don't want to hear about it."

He slapped the young man's cheek again.

"Have you really found her? Get in quickly."

Thanks to their quick reaction, the young man explained, she had already been caught at XX, and his brother had left to fetch her. Finally looking somewhat appeased, the gentleman started to fuss that he could go no further because work was so busy here, and with that he gave up his seat, along with the woman's ticket, to the young man before leaving the train himself.

The train pulled out of the station, and the gentleman disappeared into the distance outside the window.

But then the young man noticed the woman watching him, and out of nowhere and without a word he slapped her on the cheek. Her head flew back to one side, and she set to tidying her disheveled hair back behind her ears, as was her habit. Another slap resounded. This time she lost the grip on her cigarette. The hand moved a third time. She bit down on her quivering lip. Even in the smoke-filled light, red finger marks were clearly visible on her cheek, which was twitching with spasms. Her white teeth clenched her trembling lips, as if to suppress a rising sob. But when my eyes met hers I saw what was without any doubt a smile. Even her twitching cheeks and clenched lips seemed to suppress an irresistible laugh. Forgetting myself, I could not take my eyes off her face. At last tears began to gather in her eyes. She had only to blink once and down they would pour. I could look no more and turned away.

"Where are you going?"

The young man shouted a moment later.

". . ."

Shielding her tear-strewn face with her handkerchief, she gestured toward the toilet with her chin. He watched her go, heard the toilet door close, and, sensing with his body that the train was now moving at full speed, took out a cigarette, as if beginning to relax at last.

"Excuse me."

He reached over for the matches, which were on the windowsill. Her matches had been elbowed toward my side when the gentleman had leaned out the window.

"Oh, thank you. I'm sorry about just now . . ."

He tried to start a conversation as he returned the matches to their place.

Not only did I have no reply to his persistent attempts to make conversation, but I began to feel increasingly uneasy, even dizzy. I was not going away for long, yet my whole body already felt exhausted by the journey so far, with the journey ahead sure to be more tiring.

Perhaps it was my nervous state, but for some reason a vision of the woman floated clearly before my eyes—her head was in the toilet, and blood poured from her mouth. This may well have been prompted by the earlier trivial and drunken implications of the men, who departed the train saying, "We had a good time," or it may equally have been a vision produced by my own cruel curiosity about others. Although it seemed unlikely that she would bite her tongue and throw away her life solely because of their suggestive parting phrase, I simply could not make that vivid scene disappear. When I thought of her eyes, laughing even as she bit down on her lips, it seemed as if she might just be determined enough to die. I grew more anxious, and my body began to shake with the impulse to jump up immediately and break down the toilet door if necessary.

Of course, the new occupants of the carriage did not know what had happened earlier, and even the young man might be unaware of the urgency (?) of the situation, but I was frantically anxious that someone was dying, and that anxiety only increased while I wavered helplessly, trying to decide to what extent my worries were fanciful and to what extent they were rational.

Those who had no idea of the "emergency" were simply curious to know why the man had hit her.

"What's going on?" asked one of those curious people, continuing the conversation in my place.

The young man smiled pleasantly and answered, "Oh, it's funny really. It's not just the girls who drive me crazy, but my father too. . . . What else can I do when he hits me, and I only have them to vent my anger on? That's why, well . . ."

The man who asked the question laughed along with him.

The answer was so clear that there was no need to ask any more. It was simple: those who could would do the beating, while those in the position to be beaten would be beaten.

Even while observing this most transparent reality, my vision persisted, except now it seemed that no matter how much I hurried it must be too late. Her cold, stiff corpse rolled around inside my head, behind my closed eyelids, and tumbled back and forth like a piece of baggage on the shaking floor.

Ah! All of a sudden, and most fortunately, my nightmare came to an abrupt end. The woman brushed past my knees and returned to her seat. Not only had she returned safely, but she had also touched up her makeup and dusted white powder onto her cheeks, which no longer revealed any traces of either finger marks or tears. To top it all off, her eyes looked as if they might cast one of her professional amorous glances my way at any moment. At least I was glad that she had returned alive and was looking so calm.

"Did you say you caught Okju?"

It was the first time I heard her speak.

"Yeah, so you two planned this together, did you?"

His voice was carefree, as if he harbored no grudges over past events.

"What kind of plan could we make . . . anyway, I'll be glad to see her again."

I had to struggle to suppress the urge to burst out laughing.

The Barley Hump

Sangjin kept switching the heavy bundle of books back and forth between one hand and the other on the long walk home. He had been summoned to "appear" at the main police station in K County. He was of course relieved to be returning home safely, and yet he could not help but be annoyed by the nonsensical nature of it all.

In the end, the only sense he could make of what had happened was that in order to serve yet another summons and conduct an interrogation—all while the head of the Higher Police just happened to be visiting—they had used the pretext of returning these books, which they had confiscated during a house search that had itself been conducted with only the vaguest hope of finding something suspicious. In other words, he had come to their attention by what they termed "possessing things of such little utility in these urgent times that he could hardly be viewed favorably," and with that their intention appeared to be to keep scratching away until they could manufacture some kind of incident, and if that proved impossible, they would continue their efforts until they could catch him in the act of contradicting himself. As for their "interrogation," from the time of the house search, this is how it had proceeded:

> Are these your only books?
> Have any young people borrowed books from you?
> Are you exchanging letters with anyone?
> Who are your associates?
> Have you been talking to anyone about the recent military
>   draft?

Such unfocused questions suggested they were groping in the dark, hoping to stumble upon something. And yet the bastards did not drop their guard for even a second but scrutinized Sangjin's every expression and pose for signs that he might, deep down, be harboring some treacherous thought or even some kind of plot to put such thoughts or words into action, which they might then be able to uncover.

So you bastards haven't come rushing in on the back of some kind of lead, then!

Sangjin knew better than anyone that there could not possibly be any substance to their suspicions, and yet the house search had struck like a bolt of lightning out of nowhere, and with the added event of this interrogation he could not help but feel anxious, as if he really had done something, and worry that he might have become tangled up in some false accusation or ridiculous blackmail attempt.

In the midst of all this they had posed the hardest question of all: "Why don't you write anymore?" This was different from their questions about concrete facts, when he could cut them short with a yes or a no or by saying this or that had happened or not. They watched his face ever more closely, even paying attention to the tone of his voice. Confronted by the sting of their glares, all Sangjin could do was invoke his beriberi and other minor problems and repeat, "It's my health, you see. . . ."

They knew all about that, they said, but even if he wasn't able enough for conscription or the Patriotic Corps, surely he could still write? "In other words, isn't the problem more in your head than your heart?"

Sangjin was at a loss to reply. The best defense he could muster was that he neither wielded influence among the masses nor was particularly well known in literary circles any more, on account of his health and his not having written anything for five or six years.

This provoked a snort from the head of the Higher Police, who asked whether Sangjin had ever made any attempt, even once, to cooperate with the authorities and write something that might exert a good influence on the masses.

"Ultimately all you need to understand is this one point. If you end up classified as a nonsubject because you're standing on the sidelines, the consequences will be terrifying."

This final threat was designed to tighten the screws. There was nothing else Sangjin could say. He could offer yet more flimsy excuses, but these seemed only to sully the innocence he had maintained thus far, an unnecessary scratch provoking an abscess. Timid Sangjin could feel the sweat still trickling down his back as he walked away, dismissed like a loser with nothing more to say in his own defense.

The books weren't particularly valuable or even worth carrying all the way back home, but since the police believed that they were generously returning important items they had previously seized, he had no choice but to pack up the precious books and take them with him out of the station. *The Philosophy of Melancholy*, *The Anatomy of Melancholy*, *The Philosophy of Tragedy*, *Flowers of Evil* . . . such books were not exactly banned, but their unwholesome sounding fin-de-siècle titles had aroused the thugs, who appeared to have confiscated the books on the suspicion that they were somehow acting as camouflage for something else, given their distance from the urgency of the current situation. In truth, when Sangjin had evacuated to this market town in S township, he had buried all his books in bundles of straw in the shed. But he seemed to still attract attention as a fairly well known writer—even though he hadn't picked up a pen for five or six years, since the Sino-Japanese War had broken out—and he had become worried that it might seem unnatural if his room were completely free of books, and so he had arranged a few books in a display, with circumstances like this in mind, in order to dispel any suspicions about the kind of books he might have hidden elsewhere.

He had sorted through his book collection, carefully setting aside any volumes with red lettering and titles, in addition to those written in Korean of course, and then he had chosen some from the dozens remaining as traces of his wan—yet still tidy— melancholic youth; the conspicuous display created from the selected titles acted as a kind of camouflage to cover the deep bruises and stains that had coagulated, as if from an internal hemorrhage of gloom.

Sangjin had barely walked ten ri before he was exhausted: by legs weakened from beriberi, by the difficulty of getting any sleep during the night while under attack from the bedbugs and fleas in his room at the inn, and by the stress of an interrogation that had lasted the entire previous day, due to the devious scratching intended to examine everything from top to bottom in the most humiliating fashion, to squeeze out the oil, as the saying goes.

For several days now, the surveillance in town had been unrelenting with the number of military and regular police swollen to keep watch over the inspection of all youths of conscription age—this would determine who could be drafted into the military. Sangjin had hesitated over waiting for the next day's car, but in such an atmosphere he was nervous of being questioned again and had set off on the breathless forty-ri journey immediately after finishing an early breakfast.

I t was that time of year when the acacia flowers are beginning to open while it still feels chilly in the shade, and yet after climbing up a hill, the sweat dripped down Sangjin's back, and he struggled to catch his breath. He wiped his feverish brow before stretching his legs out on the grass in the shade of a tree and lighting a cigarette.

When would the day arrive when he didn't feel like howling from sadness? The Soviet Army's occupation of the towns on the outskirts of Berlin had brought the war to an end in Europe, but the Pacific War lingered, with the U.S. Army still far from the main islands of Japan, even after the fall of Iwo Jima and the Okinawa landing. Perhaps it was Sangjin's impatience that made each day feel like a whole year, but the bastards were claiming that the war would drag on, because even if the Allied forces were to land in Japan they would need time to make further preparations before advancing, and even though Sangjin thought this mere propaganda and lies intended to deceive the people the uncertain future still looked dark. This latest incident aroused the fear in him that the longer these days were to continue the more likely their threats might become reality, and he could no longer see through the darkness to the next moment even. Why wasn't there any way to shorten time, just as there had been methods to bridge distances in the past? And how could he make it through these turbulent times in an honorable fashion? Such were the thoughts occupying him when a group of seven or eight youths appeared over the hill. Judging from their cotton khaki fatigue caps and gaiters, they were clearly youths of conscription age who were returning from the military draft inspection.

"Right, why don't we stop for a rest here too?"

They all threw down their hats at this one youth's suggestion and plopped down on the grass, as if following an order. Despite being in the full bloom of youth, dark shadows seemed to haunt their spotty faces, and their strong shoulders seemed to sag, as if troubled by stress and exhaustion. Sangjin spotted a familiar face or two among them.

"I'm so exhausted I could die."

"Well, we're not likely to live long in any case, so might just as well go and die early."

"Hey, let's cut the gloom and doom."

While chatting away like this, several of them lay down on the grass and covered their faces with their caps. Some emptied tobacco crumbs from their pockets, fashioning roll-ups with scraps of newspaper, before poking the others in search of a match or a flint.

"Here's a light."

Sangjin proffered the cigarette he had been smoking.

"You brat, puffing away at your age like a little goat!"

"You only started smoking the other day and already you're hooked."

"Hey Sŏkchu, what are you doing smoking in front of a grown up? You've got no manners, just like a monkey farting!"

This Sŏkchu blushed at their teasing, and retorted, "Well, once we're soldiers, tobacco's all we'll get to eat anyway . . ."

He exhaled a trail of smoke, all the while spitting out the tobacco crumbs that kept sticking to his tongue. Now the non-smokers who had teased him began saying, "Perhaps I'll have one too."

And they shook every last speck of dust out of their pockets to make up a cigarette. Those with no tobacco at all waited their turn for a drag.

"I've got some here, why don't you take one each?"

Sangjin placed his pack of cigarettes in front of the group. At first not one of them would touch it.

"Go on, take one."

He offered the pack to the youth sat closest to him.

"How did they rank you?"

"Top grade."

"Top grade! You've got a good build."

What a precious young man! With this thought, Sangjin took a closer look at him. He wasn't that tall, but his body was solid, and his bright eyes and clear face seemed quite familiar.

"Ingap's not the only one. They said we're all top grade."

"As long as you're not a complete cripple and all the bits are there, everyone gets top grade."

"Yeah, as long as you can move around on your own feet and are ripe for a bullet, anyone will do."

"It's true, even if you come from nowhere, like that bug-bitten wild melon from a ditch Kilson over there, it's still top grade, what else is there to say?"

The young man who looked the fittest, even sitting down, gestured with his chin toward a youth sat on the other side, who was clearly the butt of his joke. Kilson blushed like a young boy and wrinkled his nose up like a cock's comb, as he retorted,

"You bastard, Tongsŏk, a pooping stick like you would cost a don and a half, no less than me."

"A don and a half?"

The bug-bitten wild melon called Kilson explained himself.

"They say that Chiang Kai-shek's bullets cost a don and a half."

At this they all burst out laughing, "You idiot, how do you come up with these things?"

They really were young.

And yet, "All this laughing's making me hungry."

"Me too, I can hear the clock in my stomach fret, it's turning so fast."

Tongsŏk grabbed a fistful of grass, rubbed it into a ball, and threw it away before stretching out on the ground. With these words they all seemed to return to reality, and their laughter transformed into something more sullen.

"It's looking grim until we get over the barley hump."[1]

This low murmur originated from the youth named Ingap, who had been sitting in silence, blowing on a grass flute, his arms wrapped around his knees. His eyes surveyed the still green ears of barley in the field. Not only was the barley still young, but with the shortage of hands due to the military draft and the lack of fertilizer, it didn't look as if this barley would ripen much.

"Barley hump is old talk now. What's the point of harvesting barley these days? We'll not see more than the dust, will we?"

Tongsŏk sounded listless. Sŏkchu pretended to ignore him,

"I wish I could eat my fill of barley, even if I fart myself away."

"Huh, you think there'll be enough to make us fart. If we can just pay our quota without getting punished, it'll be a miracle."

"We just have to eat it all up early, even if those bastards get us for it."

"You idiot, you think they're gonna leave you alone long enough that you can eat it all up early. They could call us up any day, and we'll have to go along with whatever they say."

Kilson interrupted, and the boyish face reddened once more. "Still . . ."

One youth had covered his face with his cap and appeared to be dozing, but now he turned over and muttered in annoyance, "How do you kids keep coming up with such depressing talk?"

A heavy silence descended over this strip of arboreal shade, like thickly congealed air, even though they were in the middle of a wide field under a clear sky. The youths all lay down and languidly rested their heads on their fists, leaving Sangjin sitting

---

1 "Barley hump" refers to the last days of spring, when the previous year's rice has all been eaten and the new harvest is not yet ready. During that time barley became the main foodstuff, and the term "climbing the barley mountain" referred to the spring hunger.

upright and alone. He felt as if he spoke a different language; even his emotions felt disconnected, as if he originated from another country and could not even sense this atmosphere; and he shuddered at the realization that he was listening in like an idiot to the groans of these young compatriots, who were being compelled by a terrifyingly oppressive force to stamp out the light of their own lives.

Just then, the jingle-jangle of a bell heralded the appearance of two bicycles coming side by side over the hill.

Somebody said, "Look out, it's the head of military affairs!"

The youths all stood up and bowed in greeting. The other bicyclist turned out to be the mayor of the township. The two bicycles slowed down at the sight of the youths and approached the group. Sangjin had no choice but to stand and acknowledge them as well.

"Uh um . . ."

The mayor spoke first and asked them where they had come from. He could barely suppress the knowing smile taking shape on his lips. He proceeded to chat away in Japanese as if he had something interesting to say. Sangjin only saw the mayor once a month or so—whenever he delivered his medical certificate from the community doctor to prove his exemption from military service—and he always found him to be a most unpleasant man. It was that slimy appearance and attitude, like a greasy dog that would not hesitate to worm its way through the messiest of worlds and the narrowest of alleys for its own benefit, even if it meant crawling between someone else's legs. And then, there was that ever-present smile on the thin but glistening lips, which would gab on as if he were always up to something.

"I was just resting my legs."

Sangjin's reply seemed all the more awkward because he spoke in Korean. The mayor didn't even pretend to listen but whispered something to the head of military affairs before excusing himself with an "uh um" and cycling away.

"What are you hanging around here like this for, instead of hurrying back home . . ."

The remaining head of military affairs directed a pointed stare at Sangjin before issuing this order to the young men while he brushed off his cap and returned it to his head. The young men all hurried each other along in the wake of his bicycle. Sangjin was annoyed, as if he too had been scolded. It was even more aggravating to think that the head would probably not have puffed out his cheeks to shout at the resting youths if Sangjin himself had not been there. What a wretched world! Sangjin tutted his annoyance and stood up to retrieve his bundle of books.

He had taken no more than a couple of steps before the group ahead of him looked back in his direction and called out, "Ingap, aren't you coming?"

"Mm, I'm on my way . . ."

Ingap was still sat down on the grass, putting his shoes back on. This was the youth who had earlier lamented the barley hump.

"Don't forget you're being watched, *niramarerujyo* . . ."

They all turned in the direction of this voice shouting in heavily accented Japanese, only to see the head of military affairs leave a trail of dust behind as he sped over the hill. Sangjin listened to the exhalation of his own meaningless sigh. Each one of these sighs seemed to expend just a little bit more of his power to resist. He plodded forward, switching his bundle of insignificant books from one hand to the other and contemplating how the shadows clinging to his toes seemed all too thin and solitary. He felt so alone! Sangjin had no reason at all to embrace any pride in remaining aloof or upholding his integrity where others failed; instead he just felt shabby and alone. He could hear someone behind him, blowing on a grass flute. It was Ingap. The shrill sound of his flute sounded lonesome in this broad field under the blue sky.

Once the group ahead had disappeared over the hill the flute grew quiet, and all that remained within Sangjin's earshot was the stomp-stomp of quickening footsteps. Ingap was catching up with him. Ingap blushed when he finally reached Sangjin's side.

"Sir . . ."

"?"

"Er . . . in English . . ."

"Mm, in English?"

Ingap blushed even deeper and hesitated.

"Er . . . how can I say . . . er . . . 'I'm Korean' in English?"

He looked warily around, as if surprised by his own voice asking this question. When he turned back to Sangjin, the light in his eyes proved this was no idle curiosity. Subjected to eyes like that, Sangjin was forced to think more seriously about this encounter. For just one moment, he wondered why this young man felt safe enough to reveal himself like this and even thought his face seemed familiar from some memory of having been recognized by someone like him in the street; moreover, those eyes reassured Sangjin that he, too, had nothing to fear. To ask Ingap why he wanted to know could easily be misunderstood as a sad joke right now.

"I mean, if I wanted to say, 'I'm not a Jap, I'm Korean'?"

"Oh, yes, yes, I see."

Ingap seemed pleased that Sangjin understood what he meant.

And he eagerly repeated after Sangjin, "*I am a Korean.*"

"You've learned this before somewhere, haven't you?"

It was only a simple sentence, but from the way Ingap repeated it immediately, after hearing the words just a couple of times, and from his smooth intonation, he didn't appear to be an absolute beginner.

"I used to go to middle school."

Ingap blushed again and, scratching beneath his ears, he continued, "But I had to stop early on, and I don't know my ABCs so well now."

It turned out that he had already learned how to say the same sentence in Chinese, *Wŏ shì hánguó rén, wŏ bù shì rìběn rén*.

The two of them walked along in silence for a while. Ingap had a smile on his face and kept repeating another phrase he seemed to have learned recently, as if chanting in his sleep, "No Jap!" With each invocation, Sangjin wondered about the efficacy of such emotional behavior. He had to fight the impulse to take hold of Ingap's hand.

"How big is your family?"

"Counting me, there's four of us. My mother, my father, and my older sister."

"No older brother?"

"He died seven years ago . . . if only he'd lived, then I might've . . ."

Ingap explained that his family was so poor that it was only thanks to his older brother's obstinacy that he had been able to dream of going to middle school in the first place. His brother had given up school at a young age to follow their parents into farming, but he was absolutely determined that his younger brother would be able to study and had enrolled him at XX Middle School in Pyongyang.

Then, the older brother had died suddenly of acute pneumonia in the winter, when Ingap had been preparing to take the exam to move into his second year. With no way to pay the school fees and no one to help his parents in the fields were he to try to pay his own way through school, Ingap had no choice but to abandon his education too.

"How old are your parents?"

"They'll both be sixty next year. But you know my father, don't you? He helped rethatch your storehouse roof last autumn . . ."

"Ah . . . that old man . . ."

Sangjin just stopped himself from completing the sentence with the words, "That Old Screw Fist?"

I t was one day last autumn . . .

The house was old and consisted of two separate buildings of three rooms, each facing one another in the shape of the character for two, 二. Although the inner row of rooms was roofed with tiles, the front three rooms were thatched and would not withstand the winter without the thatch being replaced. Yet both straw and rope were as hard to come by as manpower. It did not help, either, that Sangjin was new to the area.

Sangjin knew no one apart from an old middle-school classmate who was the director of a coop and a neighbor since Sangjin's so-called evacuation; the community doctor, who on the introduction of that classmate now signed Sangjin's medical certificate every couple of months; and the people in the house next door, whom he would greet each morning and night. Sangjin had worked as a middle-school teacher in Pyongyang, but with the onset of the Pacific War and the reduction in English classes he began to spend more and more time idling the hours away as a surplus teacher, until finally his school's Korean head teacher had been replaced by a Japanese head teacher, who had suggested that Sangjin might as well offer up his resignation on account of the bad influence he exerted on young Koreans for having published in the Korean language. With a salary that barely covered his living expenses and no additional income since he'd stopped writing long ago, there was no way he could remain in the city after the loss of his salary, even if he hadn't already decided to evacuate. As for assets, he owned nothing besides his books and his house. Luckily this was before the trend to evacuate took off and house values plummeted; his calculations had allowed for a house in the country and two rudimentary meals per day for about two to three years. If he could only survive another three years, which was the longest he reckoned Japan could hold out, then liberation would follow—and what would he have to worry about in his own country once free? And so, on the advice of Pak, the director, Sangjin had bought a house in this village and begun the long wait for time to pass. The problem was this: the speed with which prices rose greatly outpaced that with which the days passed. Sangjin was clueless about generating money and had earned nothing in his forty-something years apart from his salary and a trickle of payments for his writing barely larger than a sparrow's tears, and yet the days continued to roll on, growing harder to bear as his anxiety increased, and suddenly it was autumn and he had to worry about rethatching.

All straw and rope had to be sold to fulfill the government quota, leaving even farmers worried about how to repair the thatch on their own houses. Workers were scarce, too. Almost all the young men with any strength in their arms had been swallowed up into the Patriotic Corps, and those left behind were so busy with threshing and the pressures caused by the government quotas that they didn't have a moment to blink. In addition to the burden of work, anyone with fields was panic-stricken over taxes. The head of the police substation, Kawamoto, and the mayor of the township, who was renowned for delivering the best quota results in the whole of K County, were two of a kind when it came to exacerbating the already dire situation: the mayor reported every single peasant who could not fulfill the impossibly heavy quota, and the police head specialized in the whip. To make matters worse, this Kawamoto was an alcoholic and rarely in a sober state of mind; he would pick up the whip at the slightest provocation, with the result that few people, once caught, walked out of the station on their own feet. Heads were sliced open, legs wounded, and ribs broken. Because of this chaotic situation, those peasants who could not fulfill their share of the quota would even sell their oxen or houses in order to buy extra rice to hand over, and any peasants unable to do this had no choice but to go into hiding. Everyone was rushing around in a state of panic; hiring extra hands was no easy task.

Sangjin wondered whether it was worth the effort to rethatch a house that he would leave behind without any regrets if the war were to end today, but the roof had begun to leak at the slightest hint of rain, and the Japanese were still holding out in Rabaul, while there was no news of the much-anticipated second front in Western Europe, which teased like an impending storm.

Ch'unsik was the nearest of those neighbors with whom Sangjin exchanged greetings and the one who suggested that Old Screw Fist might be available for a day's work when Sangjin had found himself in a quandary over his inability to take care of the thatching. Old Screw Fist had gotten hold of the straw and rope and woven the thatch the very next day.

"Today the master will have to play his part too."

The old man was there waiting from early morning, having already measured the length of the roof and finished all the preparations, including tidying and twisting the rope for the thatch.

"The straw bunches have got to be even or the rain'll come through."

The old man grumbled at every bunch of straw Sangjin assembled in his clumsy fashion, complaining that this one was too big and that one too small. When the old man all but snatched the increasingly shoddy bundles of straw from Sangjin, his hands, as black and as strong as cast iron hooks, proved nimbler than Sangjin's slender white hands, unbelievably so.

"And they call you Old Screw Fist . . ."

"Ha ha ha, if these really were screw fists, would I be going round working like this? It's only 'cause I can't open both hands properly that they started calling me that."

He looked to be trying really hard to straighten out his hands, but they would unfold enough to hold only a large egg in each hand.

"What happened to your hands?"

"Well, I've worked with 'em since I was little and they've hardened up . . . so if these here hands are screw fists, them there novice hands must be flat fists, ha ha."

He was clearly proud of his hands, but his fingernails were truly a sight to behold. These were not fingernails perched upon white hands, the kind of nails that assist with the scratching of an itch. These nails were weapons, bulwarks of defense positioned on the tips of his fingers. His thumbnails looked as strong as black clam shells, and deft too, able to cut the ends of the straw and even slice through the thatch as well as any small knife.

"Shall we take a rest?"

Sangjin asked less out of concern for the old man than because he himself was struggling to keep up, but Old Screw Fist glanced up at the sun and said, "They'll all be laughing when we've blocked all them holes with this here straw, ha ha ha."

With each toothless guffaw his mouth cavity grew deeper and his laughter sounded more optimistic. But the end of laughter hardened his face into a dark and heavy mold, with wrinkles deeply etched into his forehead and cheeks. He would lower his eyes, moist with tears from laughing, and the mechanical movements of those cast iron hooks would quicken. Even while Sangjin chattered on, the old man's concentration prevented him from talking or looking away from his work.

After lunch they sat down on the sheaves of straw to have a smoke and a rest. Just then Ch'unsik, the neighbor who had recommended Old Screw Fist, came limping along.

"Something's ticked him off again."

Old Screw Fist laughed when he caught sight of Ch'unsik. Ch'unsik always carried a slight limp, but if he was in a rush or angry about something, that limp became more pronounced. Today he was muttering to himself, "Dammit, is this quota or what? Now even selling three piglets isn't enough, what a game . . . dammit, it's not as if I can stop living just like that . . ."

He had been born with no strength in his left ankle and had to lift up his leg to drag his trailing foot along. The family was poor, but his parents believed he was in superlative possession of the five spiritual powers and wanted him to study so that he would be able to make a living at a less arduous job; with this in mind, they tried to enroll him in a commercial or technical school as soon as he graduated from the regular school. But he was rejected on the pretext of that leg. His angry parents had sent him to the neighboring village school to study classical Chinese for two years, thinking that it was all writing anyway. Despite all their efforts, Ch'unsik ended up farming. He had worked for several months as a scribe's assistant but stopped when he realized the number of scriveners' offices in any township was limited and his turn was unlikely to come any time soon. The township office had positions for scribes but was not interested in him because of his leg. With such a meager résumé, he lacked the courage to go to other towns in search of work. In the end there was only farming. And yet, even if he was unable to plow fields or rice paddies, few villagers matched him for energy; there was little that could put a stop to him. Strong by nature but brusque in his speech, his invalid's lack of empathy could occasionally invite misunderstanding, but when his leg freed him from the worry of being drafted into the Patriotic Corps, his good humor allowed him to compare his own fate to that of the fabled old man who let his horses run wild only to lose some and gain some back. He was also generous to a fault, and when the role of head of the neighborhood association fell to him, on account of the fact that he could at least write his own name, he passed along his quota exemption for the gathering of pine resin knots, grapevines, and oak bark to another youth on the basis that he himself had already received an exemption from the Patriotic Corps.

"You old man you, I knew this would happen."

Ch'unsik dropped down onto the straw sheaves, looked around at the thatching, already woven and standing up in one corner of the yard, and waved a finger in front of the old man's nose.

"There's really no one as enthusiastic about work as you . . . still, I need to give a thought to others sometimes . . ."

"Ha ha ha, there's a reason why I work, you know!"

"I know, you're really hard up . . . well, you old man you . . ."

"Everyone says they're busy, but what they're up to, I don't know."

"Just listen to this hard up old man's story, won't you, sir?"

Ch'unsik started to tell the story in his usual animated fashion.

"No matter which way you look at it, however hard the old man's worked, it's all been to no avail. That top rice paddy that he tended so carefully, swept away in a flood . . . the only son—the one he'd been relying on like a guardian spirit to look after him in his old age—he's been drafted, and we don't know if he'll come back dead or alive . . . and now that girl, his daughter-in-law to be, is all but a stranger, and even though he's got a daughter, who would take on a widow at her age? No chance of bringing a son-in-law in when the old man doesn't have enough land to plant even a few lettuce seeds or grapevines, is there? . . . Could there be another man with such an unfortunate fate?"

He roared with laughter, inexplicably. All that he said was true, of course, but when it came to trying to comfort someone in pain his words were as rough as the two men's hands, for what had begun as praise for the hardworking old man he had recommended to Sangjin ended up sounding more like a tale of misfortune, though Ch'unsik clearly sympathized with the old man's sad fate.

"That's right, that's right, that's how it goes . . ."

Old Screw Fist opened his gaping mouth once again and laughed too. Perhaps this was what was meant by young and old getting along together? Or perhaps such coarse and brusque words helped them to laugh at something which would otherwise make them cry?

"It's grim, isn't it? He even used to taste the water in the stream by the well just to check how rich it was before it flowed into his paddy . . . what else can I say?"

Ch'unsik spat, as if just saying this upset him.

Apparently there was no one around here who didn't know about the famous "top paddy," which Old Screw Fist had cared for so deeply. As the name suggested, this was the first of the paddy fields in the village to receive the wastewater, and that water was so plentiful that there was hardly any need for fertilizer; they said even an ox could drown in the rich soil, and no tool bigger than a hoe was necessary for plowing the narrow paddy. Since ancient times wealthy men have boasted of such paddy fields as if they were toys. From the plowing in spring through the autumn harvest the landowner didn't have to argue with his tenants over anything, not even the seed or fertilizer, which had long been the tenant's responsibility, and yet, as the owner of the rights to the land, the landowner would receive his half share of the harvested rice, delivered to him on the tenant's back, and accompanied by a young chicken for the midsummer's day outing and even a fattened hen for the harvest festival. There was no obligation to provide an ox, because none was necessary for plowing this paddy. The landowner was quite happy to lie around like a cricket, taking his pickings and arrogantly relying on the spoils of the vegetable fields, which he had his tenant farmer work as well.

Consequently, those with money who wished to buy land in the area wanted more than anything to buy this particular field, which was the yolk of the egg as it were, even if it came at a price.

The paddy was the envy of all to the extent that if someone made a lot of money or their circumstances went downhill, the local people would use phrases such as "He's bought himself the top paddy" or "He had to sell off the top paddy." The farmers were so envious of this paddy that when they were drunk they would grumble and sigh, "Dammit, if I could only buy the top paddy, I'd be doing okay." Above all, the paddy guaranteed a good harvest, even if the farmer had to buy the seed and fertilizer. There was no comparison to the other fields, which were irrigated by rainwater alone, because for those fields just two weeks of dry weather meant the efforts of spring and summer would end in invocations to the Buddha and a year's farming would come to waste. Then there was the convenience: the top paddy was so close to the village that it was literally just out the front door, which saved on the time needed to care for it.

Old Screw Fist had taken over the paddy the year before last. He had been allotted the very best strip, having caught the attention of the landowner as a hardworking, diligent, and intelligent worker who played no tricks. He was overjoyed; it was as if all his dreams had come true to be able to work the paddy he had envied all his life. But that year saw the imposition of the murderous government quotas. Because the paddy was of famously high quality, Old Screw Fist was allocated a quota almost double that imposed on other fields, and he continued to struggle, seeing barely any improvement in his life. Then he suffered a further blow when the landowner suddenly departed that winter and the management of the land changed hands. This landowner was one of the two highest taxpayers in this small place, and moving his family to Pyongyang helped him to hide his riches. He passed on the rights to manage his land to the family retainer, Kim Chusa. Now for tenant farmers, all hinges upon the landowner or tenant supervisor, but a manager has to try to make some profit in the middle, and so not surprisingly this Kim proved one very prickly small fish. Always on the lookout to extract more free labor from the tenants, he would not let them pass with even a grain of rice left behind on the threshing floor. What was most unnerving to Old Screw Fist was the fact that Kim appeared to have his eyes set on the top paddy. For a while Kim avoided revealing his true intentions, probably thinking he might look bad, but his chubby-cheeked nephew, Pongdŏk, strutted around as if he were the real land-owner and began spreading the word that his family would soon take over the top paddy. Words were not his only ploy; as deputy head of the Civil Defense Force he conspired with the township clerks to impose an outrageously high quota in a strat-egy likely to make the old man's life unbearable.

In the face of these efforts, Old Screw Fist maintained his faith in the future. He had no way of knowing when or how, but surely these quotas, which had been unheard of in the past, would not remain in place for another hundred years? Even though life might be hard at the moment, if he could only forebear, then when there was no longer any quota to deliver, the top paddy would remain the top paddy, would it not? No matter what that Pongdŏk got up to, surely the landowner would not take the top paddy away?

Trusting like this in human nature and the passing of time, Old Screw Fist stood once again at the sluice gates to the paddy, shovel in hand, the moment the ground started to thaw in the spring. He dipped his finger into the cloudy, mushy water of the flowing snowmelt as if he were tasting some kind of soup. This water flowed down from the back mountain, passing a street on the slope and merging with the ditch by the well. The fouler the taste of the salty water flowing into his paddy, the greater was Old Screw Fist's satisfaction. And when time came for plowing and he watched the others drive their kitted-out oxen down the main street, Old Screw Fist—a mere pitchfork slung over his shoulder—did not wait to be asked but would laugh to himself, "Ah, just look at that son-of-a-gun soil in our top paddy . . . can you imagine putting an ox to work in that!"

When the time came to transplant the young seedlings, Old Screw Fist roared with delight at the sight of his old wife carrying a whole bunch in her hands; she had fallen over in the middle of the paddy and couldn't make it back onto her feet. After laughing to his heart's content, he took hold of her hand, only to slip himself and emerge with his face covered in mud. It never occurred to him to spit the mud out from his mouth; instead he noisily licked on it and roared with laughter some more.

"This darn soil here, I could chew on it all day, I swear, and not find a single grain of sand."

During the rainy season, this paddy, which he loved so much, was buried in sand by a landslide.

The floodwaters were not necessarily greater than in previous years. The problem lay with the embankments and levees that separated the fields; tens, perhaps even hundreds, of years of footsteps treading down grassroots had shaped these banks, but now they had eroded. Because of the vicious government quotas, the fields and paddies listed in the land register no longer sufficed to ensure the peasants' survival, and those peasants had set to reclaiming hillsides and stripping levees and embankments bare with the goal of planting even one more corn or beanstalk. The levees on the far side of the embankment by the top paddies, which were irrigated by wastewater, were no exception, and bare earth had been exposed on them too. Even though the levees were on the far side, this was a cause for concern. If the tall embankment were to collapse and block the ditch underneath, the seasonal rainwater would overflow or even destroy the low and narrow levees on this side, thus flooding the paddies. All the farmers working the paddies connected to the ditch, including Old Screw Fist, had opposed the reclamation of that embankment. There had almost been a fight when they tried to block it. But for destitute peasants with little or no land at all, planting even one more stalk felt like a matter of life or death, and there was no leeway to think about the consequences or to worry about others.

"Don't you have anything else to worry about? It's not as if anybody owns this land, we're just trying to live off the land of our country, so how's that any business of yours?"

It just happened that nobody owned the field with the wide embankment, on which there was only a path.

"You, with your rich paddy, you don't know anything about feeding an empty stomach. It's only by clearing empty land like this that we can get a little something to add to our gruel. Come on, can't we just live together somehow, please?"

What could they say when a comrade's widow made a desperate plea in such pitiable circumstances?

After hearing such stories they could hardly continue to block the planting; perhaps they were too absorbed by their own futile worries. And yet Old Screw Fist could not help but shake his head every time he looked at the embankment and saw the protruding threads of broken grass roots, which were trying to hold the dirt back, and the increasing erosion around the sluice opening to his paddy.

However much he sympathized with the pitiable circumstances of those whose only hope lay in reclaiming the embankment, Old Screw Fist could not simply let this pass, and he raised his concerns with the manager several times. Kim Chusa said there was nothing they could do, although he did visit the mayor on one occasion to discuss the situation, but the mayor seemed annoyed, saying it was not his responsibility and in any event it was now state policy to increase food supply by planting everywhere, even around kitchen stoves. Old Screw Fist grew so worried that, though it pained him, he decided to seek help from Pongdŏk, who was after all the deputy head of the Civil Defense Force, but Pongdŏk said the old man was worrying over nothing and seemed equally annoyed.

Yet this did not seem to be a simple case of worrying about nothing. An ox carrying a heavy load only had to pass by and the eroded embankment would start to crumble, and whenever rain fell during the night, the next day several spadefuls of dirt would have fallen down into the narrow ditch. As soon as the seasonal rains began, work increased for Old Screw Fist and the other farmers looking after the paddies, who had to increasingly shovel dirt from the ditch and pile it up on their side of the embankment.

Finally, after several days of intermittent rain had washed the loam from the riverbank downstream, the rain seemed to pause early one evening, though it had been falling since morning on that day too, before an absolute downpour was unleashed in the middle of the night. Old Screw Fist had not been sleeping soundly for several days and now leaped up at the unusually heavy sound of rain; he rushed outside, carrying just a few straw mats and a shovel that lay to hand, with no time to wake anyone else to accompany him. By the early evening the water had risen halfway up the riverbank, but now the banks had burst and water was gushing down the street. He raced through a cacophony of sound—rushing water, lashes of rain—unable to see even one step ahead, and yet somehow his feet found their way to the sluice opening. At the moment of arrival, as if it had been waiting for him, there was a crash in the distance, and he heard the sound of the entire embankment collapse. A current of water that had reached his shins now smashed into him, wrapping around and above his waist. Old Screw Fist was startled by the shock. A fresh smell of dirt now mingled with the drops of rain that were beating down so hard he could not even open his eyes. There was not even enough dirt in sight to fill a shovel to try to block the sluice opening. There was nothing he could do but try to place the straw mats over the opening and sit down on top of them. Just then, the farmers of the neighboring paddy appeared. And Ch'unsik showed up at the first paddy. But even all of them

THE BARLEY HUMP

176

together could do nothing. Old Screw Fist sat on top the levee with the opening, which now began to wobble beneath his mats, like an enormous turtle. The levee was dissolving into the water and began to rush out from beneath Old Screw Fist's buttocks. In an instant it whirled around his waist and swept down into the paddy. Everyone rushed to grab hold of Old Screw Fist, who was wailing like a toddler. Daybreak revealed that the levee close to the sluice opening had collapsed into the ditch across a span of almost twenty feet. There had been worse rains in the past, but this time the back mountain had been stripped of trees in attempts to meet the firewood quota and used for slash-and-burn farming, with the result that the rain had gushed down in a torrent like the proverbial bull and rammed into the corner of the embankment, decimating it instantly. With its path forward blocked, the water had overwhelmed the low and flimsy sluice openings, sweeping them away and depositing a layer of red mud from the mountain over the entire top paddy, and then the second and even the third paddy. Old Screw Fist alone lost two thousand p'yŏng, but altogether around five thousand p'yŏng of rice plants, fat with grain, were buried under the mud. In many other places too, paddies irrigated by wastewater suffered the same fate under similar circumstances.

A whole year's worth of farming had been lost in one night, but they had also lost their farmland and there was no one to whom they could appeal. Nothing was to be gained by blaming anybody. All they could do was sit down at the corner of their fields and cry.

"What good can crying do now? Even our tears are steeped in the grain. Let's not waste such precious stuff."

Ch'unsik did not lose his sense of humor, even under such extreme circumstances; instead, he urged everyone to find a way to fix their paddies as soon as possible, and so they came to visit Kim Chusa. In these kinds of situations the landowner customarily bore the expense of restoring the land. But Kim Chusa said he could not make any promises about when those repairs would start, or even if they would happen at all, without first consulting with the landowner, because in this case the work necessary was huge and would require an enormous amount of paid labor. They had met again several times, but Kim Chusa seemed hesitant to even broach the subject with the landowner, most likely because as manager he, too, bore some responsibility for the colossal amount of damage. At this point the tenants were planning to approach the owner directly, since they could not trust Kim Chusa.

"Dammit, a paddy no bigger than my eldest's buttocks wouldn't make much difference to me, even if it's the best paddy, but it's been hard for this old man. Ever since he lost that paddy, well, he used to be as tough as iron, but some cracks have appeared and he's aged . . ."

Ch'unsik exhaled a long trail of smoke from a newly lit cigarette. He couldn't resist one further small jab.

"Still, at least this old man's got one less worry thanks to that damn disaster . . ."

Old Screw Fist waved his hand. "I said I don't want to hear it, what are you gabbing on about that for now? . . ."

"But it's true, isn't it, granddad? Dammit, this old man here's daughter-in-law has feet so tiny it was quite a worry . . ."

The story here turned out to concern the girl who had been promised to Old Screw Fist as a daughter-in-law; although she was pretty to a fault and in no way deformed or even abnormally small, there was the question about the size of her feet.

"Ha ha ha, those feet, like tiny little seashells, how could she have worked in our top paddy? She'd need shoes at least the size of a hand to stop her from sinking right down to the bottom."

Ch'unsik was teasing again. Whenever Old Screw Fist passed by the well, it seemed, he would stand for ages and watch the girl draw water or do laundry, chuffling at the sight of her buttocks, which to his glee were fattening out day by day.

"Well, that's all that really matters, isn't it!"

Old Screw Fist tried to defend himself, but that toothless, empty mouth revealed itself again with his laughter. He had wanted to conclude the marriage ceremony as soon as possible and move that oh-so-sweet daughter-in-law into his home, but now that the year's farming had come to nothing, how could he bring someone else's precious child into a home where she might go hungry? And now that his son had been caught up in the draft and might be dragged away at any time, Old Screw Fist had as much as given up for good.

"How could we bring her here from greed and watch her mother and father suffer?"

"That's right, that's right. That kid is heading off on a path of no return . . ."

Back then, Ch'unsik had cracked jokes from the moment he had started to tell the story and he liberally sprinkled his tale with coarse language, according to the fashion by which villagers like these customarily rub stinging red pepper into wounds. Old Screw Fist himself had laughed along, as if the story concerned someone else, but Sangjin's heart still ached from the vivid memory of a deep wound, which still oozed blood no matter how much pepper was rubbed in.

That's all that really matters, isn't it!

As long as such desperately heartfelt words still resounded in Sangjin's ears, it was impossible for him to look upon Ingap, now walking by his side, as simply a fellow traveler whom he had met on the road for the first time.

A precious son! This was Old Screw Fist's one and only precious son. Yet, in this time of national crisis, wasn't he one among so many sons in Korea? He was one more young Korean who had no choice but to tread a tragic sacrificial path, abandoning ties that were otherwise unbreakable, as if tearing a living branch from a tree, and all because of a history of deeply rooted mistakes. Was it correct to say that those responsible for this sacrifice belonged to the past and were no longer around? Was there no one who could halt this cruel sacrifice even now? If not us, then would that mean we have to wait for someone to appear in the future? Sangjin's thoughts led him up a dead-end alley yet again, as they always did. He struggled to breathe; he felt like he was walking inside a sealed vacuum tube.

"Did that top paddy, or whatever it was called, ever get restored?"

He was thinking about the story he had heard back then.

"What?"

Ingap turned to him, his face flushed, as if roused from some absorbing thought.

"What do you mean, restored?"

They had visited the landowner twice as planned, it seemed. When they had seen him last autumn he was furious at the enormous scale of the damage. Although he had already heard the news from Kim Chusa, he had not realized just how great the damage was.

"Of course not, he started asking if we were trying to ruin him, spending his money, asking him to pay the labor, not to mention everything that had already been lost."

The landowner flew into a rage. He said that if they needed several hundred times the market labor price of seventy won, then labor alone would end up costing more than the paddy was worth—the belly button was bigger than the child, as it were. And did they know that he earned barely more than a few pennies from that field anyway, once the rice had been sold at a fixed price to the government, and that it had been a pointless enterprise from the beginning?

They had asked, "So, that valuable paddy is going to be left to grow weeds?"

He retorted, "And who made that valuable paddy unusable?"

He was acting as if the accident during the heavy rain had been the tenants' responsibility. Finally he had added, apparently to save some face, "If you really think that field is valuable, then why don't you fix it first? Then perhaps we can talk again."

With the loss of the harvest they had no way to make a living. Forced into having to sell their labor day by day, to start a project that would take more than a year to complete by themselves was impossible.

The landowner's attitude showed no change on their next visit, when the ground was thawing in the spring. It was not clear whether there was any real possibility or whether he was just making excuses on the spot, but at best he had said, "Well, given that increasing food production is national policy, perhaps if the authorities were to provide some kind of assistance, then who knows . . ."

He diverted attention to the so-called authorities and said that without help there was no choice but to wait until the war was over, the cost of labor had fallen, and he was free to dispose of the grain as he liked so that profits came back in line. And that was the end of the conversation.

"For the landowner, land is all about profit. He calculates his own interests and if there's no profit then he's fine with simply letting it go, but for farmers like us it's different, isn't it? Without land a farmer can't survive. But we need some help to bring that paddy back to life."

According to Ingap, the family that worked the second paddy had already left to work in some mine, and his family, too, would have joined the labor market, except that he might be dragged away any day, leaving only his elderly parents behind, and if they had to sell their labor, then it would be best if they continued in the farmwork they were familiar with.

Struggling to remain calm, Ingap ended his account with a heavy sigh. He hadn't taken many more steps before he turned to Sangjin and said, "We're not the only ones to have suffered like this. So many old paddy fields around here are lying in ruin. I'm not saying that the owner of our field is any worse than others. It's just that landowners think about the earth and relate to the earth in a fundamentally different way from farmers like us."

These words took Sangjin by surprise, and he could not help but look at Ingap through new eyes. What a profound observation! It might seem like the natural conclusion to their conversation so far, but Ingap could only have reached this awareness through bitter experience and not as a result of some theory. Ingap was blushing like a schoolboy from the excitement of their conversation, but when Sangjin looked at him, he thought, Ah! What a young peasant! Those eyes that observe reality with such accuracy, and that clear awareness of his own situation! Wasn't this a sign that a new history might be created in the not too distant future? Ingap's words reminded Sangjin of a slogan he had read about in a book: "Land to the peasants."

By this time, they had climbed another hill.

"I'm going to have to rest again."

Rubbing his aching legs, Sangjin was apologetic. He had already asked them to stop several times.

"I'm sorry, you must be busy."

"I'm not busy, and don't want to be, either . . ."

Sangjin smiled at Ingap's reply, and they sat down side by side. These did not seem like words spoken by a young man. Ingap accepted a cigarette and started looking through Sangjin's bundle of books with a schoolboy's curiosity.

"By the way, I've read several of your stories, sir."

"Ah, how on earth did you find time for that?"

When Ingap could not attend the school to which he had been admitted after so much effort, he still wanted to learn and had asked an old friend from his dormitory to send him any discarded magazines or novels; Ingap had read these together with Tongsŏk, asking Ch'unsik for help with any unfamiliar Chinese characters. They had persevered for a couple of years before restrictions were imposed on students reading Korean books and the books subsequently became hard to acquire. So this was why Ingap had approached Sangjin in the first place and opened up about his feelings. Sangjin wondered why he had never thought to write something more enlightening and accessible for young men like this back when there had been relatively more freedom. Once more he found himself full of regrets.

"Oh, sir, you need to be careful."

Ingap seemed to guess the reason why Sangjin had been summoned this time.

At the most recent "Lecture on the Current Situation," Ingap had been on duty for the Civil Defense Force and served at the banquet that followed. Once inebriated, the local head of the Higher Police apparently had started asking what this person called Yi Sangjin was up to, complaining that his heart problems or beriberi were likely feigned and an unnecessary nuisance. Chief Kawamoto had replied that such riffraff were no better than weeds to be extracted by the roots and should be subjected to martial law. On the following day Sangjin's house had been searched.

"You shouldn't go yourself to buy rice on the black market, sir."

According to Ingap, Kawamoto took a particular interest in people like Sangjin who had evacuated here from elsewhere, describing them as arrogant bastards.

Hearing all this made the world feel even more suffocating than usual and life ever grimmer. If only Sangjin had wings so that he could fly away. He wanted to disappear somewhere on the other side of the earth, far beyond the reach of Jap hands. Perhaps Ingap felt the same way, because he gazed at the distant mountains on the horizon before turning to Sangjin, who was now lying down next to him.

"Sir."

"Mm."

"That Kim Il Sung . . . his troops, they'll keep fighting the Japs at Mount Paektu, won't they?"

Sangjin sat up with a start.

"Kim Il Sung's troops!"

Sangjin repeated the words and looked directly into Ingap's eyes. He could hear a voice inside him exclaim, "Ah, this young man really does have wings!" What dazzling romance, what brave leap of faith allowed Ingap to believe in Kim Il Sung, when he was being stifled in this vacuum tube?

"Of course he'll fight. His men must be fighting even harder right now!"

Sangjin pictured the figure of a fighting hero lighting a beacon for the liberation of their homeland on behalf of all his compatriots on top of Mount Paektu, that ancient Korean peak and treasure trove of magnificent ancestral legend.

"If I get sent to the north or Manchuria this time, I'm heading in that direction, even if I die on the way."

"Well! That's good thinking. That's the right thing to do."

"From what I can tell just looking at the newspapers, if we can escape, then the only safe place to go is to join up with Kim Il Sung's troops. If we can just reach them, at least we won't die like dogs."

How could these young men possess such acute awareness? After languishing and suffocating in the darkness with no escape hatch in sight, these young men had searched and searched until they had finally managed to open a window within their own hearts through their own will and judgement. Sangjin could feel a window open in his heart, too, at the thought of the heroic Kim Il Sung lighting a beacon for the nation so high up and far away that its light could shine into their windows and the shouts of his troops could rouse young hearts. The freedom and liberation of the nation was being won through the efforts of Sangjin's compatriots at this very moment. Because of the one and only Kim Il Sung, we were no longer a nation in shame.

Sangjin walked on, inhaling and exhaling deeply in the fresh atmosphere created by the light shining into their hearts. His was no feeble sigh.

They climbed one more hill before catching up with the group, who had gone on ahead and were now chasing each other around in high spirits in front of a tavern at the bottom of the hill.

"Look at them. Looks like they've been at the rice wine again."

Ingap blushed as he mumbled this. On closer examination, the sweat was running down the young men's faces, which really were as red as carrots, while they attacked each other in jest. They were running after each other, pretending to be holding clubs and stabbing with bayonets, to which one responded by holding up both hands and shaking his head, saying, "*Wŏ shì hánguó rén, wŏ bù shì rìběn rén.*"

"Ha, ha, ha."

The attacker rocked with laughter. Meanwhile, on the other side of the path two of them sat with their arms around each other, foreheads touching, crying. Sŏkchu and Tongsŏk. For some reason, blood was trickling down from Sŏkchu's nose. Yet it was he who was hugging Tongsŏk and wiping away his tears and snot with his own sleeves and the palms of his hands, all while gently sobbing himself.

"You idiot . . ."

"Mm, you idiot . . ."

"If we've got to die, let's die together."

"Mm, if we've got to die, let's die together."

Their tears fell as they looked into each other's eyes and talked to each other fondly. Then they rubbed their foreheads together and sobbed even more.

"What's going on?"

Sangjin asked Kilson, who was standing to one side. Kilson was silent; he simply lowered his face, which was also flushed the color of a carrot. Eventually his shoulders began to shake, and he looked up at Sangjin with tears in his eyes. His face puckered up, and his lips began to wobble, and he said, "We've always hidden our sadness."

He turned his face away and began to cry.

"Kilson!"

Sangjin gently shook the boy's heaving shoulders and spoke in a low voice,

"Kilson. *Nǐ shì hánguó rén.*"

What he meant was, have hope. A smile momentarily lit up Kilson's eyes. Then, he burst into tears like a small child and buried his face in Sangjin's chest.

"Sir . . ."

"?"

"We've been drinking, and we're drunk . . ."

". . ."

"Now, now we've messed up."

He burst into tears again. Ingap teared up too. The fact that they were not used to drinking was certainly having an effect, and yet how anxious and frustrated they must feel to pour out their sadness to a stranger like him? Sangjin tried to hold back his own tears while he hugged Kilson and rubbed his back.

I t was the middle of June by the time Ingap and Kilson were called up. The war was already over in Europe, and Okinawa was under siege. The Japanese imperialists were launching their final desperate attacks.

The season to harvest the barley began. Having crossed the peak of the "barley hump" of hunger in the spring, the peasants could finally breathe a little. But then came the mobilization: the police, Civil Defense Force, township clerks, borough and neighborhood association heads, all were tasked with relentlessly harsh surveillance over farms and barley fields. Not a single ear or grain was to be damaged. Although the peasants had cultivated their fields, the longed-for end of the barley hump now seemed more distant than ever. In villages and neighborhoods here and there minor clashes broke out between draftees and the police, clerks, and the Civil Defense Force. Resistance came mostly from those of draft age who refused to stand by and watch while their fathers and older brothers were beaten for eating the grain early. The police were unforgiving, even though the young men would be dragged off to war within a day or two. In the most extreme cases some young men had to change into their uniforms in prison and leave directly to join the army. The brutality had reached its peak when Ingap joined the army. He visited Sangjin twice before he left. On the first occasion he sought advice on a plan to withdraw his offer of marriage to his fiancée before leaving. His reasoning was that he wanted to offer her freedom. He would feel grateful if she were to wait for him of her own accord, but if he did not free her and then failed to return, then according to village custom she would end up a wretched virgin widow, marked for a life of unhappiness. He felt guilty about this.

Sangjin asked whether Ingap had sought out her opinion. Ingap replied that the idea was his and he was unsure whether to confer with her or not—she was still young and unlikely to be stubborn or have any strong opinions, so the decision was as good as made if he said so. Sangjin voiced his opposition.

"I understand that you are trying to do your best for her, but without asking her about her feelings, this could be seen as cruel. There's a whiff of the Japs in what you're saying too. Back in the times of the samurai, who loved to fight and kill people, they even killed their wives and children before leaving home to fight so as not to leave behind any lingering attachments . . ."

In Sangjin's mind, even if young Koreans had little choice but to be dragged away to die on the battle field alongside the Japanese bastards, their position and thoughts should remain fundamentally different from those of the Japs; it didn't feel right that the Koreans should be prepared to die in advance. In conclusion, he added, "Anyway, you have a greater ambition, don't you, Ingap?"

Then, several days later . . .

"Kids these days are tough . . ."

"They've got to be. Why should she listen to her older brother if she doesn't want to?"

"But still, if that had been us, it wouldn't have been easy to speak up about our betrothed."

The old people in the neighborhood were all talking about Yugami. Apparently Ingap had felt troubled enough to speak with her older brother. Although her aging mother was still alive, her father had passed away, and everything hinged on this older brother's opinion. His initial response had been rather vague, a simple "Don't worry about such things."

But later that same evening he had returned after a few drinks, saying that he would hand back Ingap's letter of proposal after all, along with the letter containing the four pillars of Ingap's time and date of birth. Shortly afterward Yugami had run away, clutching both letters and refusing to hand them over, even when her brother had brandished a whip.

Two days before he was to join the army Ingap visited again, accompanied by Ch'unsik. In fact, Ingap was not visiting of his own accord but had been dragged along by Ch'unsik.

Ch'unsik set to grumbling immediately, "Sir, have you ever seen such a morose idiot? Instead of keeping quiet he has to go and beat all his good fortune away with an iron, and now he's gone and caused even more fuss, saying he's made a mistake, what with this girl about to hang herself with her belt . . ."

Although he remained silent, Ingap appeared to regret his actions and had grown noticeably thin and listless in the meantime.

"I know what's going on inside your head Ingap, I really do."

Ch'unsik puffed away on a cigarette before continuing, "Don't worry, your brother-in-law will come around if you just work on him. He drinks a lot, but if he doesn't listen to you, then I'll show him my fists if I have to. He'll wait for you to come back, don't you worry about that."

The fact remained that Ingap would now be leaving in an even more depressed state of mind on account of these most recent events.

When it came time for his departure, Sangjin stood on the hill by the new road, where the truck was waiting to take the draftees away. He didn't want to go as far as the police substation and risk running into Kawamoto.

Old Screw Fist was waiting, leaning on a young woman who was most likely Ingap's older sister.

Ch'unsik declined to go as far as the police substation, too, but waited at the road instead, saying, "What's the point of following him all the way there? Let's wait here." A young girl stood off to one side several steps behind them and facing the other direction; Sangjin guessed this must be Yugami. Tall and slender, with an intelligent face sitting on top a curved neck—she was in her prime, her buttocks "fattening out," just as Ch'unsik had once teased. There was no sign of Ingap's elderly mother.

Despite the extreme heat of the early summer midday sun, Old Screw Fist shivered in a faded cotton-padded jacket. His face seemed to have shrunk since Sangjin had last seen him; deep wrinkles were carved into his forehead and cheeks; his eyes were blurred with tears and focused on the ground; his hooklike hands trembled; even that bushy pine of a beard was shaking. Instead of small beads of sweat his forehead was coated with a cold frost, enough to make anybody shiver. Sangjin could not bring himself to greet the old man in his usual way, but simply gestured with his eyes.

"Our boy's always talking about you, sir."

It was Old Screw Fist who broke the silence.

Cheers of "banzai" rose up from the yard in front of the substation, followed by the singing of the primary schoolchildren, and finally a procession led by several banners began to wind its way through the street and head toward them. Ingap, Kilson, Sŏkchu, and Tongsŏk were all there along with two other young men. Their puffy-eyed families followed, the women all sobbing out loud. It was our own funeral procession. Banners fluttered like heavy funeral streamers. And then, when the procession reached the front of the truck, it came time for final farewells.

Ingap stood before his father with his eyes closed and head bowed. Neither of them spoke. The young woman who appeared to be his older sister ran up to him and pressed her forehead into his shoulder, unable to suppress her sobs.

"I told you not to come."

It was Old Screw Fist who broke the silence once more; he stood still, emotionless, like a dead tree or perhaps a rotted totem pole. Ingap shook his head once, as if to clear his thoughts, before turning to Sangjin. Sangjin took hold of his hand. And as Ingap moved his lips close to Sangjin's ear, he whispered, before laughing, "*Wŏ shì hánguó rén.*"

Sangjin smiled in return and grasped Ingap's hand more tightly. Then Kilson ran over to them. He whispered exactly the same words in greeting. The three of them could not suppress their inappropriate laughter. Just as the young men were climbing up onto the truck, Ch'unsik came running over.

"Ah, what about this little one . . . you'll be back soon enough, but how can you leave without saying goodbye to your little wife?"

He prodded Ingap in the back to push him toward the young girl. She lowered her face, flushed the deep red of a hot pepper pod. And that was their farewell. Ingap looked even more embarrassed and brushed away Ch'unsik's hands in order to jump up onto the truck. For a moment everyone standing around forgot their sadness and laughed at the young couple. The truck departed. The remaining families resumed their wailing. Sangjin waved his hand high in the air as he watched the truck disappear into the distance. He prayed for these young men—glancing back at their hometown, their parents, their siblings, and their wives until the very last moment possible—and he hoped they were not heading off to have the light of life stamped out of them but would be able to pour the oil from the lamps inside themselves high up onto the beacon of the nation built by the heroic Kim Il Sung. When the last trace of dust had vanished around the corner of the mountain, the families had no option but to head back home. The fondness with which the young women caressed that young girl's trailing braid in front of so many people left quite an impression on Ch'unsik and Sangjin, who walked back side by side.

Afterward all the old people in the village were talking about what had happened.

"Young people these days, they know what they want!"

"She likes him all the more since her brother said to wait a while."

"Still, when we were young, would we have looked at our husbands in front of anyone else, even after we'd married?"

Yugami's appearance at the sending off was the talk of the whole village.

Almost a whole month passed before any news from Ingap arrived. Old Screw Fist carried the postcard to Sangjin with trembling hands, but Ingap had simply asked after everybody and explained that he too was well, in Japanese. When he looked up at Old Screw Fist, whose eyes were opened wide in anxious anticipation of more words to follow, Sangjin was embarrassed there was no more to read out. Ingap would not have been free to write any more. Nevertheless, the fact that his son was still alive and in Taegu now could not but be good news for the old man.

"Taegu . . . that's Kyŏngsang Province. . . . So he's still alive and here, in our country?"

Old Screw Fist shed tears of relief.

A fortnight later a second card arrived, this time from Sunch'ŏn. This one also inquired after the old man's health; the only difference was that in addition, Ingap asked his father not to think of trying to raise the money to come and visit.

"Ah, are they really going to drag him off to war?"

Old Screw Fist's sigh was tinged with desperation upon hearing the contents of the postcard. The route from Taegu to Sunch'ŏn was the exact opposite of the direction in which the boys had set out. Kilson, Sŏkchu, and Tongsŏk's cards arrived from the same place. At that point the focus of the war still lay in Okinawa. Even after the Japanese imperialists had lost Naha and Kitazato, they persisted, dispatching their commando forces and suicidal shock troops to gasp their final breaths and relentlessly pouring our people's blood into the desperate fight. The battlefield lay not only in Okinawa: Kyushu, Osaka, Tokyo, and the entire Japanese archipelago were huddled beneath a sky raining down fire. Despair and anxiety hit exorbitant levels as soldiers lost all hope of returning home, no matter whether they were dispatched to Okinawa or elsewhere in Japan.

At the beginning of July the explosions reached T'aejŏn and Kwangju, and with the formation of the so-called National Volunteer Corps around the same time, people grew increasingly uneasy about the imminent transformation of the entire Korean Peninsula into a battlefield. In the midst of all this, the deadly extraction of the barley quota began. The police had taken over the Civil Defense Force and were moving in groups from house to house on a daily basis, conducting searches, confiscating any food, and dragging people away trussed up in ropes. Even Ch'unsik was caught and returned home with a broken nose, and Old Screw Fist was beaten when a small amount of rice was discovered at the bottom of a jar, despite his having been unable to farm that year. He could not bear to eat all of the rice acquired with such great difficulty for the son he might never see again, but which the son had been unable to finish before he left. It was the chubby-cheeked deputy head of the Civil Defense Force, Pongdŏk, who had given the old man a slap, and although the peasants had gotten used to beatings by Pongdŏk, there was an additional reason why the incident fueled rumors and brought a frown to the face of everyone who heard what had happened.

After Ingap had left, Yugami's brother, Sunch'il, had taken to drinking with Pongdŏk more frequently and in a drunken state had asked Yugami to hand over Ingap's letters of proposal and the four pillars. At first Sunch'il had tried to cajole her, then badger her, and finally he even gave her a few lashes. Pongdŏk began drinking at their house or drinking elsewhere before returning to the house arm in arm with Sunch'il. Upon arrival Pongdŏk would lie down on the warmest part of the floor, as if it were his own home, and start to harass Yugami. Each time this happened Ingap's perceptive older sister would guess what they were up to and contact Ch'unsik. Ch'unsik would then turn up even in the middle of the night, announcing his appearance with a cough, and find a way to make the party peter out and send Pongdŏk stumbling back home with a scowl on his face. One time Yugami was fleeing her drunken brother's lashes when Ingap's sister suddenly appeared at the corner of the house, grabbed her by the wrist, and helped her to seek shelter at Ch'unsik's house. Around this time, rumors arose that Sunch'il and his taut leg muscles had managed to avoid both the military draft and the Patriotic Corps with Pongdŏk's backing and that Pongdŏk's assault on Old Screw Fist, on the pretext of discovering such a tiny amount of rice, resulted from some kind of secret agreement between him and Sunch'il as much as from his envy of the old man's top paddy.

After the slap, Old Screw Fist visited Sangjin and sighed, "Is there anywhere we can survive these days? When will it ever all come to an end . . ."

Several days later, Old Screw Fist visited once more and asked, "And what do the newspapers say lately?"

What he was really asking, as he waited with as much restraint as he could summon, was "When will it ever all come to an end?" Whenever he asked this, Sangjin would pick up the newspaper on which he was scribbling or which was already black from his doodling, choose a couple of important articles that were concrete enough for the old man to be able to understand, read them out loud, and then conclude, "Whatever happens, it clearly will not be long now."

Yet these past few days he could not find a single article that would suggest the tedious era might be drawing to an end any time soon. Instead the bastards continued to make noises that the war was going to continue for a long, long time; there were reports on the inspections for volunteer navy cadets, the increased production of pine oil, the successful fulfillment of the barley quota, and how many thousands of wooden airplanes were being built each month. Sangjin suspected this was all propaganda, attempting to deceive the people until the last day possible; nevertheless he felt intensely threatened by the prospect of having to bide his time longer still, having already endured the tedium thus far. In reality, Sangjin had been feeling threatened by his living circumstances for a while now. When he had calculated his budget for three years, it had challenged his imagination to set one hundred won as the presumed price for a sack of rice, but he was running out of money before even the first year had come to a close. His wife had to restrain herself when buying even the tiniest bowl of salted shrimp or cabbage for making kimchi.

"We're not even allowed to sell a needle on the black market, but everything we buy has to come that way."

His wife constantly sighed with the worry of how they would survive if the situation continued. One of the slogans in the competition for survival at the time was to resist *yami* with *yami*— resist the black market through the black market.

"Have you any idea how much money we have left?"

At quiet moments, when Sangjin would be doodling on the newspaper while his wife sat beside him sewing, she would start to worry about how they were going to survive.

"Well . . ."

This was hardly an appropriate answer, but Sangjin could find no other, and stuck for words he would take out another cigarette and place it in his mouth. When he looked as if he might be searching for a precious match, his wife would hold the brazier out toward him and laugh, "You really are calm, aren't you?"

Sangjin could not help but laugh to himself at the thought of him sitting there on a sultry summer's day, lighting his cigarette with a brazier so hot it felt as if his forehead was being burned off.

"Well, as they say, *harotongsŏn* . . ."

He calmly launched into an unnecessary explanation when his wife looked puzzled.

"You don't know the saying? Like a brazier in the summer and a fan in the winter . . . That's how useless I've become."

She laughed—he was not someone with whom she would be able to share her worries.

Not that worrying helped one bit. There were still some clothes left in their wardrobe, so they should be able to survive by selling some of those and living on millet and bean paste until liberation, surely? Sangjin was calm, feeling they had the grit to survive, if not the budget. He wished he could read something, but after the last house search his wife had confiscated all the books he had hidden away and would not let him so much as contemplate taking a look, saying that the police might show up again at any time. And that was how he began his preparations for the new age with some doodling, just like a brazier in the summer or a fan in the winter. Wetting an inkstone of some antique value, which had been passed down through the generations, and quietly grinding ink for who knows how long like a madman just to practice some calligraphy, even on scraps of newspaper—this seemed a fine pastime for forgetting the sultry heat in such tedious times, when he had no choice but to fancy himself peacefully withdrawing from the world until the turbulent age had passed.

Eventually the rainy season drew to an end and a glimpse of autumn color appeared in the distant clear blue sky.

Sangjin was doodling again.

"What, writing again? Don't you think we should think about escaping to somewhere safer?"

His wife had been worrying on and off for several days now.

On the ninth, the Soviet Army had finally overrun the Soviet-Manchurian border in both the east and the west and crossed the Tuman River to begin entering Korea. Around the same time, the cities of Hiroshima and Nagasaki in Japan had suffered horrendous damage inflicted by some kind of new bomb, and on the tenth martial law had been declared in Tokyo. By the eleventh, the Soviet Army had already entered the port of Unggi. They really were sweeping away all before them, as if they were slicing through a forest of bamboo. The long-awaited liberation of our Korea was becoming reality hour by hour, starting from the northern regions and enacted through the great strength of the Red Army. But wasn't this exactly the moment when the Japs were likely to begin their final throes? There was no reason for those thieving imperialists to politely return what they had stolen and withdraw of their own accord. If there were to be large scale destruction and a massacre of the starving ghosts, then this would surely be the moment.

Let's bring in martial law! The martial law craved by the bosses here for so long had already been announced in Japan. Sangjin had no radio, and the newspapers, which had always reached him late anyway, were now arriving four or even more days late, leaving him completely in the dark and not without suspicion that martial law might already have been imposed in places like Seoul.

He believed in the rational behavior of human beings, but sitting here in the midst of a total news blackout, he could easily imagine Kawamoto issuing the command "Die!" in some drunken stupor, and anything might happen. He contemplated escaping somewhere temporarily with his wife, but they had nowhere to go. Everybody was trying to escape from cities like Seoul or Pyongyang: even if the two of them were to move to the city, staying at an inn made no sense, and all the friends with whom they might stay had already evacuated or were equally anxious about remaining behind. They also had no way of knowing how sympathetic their friends might be, because they had not been able to exchange letters for more than half a year. Yet there were no other villages in which they could seek shelter. While he mulled over this and that possibility, Sangjin's anxiety increased exponentially until finally he wondered whether he had fallen into a state of paranoia—after all, did he really attract enough attention to justify this much worry? As long as that deranged alcoholic was walking around with a bayonet like a mad dog, however, Sangjin could not possibly remain calm. For several days in a row he had climbed up the back mountain after breakfast and spent the day dipping his feet in the mountain streams, which were swollen with seasonal rain, but people were foraging throughout the woods for pine resin knots, grape-vines, and oak and bush clover bark, watched over by the Civil Defense Force, dashing around trying frantically to reach the yet-to-be fulfilled quota; in their eyes, who on earth was this man with nothing to do but bathe in the streams all day long? The past two days he had stayed at home. Through all this his wife had not been able to sleep and kept pestering her husband, who was still doodling away as if without a care in the world.

"What are you writing for? If that's all you have to do, why don't you walk up the mountain again?"

She was interrupted by a dog's bark, followed by the sound of footsteps outside the gate; the blood drained from her face and her eyes opened wide.

"What are you doing now? What if someone sees?"

Sangjin was writing in Chinese characters, "No family, no country, where can we settle?"

A cough outside the gate heralded the arrival of none other than Ch'unsik, walking into their yard in the twilight.

"Sir, are you at home?"

"Please come in."

"You haven't heard the news, sir?"

"What news?"

"Ha, it's all over."

"?"

"Everything."

Ch'unsik kowtowed and pretended to be begging for his life.

"No, what do you mean, everything?"

Sangjin dropped his brush and sat back.

"Surrender. It's unconditional surrender. They say the Japanese emperor went on the radio today and said they'd surrender."

Sangjin closed his eyes for a moment, then shook his head with a shiver, before taking a deep breath and telling himself, in an attempt to calm his quivering heart, "Be still."

"Where did you hear that?"

According to Ch'unsik, he'd heard the news from someone who had just arrived from Pyongyang and reported having listened to the broadcast with his own ears at noon that day. The bus had arrived from K town a little earlier, and the passengers all confirmed the news.

"Can it be true?"

This unbelievable dream of a day was August 15, 1945.

C ould it really be true? Was this the day for which he had waited half his life, not a longed-for dream but actual history unfolding before his very eyes? The dark past seemed even more dismal now that a bright and dazzling future promised new paths from this day on. Having wasted his youth, half his life, wandering helplessly in the darkness of subjugation, Sangjin still could not wrap his head around reality the following day; he paced around his narrow room and yard, as if caught in the daze of a rapturous dream.

At one point, Ch'unsik interrupted to report that all the men had returned who had been sent to the Yonggang airfield as part of the Patriotic Corps, and now several people who had been dragged off to some mine had also reemerged.

"I guess Ingap and all the soldiers sent to Japan will be back soon, as long as they're still alive?"

"Of course, of course."

Despite this optimistic reply, Sangjin felt more hopeless than curious about Ingap's fate. There had been no more correspondence after the postcard from Sunch'ŏn. The two of them had kept their ominous thoughts to themselves, but clearly Ch'unsik shared Sangjin's worries. He added, "What with the drafted men coming home like this, Old Screw Fist seems even more upset. I just went over there, and he's sat smoking, not saying anything . . ."

"Of course, who wouldn't feel that way?"

Sangjin realized it was no longer a dream. Perhaps because half of his life had been so distorted that he had grown accustomed to the stinging pain of facts instead of states of enchantment, he could not help but worry that this might be yet another case of the saying, "The things of the world do not follow one's intention eight or nine times out of ten." But if this was not living reality, then what could it be? For the first time he could feel reality.

The following day saw the formation of the S Township Committee for the Preparation for National Construction. The head of the police substation, Kawamoto, had taken fright and fled during the night, leaving his wife and children behind. The school headmaster and the postmaster had followed in his wake. This meant that all the Japs who had lived there were now gone. The Committee for the Preparation for National Construction took over the running of the school, the post office, and the police substation.

T'aegŭkki flags fluttered high above every house, and patriotic songs and cheers rang out continually from morning until night.

While all the people were jumping up and down with joy at this reversal of fortune, the mayor and other lackeys of the former colonial government were unable to share in this happiness. Their pale faces exposed their identities no sooner had the power of the Japs come crashing down, inflaming the people's desire for revenge and increasing the determination of Ch'unsik and some of the other youths to impose strict restrictions. But instead of continuing to forge his slimy path through their world, that oily puppy of a township head had slipped right out of it and fled that very night. A rumor circulated much later that he had fled across the 38th parallel to the south in an equally slippery fashion.

In the meantime, Sangjin had been asked by the Preparatory Committee to produce some Korean-language teaching materials for the school that was to open before long. Given that Sangjin himself had no confidence in his spelling ability and his collaborator teachers had shown little previous interest in our language and writing, the materials were not likely to be adequate, but Sangjin had accepted the challenge, believing that anything would be better than nothing at all. More authoritative experts would be sure to undertake such work in the central regions, but their efforts were unlikely to reach a secluded area like this any time soon.

On his first day working on the project Sangjin went to his shed to look for some reference material and found a box; when he broke it open, Korean books came tumbling out. In the heap, he found novels such as *Im Kkŏkchŏng* and *Hometown*, short story collections including *Crows* and *A Small Boy's Journey*, old magazines such as *Writing*, as well as his copy of the *Korean Dictionary* and *Collection of Standard Vocabulary*. He was overjoyed to see them all again. These books, covered with grimy fingerprints, had been sheltering along with him in anticipation of this day. They had survived two rainy seasons buried beneath piles of straw in a shed and were dusted with mold spores; their pages stuck to each other and some of the books were glued together too, like sticky rice cakes.

"Now then, let's go outside and see some sunlight," Sangjin muttered, as he carried an armful of our liberated language and writing out onto the porch, where the distant autumn light would be even brighter.

They decided to begin the textbook with several phrases:

Country
Our country

And then advance a level to:

Korea is our country
We are Korean children
Smart children

Even such simple sentences could not help but impress upon them the awe of what they were doing.

A couple of days after he had finished preparing the teaching materials, Sangjin left for Pyongyang. There was still no sign of Ingap or any of the other young men who had left along with him.

At their parting, Old Screw Fist said, "As soon as our boy gets back, he'll be sure to come visit you." He added, "Now that we have our country back, we have to get on with fixing the top paddy, and his mother's waiting for him too."

Tears gathered at the end of his bushy pine of a beard. Ch'unsik was standing at his side and teased him, "Oh, here you go again. Now that good fortune is shining on our country once more, what's happened to all the young people who are going to do all the work?" He turned to Sangjin and said, "Sir, you must be sure to come to our little Ingap's party. Yikes, back then that Pongdŏk bastard was supposed to lead the ceremony, well, he had his mug broken yesterday . . ."

Angry at the mayor having slipped out of their grasp, the young men had apparently picked on the chubby-cheeked deputy head of the Civil Defense Force.

Two days after Sangjin returned to Pyongyang, Soviet troops entered the city. They had resisted the fascists' invasion and protected their own country in Europe, then they had pushed on to the invaders' den in Berlin and liberated the small and weak countries in between, and finally they had turned to the East, where they destroyed the army of the Japanese imperialists and entered this city as upholders of peace and freedom. The Japanese Army and police had been disarmed, and we had been liberated.

In October, General Kim Il Sung made his triumphant return. When Sangjin watched the general from a distance at the great rally of the people, held in the wake of his victorious return from single-handedly upholding the honor of thirty million of us among the ranks of the world's nations, Sangjin was bothered once again by his recollection of the previous spring and of Ingap, of whom there was still no news. This was the general for whom the young man had longed from afar through the window of his depressed heart, and now this general had appeared in person before Sangjin's own eyes.

It was the following January when Ingap suddenly walked into the meeting hall of the General Federation of North Korean Arts. At first, Sangjin thought it must be a dream. There was Kilson too. They both laughed as they recounted that because they had been sent to the Kansai region, they had never had the opportunity to use the phrase, "*Wŏ shì hánguó rén*," which they had learned to help them reach General Kim's troops; neither had they been able to recite "I am a Korean," because in Kansai the bombs had fallen from airplanes in the sky.

They had returned only ten days earlier, but they looked energetic and showed little sign of exhaustion. They really were young, except now they looked like hearty young men. The bug-bitten wild melon from a ditch, Kilson, was almost unrecognizable with his broad shoulders and thick chest.

THE BARLEY HUMP

203

They said both Sŏkchu and Tongsŏk had returned safely with them.

Over lunch in a restaurant, Sangjin asked them about their plans for the future in this new Korea. Ingap would have to look after his parents and their fields, he said, and claimed this was what he really wanted to do. As soon as he had arrived in Pyongyang he had visited the landowner to discuss the top paddy, but the landowner had again complained that income and expenditure were not adding up—it was already awkward to manage existing land, he grumbled, and he seemed far from convinced of the value of spending money to fix land that had already been discarded. In other words, this landlord seemed to hold a preference for money, which could be freely moved around on foot at any time were the atmosphere in the north to turn against him.

Ingap would have no choice but to find land to cultivate elsewhere this coming spring, even if it meant leaving his hometown.

"Nothing has changed since liberation . . . it's not just those of us who have no land to farm who are struggling at the moment, but even those who are already farming. They say it's a new country, but don't the villagers and farmworkers need some new hope?"

In Kilson's case, his two older brothers were already working the land and he was hoping to move in a different direction; he had applied to join the security forces. He added, "It's true. Since we returned, all the farmers without their own land are saying that there's no real independence, even if we've been liberated. . . . They're playing cards and gambling, and drinking and getting drunk, just like during the Japanese occupation"—he blushed, as if recalling the events of the previous spring—"And it's true. We were as good as dead, but we survived and made it back home, thinking everything would have changed with liberation, but nothing feels new at all."

Their thoughts were really another expression of that slogan which Ingap's words had brought to Sangjin's mind when they first met on the road the previous spring: "Land to the peasants." It was clear that the peasants, who made up about 80 percent or more of the entire nation, were still unable to enjoy liberation.

Kilson said they could meet up more often if he stayed in Pyongyang. Then, on parting, Sangjin asked Ingap about his marriage plans, but he merely blushed and replied, "We'll see."

The response did not reflect bashfulness so much as his situation, still far from liberated from the endless orbit of the spring hunger.

In February the Provisional People's Committee of North Korea was established with the support of the entire people and with General Kim Il Sung as its chair.

The first anniversary of the March First Uprising since liberation came around. A tower was set up in the center of town and marked "Day of Blood." After a memorial service held in front of the station, everyone walked back through the town. Sangjin marched beneath the flag of the General Federation for the North Korean Arts. As his group approached the central party headquarters a procession of peasants appeared, towels wrapped around their heads, sickles and hoes clasped in their hands. The cultural workers gave way to the rows of peasants and cheered them on with shouts of "Hurray for the peasants of Korea!"

The procession moved forward behind a tall banner carrying the words, "Land to the peasants!" In the middle there was one flag that read, "K County S Township Peasant Association." Sangjin took a step forward for a closer look. The first person he recognized was Old Screw Fist. He found himself running toward the old man. Old Screw Fist was startled when someone grabbed his arm, and his surprise only increased when he realized that someone was Sangjin.

"Ha, I'm so glad I lived to see this happy day, and to meet you again, sir."

And laughing all the while, he added, "Our Ingap is right behind."

Just then Ingap himself ran up and clasped Sangjin's hand. In his other hand he held a large streamer that also read "Land to the peasants!" He had perhaps always been vaguely conscious of this demand, but he had been unable to formulate words for it other than through suggestion or paradox. Today it had taken shape in a clear slogan; its time had come to be pronounced clearly and concretely. Sŏkchu and Tongsŏk also stepped cheerily out of the procession for a short while to greet Sangjin. And then, just at that moment, a police guard rode up on a horse. He seemed to want to bring this part of the procession back into order.

"I'm sorry."

Sangjin apologized, but when he looked up, he saw that the guard was Kilson.

"You bastard, Kilson, don't you recognize us?"

Sŏkchu merrily greeted him with this question.

"You riff-raff! Who calls a guard protecting the people a bastard?"

They all burst out laughing. Kilson bent down to shake hands with his comrades. Sangjin also took hold of his hand.

Ingap reported that the Peasant Association, the National Youth Association and, of course, the township's People's Committee were working together to open a middle school in S Township.

"Ch'unsik's the clerk of the Peasant Association, now and he's working really hard for the school. When the school opens," he added, "be sure to come along."

And with that, they rejoined the procession.

"Hurray for the North Korean People's Committee!"

"Hurray for General Kim Il Sung!"

"Land to the peasants!"

The shouts resounded as the march continued. And police guard Kilson, of peasant stock, slowly rode his horse beside the procession of peasants, most protectively.

Sangjin returned to his group and started a new chant, "Hurray for the liberation of Korea's peasants!"

Four days later, on March 5, the People's Committee of North Korea, which was now the people's government, announced the historical Land Reform Law in response to the demands of the peasant masses. On this day the peasants were liberated and took possession of their own freedom and land.

At the beginning of April Sangjin received a letter from Ch'unsik and Ingap inviting him to the opening ceremony of S Middle School. The school was housed in the old Civil Defense Force building, and classes were to begin the following day. Sangjin arrived to find Ch'unsik busy in the schoolyard overseeing the carpenters, who were putting together new shelves for the students' shoes. He turned to Sangjin and asked, "Sir, may I show you a truly fine sight?"

He pointed to the fields just outside the village entrance, where dozens of farmworkers were busily constructing something. He explained that recently, when the peasants had divided the land as part of the land reform, Old Screw Fist and the top paddy had raised a problem. They could not give the discarded top paddy to Old Screw Fist in its current condition, but there had been no surplus land, and so they had decided to take a small portion of land from each person with more to give to the old man. This did not satisfy Old Screw Fist, however, who seemed unable to give up on the top paddy and said, "Even if I have other land, there's no one going to farm this . . . does that mean this precious paddy will stay a field of weeds forever? That's our country's land, isn't it? This isn't the way we farmers do things."

The peasants had been concentrating on how to divide up each other's land and now hesitated somewhat awkwardly.

"Okay, how about we do this?"

Tongsŏk and Sŏkchu were executives in the National Youth Association and came up with a proposal. Although it might be difficult for one or two households to restore the paddy, if the members of the Youth Association all pitched in, the situation would be different: three hundred days of labor were necessary, which meant that if the more than one hundred members of the Association each took on two or three days of work the field could be restored. Because the farming season had yet to start in earnest, it would not be a great hardship for that many people to promise two or three days each. Once restored, the land would be handed over to Old Screw Fist, but the youths would not be working for the old man alone; they would be restoring life to the land of our country. All the members of the Youth Association agreed to the proposal.

"Let's revive our country's land with peasant hands!" This new slogan emerged organically. When the Peasant Association saw what was going on, they agreed to collaborate. And so the new slogan became reality. The scene outside the village was the work of the peasants reviving the land of our country.

Sangjin followed Ch'unsik to the site to view the wonderful spectacle. To reach the top paddy they had to pass the well, where Old Screw Fist had said he dipped his finger into the ditch to taste the water. The sun was beginning to set, and the village women had gathered to fetch water and rinse rice, along with the shepherd's purse, water parsley, and other herbs they had picked on the mountain that day. Ch'unsik limped straight into the middle of the lively scene and called out to one of the women in his usual joking manner, "Ah, my sister-in-law from the Women's Association . . ."

The crowd of women around the well erupted in laughter. One young woman spoke up in response, turning to face the men with her water bucket on her head: "Ah, so did we form a Women's Association to keep the women separate? You haven't even introduced your visitor . . ."

Here was Yugami. The braid that Ingap's sister had stroked so fondly back when Ingap had been dragged off to the army had been replaced by a chignon, suggesting that this girl was now a daughter-in-law, this girl about whom Old Screw Fist had once said, "That's all that really matters, isn't it?" Ingap, it seemed, had recently married her. She put down her water jar to greet them. Sangjin was delighted by this first introduction.

Old Screw Fist had been standing on the bank of the top paddy holding a shovel, but now he shaded his eyes with one hand to see who the visitors were and climbed up the hill to join them.

"It's been a long time."

Sangjin greeted the old man, who laughed and grasped Sangjin's hand firmly before wiping away the tears that had gathered in his eyes.

"I'm so glad to see you," the old man replied.

All of the dozens of young men, who were busy removing dirt with shovels, spades, buckets, and other tools, now stopped for a moment to acknowledge Sangjin with their eyes or ask him in place of a greeting, "Ah, when did you get here?"

A few of them threw down their shovels and ran up to him. These included Ingap, naturally, and also Tongsŏk and Sŏkchu. Everybody clasped each other's hands.

"I can see that this ruined land of ours is now being brought back to life through all of your efforts."

Sangjin was truly delighted.

"You must be so happy? Of course, it's a lot of work for you too . . ." he said.

"Ha ha ha, what's that to me . . ."

Old Screw Fist had lost a few more front teeth in the meantime, and his laughter revealed an even bigger hole in his mouth.

"From now on this land belongs to all the farmers, and the young men are working on it like it's their own."

"That's right. Now the peasants are no longer thinking in terms of you and me."

Sŏkchu affirmed the old man's words.

Ingap, too, sounded much brighter and explained what was happening,

"Back then, when the top paddy was destroyed, the fields behind the village went unused, too, and stayed like that for a couple of years, but now the Youth Association is working to bring them all back to life. This year probably not a single paddy will be left unfarmed."

How depressed and furious he had felt about this top paddy back last spring, when they had walked side by side.

"I say, Kilson's in Pyongyang!"

Standing before them all like this, Sangjin had suddenly remembered their friend.

"It won't be long before that rascal comes back to the substation here and starts throwing his weight around."

Sŏkchu's response made everybody laugh.

"Well, let's all clear away at least one more shovelful before we finish up for the day . . ."

Sŏkchu glanced up at the sun, which was slowly disappearing over the mountain to the west, and stepped back into the paddy.

Sangjin followed Old Screw Fist and Ch'unsik to the bank across from the whetstone, where they sat down. The once bare collapsed bank had already been rebuilt, and footsteps were beginning to restore the line of the interrupted farm path, where green shoots of grass poked up from roots that were crisscrossing the bank and gradually pulling the entangled dirt back into place. A red evening glow slowly sinking down in the western sky harbored the promise of fine weather the next day, while in the village, nestled snuggly at the foot of a mountain, smoke wafted up from the chimneys, as if the houses had each lit up a pipe. Hearing the distant tweets of birds flying across the clear sky and the quiet lowing of the oxen, Sangjin was struck by a sense of the earth's magnitude. He stretched his legs out on the grass and felt as if he might drift off into a comforting sleep at any moment, so pleasant was the tiredness enfolding his body and the faint hopes relaxing his mind.

"And how is our General Kim?"

Old Screw First suddenly asked the question. His inquiry was sincere. It was just awkward that he presumed Sangjin would know the latest news of General Kim.

"I haven't seen him often, but he's fine, I'm sure."

"Well, because of that fine . . . because of that fine man, peasants like us feel like we've had rice cakes thrown into our huts. I couldn't believe anything at first . . . we were at a loss . . . it was like a dream."

Old Screw Fist laughed again, and Ch'unsik interrupted.

"But now it's real, isn't it? Watching this top paddy being fixed."

"It's real, seeing this field of weeds brought back to life through peasant hands, at last the land has found its owners."

Sangjin nodded in agreement while watching the young people spread out in rows across the paddy field, gradually stripping it clean of mud. They pushed their shovels horizontally to try to avoid treading the mud down into the original soil or digging so deeply that they might remove any of that soil, and then they carried the mud away in the waiting buckets. With each shovel load, they removed the rough mud and sand, full of weeds like mugwort and crabgrass, until the old top paddy reemerged, glistening like the best-quality ink.

"One strip of our nation's land brought back from devastation and restored to fertile earth by peasant hands!"

Sangjin recited this phrase to himself, almost as if it were a line of verse.

More and more people were walking back along the path where Sangjin sat; they each carried pitchforks and hoes over their shoulders or drove oxen. The farmworkers were returning home from their day's work. Those working on the top paddy lifted their plows onto their shoulders. The scent of soft earth wafted up from fields neatly dug right out to the edge on either side of the path at the end of the embankment. Barley fields could be seen here and there. It was still too early for their green waves. Neither had the acacia flowers at the side of the path bloomed yet.

"Ingap, do you remember when we first met? It was a little later than this, but you said the barley hump loomed grimly on the horizon."

"Ah, yes, I do remember."

"Back then you were referring to something else, but perhaps the barley hump really will become a phrase belonging to the past?"

"I think so."

"It's true, it really is."

Ingap and Tongsŏk agreed.

"Ha ha, that barley hump was really hard to get over. I wonder how many of those humps I must have climbed up!"

Old Screw Fist let out a sigh at the thought of the dark past. At the same time he did not forget to laugh as well.

"But now the future looks bright. Because we've gotten through all of that. Perhaps the children growing up now will hear the word barley hump and think it's an ancient word."

How things had changed! Until last spring life had been so hard, but this spring it was simply delightful.

Thanks to the land reform, North Korea's peasants had finally crossed the barley hump, which had caused them so much suffering, and they had left behind the annual pain of the spring hunger, which they had once believed to be their unavoidable fate.

The Engineer

The bastard from the police unit returned to the cells, another piece of paper in hand. It was the same man who had led in the officers a short while earlier while they joked about coming to get their share of the "rations" and wanting "to kill someone." Even before the stench of alcohol left in their wake had dissipated, this man walked in with yet another scrap of paper bearing the name of the next person to be dragged out.

These prison cells had been created by sectioning off a warehouse so that fifty to sixty people could be stuffed into each of them. Now the air congealed in an instant with an asphyxiating tension, like pond water lurking beneath layers of deeply frozen sheets of ice.

"What, more? A few extras now that they're done with their rations?"

A guard took the paper and grumbled his annoyance at the repeated bother before checking the name against his roster and

"The Engineer" was first published in 1951. The unbracketed footnotes that follow are additions to Ch'oe Myŏngik's 1952 book *Kigwansa* (The Engineer).

glancing around the different cells. Eyes shone through the bars surrounding him as everyone waited with bated breath and ears pricked up for the name to be called. "Who will it be this time?" This same question was on everyone's mind, but it didn't hold half the urgency as the thought that it might be "my turn." The guard noisily unlocked one of the cell doors and shouted inside.

"Hyŏnjun, where's Hyŏnjun? Out here now!"

In the far corner a young man stood up. The prisoners were packed in so tightly that in order to make his way through the seated crowd he had to push down on their shoulders with both hands and step over them. All the eyes that had been peering at the guards through the bars now redirected their focus onto this young man.

At first glance he looked as sharp as a chisel: tall and slender, the lack of any trimmings or pockets on his jacket and trousers only emphasizing his upright and smart appearance, while his dyed indigo work clothes, displaying the strong white stitching of a thick needle, endowed his broad shoulders and firm chest with a dignified solidity.

Deep sighs resounded through the cell, and the already thick air seemed to grow even heavier. Hands reached out toward the young man, who bent over to choose his step. Hyŏnjun grasped each hand firmly as he moved through the cell. Eyes bid a silent farewell. Yet this was both first greeting and farewell, because Hyŏnjun was not from the area.

Unrelenting surveillance by the bastards had prevented any opportunity for the prisoners to introduce themselves to each other properly, even though they had spent almost a week together in the cell. Despite this, even complete strangers were now treasured comrades because of their shared suffering at enemy hands.

Another comrade dragged off by those bastards! What kind of plans for heinous slaughter would the bloodthirsty enemy be holding in store? What kind of torture rack awaited this sharp young comrade now making his exit? Unable to voice such thoughts, those who shook the young man's hands could reveal their care and sadness only in their eyes, looking up at him, alongside their belief that in the final instance he would not succumb. Comradeship, trust, and silent support sparkled like dew and entreated him to fight back, no matter how bad a turn events might take.

The recipient of these farewells clenched his lips, hardening his angular chin, which looked as if it had been carved from stone. But a sparkle in his eyes seemed to send out a cheerful smile.

A sudden explosion of gunfire. From the usual place on the hill out the back. The bastards had executed the prisoners dragged out a little earlier.

"Quick, get out here now!"

Two or three gun muzzles pointed into the cell through the doorway, where the guard, waiting with lock in hand, now stamped his foot to hurry things along. As the young man quickly stepped out, the muzzles turned and followed behind him. These bastards were truly frightening.

When one of the guards holding a gun muzzle to Hyŏnjun's back slowly opened the door to the office of the Special Investigations Unit, rounds of raucous laughter burst out. Several tables were scattered around the spacious room. But not one of the bastards was sitting down properly. Instead, they half-perched or leaned against the edge of the tables and talked rabidly. In addition to the members of the Special Investigations Unit working here, there was a host of clingers-on, officers and military policemen, waiting for the used bathwater, so to speak.

At the center of the group, in the manner of a wrestling match, a young American soldier jumped around, punching the empty air. He appeared to be trying to box. Red hairs glistened on the Yankee's two fists as he busily threw his punches. The rabble surrounding him clapped and laughed and nodded their approval, while they each tried to catch the eye of the American soldier spinning in circles. This only excited the young Yankee even more.

"So this is what those bastards call the police. With this sort of chaos there can't be much order in the squad!" Hyŏnjun murmured to himself as he walked through the door. "Slaughter, looting, rape, alcohol, destruction, the futile competition to suck up to those American bastards . . . that's all they can do, will do. So many comrades have been killed. Perhaps they will kill me too. But we'll have the last laugh when we destroy them. It's obvious. They'll soon lose."

"What's this?" One of the officers suddenly shouted out angrily. He seemed to sense the disdain in Hyŏnjun's smile and almost barked out the words while a murderous look settled into his glaring eyes.

"Well, well, if it isn't another one of those Reds that needs to be sent back home."

Just then a military policeman called out from where he was sitting astride a far table, "This one's for me." And pulling a pistol out from his waistband, he walked up to Hyŏnjun.

"It looks like time for a game of rock-paper-scissors."

The interjection came from someone behind the two of them, who was yawning as if possibly stretching. Everyone burst out laughing. Until someone from the Investigations Unit spoke up, "Hold on, not yet."

And he waved a hand as if to say, don't touch.

"If I could just get even one of those bastards . . ." Hyŏnjun thought to himself in his excitement, and he felt as if he could wring someone's neck there and then. But then he thought again, "Just hold on. If things really don't go well, I'll at least get my pound of flesh." He slipped a clenched fist into his trouser pocket and turned to face the window with a silent shout, "Even if I have to use my bare hands, I will not die for nothing."

This was Hyŏnjun's first interrogation, although he had been brought in the previous week. He could see all his belongings on the desk of the Chief of Special Investigations, taken from him in a body search when he had first been caught: his citizen's card, ID card, some hundred and something won in cash, his big shiny nickel pocket watch on its thick nickel chain, even the tiniest scraps of paper.

From the beginning the interrogation seemed to hold no purpose other than to establish whether or not he was a party member.

Hyŏnjun denied this. The Chief took a shiny black, steel-colored pistol out from the back of his trousers and placed it within reach on the edge of the broad table. Only then did he commence the interrogation, threatening to shoot at the end of each sentence. He contended that Hyŏnjun must be a Red who had abandoned his house and family in order to retreat. Hyŏnjun feigned innocence, countering that he had certainly not been in retreat. He explained that he had sent his wife and children to stay with her family in a mountain village in Yŏngwŏn a long time ago, when his house had been blown up, and that was where he had been heading too. He was even asked how many times he had driven a military train during the war. But this was merely another way of trying to find out whether or not he was a party member. He responded along the lines that even during the war he had only driven his usual passenger trains between Pyongyang and Namp'o.

The Chief looked over Hyŏnjun's ID and citizen's card once more. Hyŏnjun was not from the area, and there was no particular reason for his arrest. He had simply been one among some dozens of people loaded onto a truck and handed over by a

National Defense Force scouting party, which had passed through a while before and "caught some retreating Reds" on the way. As a result, the bastards had been unable to discover any evidence or find someone who could snitch on him.

In the end, the Chief had asked why he hadn't become a Red if he really wasn't one. Hyŏnjun replied first that he was ignorant and second that he wouldn't be able to stand the strict discipline.

The Chief had been looking down at Hyŏnjun's rough hands, fingers forked like a goat's horns, but now he picked up the telephone receiver on the table, where his two legs were resting.

By evening Hyŏnjun had been handed over to the Railway Security Unit, which was based in the same location within the premises of S Station. There he underwent another interrogation before being put to work at the station the following day.

Hyŏnjun was given the job of shunting train cars to tidy up the station yard. When he first entered the yard he found cars scattered all over the place in no particular order and only one main artery, running from east to west, completely clear. It wasn't that nobody was around. But there were no workers. Several locomotives had even begun the work of shunting. However, the unfamiliar engineers must have been beginners, because their engines huffed and puffed around the complicated shunting lines, all the while achieving nothing.

Hyŏnjun was assigned an engine plus a dwarfish Japanese for a fireman. Rail workers were in short supply, and this one had been chosen from the army because he said he had some previous experience firing engines in his own country. Kang, the lieutenant in the military police who had led in the dwarf, had asked Hyŏnjun whether he knew any Japanese. Hyŏnjun had in turn replied that he did not know a single word and before liberation had farmed in a secluded mountain valley where no Japanese were to be seen.

In truth, before the liberation Hyŏnjun had worked under Japanese engineers for four or five years and was not completely ignorant of their language. He had said he knew nothing in order to prove his ignorance, and because he had no desire to talk with some Japanese bastard again in a language that he had experienced only as a form of abuse and contempt. The military policeman and the Japanese soldier both seemed nonplussed until Hyŏnjun said they would be able to work together without any problem by communicating through hand gestures; thus, he began the work of shunting alongside the Japanese fireman.

Hyŏnjun was only to drive the engine at slow speed within the station limits, yet when he sat up in the driver's cab by himself and took hold of the lever for speed control, he inhaled deeply on the pure breeze that gently grazed his face, as if swallowing sweet water. Mixed in with that same gentle breeze however, he could also detect the smell of burning.

The small town of S, situated on the left-hand slope of a narrow plain onto which he could look down, had for the most part been reduced to a pile of ashes. Singed foundations were all that remained of the small villages, which had once been snugly tucked into the valley slopes on either side of the railway tracks. It wasn't only the houses. Even the surrounding mountains revealed little of their former appearance. The autumn leaves should now be in full color; instead, lone crimson streaks on burned black slopes flared up like the flames of a mountain fire, and the air was thick with the smell of the jellied gasoline those bastards had thrown everywhere.

Hyŏnjun had driven trains down the Pyongyang to Kowŏn line regularly for several years and had memorized every detail of the mountains alongside the railway tracks and the villages below, just as he knew exactly which mountain bend was followed by a steep gradient and how many kilometers remained before a certain tunnel or bridge would appear. He might not know their names, but he could even recognize the faces of the women and girls he saw at the wells in the villages alongside the tracks. He knew which village had a chestnut grove out back and behind exactly which house there was a large jujube tree growing, and he could take a pretty good guess at which houses in each village hoarded the largest stores of grain.[1]

But now it was impossible to distinguish anything; all that remained was a heap of ashes. Where were the people who used to live in these villages, in these houses?

An image of his wife and son flickered before Hyŏnjun's eyes. They were turning to look back at their house and hometown when they set off on the road to retreat a few days ahead of him. She carried a small bundle on her head and held little Poksŏk's hand as he trudged along. Hyŏnjun had to refocus and take a proper hold of the lever with his hands.

"Oh, *umai*, that's good!"

To one side the Japanese fireman made repeated exclamations in his own language. On top of everything else he was pigeon-toed, his stumpy shins turning inward. Now the dwarf kept calling out *umai*: for how well Hyŏnjun drove his engine across the points to switch rails with barely a rattle, as if the pattern of complicated shunting lines was engraved on his mind, and for the delicious taste each time the dwarf chewed on the chestnuts for which he rummaged in his trouser pockets in between shoveling coal into the firebox.

To Hyŏnjun the taste of that chestnut, which the dwarf now ate with such delight, recalled the taste of the old Japanese "colony," and the dwarf inevitably seemed like just another Japanese bastard still licking his lips on snacks. Hyŏnjun could never let his watch down, knowing that the dwarf was not only the fireman for this engine but also a guard and informant on his own behavior, as well as a dog lured into place by those bastards to

1   And he even knew which of those thatched roofs had been covered in bright red peppers left out to dry around this time last year.

be the first to bite Hyŏnjun's hand and block his way were he to try to seize an opportunity. Despite this, Hyŏnjun thought that under certain circumstances it might be rather good that the dwarf counted for little more than a dog.

The day's shunting work was done. The cars, which had been scattered all over in chaos, had now been returned to order, and the yard looked as if it had been given a good cleaning; with not so much as a shadow remaining on the brightly shining rails, Hyŏnjun felt satisfied that he had finished the job.

That evening a military train passed through.

"When do we get to take the engine out for a run? When you're up there, it feels good to move along a bit . . . it's a bit dull being stuck in this narrow yard, where it's forward, stop, backward, stop . . ."

The dwarf was speaking to Kang. The dwarf's question was the very one that Hyŏnjun wanted to ask but could not, and so naturally he pricked up his ears.

"Just wait and see."

This was the MP's response.

"Oh, right, of course."

The dwarf slapped his forehead with the palm of his hand and glanced over at Hyŏnjun, as if to say, "How could I have been so slow?"

"In any case, his technique is solid . . . So, mmm, how are things going? Is America . . . no, our UN troops, are they still at . . . now where was that again? Have the troops that were cut off to the east and west been able to join up again?"

"You mean at Yōtoku?[2] Not yet, not yet."

2. [Yōtoku is the Japanese pronunciation of Yangdŏk, a county in southeast P'yŏngan Province that was subject to fierce aerial bombing during the Korean War because of its significant railroad infrastructure.]

"Oh. So they're that strong? How long has it been now since those partisans, or whatever they're called, got going? Isn't there any other way?"

"Another way . . . well, just attack and attack. That's why we're concentrating all our efforts over there now. . . . So, how's it going?"

Kang had been chatting away with the dwarf in Japanese up until this point, but now he suddenly steered the conversation toward Hyŏnjun and spoke in Korean.

"With what you're doing?"

Hyŏnjun was just then tightening a driving wheel axle and merely glanced at Kang while he continued his work before finally responding in kind with a question.

"How is what?"

"I mean, how are you enjoying the work?" The MP's tone immediately turned sour.

"It's what I've always done." Hyŏnjun's reply was as unelaborated as ever.

"What you've always done, you say? Do you think I don't know that? . . . What kind of an answer is that, eh?"

". . ."

Hyŏnjun could not understand why the bastard had reacted so angrily.

"What kind of impudent . . . when your superior is good enough to address you. Let's try this again."

Now Hyŏnjun understood. Nevertheless, all he did was stare silently at Kang while he straightened his back to stand up, still holding an enormous hammer in his oily hands.

"You mean you can't reply, 'Thank you, sir. It's very interesting'? You'd better think about just whose sky you're living under." By this time Kang was shouting.

"I think it's enough if I do my job properly." Hyŏnjun's words were weighted carefully. He was not unaware that sucking up to these rotten bastards with conspicuous flattery could constitute one tactic in the battle against them. But the words that he should force himself to utter did not come easily to Hyŏnjun, who had lived and worked through the five years since liberation, when such flattery served no purpose and was even perceived to be a crime.

"What? 'If *I* do my . . .' You arrogant bastard! What the hell do you mean by this I, I, I . . . ?"

". . ."

"I don't know much, sir, but it seems to me that this one's attitude is indeed a touch arrogant. Perhaps these North Korean laborers have got a few too many guts, sir?"

The dwarf spoke in an exaggeratedly fawning manner off to one side.

"You need to change the way you speak to your superiors. Now, let's try it again."

Kang placed both his hands on his hips, as if to alter his posture, and took a step toward Hyŏnjun.

"Uh, um, Mister Kang."

A sudden whiff of alcohol wafted in from one side, along with this nasally voice. An American soldier had shown up from out of nowhere. He, too, placed both hands on his hips and moved his head from side to side, as if to humor the lieutenant.

"Uh um, Mister Kang, drink, oh drink is good."

Kang seemed suddenly cowed by the American bastard and said something to him in a low voice, as if imploring him. "Oh, no no. No good. Drink, drink is good."

The American soldier shook his head violently and reached out a finger to pluck Kang's tie out from beneath the collar of his uniform, which was secured by two rows of buttons. Kang looked to be embarrassed in front of Hyŏnjun and turned away in order to hurriedly stuff his tie back into place. But the American soldier would not leave it at that. In an instant he had pulled Kang's pistol out of its leather holster on his waist and jabbed it below his beltline. Kang tried to push his hand away. But the American waved a clenched fist in front of the lieutenant's nose, shouted something as if to give the order "forward," and twisted Kang's shoulders to turn him around. Then he marched Kang away ahead of him, kicking his buttocks alternately on the way.

"Oops, disarmed so easily just as he was bragging to the hilt, that brought an end to the party, didn't it?" The dwarf murmured to one side. He had just reemerged from behind the engine, where he had hidden the instant the drunken American soldier had appeared.

"Well, well, even a complete idiot like that is the American master, so there's not much can be done." After this, the dwarf seemed to grow bored, having nothing else to do, and began to absentmindedly whistle the tune, "*Sake*, a teardrop or a sigh?"

That evening the dwarf disappeared somewhere and returned so drunk that he collapsed, feeling sick. Hyŏnjun lay next to him but could not fall asleep. His head was full of too many thoughts. The moon cast a cold light aslant through the window facing him. There must have been clusters of black clouds racing across the sky, because the blue moonlight would disappear from time to time. The same window also admitted an endless reverberation of shrieks and yells from drunken bastards and the humming of vulgar popular songs, both nearby and afar. Gunfire and ugly outbursts of laughter intermingled, like violent melodies splicing into the sounds of people speaking the Korean that he could understand and the scattered voices of those debauched Americans, whose melodies made him frown, even though he didn't understand the words. This must be their so-called jazz. It was no mere sound of decadence; it was the sound of the despair that arises from neither knowing life's rewards nor holding any hope for the future.

"I must get to Yangdŏk!"

Hyŏnjun murmured aloud, and he lifted his head from his pillow, as if to shake off the noisy disturbance.

"Whatever it takes I must find a way to get to Yangdŏk and fight alongside our people and comrades!" Hyŏnjun realized that even with the tasks he was being assigned now it was not impossible that an opportunity might arise. This was the same Hyŏnjun who only a day previous had been watching out for a chance to "get just one of those bastards for my pound of flesh!" His heart had throbbed with joy when they told him he was being sent to the yard, and when he sat up on the locomotive engine he had thought, "If I could destroy even one of these engines!" Each time he waited for the points to change, his hand would clench the lever with the impulse to defy the stop sign and drive on, thus overturning the engine and destroying it.

But Hyŏnjun's heart had jumped when he heard that our people were fighting a guerrilla war against those bastards in Yangdŏk at that very moment; now, one measly engine and a few empty cars no longer seemed enough. Yet, according to the dwarf and Kang's earlier conversation, there might not be a better opportunity coming up.

Yangdŏk was no more than sixty or seventy ri to the east. Holding a gun, throwing grenades, destroying the bastards' tanks, or overturning their trucks so that he might stab the enemy soldiers in the chest with his bayonet when they came pouring out—if he could only escape and join our comrades' fight, then what a glorious chorus of cries would resound!

Just the thought of fighting alongside comrades while they talked about the victory to come! Even if he were to die in battle, he would be dying in front of or next to those comrades! "I must get to Yangdŏk," Hyŏnjun resolved once again, and he decided to bide his time in order to seize an opportunity in daylight to steal at least a couple of rifles and some grenades to take with him.

It was the middle of the night. Hyŏnjun had been deep in thought and staring at the ceiling when suddenly flames lit up the window facing him. Two or three loud gunshots sounded out nearby. Then he heard a young child crying for its mother.

Hyŏnjun pushed back his blanket and went to the window. A thatched hut had caught fire no more than twenty or thirty meters from the wooden fence that surrounded the yard. The blazing red flames seemed to tower even higher into the sky when black clouds momentarily shaded the moon. Another gunshot clearly rang out from the same spot. Then he heard a young woman scream. That scream, which had now replaced the young child's cries, was even more bloodcurdling than the sight of the flames flaring up into the night.

Before he even realized it, Hyŏnjun had kicked the door open and rushed out into the entranceway.

"Who's there!"

Suddenly, a shout resounded from the shadows beneath the eaves and his chest felt the thrust from a bayonet, shining all the more sharply in the light cast by the distant flames.

" . . . "

Hyŏnjun did not even have time to reply.

"Where are you going? Not so much as a footstep without permission, don't you know that?"

The bastard was wearing a military police armband.

"Get back inside."

The man barked and all but poked Hyŏnjun in the shoulder with his bayonet before pulling the door shut again. Hyŏnjun had no choice but to return to his room, where he stood transfixed to the window and watched. A human shadow flickered in the light of the flames, which began to spread from the rotten protruding eaves toward the supporting columns of the hut inside its collapsing fence. The shadow seemed to be holding a large bundle in one arm. It turned out to be another person. An American bastard was clearly visible, emerging from the shadows of the fence with his back to the blazing flames and striding in

Hyŏnjun's direction; the bundle he grasped on one side was, in fact, a disheveled-looking woman whose pale blue skirt dragged in the dirt. The bastard used his enormous boots to tread straight through the partially collapsed fence and enter the yard, carrying the woman with one arm, while her arms and legs, as well as her skirt, were dragged along in the dirt. Judging from his enormously broad but hunched shoulders, into which a reddish-white haired head had been pressed down, it was clearly the MP officer from the Railway Security Unit.

The young woman let out a shriek, apparently startled back to life from her terror-stricken faint. Just then, the moon emerged from behind black clouds and, with additional back lighting from the towering flames, Hyŏnjun could see the woman struggle to escape the bastard's grip. The man's stride accelerated. The glistening reddish-white hair on his bare head flapped, falling down over his forehead, even as far down as his nose. He had not gone far before he stopped dead in his tracks, emitting a scream that resembled the howl of a wild beast struck by a non-lethal bullet. For a few seconds he staggered, unable to control his body, before suddenly raising one arm and letting fire glitter forth from his fingertips. Shots rang out one after another, apparently directed into the face and chest of the woman, whose waist he still cinched with his other hand. Then the woman's silent, lifeless body was cast down, catching on one of the railway switches.

Hyŏnjun watched the scene unfold before his eyes and felt as if he were in the middle of a nightmare. "Can this really be happening?" he thought to himself, but the hideous beast, the like of which he had never seen in his life, still moved before his very eyes.

The two-legged beast looked down, as if unable to give up on the woman's corpse, which lay in a heap torn asunder beneath the bright moonlight. Then he slowly turned his head to look around, his hair still glistening despite its faded color. His eyes reflected both the red flames and cold blue moonlight through his disheveled hair, eyes that shone like those of a beast in search of the scent of blood to drink. As he began to withdraw, one hand at the end of a long arm dangling from hunched shoulders clutched a blunt pistol, while something like blood dripped from the other, which was as black as if it had been soaked in ink.

A bayonet tip passed by the window in front of Hyŏnjun's watching eyes; it belonged to the beast's guard, a policeman from the National Defense Force.

T he following morning Hyŏnjun and the dwarf fireman were firing up the steam engine when Kang appeared and ordered Hyŏnjun to prepare some dozen empty cars for immediate departure. This was unexpected.

"Well, they're empty cars . . ." he thought to himself. The cars were already in place and the engine had been started, so they would be able to leave immediately.

By the time Hyŏnjun had got up into the driver's cab and placed his hand on the lever, Kang, who had momentarily disappeared, returned with an American MP, and they stepped up into the cab together. It was the same bastard from the night before. Hyŏnjun sat looking straight ahead, his back to the two of them; he could feel his teeth quiver.

"Hey!"

The American suddenly shouted. Then Kang shouted, "Turn around!" But before he even had time to do so, Hyŏnjun felt the knee of the long-legged MP in his back. He jumped up and turned around to find the blunt muzzle of a large pistol pointing toward him. The MP muttered something.

"Do you know what this is?"

Kang translated. Hyŏnjun saw no need to reply. He looked back and forth between the pistol and the bastard's eyes instead. The beast of the previous night had bloodshot eyes and a white bandage wrapped around his hand, which now held the pistol. Beneath those bandages were most likely impressed the vengeful teeth marks left by the woman, who had died by his hand the previous night.

"If you make even the slightest mistake or cause trouble, just you see! There'll be a hole in your head immediately. Understand? Right, let's go."

Yet the order given was not to move forward but to back up.

Even after they had left the station, Hyŏnjun had to keep looking back at the green safety light, which flickered at the back of the train of some fourteen cars; it was as if he was shunting. Armed soldiers stood guard on both sides of the tracks between each telegraph pole.

There must have been some kind of accident on the railway. Perhaps a military train had come to an unexpected halt on this track to Yangdŏk, and now the bastards wanted to back up the empty cars in order to switch troops or some other load. Suspecting this to be the case, Hyŏnjun drove the engine in reverse, contemplating all the while "What if . . . ?" They could not move at full speed backward so the needle on the speedometer hovered gently between twenty-five and thirty kilometers an hour. Because the cars were empty there was little pressure on the springs in the running gear, which were clearly visible, and the speed allowed for a leisurely counting of the clunkety-clunks as they passed over the joints in the rails.

"How far are we going backward like this?"

The dwarf put down his shovel and wiped the sweat from his forehead.

"Until we get to where we're going."

Kang replied briefly with a click of his tongue, as if it were some kind of military secret.

Hyŏnjun had, of course, been listening in, but Kang's reply returned him to his own thoughts. "I wonder if they'll leave me

at the controls when we return loaded with weapons or troops?"
This was his first thought. Of course, the engineer of the train
coming from the other direction would most likely sit in the
driving seat, unless he had been injured or even killed in some
unexpected incident. That engineer would be someone the
bastards trusted, whom they would have brought up from the
south specifically to take charge of their military trains.

Yet, given that there were two bastards guarding him in the
narrow driver's cab, it seemed possible that he might be asked
to drive the train not just when it was empty, as at the moment,
but on the return journey too, loaded with cargo.

There were no military police in the driver's cab whenever
someone they trusted was in charge.

If this turned out to be the case, then this just might be the
opportunity for which Hyŏnjun had been waiting. He resolved
to follow his heart through to the end, even with two armed bastards watching over him. The green light had gradually shrunk
as the train wound around the foot of the hills, but about ten kilometers from S Station the tail of the train straightened out once
more, and they immediately began to enter what looked like a
cave full of people. It really was just like a cave, lacking any ceiling, but with soldiers packed tightly together along both sides
of the rails. Hyŏnjun pushed down on the lever in his hand. A
red stop light appeared at the tail end of the train. He pressed
down on the air gauge, causing the brakes to exert pressure on
all the wheels and bringing the train to a halt with a screech.

As soon as they had come to a complete stop, the American
MP and Kang stepped down. Hyŏnjun also stood up from the
driver's seat to take a good look outside, holding on to the side
of the door. A folding screen of human figures—of all shapes
and colors, just as the saying goes—stretched out in layers from
the front to the far end of the train. American bastards, including the conspicuously black Negroes, National Defense Force

bastards, and, in their midst, a load of Japs talking away in their own language.[3]

Hyŏnjun looked around to find their engineer. He was still nowhere to be seen. But he might show up at any moment, because the soldiers from the National Defense Force and U.S. Army—Negroes prominent among them—were still swarming forward, either dragging or carrying on their shoulders heavy and light machine guns and small caliber mortars, with their various gun barrels and mortar plates disassembled.

Now Hyŏnjun noticed that the American MP and Kang had reappeared at the foot of a small hill on the far side, having jumped down from the engine and disappeared into the crowd of soldiers. A flash of wings rose into the air on a cap, and gold edging sparkled on large, palm-sized badges; seven or eight American officers were standing together on the hill.

Hyŏnjun wondered what on earth had happened, but he could only see about three or four hundred meters further down the track before it disappeared around a bend in the foothills.

He removed a hammer from beneath the driver's seat and climbed down from the cab. As was usual when his train came to a stop, he went to inspect the running gear on each car. Beginning with the driving wheel, he tapped the axle of each wheel with his hammer, lifted up the covers on each axle and checked the compressed air hose linking each car to the next. He had been moving down the train, bending over to look beneath each car, when he suddenly straightened his back and stood up. He could clearly hear the sound of a train moving on the other side of the mountain. The sound grew gradually louder as he strained his ears, but it was clear that, wheel by wheel, the train was moving further away. It was the sound of an engine struggling.

While he strained to listen, Hyŏnjun's long eyes narrowed even more than usual beneath his brow, which glistened like a

3   At a glance they looked to number around two thousand.

thick stroke of ink. A deep blue sparkle in his eyes, pupils sharpened like a needle tip, gave the appearance that he was looking nowhere other than inside his own head.

The order appeared to have been given. With a chaotic sound of tramping boots and the clanging iron of weapons, soldiers surged toward the train.

Hyŏnjun had taken a towel from his waistband in order to wipe his oily hands, but now he hung it on the valve of the brake pipe at the end of the tender and picked up his hammer again. The bastards were loading boxes of ammunition into the car next to the tender. There were no tanks or artillery, but they still seemed to have plenty of weapons, at least one large load of light and heavy machine guns and mortars for each half-dozen men.

By the time nearly all the soldiers were on board, Hyŏnjun had also finished his inspection of the running gear. He returned to the cab to find the American MP and Kang already there, standing out front talking with the dwarf fireman. Hyŏnjun could not work out what they had been saying, but he did hear the dwarf's final words.

"Oh, don't worry."

"Well, it's only as far as S Station . . ."

It was Kang who interjected, looking back and forth between the American MP and the fireman.

"Yes, of course. You'll have seen for yourself on the way here, but on an even track like this it would be hard to cause an accident, even if you tried."

"They're talking about me," thought Hyŏnjun, and he picked up the towel he had hung behind the tender as he walked by. At the same moment, he gently closed the valve on which he had hung the towel. It was so simple. And it was something that an engineer or fireman would never do on a train in their charge. Each car has such a valve, but if just one is disabled, the brakes on all the cars that follow will fail. Yet the dwarf had no opportunity to notice what had been done. Everyone was on board.

"Hey!"

Hyŏnjun heard the American MP shout behind his back. He had just sat down and grasped the lever, but now he stood up politely without waiting for Kang's translation.

"Remember this?"

This was Kang's translation of the American MP tapping his hairy fingers on his gun holster, which was so big it looked like some kind of sawed-off leather saddle perched on his disgustingly fat stomach.[4]

"Yes, I understand. Don't worry."

Hyŏnjun aimed a ready smile at the American MP, whose wide open eyes glared out from between folds of red skin and gave the impression that he might swallow Hyŏnjun up at any moment.

"Right, S Station!"

Kang translated the American MP's command.

"Let's go."

Hyŏnjun pulled gently on the lever.

"Whoosh . . ." Amid puffs of steam, the strong arms of the pistons began to push the axles on the huge driving wheels, which slowly started to roll forward. Soon the pebbles on the ground between the railway tracks were flowing by, and the mountains on the far side began hesitantly to move. The speedometer needle gradually pushed higher and higher until it hovered around forty kilometers. The small distance signposts, placed at intervals of two hundred meters alongside the tracks, flitted past like spots, dizzying the eyes. At this speed it would take only around ten minutes to reach S Station.

All the scenery looked familiar to Hyŏnjun, who rested his elbow on the window as he looked out. The blackened remains

4 "From now on you need to understand under whose sky you are working if you want to survive," Kang translated once more.

of villages appeared burned beyond recognition by the bastards' bombs. Even the mountains revealed the scarred remnants of fire here and there. Yet, despite this, these were the same mountains of the past, and the pure water of the mountain river would still be flowing around the following bend. Clusters of mountain strawberries grew in the woods along the banks of that river. Each time Hyŏnjun saw the masses of ripe red strawberries he thought of his son Poksŏk. He had no idea where Poksŏk was now. The season for strawberries was on the wane, too, and they were nowhere to be seen. In their place grew a plain of yellow wild chrysanthemums. An armed soldier guarding the railway suddenly flashed past; he was standing in the middle of the flowers, trampling them down.

While he looked out the window, the sudden sound of the word "partisan" made Hyŏnjun pay attention to the dwarf and Kang's chatter.

"So the accident on the tracks was the partisans, eh? Mm, so they've reached this far? Ha."

"Well, things like this can happen as we go along. But the decisive rout has begun, so there won't be any further problems."

Hyŏnjun had been listening in to their conversation, but he now interrupted the fireman by pulling at his sleeve and pointing to the furnace to tell him to shovel some more coal. The fireman seemed to have no intention of adding more coal because the train would soon be arriving at S Station. Hyŏnjun, however, needed much more steam.

"*Ha-i, hai.*"

The dwarf sounded more than a little irritated by the engineer's order but began shoveling nevertheless. Hyŏnjun now pictured to himself the dwarf's movements a few minutes from now: how the dwarf would run toward him and how he himself would resist.

In no time at all, the shining red and green glass balls of the safety lights came into view, hung high over the entrance to S Station.

"We're here!"

Kang mumbled, as if he had been on a tedious journey; he must also have been looking outside and now stifled a yawn, dropping his cigarette butt as he stretched his fingers. At his side, the American MP brushed away the ash and coal dust that had settled on his shoulders and chest before exhaling his cigarette smoke along with it and blowing the dust from his gun holster.

The safety lights that Hyŏnjun had been watching seemed to graze his eyes as they flashed past. The station came into view ahead. In front of the station was the long platform at which the train was to stop.

Hyŏnjun gently pulled on the lever, and then cranked it open. The skin surrounding his pursed lips trembled slightly. The needle on the speedometer had been hovering around forty, but now it shook, as if with convulsions, and jumped alarmingly up to sixty and then seventy. Bang went the sound of the American MP's round back, hitting the iron plate that formed the back wall of the car. Kang had been straightening his belt, but now he unwittingly grabbed hold of the MP's arm at the force of the jolt. The dwarf had already put down his shovel in expectation of their arrival and was standing with his hands on his waist, but now he hopped like a sparrow and spread his stumpy pigeon-toed legs in order to remain on his feet, swaying back and forth like a man with experience. A military policeman who had been holding the green and red stop and go signs and waiting for the train to stop at the end of the platform fell backward, apparently caught by the driving wheel.

"Stop, stop!"

The dwarf was the first to shout out in his own language.

"Why haven't we stopped?"

"Hey, STOP! STOP!"

Kang and the American MP both shouted at once. Hyŏnjun neither replied nor looked back but merely raised his elbow to block the bastards behind him from touching the lever, which he held in his hand.

The train headed into the wind. Embracing the wind, it raced forward. In an instant, the signs on the far side had rushed past. Now the station had been left behind.

"Why are we still moving? You bastard, stop the train," Kang shouted as he grabbed Hyŏnjun's shoulders and shook him.

"You're not going to stop?"

Hyŏnjun glanced back briefly; a smile sparkled in his eyes, cold enough to make anyone shudder, and he made no attempt to shake off the military policeman's hands.

"We're done for, MP *san*! If we continue like this, we'll either roll over or explode."

The dwarf screamed, but there was nothing he could do, even though he looked back and forth at the speedometer needle, which had now reached its peak, and the brake, which was next to the lever held in Hyŏnjun's far hand. Though he glared at it, the dwarf could not bring himself to touch the brake, for he knew all too well that at this high speed to pull on the brake and attempt an emergency stop without first closing the lever to reduce the speed would cause the train to leave the tracks and roll over.

"I'll shoot!"

". . . STOP . . . STOP STOP . . . STOP."

Of all the American MP's shouts, Hyŏnjun could only understand the word "stop," but he felt immediately the hot press of a blunt muzzle in his back. The bastards still will not shoot. They have not given up hope of living and do not have the courage to kill the engineer on the spot. But in the next instant the dwarf attacked like a dog trying to bite Hyŏnjun's hand, which retained its hold on the lever.

Hyŏnjun landed a well-planned kick in the vital parts of the dwarf's stumpy groin. When the dwarf had attacked, he had been in the midst of shouting, "Aah, on this steep slope . . . this is deliberate. You've done it on purpose! Murderer!"

Now the dwarf gasped as he was thrown into the air, before landing in front of the blazing furnace, where he rolled over, grasping his groin with both hands, eyes swiveling backward.

The train raced on until it finally entered a steep downhill descent. This was about two kilometers further on from S Station. The tiny white distance signposts, placed at two-hundred-meter intervals, were no longer individual floating spots but a string of beads flowing past.

The American MP grabbed Hyŏnjun's arm, which was holding onto the lever, and pulled himself up. The train would charge down the steep hill on its own strength regardless, so Hyŏnjun now let go of the lever, stood up, and glanced backward at the bastard's face while taking hold of the brake with his remaining free hand. Kang rushed forward to grab that arm. But Hyŏnjun did not try to pull on the brake just yet. By this time the train was no longer racing; it had begun to fly like a shooting star.

Both the American MP and Kang had grabbed Hyŏnjun's arms, but there was nothing they could do. Outside the window was a whirl, all things mixed up beyond distinction.

The sky, the mountains, the green pine trees, the red maples, black rocks, telegraph poles, those bastard guards, even the water of the mountain creeks . . . everything crushed together haphazardly, flowing past as in a whirlpool. Such a gale hit their faces that it took their breath away, as if it might blow away their ears along with their hair. The bastards' military hats had long since disappeared.

Hyŏnjun felt the American MP let go of his arm. For an instant there was a burning flash in his side. Gunshot! The smell of gunpowder!

Hyŏnjun felt the energy drain from his whole body at once. His legs gently coupled, as if to sit down. Still he did not pull on

the brake, but instead he tried to endure and kept looking outside. He wrapped his fingers more firmly around the brake so
that were he to lose consciousness and collapse, the weight of his
body would pull on it. The bastard shot repeatedly into his back.[5]

For an instant, Hyŏnjun felt his upper body reel from the waist
up. But he knew that he was still conscious, and with his mouth
burning so badly he could almost smell the smoke, he barely
managed to whisper, "Just a few more seconds . . ."

He shook his head, now growing faint, and looked outside
again.[6] At last a section of the faded parapet of a tall iron bridge
leaped into his dimming eyes.

"This is it!"

Beneath a brow sticky with the sweat of exertion, Hyŏnjun's
pupils had dilated with his dimming consciousness, but a smile
still rose in his eyes. This was the bridge that Hyŏnjun had pictured to himself as the site for the decisive battle, as far back as
when he had closed the valve. And it was the bridge for which
he had waited, grinding his teeth to dust in order to endure the

---

5 With a bestial howl [the bastard shot repeatedly into his back].
   Although he let forth two rounds of fire, he didn't have the guts to hit
   Hyŏnjun directly in his vital parts, because killing the engineer
   would mean giving up on his own fate for good.

6 While this fight to the death was taking place, an uproar broke out
   inside the carriages pulled by the engine. All of the windows and
   doors on the freight and passenger cars burst open. What kind of
   speed was this? Faces thrust themselves outside the windows, almost
   breaking through the frames, and on those faces eyeballs popping
   out from the terror of staring into the void of imminent annihilation,
   and mouths frozen into a scream; and then, squashed between the
   faces, handguns and automatic weapons, clutched by hands, discharged
   their warning fire. Those hands and guns, poking out like the spikes
   of a startled hedgehog, their gunshot and gunpowder! And those ugly
   faces, screaming with despair, plastered all over the fourteen cars of
   the bastards' winding military train, which was now hurtling forward
   at terrifying speed toward the void of annihilation, driven by our
   engineer Hyŏnjun.

hot blood spurting from his back for these past four or five seconds.

Hyŏnjun pulled on the brake. Or rather, he pushed down with the weight of his body.

This was the moment.[7] The brakes pressed down on the wheels of the engine car. The force of racing along at such high speed caused the train to slide for a while; there was a terrible noise and sparks shot up from the wheels that were grinding on the rails, flaring up into the sky in the shape of a cypress broom.

The cars behind still raced along at high speed and pressed into the tail of the sliding locomotive, which lifted its head and stood up stiff, still holding onto its driving wheels, like an angry devil fiercely lifting its legs in defeat. The instant it rose, it twisted from the impact of the cars slamming into it one after another.

"That's it! Now those bastards will get what they deserve," said Hyŏnjun as he looked back.

The American MP held onto his gun, which was still blooming gunpowder smoke, but his eyes had already frozen over like those of a fish in a freezer, cloudy from the terror of death.[8] A flying fireball had set fire to the hair of the collapsed dwarf.

At the moment of twisting, the locomotive began to break through the parapet on the towering iron bridge and seemed to fly through the air, drawing a huge semicircle like strands of a rainbow in the sky. The fourteen cars behind the engine crashed into each other, tail into tail, and flew up into the air, just like a dragon of legend—a black dragon with a surging black back at that—and then fell back down behind the posts of the iron bridge, which were more than twenty meters high.

The engine car thrust its nose down into the dry gravel on the far side and exploded, still standing on its head. Fire broke

7 [Sentence missing in 1952 version.]
8 Even Kang's scream had frozen, his gaping mouth revealing his uvula.

THE ENGINEER

out on the tender behind it. The stack of flames from the coal set fire to the mounds of bullets and shells that had poured out from the flattened wagons, and they began to explode like thunderbolts. The running gear on both sides was exposed, like the belly of a large centipede, and the wheels on the upturned cars spun through the air like lightning. Gun barrels from the machine guns and mortars flew out, scattered, and rolled around. Some of the cars had rammed straight into the car ahead of them. From those cars, rammed into each other like matches sliding into a matchbox, fragments of flesh and bone flew out through ripped walls and windows, blood spurted. Water bubbled up from the cars that were submerged in the river with only their roofs showing; blood had already dyed the water red.

Part of the parapet looked as if it had been sawn in half by a rough blade, and Hyŏnjun watched as the iron bridge collapsed and was swallowed up.

Hyŏnjun had been plucked from the inverted locomotive and fallen flat on his back on the gravel to one side, but now he opened his eyes. He saw before him the spectacular fruit of his victory.

As those eyes began to dim, he gazed up at the blue sky. It felt like the first time he had seen a sky so clear and high, so deep and blue. Shiny white puffs of cloud floated across that blue sky.[9]

---

9 [From this point, the 1952 version concludes as follows:]
"This sky is ours. No matter what you bastards try to do, this sky belongs to our fatherland."

After crying out loud, Hyŏnjun suddenly grew very tired, and his eyes began to close. Just then he heard the sound of something scratching around nearby. He lifted his head to see the MP, who had collapsed by his side, attempting to pull himself along through the gravel. Hyŏnjun reached for a nearby stone and tried to stand up. But his lower body would not obey, as if it were no longer his own body. Pushing down on his elbows with all his remaining strength, he managed to lift his back off the ground, twisted his upper body, and threw the stone onto the MP's head, as if to ram his fist through it, and then he collapsed on top of the bastard.

Hyŏnjun grew very tired. As his eyes began to close, he seemed to remember something and barely managed to move an arm to feel the sleeve beneath one of his armpits. He felt something small but hard. It was his cherished party badge, which he had stitched in there. A smile of satisfaction and comfort flashed across Hyŏnjun's face and slowly froze there as he closed his eyes for the last time.

(May 1951)

Deep in a mountain valley, behind a small village about five ri from that iron bridge, a new grave was dug beneath a large oak tree. In front of that grave a neatly trimmed oak marker was inscribed in vivid ink with the words, "Workers Party Member Hyŏnjun."

When the Americans found out that their military train had been overturned, they had mobilized the local peasants and forced them to tidy up the scene.

At the sight of a solitary worker's uniform collapsed amid the enemy bodies after apparently fighting them until the very final moment, the peasants had realized that our engineer had sacrificed his own life in order to destroy thousands of the enemy by overturning their military train, and several peasants had returned secretly that night to extract Hyŏnjun's body and bury him safely in this spot. At the burial they discovered a party badge hidden away in the armpit of his worker's uniform, which they passed on to their local cell head, who had taken part in the partisan struggle at Yangdŏk, and then they had erected this grave marker.

(May 1951)

Young Kwŏn Tongsu

A sharp wind blew on the dark and dismal day.

Young Kwŏn Tongsu was walking down the street, his head tucked down to ward against the cold wind piercing his collar, his chest wrapped in his arms to try to avoid the drifting snowflakes. He stopped to look up.

He was standing in front of the enormous intersection at Sŏngyori. A fountain had once stood here in the center of a tidy stretch of lawn, and on clear days beautiful rainbows arced the wide expanse of road, painted in the air. There was no trace now of any fountain; even the rows of houses, which used to line the road at the far end of the beautiful rainbows, were nowhere to be seen. Here and there a chimney poked up alongside the wide stretch of asphalt that encircled the intersection, but only the foundations remained of the ruined houses, making it hard to recall what building had stood where. Nearly all of the houses on the once bustling street had collapsed under the merciless enemy bombardment and now barely a single house remained intact. Houses whose walls were still standing but whose roofs had flown away, their bare rafters and crossbeams reduced to charcoal all that remained from pieces of wood that had once measured more than an armful in circumference; houses that looked down onto the deserted street through empty window frames in their remaining roofs and walls without a single pane of glass, dark and deeply receding like eye sockets missing eyeballs; houses that had survived intact only by dint of being small and low and squeezed between much larger buildings, but whose doors were boarded up, devoid of any sign of life—the once bustling street was now deserted and lying in ruins. Only the wind roamed about, chasing snowflakes and licking the ground. Any remaining movement belonged to the trucks and jeeps driven by those bastard Americans and National Defense Force soldiers. It was forlorn. And it was brutal.

Young Kwŏn Tongsu had walked solitarily up one side of the wide street and now muttered to himself, "Why have I come this far?" He had no particular purpose; he had stepped out into the cold air in an attempt to calm a restless feeling, and his feet had carried him all of ten ri to this neighborhood before he realized it. If there were any particular reason, it was simply that he had been born here in Pyongyang and lived here all sixteen years of his life. Both the house which he had called home until just one month ago and the place where he had worked until several months before that had stood here in Sŏngyori. Now there was nothing left. Neither his home nor his workplace remained. Not his older brother or older sister, not his mother, not even he himself could stay here anymore.

His elder brother, Kwŏn Kil, had been a cell leader in the engine room of a grain factory and had disappeared without a trace after volunteering for the People's Army as soon as war had broken out. The whereabouts of his elder sister, Kwŏn Kŭmju, were also unknown; she had led the Workers Federation in a state-run rubber factory but had been dragged away by the so-called police just days after the occupation of Pyongyang began.

According to those thugs, as a cell leader who had joined the People's Army, Kwŏn Kil must be a Red, and Kwŏn Kŭmju, being a Workers Federation leader and a woman at that, must also be a Red, and so the mother who had given birth to them and the younger brother whose eldest siblings were both Reds must themselves surely be Reds; and they were both subjected to a merciless beating as a result. But that was not all. The bastards had then taken possession of the house in which young Kwŏn Tongsu lived together with his elderly mother.

Among their neighbors was an evil reactionary named Kim Inhwan, who had been appointed president of the neighborhood association when the bastards took over the city of Pyongyang; once he was president he had committed all manner of violent acts, swearing that no Red family would be allowed to stay in the neighborhood, and then he had subjected this mother and son to various forms of harassment before calling in the police. Finally, mother and son had been beaten and driven out of the neighborhood.

Having been chased out, the young boy and his elderly mother had no choice but to borrow a room in a relative's house located ten ri outside the city.

What with the sudden loss of her daughter, followed by that of her home and possessions, and still suffering the injurious effects of a vicious whipping, the elderly mother had taken to bed. Young Kwŏn Tongsu had been nursing his mother for almost a month now, and on this day he had taken advantage of her finally falling asleep in daylight hours to go outside for some fresh air.

From his first step beyond the entrance to the village he could clearly see Pyongyang in the distance and had forged a path from the initial hut-lined street to the next house and then on to the next, gradually savoring the joy of seeing his hometown again until he discovered he had walked this far. Upon arrival, though, he had felt pitifully lonely; he was also freezing cold.

Then all of a sudden he heard the sound of a clock striking somewhere. The street happened to be empty, with no enemy jeeps or trucks passing by, and his ears naturally gravitated toward the chimes, which must be coming from inside one of the houses.

"One, two, three . . . three o'clock!"

He counted to himself.

"Three o'clock! Oh, it must be three o'clock in the afternoon!"

He repeated the phrase to himself and looked up, a spontaneous smile spreading across his face, as if he were glad to meet someone. An enormous electric clock, which had hung high up in the center of the broad, white wall of the coiling room in the state-run sock factory, now hovered before his eyes.

The electric clock had been silent. But the factory workers whose job it was to disentangle and wind the thread, young Kwŏn Tongsu among them, knew exactly what the time was without even having to look up at the electric clock in the room. The young boy could tell the time almost as accurately as that clock just by counting the number of spools he had already wound and the thickness of the thread on the spool then spinning on his machine.

The "three o'clock in the afternoon," which young Kwŏn Tongsu had synchronized with the time of the clock, had been the tensest yet most interesting part of his workday. A mere hour had passed since lunchtime, when he had been able to ease some of his fatigue from the morning and gather up new energy, while a couple of hours still remained before the end of the workday. Those remaining two hours would determine the parameters of the day. From the moment that the trusty hour hand on the handsome clock face hit the fat numeral three, tension would build; the workers were approaching the hundred percent mark of the workshop's planned quota for the day, and then the fun would begin. How far above the quota could they go? How proud of their excess production rate would they be feeling on the walk home? "Three o'clock" brought the greatest joy, and the utmost feeling of urgency, to young Kwǒn Tongsu's work in the factory. Shouldn't such memories remind him just how cozy his factory had once been?

Instead those memories merely made young Kwǒn Tongsu quiver and feel the biting chill even more, as if he had never once found himself in the cold outside the freezing factory at three o'clock in the afternoon. And wasn't it, in fact, true? He had never before wandered these streets at this time of a day in such a solitary fashion and with no purpose. This was the case not only for him but also for the more than one hundred comrades who had once worked alongside him in the factory, where several hundred spinning machines had never ceased their turning and thousands, tens of thousands, of threads were in the process of being coiled and wound every day.

The factory where he had once enjoyed working at the heart of such joyful tension! Right now, young Kwǒn Tongsu's yearning for that place was extraordinarily strong. The building had long since been badly damaged by the enemy bombardments, and when the Americans showed up the machines had been destroyed as well. Yet, even if the factory were empty, he still felt an urge to go and see it. He turned into a back alley, realizing that at this moment his desire to see the factory was more urgent than his longing for the house out of which they had been chased and which now housed new occupants.

In the back alleys, more houses seemed to be inhabited than along the wide road. There were even some small shops open, a sight not to be found on the main street. The sight of those small shops prompted young Kwǒn Tongsu rather suddenly to realize he should be avoiding this particular alley. At the far end the alley was sliced off by the intersection, and the first house over the crossing contained a small shop run by the evil Kim Inhwan. Kim Inhwan hardly ever seemed to be sat keeping watch over his shop, however. He had moved to this neighborhood only after being chased out of some rural village at the time of the land reform, when he had been accused of being an evil land-lord, and yet he had never abandoned his habit of living off others while sitting around on his hands; having bought a small shop for his concubine, he failed to take care of it, because he stayed up all night drinking and slept throughout the day. Young Kwŏn knew all of this, but he was still afraid of the violence that might be inflicted upon him if he were to come across that thug. It was all the more unfortunate, then, that he decided to deliberately avoid this street and enter an alleyway to one side.

He was walking down the narrow alleyway, alongside the wall of some house, when he turned a corner and was startled to find himself face to face with the bastard Kim, urinating while standing at the side of two very drunk National Defense Force soldiers.

"Well, well, isn't it that Red bastard?"

They were first to recognize him. All the more unfortunately for young Kwŏn, Kim was not alone. Kwŏn still thought he could make an escape and swiftly turned on his feet to run away.

"That bastard's a Red! Catch him!"

Kim's harsh voice reverberated.

"A Red?"

A stinging sensation in his left shoulder followed swiftly upon these words, and Kwŏn tumbled forward in the same instant that a gunshot resounded throughout the narrow alley.

"Hey, you bastard . . ."

Kim came running up and dragged young Kwŏn onto his feet, encircling his throat with his hands. This brought young Kwŏn back to his senses, and he groped the front of his shoulder. Warm blood was rushing down through his sleeve and over his hands before dropping down onto his toes.

"What are you doing here? You little bastard, did you finally come back to see what happened to your house?"

Kim slapped young Kwŏn on the cheek. Kwŏn clenched his fists with all his might. He could feel the strength in each fist.

He was buoyed by the thought that he could not be seriously injured, even though his shoulder throbbed with pain inside his drenched sleeve, and he gritted his teeth.

What should I do with this thug? Should I butt him in the nose and make a run for it?

For a moment, young Kwŏn felt the urge to do just that. But the National Defense Force soldier stood at Kim's side was stroking his moustache with the tip of his gun, as if to savor the scent of freshly fired gunpowder, and now he stared at young Kwŏn through dark glasses.

In the end they dragged Kwŏn away to a building located just behind them, which had once been used as a warehouse office. The interior was packed full of American MPs and National Defense Force soldiers. No sooner had he been dragged into the building than he was set upon twice over. The first beating was on account of his being a Red; the second, they said, was to demonstrate what would happen if he were to fail to submit.

His entire body bloodied and bruised from the relentless beatings, Kwŏn looked as if he had been drenched in ink. Blood poured from his nose, and one eye was so swollen he could not see. When they judged him half dead, they threw him into a room where some odd-job workers were sitting around.

When he finally regained consciousness, he had no idea where he was. He struggled to open his less swollen eye but could see no more than a dim light. What kind of room was this? From feeling around with his hands, he discovered that the floor was concrete, ice-cold. Where was he? He tried to lift his head in order to see more.

"Looks as if he's coming around at last."

A voice sounded above his head and was succeeded by the tickling sensation of a long beard on his burning cheeks. Finally an old man's face appeared.

"Who are you?"

A startled young Kwŏn attempted to speak out loud, but a tiny, mosquito-like whine was all that penetrated the phlegm stuck in his throat.

"All in good time . . . why don't you try to drink some water first?"

This voice was different. Kwŏn nodded. The old man held a cup of water to Kwŏn's mouth with great concentration. After a few sips young Kwŏn was finally able to raise his head a little to look around and discovered four old men sitting beside him where he lay. As for the room, he could see the concrete floor, which he had only felt before, and he could see that he was lying in one corner on top of a pile of two or three straw bags. The walls and the ceiling, from which a dim light hung, were all made from wooden planks. This was not a proper room. As his mind gradually regained some clarity, he began to recall being dragged to this place, and he wondered whether this was some kind of shed attached to the larger warehouse.

"Who are all of you grandpas?"

After asking just this one question, young Kwŏn dropped his head back to lay down again. Before they answered, he realized that his head was being supported in one of the old men's laps and not by a pillow, not even a wooden pillow. At the thought that these old men must have laid him down and supported and nursed him from the time he had been dragged in here unconscious, tears gathered in his eyes, and he could not refrain from sobbing.

"Oh dear, don't cry, what's to gain from crying . . ."

This was the old man who was still holding the cup of water from which Kwŏn had drunk.

"Old folk like us, we look to our young people and believe in them. . . . This is no good."

This was the old man who cradled young Kwŏn's head in his lap. Young Kwŏn could not help but shed even more tears upon hearing his words.

"Now what young man would not feel like that when they've been beaten into the shape of you!"

This old man bit his tongue as he spoke.

"No, grandpa, it's not that."

Young Kwŏn struggled to speak through his tears.

"I'm not crying because it hurts. And I'm not crying because I miss home."

He just managed to stifle his sobs enough to roughly explain his family's situation and how he came to be captured and dragged into this place.

The old men gave the boy something to eat, even though all they had was cold rice, and told him their own stories. All four of them were of a similar age, approaching sixty. Three of them were peasants who came from a place called Kujang. They had heard a rumor that their sons, who had all joined up with the People's Army, were somewhere in Sariwŏn, and they had set off at the beginning of October to try to find them without success, only to be caught on their way back home by the Americans. The fourth old man lived in Pyongyang but had traveled as far as Haeju before being caught and brought in under similar circumstances.

Kwŏn had been brought to a prisoner of war camp which held soldiers from our People's Army who had been injured on either of the frontlines. The bastards were now forcing these old men to work for the camp under the pretext of calling them odd job men.

On the following morning, young Kwŏn helped the four old men carry food into the imprisoned People's Army soldiers. The old men had begun preparing breakfast as soon as the light began to dawn in the east. They arranged cooked barley by fistfuls on wooden trays. When the MP bastards opened the doors to the warehouse, young Kwŏn stepped inside for the first time and was immediately overwhelmed by the fetid smell; hearing the groans and witnessing the appalling state of the prisoners made him feel dizzy. The interior of the warehouse was wide and dimly lit; a corridor ran down the center and iron bars divided the space to each side, which was packed full of injured soldiers.

Who knows when their bandages had last been changed? Most of the arms, legs, and heads were swathed in bandages that had hardened from oozing blood. But many soldiers had no bandages at all to speak of; their wounds were simply exposed, oozing blood and pus. Without exception they were barely dressed despite the winter cold. Barefoot on a cement floor, which differed little from an ice sheet. Faces had shriveled, clinging to skulls . . . yet somehow those faces were still swollen and sallow, as if yellowish fluid might gush out were the skin to break . . . groans and screams merged into a deafening racket . . .

Young Kwŏn felt as if he was looking at the kind of living hell he had only heard about in stories.

Meals were served twice a day, in the morning and evening, but consisted of no more than a lump of barley smaller than a fist, with a few grains of salt on the side.

Removing the corpses of those who had died during the night was the first order of things after breakfast, while the corpses of those who had died during the day had to be carried out after dinner.

That evening young Kwŏn cried all night, unable to sleep. His heart felt as if it would explode, and not even wailing and punching the floor with his fists seemed likely to bring any relief. Not that he was free to wail out loud. The old men, too, cried in the silence.

"I would give up this old life in an instant, if it meant saving even one or two of our young people . . ."

This was the bearded old man's lament, the one who had the night before said, "We look to our young people and believe in them."

"That's the least we can do. When I think that our children have joined the same People's Army, I can hardly bear to stand by and watch."

"If we could only take their place, I would happily die ten times over with no regrets!"

"Who else in the world would value our lives so little?"

"Isn't that why they are the enemy?"

"Bastard enemies . . . grinding their bones and eating them up wouldn't be enough to make me feel better."

"Stop . . . what's the point of living like this . . ."

The old men sighed bitterly. Then they discussed whether it might be possible to rescue some of our soldier comrades. But the discussion trailed off when the subject arose of the thirty American MPs and sixty so-called National Force soldiers guarding the prison and how altogether these ninety thugs were taking turns on patrol, rifles slung over their shoulders.

"But grandpas . . ."

Young Kwŏn had been listening and now spoke up.

"What about the doors? The main door to the warehouse and the doors to the cells can't be opened from the inside, but they're not very strong and would open from the outside if the bolt is taken out."

"You're right. We've been wondering about that too, but even if we could get people out, there's still the problem of what to do next."

For young Kwŏn, at least, the mere fact that it would not be difficult to open the door to the warehouse, where the prisoners were locked up, raised the hope that the next step would not be impossible to find.

The following morning, as soon as he had finished carrying breakfast into the prisoners, Kwŏn had to take breakfast to the guards manning the office just inside the front gate. The old men also prepared their food.

After loading the wooden tray with several bowls, he was walking past the warehouse when he suddenly slipped and landed on his buttocks, all the while managing to keep a hold of the tray. Even though he did not lose his grip, several breakfast bowls dropped to the ground. He hurriedly retrieved them, only to find that some dirt had made its way into the food. It never occurred to him to fetch new bowls of rice like a devoted servant. Instead, he picked the dirt out with his fingers right there and then and tried to cover up the resulting holes by adding a bit more rice from the other bowls. He then delivered the rice, along with bowls of soup and side dishes. No sooner had one of the bastards gulped down his soup and swallowed a first spoonful of rice than he spat it out onto the table, gave it a probing prod, and then rushed over to young Kwŏn, slapped his cheeks, and lifted him up by his ears.

"You Red bastard! So you've poisoned our food? I'm going to kill you!"

The charge was false, though it was true that some dirt had made its way into their rice.

"Poison?"

"Poison in the rice?"

The thugs around the table all hovered over the regurgitated rice in an uproar.

"Kill the Red bastard!"

"Let's do away with him right here and now."

Incensed by their anger, they weighed in on him with their boots, kicking and stamping, easily subduing him, as if seizing a precious opportunity to vent their cruelty. The old men were taken aback by the commotion and came running to the front of the office. But they all stopped outside the door, not knowing what to do. Until finally, the old man with the beard carefully stepped inside, picked up the bowl of rice, which the bastards all swore was poisoned, and began to silently eat a few spoonfuls.

At this the thugs set upon the old man too, hitting and kicking him. Yet they had lost their excuse for shooting young Kwŏn on the spot and had no choice, they said, but to postpone that to a later date.

Later that evening the old men begged young Kwŏn to run away.

"We're old men, we've lived our lives, and if we die we've few regrets, but a young man like you, why are you waiting around for those bastards to kill you?"

"We can stay here and repay our life's debt by trying to get even the tiniest extra drop of water to our People's Army soldiers in the prison here, but a young lad like you, you must get out of here."

"But if I ran away, wouldn't they kill you grandpas for letting me go?"

Young Kwŏn's eyes widened with his response. The bastards had threatened everyone in and around the camp that if any one of them were to escape, those left behind would all have to take responsibility and die.

"But that's what we've been saying, isn't it? No one will miss old men like us. . . . If we could get even one or two of our young people out of here, then we don't mind dying . . ."

It was the old man with the beard who explained their feelings the most directly.

"I understand what you are saying grandpas. But if there is a way to get out, where is it? And if that way exists, then shouldn't all of you, and our comrades in prison here, come with me?"

He was sat in front of the sighing old men, but all the while he was speaking, in his head young Kwŏn was walking around the steel fence that surrounded the warehouse. He could not see any gap through which they might escape, not in the entire fence beside which the guards stood holding rifles at two- or three-meter intervals.

"Even if we can't all get out, you at least could. If an opportunity arises, even if it's only for you, then you must choose to live."

The old man with the beard seemed alone in his thoughts for a while before nodding and speaking in an even more urgent tone, as if to command Kwŏn.

"Don't argue, just do as I say."

The following evening, a drinking party had carried over from daytime and was still in full flow in the office at the main entrance, when one of the drunken bastards peered out into the backyard and shouted harshly for someone to go buy some cigarettes. His order was not aimed at any one particular person. But the old man with a beard replied immediately before standing up with a tug on young Kwŏn's sleeve.

The bastards would send the old men on such errands quite frequently. And this opened up an opportunity for escape. Fearing that revenge would be wreaked on those left behind, the old men had never once thought of saving themselves but had always returned to the camp. The bastards had such faith in their control that this time too they simply threw some money down outside the door without any particular sign of concern.

The old man who had grabbed hold of young Kwŏn's sleeve picked up the money and placed it in the young boy's hand, while speaking loud enough to ensure that the guards at the gate heard him.

"Cigarettes, you say?"

He pushed young Kwŏn in the back, propelling him out the gate while he himself turned around to go back inside.

Young Kwŏn did not have the chance to utter even one word, but simply bade the old man's back farewell with eyes suddenly bathed in tears. After turning into a side alley out of sight of the guards, he hesitated for a moment and then began to run in the direction of the Taedong River. He could not be sure they would not come looking for him, which made it too dangerous to go to the village where his mother was staying. He thought it better to cross over the Taedong River either on one of the wooden bridges or by boat and enter the main city of Pyongyang. He was running along the riverbank path when the sight of water gushing out of an enormous sewer in the slope of the opposite bank, close to Ryŏngwang Pavilion, stopped him in his tracks.

"Of course!" As if he had suddenly recalled something long forgotten, he jumped up in the air on the spot before turning around and retracing his steps at high speed. Along the way he managed to pick up some cigarettes at a small store, and then raced back into the camp.

When they saw young Kwŏn return, the old men leaped up in surprise. The old man with the beard took the pack of cigarettes, unable to hide his sadness.

"Do you really think that you're helping us by caring so much for our lives? By coming back here, where you're bound to die? You've made a mistake. Yes, a big, big mistake."

But young Kwŏn simply waved him away, as if he didn't have time to listen to a reprimand, and ran toward the back of the warehouse.

So that was it. He was happy to see that his memory had been correct. In the exact spot where he had slipped up while carrying the breakfast the day before he found a large cast iron lid, which covered a hole leading into the sewer system.

When he saw the sewer opening in the riverbank, he had suddenly remembered slipping on this manhole cover; if they could just escape through this hole into the sewer below, then they would be able to make it all the way to the Taedong River.

That evening young Kwŏn shared his thoughts with the old men, and together they decided that he would go down through the manhole alone at first and see if he could reach the Taedong River. When they heard his story, the old men realized that he had sacrificed his long-awaited chance to save himself and returned to them as soon as he thought he might have discovered a path through which all the imprisoned soldiers could escape.

He waited for the bastards to go to sleep for the night and then worked together with the old men to open the frozen manhole cover; they had to all but melt it with their own breath and the warmth of their bodies. Kwŏn then took a candle and the matches they used in the kitchen and climbed down into the sewer. Using the candle to light his way, he descended into the dark cement pipes, buried deep in the ground, and walked along following the water's current. The water was not too deep, perhaps because it was winter. In the deepest places, it rose just above his knees. And it was not as cold as he had expected, perhaps because he was so far underground. The further he progressed through the dark pipes, the fewer the number of pipes joined in from the sides; instead the main pipe expanded in size enough that he could finally straighten his back. After walking for about twenty minutes, he rounded a bend and suddenly, a wave of cold, fresh air hit and the candle in his hand flickered. He immediately blew the candle to extinguish it and stepped forward, feeling his way with his hands. Eventually, a cold wind grazed his face. The water, which had been flowing past his shins, now fell into something like a small waterfall, and at its foot, right in front of his eyes, there appeared the Taedong River with two or three stars reflected in its waters. The slope leading down to the surface of the water was not too steep, and there were no houses visible in the surrounding area. Relighting his candle, young Kwŏn began his return journey and even discovered some pipes leading off to the side where the water level was low; in the event that the prisoners were not all able to escape out onto the riverbank during the course of a single night, they would be able to sit in these side pipes and wait for darkness to fall the following evening.

The old men had closed the cover again for fear it might attract the thugs' attention, but they took turns waiting beside the iron manhole cover for Kwŏn to return, and when he did finally appear they felt even more confident after hearing what he had to say.

The following evening the old men fetched extra rice to cook while the bastards were asleep. Young Kwŏn carried the cooked rice down into the sewer. Because our soldier comrades had been starved, these preparations would ensure that as soon as the prisoners entered the sewer they would be able to fill their stomachs and gather the energy necessary for their flight.

The next day was the third of December. Our People's Army was on the counterattack, and the sound of gunfire was drawing ever closer. The bastards were rushing around preparing to flee. Everyone was distracted by their own preparations to escape the camp—both the American MPs, who were acting as guards, and the military police from the so-called National Defense Force. Young Kwŏn and the four old men were so overjoyed at the sight that they could hardly stop themselves from bursting into cheers right there and then. At the same time they felt a growing anxiety. The bastards were clearly preparing their trucks so as not to flee alone and were most likely planning to drag our captured comrades along with them. If the opportunity to escape through the sewer were to be missed, who knows where the soldiers would be taken and how they would be disposed of.

The situation had turned even more urgent and the next day harder to predict; the old men and young Kwŏn decided to execute their plans that same evening, even though they had wanted to prepare more food supplies.

With our People's Army on the counterattack, the bastards were on the run, and surveillance had grown even more severe in the midst of the confusion. Even more guards than usual had been posted along the wire fence. To cap it all, the thugs were so upset and excited that they were still babbling on and rushing around way past their usual bedtime. Yet their angry watch focused mostly on the boundaries of the prison camp. They appeared to be paying scant attention to what was going on inside the camp, having most likely calculated there was little threat, what with doors that could not be opened from inside the cells and the presence on the outside of only a few old men, more than sixty years old, plus the young boy the old men so adored. But young Kwŏn and the four old men were still anxious about their plans. It felt like a waste of their time to have to wait for the bastards to sleep.

At last Kwŏn went into the warehouse and began to tell the imprisoned comrades about the night's plans for a great escape, taking hold of them one by one and whispering into their ears. More than one hundred and fifty comrades heard the boy's words, unable to burst into shouts of joy but equally unable to hold back their tears while they grasped his hands. They even decided upon the order by which the stronger ones would carry out their weaker comrades.

By dawn on the following morning, the bastards' fate had suddenly taken an even more desperate turn when the advancement of our People's Army became reality. They brought their trucks out with the plan to drag our soldier comrades away with them in flight. But the doors to the warehouse had already been opened and more than one hundred and fifty prisoners had disappeared without a trace. The thugs' eyes turned inside out, and an urgent search party was dispatched to examine the entire area surrounding the warehouse.

Nobody knew that underground, beneath the cast iron manhole cover over which their feet trampled during their search, young Kwŏn was lighting the way ahead with a candle and leading a procession of our soldier comrades.

Voices of the Ancestral Land

Four or five days had passed since we crossed the Ch'ŏngch'ŏn River.

At the sight of rich autumn colors reflected in the river's crystal-clear waters, the hometown we had left behind suddenly felt even more distant. Across the river, in the hills beyond the far bank, the autumn foliage had advanced still further.

As we continued our journey north, the mountains surrounding us on all sides were bedecked in even deeper and more resplendent colors. Yet, in the midst of such beautiful scenery, all we could think about was how to push forward as quickly as possible.

Our procession was shaped by files of People's Army soldiers, accompanied by men and women, old and young, either carrying or pulling along increasingly soiled bundles of belongings on an endless walk through day and night; we really were the wandering vagabonds described by the saying, "Men shoulder weight, while women bear it on their heads. . . ." Age and sex were not the only distinctions among us; all kinds of people had joined this flow of one immense congregation.

Whether from Pyongyang or Wŏnsan, Seoul or Ch'unch'ŏn, Taegu or Chinju, or much farther away in the deep south, we all moved as one in the same direction. There were even, from some farm or other, some herders of dozens of milking cows, their swollen udders swaying between their legs as they retreated. Not a single drop of milk or bite of meat was to be left behind for the enemy, who were chasing behind us.

We were approaching yet another bend in the ravine we had entered. A cliff appeared to block the path, as if its precipice had taken a step into the water, which skirted the road; and then, just as it seemed a new landscape would open up, as if one more panel of a vividly colored screen would unfold, suddenly the shouts went up, "Airplane! Airplane!" Enemy aircraft. Across the river, the mountain peak receded more deeply than elsewhere in this ravine, rising behind a wide riverbank strewn with large pebbles, and thus opening up a line of sight, which now revealed two jet airplanes flying in over the mountains like arrows shot from a bow, followed by a twin-engine bomber trailing in their wake.

Flanked by the river on one side and the precipitous cliff on the other, the sliver of new road offered no avenue for escape. People were caught unawares by the surprise attack and could do no more than attempt to cover themselves in the folds of the cliff or any indentations at its foot. There were a lot of people. Those for whom this was not the first terrifying strike they had faced on the journey so far vanished from the road instantly, leaving not even a shadow to linger. But the clamor of others remained, shouting to each other, "What's that? Who's that?" Even those cries did not last for long. Bratatat tat, bang, bang . . . the instant the sound of the machine guns rang out, slicing lines through the air, even the bubbling rapids seemed to still.

Bullets bounced in all directions, white lines crisscrossed, like sprinkled lime powder over the surfaces of black rocks where people had forced themselves into even the tiniest gaps they could find. This was not somewhere an anti-aircraft gun would be at the ready, and the bastards could let rip as they liked. The jet planes took turns racing backward and forward beside the cliff face, firing their machine guns and flying so low that even the smoke from their tails shook to the roots the stunted trees pushing up through the rocks and ruffled the hair of the people squashed into the crevices below. Bullets blasted holes in coattails that could not be wrapped tightly enough around knees and rained down in front of noses, discharging scalding hot smoke and blasting dirt from the ground into faces. Sparks of lightning pierced eyelids, so that people tried to bury their eyes in the ground. And with each strike, the ground on which everyone huddled convulsed and shook, forcing rock fragments smashed by the shells to cascade down the cliff in landslides.

For one moment, the jets had either flown off across the way or separated to the right and the left; I gently shook the shoulders of my wife, who had fallen in a huddle at my side. I was worried that the cascade of falling rocks might have struck her on the head.

"Are you hurt?"

"No."

She opened her eyes and asked me in turn, "You?"

She was worried I was hurt.

"We'll survive somehow."

The nonreply all but slipped from my mouth. As long as the enemy was pursuing us and trying so tenaciously to kill us, we would have to be equally tenacious in order to survive, if only to wreak our revenge in the end.

Searing hot smoke ascended from the wake of explosive wind funnels driven in by the murderous wings. The mountain before us had transformed into a sea of fire. The bombers had circled its waist, drenching it in jellied gasoline, and then dropped incendiary bombs from the sky. The flames had already licked up the autumn foliage in the valley and reduced even roots to ashes higher up the mountain; and then, far out on the cliff edges too, the small trees had been set alight by boiling oil from rocket fire.

Once the jets had retreated, the cries and shouts began, interspersed with much distraught calling of names broken up by sobs. Blood still poured from some bodies. People reappeared on the road.

Not long afterward, a shot reverberated at the side of the road. A moment later, a crow flew past, propelled by the inertia of flight until its greedy, stubby beak smashed into the cliff face and the bird dropped to the ground.

At the foot of the cliff the roadside was a riverbank, built up by large pebbles and an occasional protruding rock, sharpened by the mountain rapids. An officer perched on one of those rocks. From behind his silhouette created a dignified impression, enhanced by the shape of the rock. One arm rested on his stomach, wrapped in a white towel, which he appeared to be using as a bandage.

A flock of crows had flown in over the burning mountain and momentarily changed direction, startled by the sound of gunshots, before coming in to land again after circling only once; their squawking seemed designed to control mouths filling with saliva, induced by the scent of blood.

The officer was still sitting neatly on the rock, one arm hanging down with a pistol in his hand wafting smoke, when he took another shot. One more of the black pests fell from the sky and splashed into the river, which was flowing past at the officer's feet. I shared his disdain for such creatures that customarily gather at the slightest whiff of blood on a corpse.

Together with my wife, I waited for the officer to stand up in the hope of walking along beside him.

At first, he walked so silently that I did not dare attempt any conversation.

"Officer, how far south did you reach?"

I finally ventured this question, which provoked a sharp glance.

"Me?"

His reply, following upon much thought, was rather vague.

"We made it close to the Naktong River."

He lowered his head again.

After some hesitation, I tried a different question.

"Could you tell us a bit about our comrades and their bravery?"

I didn't just want somebody to talk to; I really wanted to hear about the experiences of those comrades who were actually fighting on the frontline. But this officer merely lifted his face to look at me before lowering his head yet again. After a few more steps, a low voice broke his silence.

"We can tell those stories when we've won."

I lost all courage to ask further. And so we walked along beside each other without speaking for a while. And then suddenly, the officer again interrupted the silence.

"It must be very hard for you."

I wondered whether these unexpected words had been provoked by the sight of the mountain before us covered in flames.

We had already rounded several more bends, but the same mountain fire that had been ignited by those enemy planes had spread this far. The pine trees only seemed fresh and green by their juxtaposition among all kinds of autumn leaves in various shades of yellow and red. We could almost hear the flames lick up the trees one by one, increasing our sense of urgency and the feeling that, in this ravine, we really were walking through a burning battlefield.

In these circumstances, the officer's words seemed doubly mature. He could not have been more than twenty-two or twenty-three years old, and his shoulders still displayed the traces of a recently unfolded officer's uniform, not yet faded by the sun and free of epaulettes.

At this point my wife took her chance to strike up a conversation with the young man.

"Oh, your son is one of our People's Army comrades!" He raised his thick eyelashes, and a smile of pure joy replaced the dark shadows that had hovered over his face until now. He seemed to appreciate a new dimension to this gray-haired couple, whom he looked at through eyes of clear black and white, threaded through with thin bloodshot lines. "Well, I really don't know."

My wife had ultimately ignored her promise to me and simply repeated her question when this warm-hearted young officer apologized for not being able to provide a satisfactory answer. That promise had been a vow to refrain from asking for news of our son each time we managed to speak with a member of the People's Army on our journey.

"And where is your home, officer?"

My wife asked another equally fraught question. She had promised not to ask this either. There was absolutely no need to dig into the background of people we were meeting for the first time on a journey like this.

"You mean my hometown?"

To our surprise, the young officer smiled a little awkwardly before uttering a simple response.

"We've already passed it."

"So, you didn't go home?"

"The war isn't over yet, is it? . . . We're marching behind the unit ahead of us."

Changing the subject somewhat, the young officer struck a match with his bandaged hand and lit a cigarette.

His words, which hinted that the enemy might be listening in even now as we retreated, seemed to exert a positive effect on my wife, who had been thinking more and more about home the further away we walked.

All this while we had been climbing a steep path, which finally ended in a crossroads, where we passed over the peak of the hill and could look down at a river.

This one was painted the rich cobalt color typical of a mountain river. Although it was only about twenty meters wide, the current was fast and deep and threaded its way down between wide riverbanks built up from white pebbles, bleached by the sun and polished by the strong floodwater torrents that must rush down during the rainy season and spring thaw each year.

At the ferry point, a carpet of polished white pebbles stretched into the distance, not a single blade of grass or shrub in sight. The area was soon bustling with people, who had climbed down from the hill behind. They all had to wait their turn for the ferry, which looked as rickety as a cow trough and could only hold around twenty people at one time. If the ferry looked rickety, the old ferryman's hands were equally rugged, and his face had sweated so profusely under the summer sun that it glistened like an enormous copper-colored moon in the water.

"Hey, don't all rush at once, if you're in such a hurry, you should've got here yesterday . . ."

His voice was as rough as he looked when he scolded the people, who were all jostling to push ahead of each other. Everyone was anxious at the thought of being caught in open space with nowhere to hide. When we were floating in the middle of the river on the ferry, the situation felt even more dangerous. And even once we had made it across the river, we still had to climb over the wide, flat riverbank and up a hilly path, as we had done to reach the ferry in the first place.

At a peak about one ri above the river, all of a sudden we heard a roar of gasps and footsteps running in our direction. Was this another attack? No. There were no enemy planes to be seen

VOICES OF THE ANCESTRAL LAND

267

or heard. But somehow violence seemed to hover in the air. From the distance, another roar reached our ears, like a wave crashing down over our backs. The noise came from the hill across the river. The people still waiting for the ferry on the far side had all turned around to stare at the hill behind them. Those who had just crossed the peak suddenly turned around to look behind as well. The roar seemed to be growing louder, as if approaching closer and closer.

Dust floated up from the dry path, like yellow smoke wafting over the hill. And then, from out of that dust figures emerged, struggling to run. They tumbled down toward the ferry landing in a landslide. From their cries and screams it was not long before their words crossed the river.

"It's the enemy!"

"The enemy?"

"Their reconnaissance troops, they've suddenly shown up."

"?"

"Now there'll be a fight with our People's Army."

The words circulated so rapidly it was hard to know who had first offered the explanation, who had asked the question, and who had provided the answer.

Could it be true? But before there was time to even think of finding out more, gunshots began to reverberate at regular intervals. The shots sounded fairly distant, from over the far side of the hill, but this was without any doubt the sound of the enemy's carbines. Not only their planes, but now their foot soldiers, too, had penetrated deep into the ravine. On the top of the hill on this side we all held our breath, silent, as if momentarily paralyzed by the sound of gunfire. We glanced at each other with eyes that seemed to ask, "What do we do now?"

"Comrades, please keep moving, quickly."

The young officer spoke. He was standing right next to me and had already begun to untie the towel, which was wrapped around his arm, so that he could remove his overcoat. The sleeve caught on his bandaged elbow and would not come free.

"What are you going to do?" I asked as I helped him remove his arm from the sleeve.

"I have to go now."

And with those words, our young officer rebandaged his injured arm with the towel and began to run toward the ferry landing. Several young men who had been standing by us followed quickly in his wake.

Down at the landing, the passengers who had just disembarked from the latest crossing started to scramble up the hill. The officer was running down against the current. He wanted to stop the boat before it set off back across the river. But the boat did not make any attempt to move again, even when all the passengers had left.

The old ferryman had stepped down onto the embankment and was holding the anchor cable, despite the crowd on the other side of the river all shouting out for the boat; he stood staring at the hill opposite, where landslides of people were cascading down the slopes one after another. The gunshots were gradually approaching from that direction.

"Send the boat over!"

"Why aren't you crossing the river?"

Those waiting for the ferry across the way were screaming, waving their fists, and stamping their feet to urge him on.

The old boatman was transfixed by the sight before him and did not move until we saw the young officer, who had run on ahead, lift the old man back up into the boat with a push in the back before reaching for the pole at the front of the boat and thrusting it toward the old man's chest.

By the time the other young men on the officer's tail had reached the landing, the bow of the boat had already been turned around. The boatman was now using his pole to push the boat off the bank. In the meantime I, too, somehow found myself standing down at the landing, as if pulled by some invisible tie toward our young officer.

"What are you doing here?"

The young officer seemed surprised to see a group of us and shouted.

"Anyone who isn't a soldier will get in the way. Comrades, please go back."

He helped the elderly boatman take hold of the oars. They chatted to each other while they rowed across the deep river waters, but as soon as they reached the opposite bank the young officer leaped off the boat and disappeared into the crowd of people in a flash.

The people on the bank had been waiting anxiously, and now they all rushed toward the boat at once. A moment later, the silhouette of the young officer we had last seen vanish into that wave of people reappeared on the middle slopes of the hill across the way. His revolver was gripped firmly in his hand. Behind him trailed seven or eight soldiers with rifles and automatic guns slung over their shoulders. Their small group was clearly visible as they climbed the hill against the current of people still cascading down the path.

I was so immersed in the scene that the sudden sound of heavy breathing from behind took me by surprise, and I turned around. Two more People's Army fighters had appeared, as if from nowhere, and were standing beside me. They looked more like adolescents than young men, but each carried an automatic rifle slung across his shoulder. They struck the exact same pose— arms folded in unison across the stomach and one foot stepped forward, as if their lineup had just received the order, "At ease!" They were calmly observing the proceedings before them. Despite this their eyes did not appear to be focused on anything in particular; in fact, they appeared to be deep in their own thoughts more than concentrating on their surroundings.

Across the river, the old boatman had taken to waving his pole in an attempt to stop the people swarming his boat, and we could hear his constant shouts.

"You'll turn the boat over . . ."

Gradually, those shouts grew louder and louder.

"I'm only doing this because I believe in our comrades in the People's Army. . . . Don't all rush at once . . ."

The two fighters did not relax their identical poses, but at each sound of the coarse old boatman's voice, a boyish smile flashed across the taut skin on their robust and clear, if a little gaunt, faces. Each slight smile highlighted the dimples rolling like tiny waves over the cheeks of the fighter beside me.

Simultaneously and seemingly unconsciously, while also seeming to follow some agreement between the two of them, they both exhaled a long and deep accumulated breath that had been building for a while. It was the same deep breath that had first drawn my attention to them.

"Comrades, are you two also hoping to join the battle?" I asked in a low voice.

"Yes."

The young man next to me replied in an equally low voice, while his comrade merely nodded.

"Do you know that officer who went on ahead?"

I asked this second question.

"No."

One of them answered simply, while they both shook their heads.

I could ask no more before tears gathered in my eyes and I had to look away.

These soldiers' willingness to confront the enemy yet again was not inspired by direct orders, nor by the command of anyone here in the vicinity. Neither were they caught up in the excitement of a heady atmosphere. Instead of excitement, something closer to a weighty sense of calm had settled in their hearts at the thought of the impending battle, which their own experience had already taught them would be far from easy.

Yet they were still willing to stand up and fight the enemy who had appeared before us. They did so at nobody's behest. When the two young soldiers reached the other side of the river, after the boat had returned, they jumped into the water and raced up the hill against the tide of the descending crowd, running as swiftly as hares toward the increasingly fierce gunfire.

It was at this moment that I clearly heard the voices of our ancestral land. The voices that were calling these young men on behalf of the people. . . . And with this glimpse of the People's Army answering the call of those voices, I could also see the flames of justice, which will surely destroy the enemy in the end.

(February 1951)

Translator's Acknowledgments

M y greatest thanks to Christine Dunbar for inviting me to undertake this project, of which I had long dreamed. I feel honored that this book will sit alongside the many fabulous translation projects that Columbia University Press has supported over the years. I am grateful that, once again, Chang Jae Lee has created a beautiful cover for this book. I would also like to thank Gregory McNamee for vital copyediting.

I first read the work of Ch'oe Myŏngik alongside Ho Pyong-shik and Yi Ch'olho, who patiently guided me through some of these stories all those years ago. Around that same time, Kim Jae-yong generously sent me some hard-to-obtain materials, which proved extremely helpful as I completed this project. As I prepared the final manuscript, Yujeong Choi and Kyoungrok Ko entertained all manner of questions and queries from me about Ch'oe's often opaque language. They really went above and beyond the usual expectations for collegiality. Aliju Kim was a wonderful research assistant and helped me to compare and adjudicate between Ch'oe's different versions of his stories. Without the gift of such amazing colleagues, I would not have been able to complete this book.

I would like to acknowledge a fellowship from the Jackman Humanities Institute at the University of Toronto, which gave me the vital time away from teaching duties necessary to begin this project. This book is very much a product of pandemic lockdowns. Although I feel little gratitude for those experiences overall, I have to acknowledge that enforced isolation did foster certain kinds of writing projects. This is mine.

A Note on Sources

"Walking in the Rain" [Pi onŭn kil] was first published in the journal *Chogwang* [Morning Light], April–May 1936.

"A Man of No Character" [Musŏnggŏkcha] was first published in *Chogwang*, September 1937.

"Spring on the New Road" [Pom kwa sinjangno] was first published in *Chogwang*, January 1939.

"Patterns of the Heart" [Simmun] was first published in the journal *Munjang* [Writing], June 1939.

"Ordinary People" [Changsam yisa] was first published in *Munjang*, April 1941.

"The Barley Hump [Maengnyŏng] was published in Ch'oe Myŏngik, *Maengnyŏng* (Pyongyang: Munhwa chŏnsŏnsa, 1947).

"The Engineer" [Kigwansa] was first published in the journal *Chosŏn munhak* [Korean Literature], May 1951. The footnoted additions are from Ch'oe Myŏngik, *Kigwansa* [The Engineer] (Pyongyang: Munye ch'ongch'ulp'ansa, 1952).

"Young Kwŏn Tongsu" [Sonyŏn Kwŏn Tongsu] and "Voices of the Ancestral Land" [Choguk ŭi moksori] were published in Ch'oe Myŏngik, *Kigwansa*.

For a complete list of books in the series, please see the Columbia University
  Press website.

Printed and bound by CPI Group (UK) Ltd, Croydon, CR0 4YY

16/04/2024

14484055-0002